SURVIVING DERAEL

KJERI REES

SURVIVING DERAEL

HARBINGER OF VICTORY BOOK ONE

CAPITAL
CITY
TOWN
LOCATION
RUIN
THE EIGHT REALMS OF
DERAEL
Madel
KALAEREN
MARAMORE
NEVA
Nevaria
ENDRE
KORLIE
Khantaria
Selortia
VEYBER
Utor-Kassic
SWAMPS OF TURI
NATONA
Ballewine
SANTSIN VAL
AKVELIA
Revna
REVENAL
CASTLE KOPION
FOREMONT
Turrales
THE LARADAN SEA

Surviving DeRael – Harbinger of Victory Book One

Published by Karerr Publishing LLC

ISBN (Paperback) — 979-8-9874029-0-0

ISBN (Hardcover) — 979-8-9874029-2-4

ISBN (eBook) — 979-8-9874029-1-7

First Edition

Cover Art by www.etherictales.com

Questions, concerns, requests send to

kjerirees@gmail.com

www.kjeri-rees.com

To my family; the part I was given to, and the part given to
me. My first supporters, fans, and investors, and I couldn't have done it without
you.

CONTENTS

 A Professor of Disaster

Perhaps a small shopping mall parking lot full of college kids was not the ideal place to doze off, but as Arica leaned on the large pickup, she did just that. To be fair she'd waited an hour for Mindy during what was supposed to be a quick shopping trip before an afternoon lecture. She knew her best friend enough that she wasn't surprised, but their roommate, Vanessa, had gotten tired of waiting and went in after her. After fifteen minutes without either of them, Arica was regretting not going in herself, especially without the keys to the newer black truck that probably cost more than her yearly salary.

The painted metal gave her a comfortable warmth, so she settled deeper against the grille, her sneakers gripping dry asphalt.

Comfortable until the truck jerked forward, sending her into a parking spot next to the four Vanessa occupied. An agitating crash of metal on metal followed. Her hands scraped the rough ground as she caught herself and, too shocked to keep her weight steady, she sat on the ground.

A small blue car rested against the truck's rear fender; the entire vehicle several feet further than moments before.

"Holy—" She forced herself to her feet and ran to the driver's seat. "Are you okay?" she yelled through a crumpled door. It easily opened with a jerk.

Its young, burly occupant glanced up, dazed. Arica recognized the reddish-brown hair and matching well-groomed beard, before realizing the old brown blazer should've tipped her off.

"Professor Lannert," she said, hoping his name would jog more of a response.

"Wow. And here I thought I could have a refreshing nap in the fresh air from my windows," the professor groaned.

He was making light of the situation, fitting his usual outward attitude, but Arica was too shocked to even consider laughing.

"Oh my... Professor?"

Arica turned to the familiar voice of a petite blonde in high-waisted jeans and a frilly top, finally returning, but with enough shopping bags to justify a day's worth of shopping. Vanessa walked at her side, a tall, athletic woman that Arica could only ever guess was in her thirties despite rooming with a couple of girls in their second year out of high school.

Vanessa's sharp features were stony, unemotional, as was usual, but this time she was looking upon her victimized vehicle. She ignored the damage and nudged Arica out of the way to give Lannert a supportive shoulder as he tried pulling himself out of the vehicle.

"You're standing fine," Vanessa said. He stood on his own, so she let him go and pushed her long brown hair back behind her shoulder.

"I'm alright. Lucky too, it seems."

The question burning Arica's tongue finally came out. "What happened?"

Lannert's thin eyebrows rose as he shrugged. "I closed my eyes a moment too long, I suppose. Is this your vehicle, Miss Tanson?"

Arica answered by pointing over his shoulder at the truck's owner.

"My apologies," the professor expressed as he turned to Vanessa, hand extended politely. "Lovely pickup. Luckily, I have great insurance. We can get her fixed right up. I'm Ben. Benjamin Lannert."

"Vanessa," was all she said as she gently took the offered hand.

"I think I've seen you around campus; Mindy and Arica here are in my class. You aren't a student, are you?"

"I'm not in your class, that's all you need know," she said.

"R-right," the professor agreed as if completely thrown off by her brusqueness and not the accident he'd caused.

"I guess we should call the cops," Arica suggested, noticing a few onlookers. Their lack of panic seemed to deter anyone from running to help.

Vanessa walked assuredly to the smashed fender of her truck before answering. "No need to involve the government."

Lannert made a noise of confusion or disagreement, but none of it was an actual objection.

At only a touch, the tailgate dramatically tore itself loose from its cords and fell to the ground. With a click of her tongue, Vanessa turned back to the others. "A tow truck, though, may be beneficial. You're spilling coolant."

"Ah, good idea…" Lannert pulled a phone from his breast pocket as he walked out of earshot.

Arica followed Vanessa, intending to help even if she wasn't sure what they were doing. Mindy waved Lannert to the side as if trying to get beauty shots of the damage with the best possible lighting.

They pried off the plastic bed cover sporting a new series of cracks in one corner and laid it on the asphalt. This gave Vanessa room to elegantly hop in.

Arica wondered how fast he'd been going to achieve so much damage to the tall truck, but only for a moment before a large, glistening hunk of metal strapped to a bed anchor distracted her.

A gilded handle large enough for at least four hands stuck out of a leather-wrapped scabbard, wider than her hand and almost as long as the full-size pickup bed. The cross guard curved down, shaped like an umbrella's silhouette with tiny white jewels dotted throughout the gold with no real pattern, and while she couldn't see it, she could only assume that within the hard case there was a long blade. It looked way too big to even think about hauling around, but there was no way it wasn't fake. Ignoring that it would've had a good few ounces of gold on it, nobody would've allowed something like it on school property.

As curious as she was about Vanessa's secret cosplay life, she wasn't surprised. There weren't many things she knew about the older woman, and the few she did only urged more questions. Like how she'd gotten strong enough to haul a full-sized wheel over the truck's bed and lower it to the side with one hand.

Arica decided she'd be more help focused on the situation. "Do you have a jack?"

"Under the driver's seat."

She found the tools where she'd indicated and returned them to their owner.

"It'll only be a few minutes," Lannert informed the rest of the group as Arica stood over Vanessa, watching her spin off lug nuts. "What are you doing?"

Vanessa responded calmly. "Other than a few ugly marks and a torn tire, my vehicle is intact. Unless you're more injured than previously decided, I haven't time to wait for your ride."

Arica noticed he was staring into the back of the truck, hands casually in his pants pockets.

"That's quite the piece," he mumbled, eyebrows lowering.

"Thank you."

He pulled his antsy hands from his pockets, his voice suddenly cheerier. "Are you in some sort of production? Do you mind if I—"

"I do mind," Vanessa interrupted, slinging one arm over her knee as she crouched, but her voice was more amusement than annoyance. "What are you a professor of, exactly?"

"History. Understanding causality regarding knowledge available, the steps that achieve the good and the bad we as a world have accomplished, and sparking an initiative to drive our future from correlating with the more horrific of those achievements."

She made a little noise and left it there.

"Well, I hate to bail, but I'm gonna be late for class," Arica said. She only had fifteen minutes, and while she was only two blocks away, she didn't want to take the chance something else was going to happen. Hopefully, they wouldn't find anything else wrong with the truck.

Vanessa waved a dismissing hand and went back to wrenching.

Arica returned to the front seat of the truck to fetch her book bag. Upon grabbing the bag off of the nice black leather seats, she noticed an old book near the throttle pedal, as if she'd pushed it out from under the seat with her rummaging.

Normally, she would leave something like this alone, especially since Vanessa had a lot of curious, unmarked possessions and was generally private. But the weaponry sitting in the vehicle's bed still threw her off. She peeked through the window as the reflection of her dirty blonde ponytail shifting caught her eye. Then she reached across the seat to grab the dusty book.

The page she opened was a rough full-body sketch of a wolf-like creature. The next page read *Appetite & Afflictions*. If it had been a journal or similar, there was no way she would've invaded anyone's privacy. However, since it seemed to be more of a dossier for a tabletop game and could potentially shed some light on the sword, she felt her thievery was justified... If only slightly.

The book settled safely into her bag. As dirty as it was, it clearly would not be missed.

"Professor," she acknowledged as she returned to the scene of the fender-bender. He nodded a quiet goodbye, then reevaluated.

"Oh, while I have your attention, Miss Tanson, I wanted to invite you to my library on Friday."

She waited patiently as the professor dove into his mutilated sedan and dug into a bag, only to come up with a white card and a sharpie. He scribbled like his life depended on it. If she hadn't already been used to his inelegant scrawl, it would've been illegible.

"I apologize that it's so last minute, but you weren't there on Monday, so... It's just a casual get-together, maybe to show off the library I'm responsible for, but mostly because I need something fun to do. I hope you can make it."

She tucked the impromptu invitation into her bag, smiling in appreciation. It was a nice offer, but among one of many she'd blow off for no reason other than she could do something in her room instead. "Thanks. Sounds fun."

She beckoned Mindy as she passed since their classes were close.

The girl barely looked up from her phone as she followed, her bags already packed in the rear seat of the truck as if they were a horrible burden.

She hadn't even noticed the sword lying in the back of Vanessa's truck, but all Arica could think about was her stomach churning with uncertainty. She needed something to talk about.

"I'm gonna call Travis and tell him I was in an accident with no context," she said, then forced a snicker.

Mindy didn't look up from her phone, running on peripheral only. "You call your brother weirdly often."

"It's not *that* weird," she mumbled through her teeth.

One of the few things that would distract Mindy from herself or her own belongings was a pretty face, and being within walking distance of the campus, the surrounding shops were full of young ones.

It was one of these that distracted Mindy, her flirty smile and fluttery eyes lighting up immediately.

"What happened to Matt?" Arica asked, eyeing the young man as they passed, more annoyed than interested. Mindy turned her head to keep his eye a moment or two longer but didn't chase him.

"You mean Mark?"

"Uh... Yeah."

"We just didn't..." She clicked her tongue. "You know? Not my type." Mindy's stride lengthened, her steps more determined. Her piercing, narrowed eyes were no doubt searching the area for worthy prey. "Oh, maybe one of them is, though."

Arica followed the nod of Mindy's head until her eyes rested on a pair of guys walking towards them along the concrete sidewalk, happily talking to each other in low tones.

One of them was unusually tall, dark-haired, an active athlete, and had what was probably a permanent smirk. The other one was thinner, bouncier, and looked friendlier just from his laugh lines. He walked only a few inches taller than her with an unusual limp that he almost made look natural.

"Jake and Zak," Mindy whispered as she leaned over Arica's shoulder. "This is their first semester. I sat between them in our introductory humanities lecture."

"Sorry I quit that at the last second," Arica added with guilt. Sticking with things was not a trait she was known for, but that had been pretty abrupt even for her. "Honestly, I just needed the extra hours at the nursery."

"Ah, yes, because the hose-watered plants would die without your infinite love." Mindy giggled, then shrugged her small shoulders. "So what do you think of them—the boys, not your plants—from appearance only?"

"I don't know. I don't want to judge," she whispered as they approached.

The blond looked more towards Mindy, tipping his head in polite acknowledgment.

Arica watched them pass, locking eyes with the towering one briefly. His eyes were azure, glancing at her with amused mischief. She clasped her bag to her chest, suddenly feeling naked. The girls slowed to a stop, both of them looking attentively over their shoulders like a couple of cats watching birds.

Mindy made a sizzling sound between her teeth. "I mean, muscles, cute eyes, the blond has nice lips, probably a good kisser. What else could you want?"

Turning back into their walk towards campus, Arica did her best to express herself. "I dunno, scars or odd features, or, or... Something interesting."

"People can be interesting without looking weird. Intelligence and personality matter too."

"I should've said some*one* interesting. But if you really believed that, you'd be less focused on chiseled jaws and shoe size."

With a dismissing wave, Mindy turned the corner to face the campus, but before Arica did, she looked back towards the pickup in the distance, then at the pair of boys some ways down the sidewalk.

"Wait," Arica forced cheerfully as she chased after her, a successful but temporary distraction from the gnawing uneasiness growing in her stomach.

That night was darker than she'd expected, and of course, on the first moonless night of the semester, Mindy had stayed behind to flirt with a frat guy instead of walking with her. It wasn't the safest trip, but most of the campus was usually lit up pretty well. She could've done without the rain, however. It pounded down hard enough that she could barely hear her own thoughts and had to pull her hood up over her hair. Normally, she'd stop to enjoy the fresh scent and cool dampness on her skin, but tonight she was more in the mood for crashing straight onto her mattress.

She jogged along the sidewalk, spurred by the sight of her dorm and the inviting light shining from the windows. The slapping of her boots abruptly stopped, her heart lurching as a shadow shifted at the base of the stairwell.

A hulking figure in a black hoodie wandered across the grass towards their window, slow but unalert.

Arica released her held breath. It wasn't that strange for people to be wandering around or hanging out, and the guy didn't hold himself like a thief or a creep.

"Hey," she called, eating up a few more yards between them. "What are you doing, dude?"

As she approached, he turned slowly, and doubt ate at her stomach.

He was large, but it could've been just layered sweaters under the oversized hoodie. Then again, he also towered near seven feet. His face remained hidden in the shadow of the comfortable hood, his hands in the pockets of baggy jeans. She probably couldn't have recognized him even if he was her brother.

"You can see me?" he asked. His voice was low, resonating from deep in his chest, but it was also steady, almost calming.

"Y-yeah." She did a quick once-over of the area, checking streetlamps. She usually had excellent vision when others were struggling, but it wasn't *that* dark.

"Interesting," he murmured, turning towards the sidewalk as if she'd lost all relevance. "Is Vanessa home?"

"I don't think so. Are you one of her friends?" Truthfully, Arica wasn't positive she had any.

Hands back in his pockets, he stepped back a foot or two, still out of the direct glare from the windows. Dark eyes glinted under the concealing fabric, and as he turned, light from a streetlamp touched his washed-out temple and squared jaw, along with a strip of his black hair. "I'd guess she'd say otherwise."

"So you're a stalker."

Unruffled, the corner of his smirk appeared. "You're the little blonde she's been shadowing, aren't you?"

Her words came out as jumbled as her thoughts. "Well, I, yeah, no, I don't think she's been..."

"I was making sure she wasn't around so I could gain a moment with you."

Eyes narrowing, Arica stared at him. Everything was off about him. An accent touched his words; not unusual itself, but his wasn't familiar. Mix it in with his stature, his weird paleness and odd behavior, and her conscience was screaming for her to hightail it as far away from him as she could. But she'd never be able to outrun him if it came to that.

He snorted and shuffled his feet barely enough to notice. "Stare all you want, child. I won't be the oddest thing you'll see."

Arica balked, stepping back an extra foot just in case. "What's that supposed to mean?"

He shrugged with dismissal. "I wouldn't worry. You'll be fine, I'm sure."

"Why wouldn't I be?" she braved.

"You're young; inexperienced." Then he tsked his tongue, tilting his head enough that his eyes were revealed for a moment. Slender, mischievous eyes circled in thick paint the color of tar. "Never know what could happen with someone like you running around."

Arica placed her hands on her hips, ignoring the slight shaking. "I'm sorry, you're the creep out here… waiting outside female dorms," she retorted as confidently as her weak voice could achieve.

"I'm not trying to scare you," he teased with an annoying amusement. Was it too much for him to be serious? It felt impossible to tell if he was just messing with her, or was an actual threat.

"What are you doing, then?"

He eased a small rock through the grass with his foot. The faintest whitish-purple glow outlined his feet, like he wore light-up sneakers with dying batteries. It was odd, but Arica brushed it off.

"Thought I'd say hello before we're formally introduced. Or less-than-formally, should you find yourself in the wrong company."

"Wrong company?" Arica questioned rather forcefully. "Look, you're a weirdo, and I need to get home, so…" With every intention of doing just that, she walked into the light of the window, when the strange man reached into the front of his jacket.

She froze. *Please no, please no.*

"Can I give you something, at least?"

"I-I'd rather you didn't," she squeaked, taking another step back.

He pulled a small folded piece of leather out of the jacket, then casually tossed it at her torso.

Known for her clumsiness, she was proud to catch it, however she was a little embarrassed that it required dropping her bag and the loose book into the wet grass.

"Please don't what?" he mocked.

Arica held the strap of the piece so it could fall, revealing a rather crudely sewn bag. "This is a… a satchel? Why would you—"

She looked up, but he was walking away down the path as if they'd never had their odd little conversation.

ICEWATER

Genuine dark leather, hand stitched with thick thread, a simple little iron clasp, one smaller compartment beside the main one... It was a pretty cool little bag even though it had some wear. Arica had spent over an hour checking it over, but it gave her no clues why he'd just give her something like this. It was almost antique with no promotional label. No business cards lined the inside, and no little tiny cameras or tracking devices were tucked inside. As far as she could tell.

Maybe he'd wanted her to trust him, so she'd be more willing to talk to him again. It was an odd way of showing it, but it was strange no matter what context she put it in.

She heard her name called from the other room.

With tired frustration, she sighed and set the bag to the side of her laptop on the particle board desk. She should've had her paper done already, but she hadn't been able to focus on it.

Vanessa's book hadn't helped, instead being an efficient distraction. The further she dug into it, the more confused she got. It covered an extensive amount about strange things that didn't exist in other fiction, according to the internet, though she hadn't dug into fantasy territory.

For example, she'd been particularly interested in a creature labeled *Naitraith*; a drawn resemblance to a tall woman with beautiful hair, practically naked with long limbs. Then below her, a second figure was inked with the same silhouette, but the details described her to have a more wooden texture to her skin, with stringy hair and ragged claws. Like a horrific take on a druid, or a nymph. And although there were several pages of text for this creature, the language was completely unfamiliar, with a foreign alphabet and an unclear structure. M and F were recognizable, but that was about the only similarity to English.

Not the entire book was like this. In fact, it seemed to be about half English. She'd read up on werewolves and tropical plants all night. But she couldn't read anything interesting enough to dive into. Dragons, unicorns, and several creatures that she'd never heard of, including a black dragon-like thing called a solzetair were all unreadable past their titles.

Arica opened the book to the last page. It was an inscription in the same alphabet. But signed at the bottom in a gorgeous script was the name *Vanessa Damage.*

"ARICA!" came a high-pitched scream from the living room.

Caught up in her thoughts again, Arica tried to shake herself awake. Was it so difficult for them to knock on her door?

She hauled herself from the uncomfortable chair but paused at the mirror to make sure she looked presentable. She was okay; her eyes were a little dark, but nothing a bit of makeup couldn't fix if she needed it. She tore the elastic out of her shoulder-length yellow-blonde hair and shook it out. A little better. Before leaving, she lightly touched the lowest leaf of a droopy fern hugging the mirror. Several leaves were shinier from daily attention.

Sera and Mindy leaned over the sinks in the bathroom, chatting over an earthquake's mess of cosmetics.

Mindy caught her eye in the mirror and slammed her tube of mascara down. "Arica, you're going to be late! I can't be on you like I'm your *mom.*"

"Late?" she murmured, racking her brain, but there was nothing in there. She hadn't been planning on stopping near the bathroom door, but curiosity got her.

"Professor Lannert's *soiree*?" she giggled, returning to her reflection.

"Ah. I wasn't going to go. Are you?"

Mindy had her hair up in a fancy curled ponytail, wearing a tight pink blouse and a knee-length skirt, while Sera wore a denim jacket over jeans and a brightly colored shirt. Sera had broad shoulders and a slim waist, and she'd admitted to often trying to distract from one or the other so she didn't look quite as out of proportion. Neither outfit felt appropriate for a night at a library.

"Well, I thought you were, so we planned on popping in with you before heading to Harry's party." She made a goofy noise, then swept the mess into a pink bag.

"Why don't you want to go?" Sera asked, not taking her attention from the pins she was putting in her short brunette hair.

Arica forced a soft smile. "I just don't—"

The front door slammed shut, drawing her attention to Vanessa who walked into the kitchen at a slow gait like she'd been working out. She held a large backpack and nothing else.

Mindy and Sera finally finished packing up their makeup. Arica stood in the hall until they roughly passed her. She wasn't sure why, but she suddenly felt lethargic.

"Grab your jacket. It's chilly out!" Mindy giggled, tossing both of their jackets out of the closet.

"Where are you going?" Vanessa asked as she arranged new groceries in the fridge.

"We're stopping by Lannert's lovely little get-together before heading off. Assuming things go well," Mindy said with an all-knowing smirk.

Vanessa looked up at Arica, her question directed forcefully. "You aren't going with them, are you?"

"Well, I-I wasn't planning on it. Am I so predictable?"

Going back to her groceries, but not her own business, Vanessa said, "I apologize for asking, but you should stay away from him."

"What are you saying?" Mindy demanded, her voice almost nasally. "She's not *cool* enough to come? Or too quiet? Professor Lannert *invited* her." She waved a hand then grabbed Arica's jacket from the back of the loveseat. "Come on, you don't want to stay here."

Arica looked back at Vanessa, who must've felt her gaze because she met it, giving her a little frown. Vanessa was a little motherly, but Arica had never felt the need to prove something to her before. Arica smiled at the girls, then took her jacket. "Let's go get some wine and books."

Sera gave her a strained, toothy smile. "Sounds... so fun..."

"Do you have something against Lannert, anyway?" Mindy asked, leaning on a countertop. "Or a *crush* on him?"

Vanessa stared at the blonde, her jaw rigid.

"He crashed into her truck, remember?" Arica mumbled, giving Mindy a sympathetic smile.

"Ohhh," she whispered, the lights in her head brightening her face. "That's right. Well, why don't you come too? He's a cool guy."

Arica put on her jacket, but hesitated, as Vanessa's stare didn't shift from serious composure. There was no waiting for anything. She never did anything with them without being needed in some capacity. Never for fun or to hang out.

So her answer was unexpected. "Mmm. Of course I'll join you."

Arica regretted the decision within minutes of entering the brightly lit library. There were more people than she expected, most gathered in small groups among huge wooden bookshelves. The center of the library—normally a collection of nice couches and chairs—had been overtaken with a rustic counter controlled by two smartly dressed bartenders pouring wine into delicate glasses.

The atmosphere was more mild than most of the parties Mindy had dragged her to. There was noise, but it was a more chatty, cheerful sound instead of drunken cheers and dirty jokes. Colorful string lights lit the shelves up, ruining the dark mystery of the old books, but it made them a little easier to glance through.

The thing throwing off Arica's vibe the most was probably her own self-consciousness. She'd opted to wear a clean pair of jeans and a light gray tank top with frills under a denim jacket. This had felt like a reasonable choice until Vanessa had come out of her room in a red gown that while had a modest neckline, showed off her athletic shoulders and arms. It had an elegant, hugging silhouette with a simple slit skirt to her ankles, but a pair of tall hiking boots almost ruined the whole feel.

At least she wasn't dressed like she was going to a frat party afterwards.

Vanessa had wandered away from Arica very little during the whole five minutes they'd been there, but somehow she held a glass of red wine. "A party appropriate of a teacher who still has to be home before dark," she mused at Arica's shoulder.

She couldn't help chuckling, but kept an eye out. She didn't see a lot of people she knew, but she didn't know many.

"You were right," Arica conceded over the noise. "I don't like this kind of thing."

She turned, but where Vanessa had stood there was a long-haired fellow with a scarf and a small backpack on one shoulder. Sera had vanished as soon as they'd arrived, and Mindy was a few shelves over talking to a group of guys she knew.

So Arica had to find something to do that wasn't standing awkwardly between the entrance and the help desk. She slipped away from the gist of the crowd into a quiet row of books where she could still search for Lannert. If she could find him and say hi, let him know she'd shown up, she could go home without feeling guilty.

The presence of a few people from her psych class convinced her to duck back. She didn't need to be stuck talking about this next project due; she was already aware she was behind and probably not going to do well. But instead of sneaking away, she turned and smacked into a very tall, nicely dressed man she'd made fun of to her best friend once.

A gasp escaped her lungs as she jumped back, but the glass of clear liquid twisted in an agile hand, somehow not spilling a drop.

"I am so sorry; I didn't hear you," Arica blurted, hands open.

"I'm quiet," he said, raising the glass. He had a lazy, lopsided smile and bright eyes that only hinted a threat.

Arica forced the corners of her mouth up. "Yeah. And it's dark back there." She tried to sound friendly instead of awkward.

Was he Zak, or... Lane? Had Mindy even ever told her which was which? No, but Arica didn't see his blond buddy anywhere to help.

He passed her in the wide row, but only far enough to lean against the end of the bookshelf; a comfortable amount of space between them. He stared off in the same direction she did. The mob of young people buzzed on expensive wine and engaging conversation.

"How are you tonight?" the young man asked as if they were good friends who often conversed casually.

Arica couldn't help but stare at him with confusion. "Fine?"

Finally, he met her eye, his expression neutral as he said, "You seem a little tense. Anything I can do?"

"Nah, I just rarely talk to guys... like you," she admitted a little nervously. Her hands warmed as she rubbed them together.

He raised an eyebrow. "Guys like me?"

She set her hands between the bookshelf and her back, her fingers caressing the soft spines of some self-help books. Maybe they'd behave there. "Mmm-hmm. The kind that's already flirted with half the room. The kind that thinks they should be the center of attention because they're slightly more attractive than the guys in cargo shorts and gold chains?"

"You think I'm normal." He smirked, setting the glass to his lips.

Even though it had been a statement and not a question, Arica gave him one firm nod.

He looked a little surprised, but unoffended. "I'm not."

"Isn't that what they're supposed to say?" she asked, trying to sound challenging but not confrontational.

He shook his head a little, staring off into the crowd. The glass made a soft tinkling noise she'd heard already but hadn't registered before.

"Is that just ice water?" she asked with curiosity.

He held the fancy stem glass out to her. The ice clinked, condensation sliding down the edge. "You look thirsty," he prodded.

She shook her head. "How do I know you didn't put rat poison in it?"

"Because I've been standing here drinking it? Last chance."

She stared at him.

"If you'd prefer alcohol, why don't you go ask one of the other... guys like me," he replied haughtily. Then he downed the drink in two swallows, ice and all and flipped the empty glass around. As if it were a soda can, he smashed the glass between his large hands, and with barely a crack or ting, it compressed in his palms.

They opened, covered in a fine, sparkling powder in almost impossible perfection.

She wanted to exclaim disbelief or ask how many times he'd impaled his hands to learn that trick. Instead, she continued to stare, even as Mindy approached them and grabbed Arica's arm to pull her away.

"Hey, come talk for a moment. Sera and I are splitting. Are you okay to stay, or..."

Arica tore her gaze from the strange man and tried to jolt her brain back into functioning order. "Ah, nah, I still gotta find Lannert and say hi at least. You go; I'm good."

"Well, I think I saw him over by the computers showing Troy S. and Rand..." She pointed over her shoulder, but Arica glanced a look over her own. Her previous companion was no longer against the bookshelf but had wandered a few shelves further away, observing the room quietly.

"Were you... *flirting* with him?" Mindy teased, her voice girly.

She forced her attention back. "God, I hope not. It was awkward and weird."

"That's good!" Mindy smacked her shoulder, startling her. "You're past the awkward first meeting. Get his number or something!"

That didn't sound fun.

"Oooh, he looks older. I'll have to sneak in some questions in our next lesson..." Finally, Mindy shook her head. "Anyway, Sera is waiting. But you should go back after him. Don't worry about Lannert."

Arica almost tried to object, grab her arm and pull her back—something—but she lost her grip and had to watch her solitude solidify.

Maybe Mindy was right. She was already stepping out of her comfort zone. She glanced back at the glass-destroying hooligan in a dress shirt and windbreaker, glaring at the back of his head for a few moments. Then she made a last-second choice.

"Hey," she called bravely. "It's Zak, right?"

He turned to her, pointing to himself with eyebrows raised. "No, it's Jake. Zak is the pretty one." He winked, still straight-lipped like a teasing old man.

Then Jake pointed over his shoulder, to the dark recesses of the old library. "He's that way, I think."

"Oh. Thanks, I guess."

His head dipped politely and slipped into the crowd. Arica rubbed her temples. *What a weirdo.*

A pleasant, slow-beat blues song played at a quiet volume when Arica found her target almost ten minutes later. After ducking around a few groups, nearly knocking over more glasses with more dangerously colored liquids, she found herself on the media side of the library. Rows of computers sat in front of shelves filled with DVDs, CDs, newspaper reels, magazines, and records. The professor stood with an arm against a shiny, antique record player. A few students were close by, chatting with him.

One of them stood almost at Lannert's shoulder, holding most of his attention. It could've been the fancy red dress, but it was more likely the soft, teasing smile on Vanessa's lips and the words that slipped from them that made him look so interested in her.

It was disturbing. Arica had never seen her smile at anyone unless it was sarcastic.

Somehow, Arica's arrival tore Lannert's attention from his companion.

"Arica. I'm glad you made it," he greeted. His lightly aged features displayed casual appreciation. He'd gotten a new accessory since she'd last seen him, a black brace worn over his right wrist. He held it out for her to shake.

"Professor. Are you okay?"

He waved the offending wrist dismissively. "It's just a sprain. Bad enough I got it checked out, but it won't put me down."

"That's good to hear," she admitted. She bounced on her heels but held most of the nervous energy in. "Thanks for the invite. It's really nice, what you've done with the place. I knew when you got the job that they'd picked the right person."

"That means a lot to me." He gave her a soft smile, then clapped his hands. "Well, can I speak with you for a moment? In private?"

Before she could form a response, Vanessa came forward. "Actually, I need a quick word," she said, but instead of sweeping Lannert off, she grabbed Arica's elbow.

"I'll meet you in the back office in a few minutes?" Lannert asked, a hand sliding into a pocket in his slacks.

Arica nodded before being swept into the crowd for no apparent reason.

Vanessa let her go on the busy side of a cozy mystery shelf but stood close, leaning her few extra inches in height. "Lannert did this whole thing for you."

Arica balked, giving her roommate a look of pure disbelief. "What? Are you crazy? He didn't even invite me until the last minute," she objected, trying to stay quiet.

"Can you say when everyone else was invited?"

She paused but felt beaten. "Well, did he *say* something like that?"

"He didn't need to," Vanessa whispered.

Arica wanted to stare into her eyes and make sure there was no joke hidden there, but they darted seamlessly over the crowd as if she had to be aware of threats or criminals. "Do you think he *likes* me? He's a little older than I would—"

Vanessa finally cast her pale blue eyes over her, shifting from one rigid, military-like stance to another, barely more casual. "No, it's not that."

"Then why on earth would he have any interest in me? It's just weird." Arica slapped her hands to her thighs in defeat. The only weird thing was Vanessa's behavior. Well, and glass-hating Jake, but he was unrelated.

She didn't consider Lannert a close friend, but she'd known him for a few years. He'd been her older brother Travis's mentor and helped them out of a few rough spots. She hadn't heard from him in over a year until she signed up for his class, and while she'd met with him a few times to talk about assignments, none of it had been very personal or even necessarily friendly.

Yet she still would've trusted him over the secretive roommate she'd known for most of a semester.

"You shouldn't meet with him," Vanessa answered, but did it really count as one?

"Because he'll make me join his cult?" Arica asked, shaking her fingers for dramatic effect.

Vanessa's stare didn't break.

"Oh my gosh, you can't be serious."

"Do you know he *doesn't* have ulterior motives?" the older woman demanded in all sincerity. "Do you know there's nothing you have that he will want?"

Arica stared at her for a long, awkward pause, then shook her head. "You can go home and be weird. I'm gonna go talk to my professor about my late assignment."

She didn't give Vanessa a chance to object and left her, slipping past a hugging couple to find Lannert's office. She'd seen the blueprints and mock-ups of the building; they'd worked on them during extra moments in Lannert's class, so she knew the general vicinity it would be in.

Past the closed boardrooms and game rooms, she found another section of fiction, but there was the flight of stairs that would take her to the offices, including Lannert's. She smiled, but it disappeared as her thoughts were interrupted.

"Catch."

She turned just in time to get an object to the chest. Her instincts worked overtime, soaking the force of the throw with her arms and catching the wineglass between her wrists. "What, why would you—"

Jake emerged from the shadows of the bookshelf, a slow meander. He looked a lot more muscular without his jacket covering his thick arms. His right bicep was more defined than the left, likely the result of whatever sport he played. "I bet you can do it, too."

She lifted the glass in one hand. It was lighter than she expected. Maybe it was sugar glass like they used in movies. He hadn't been drinking anything from the wine cart anyway, and maybe the water wasn't able to dissolve the glass in a short period. "I don't know why I would want to."

He shrugged, resting an arm on top of a seven-foot shelf. "Why not?"

She chewed on her tongue for a long moment. But he'd piqued her curiosity. She cupped the bowl of the glass in her palms and applied some pressure. It didn't seem to be all that weak. Then it snapped, cracking into three large pieces. The biggest shard stabbed into her palm.

"Ouch!" The pieces fell to the floor.

"Well, that wasn't what I meant," Jake mumbled, jerking into a jog after her.

"It's fine," she grumbled, cradling it away from him as blood welled in her palm. "And are you stalking me?"

"I wanted to ask the same thing."

She glared at him as her fingers dripped. "You keep coming up to me."

Jake smirked, shrugging his shoulders and stepping closer to her. "You're right."

"Look, it's nothing," she insisted, using her other hand to put pressure on the minor cut. He must've taken this as an invitation to grab her sleeved wrists because he did, then dragged her out of the pile of glass on the carpet.

"You're making me really uncomfortable." Arica leaned away from him, not enjoying how much bigger his hands felt on her small wrists.

He grinned anyway. "Wanna see something cool?"

"I swear, if you take your jeans off, I'm calling the police," she promised.

"You really need to stop assuming you know me," he mumbled. He held her wrist tighter as he passed the other hand over hers.

Arica let him but watched with skepticism. "It's really not that big of a—" She stopped. Warmth radiated from his hand, enough to feel it without even touching him. The cut tingled uncomfortably.

"I dunno if I can do this," he admitted, focusing on her hand. He let out a long breath like he was stressed.

"What the heck?" She gasped as his hand glowed the faintest mauve color. It felt fuzzy under her skin, like a faraway strike of lightning in a rainstorm.

Jake let go, leaving her hand warm. The glow spread and covered most of it, not even a scar where the cut had been. Even the scabs of road rash had healed over immaculately.

"What did you do?" she demanded, turning it over, but the back was glowing too. She stepped back. Holding up her opposite hand revealed that it too was growing bright purple.

"Oops," Jake said with very little genuine regret in his voice.

Arica bolted. She tore down the hall, just to get away from him. Somewhere she could hide. She mounted some steps leading upwards, away from the exit but also away from people. The stairs turned back on the way up, opening out into a large study area or break room. A few lights guided her, but she didn't see anyone else.

She ran for the end of the comfy room to a door handle, forgetting all directions.

When it opened, she sighed in relief.

She got a quick glance at the interior before she slammed the door behind her, removing most of her light to see. It had to be Lannert's office; the opinion strengthened by the desk sitting in the corner and the leather couch that reflected a bit of the outside light. But there were no occupants.

Letting out a hard breath, Arica set her hands on her hips to relax a little. It felt better, the dark and quiet. Noise from downstairs drifted to her, but it was quiet enough that she could convince herself it was just a loud TV. She would've been fine if people had left her alone. They were unpredictable; she didn't like it.

She stepped forward in the dim light, hoping she didn't run into anything too small to see. Her hands felt the wall in front of her, letting one rest against it just to balance her. Her head spun.

Light flickered in the corner of her eye. She turned to see a tiny candle flame across the room, perched on the doorknob like a little butterfly. Out of curiosity, she watched it spread across the cheap metal, silent.

"What..." she mumbled. She wanted to inspect the doorknob, but as soon as her hand came away from the wall, the red-hot handprint she'd left behind distracted her. The paint had melted away already, the drywall glowing with little gold embers. Then one flared up.

Arica stumbled back in shock, tripping over the leg of an office chair. One arm caught her against the polished wood desk, the other merely brushing the fabric backing on the chair. Both caught fire immediately.

In horror, she scrambled away, looking desperately towards the door, but it was inescapable. Hungry, crackling flames had eaten halfway through the wood.

Smoke gathered against the ceiling, orange light hellishly illuminating the small office. The rug under her feet ignited next, in the outline of her shoes. She jumped away, her lungs catching in fear.

There has to be a fire extinguisher in here.

Arica searched around. There were a few cabinets, but nothing on top of them. In desperation, she began wrenching them open. One handle melted under her touch, covering her fingers in a dark liquid that should've boiled her skin off. After trying a few of the drawers of a small dresser and scorching each one, she gave up on the idea.

She ran into the center of the room, the furthest she could get away from all of it. The door was barely recognizable, but she couldn't see past it. One corner flamed from floor to ceiling. The desk was a pile of char; the window had flame licking from three of its four sides and the cabinets had papers falling out of gaping drawers into the hungry inferno below them.

Someone had to have noticed. It had to have spread outside the office, and pieces of the ceiling were burning up.

She stood still. The heat didn't bother her at much as it should've, even though orange was licking dangerously close to her left foot. The smell was obvious, like any campfire with elements of plastic, but her lungs stayed clear.

Then she noticed the fire receding from her in a perfect little circle. It drew away like a sudden wave, giving her a foot or two in every direction.

Either way, there were no escape routes. The floor would come out from under her feet in a matter of minutes.

But she was stuck.

QUEEN OF THE FLAMES

All Arica could hear was an annoying ring, like a walkie-talkie with interference. Her eyes were blurry from tears. She'd curled up on the ground, unable to move in her panic like she'd fallen asleep still aware of her surroundings, but unable to react to them.

So what had snapped her out of it?

The blaze in front of her flared up again, making her shut her eyes to it. She wasn't burned, but the light was almost blinding. Her dry lips parted to let out a noiseless groan.

Then a board under her loosened, jerking her to the right.

Her hands caught her, but one fell outside the protective bubble, sending a sharp, hot pain up her arm despite retracting it as quickly as she could. Terrified, she cradled her burned hand and looked around her at the horrible inferno. She never thought she'd die in a house fire. Especially stoned.

She took a quick, shaky breath, and the fire surged silently away.

Then it split in front of her, black smoke and flame parting for a woman with a long braid down her back, her features rigid with concentration. Seeing Arica, her expression lifted a little. She carefully stepped closer, working her way through the splotchy room.

It surprised Arica that there was even enough floor left to get to her. And suddenly she regained her conscious thought and lurched to her feet.

"Vanessa!" she cried, but she didn't hear any sound leave her mouth over the ringing.

With every step, Vanessa's body repelled the orange fire until she was almost within arm's reach. Her hands stretched out, her lips trying to relay instructions, but all Arica could do was follow the point of one hand to the floor between her little circle and Vanessa's foothold on an exposed beam. The space between them was empty, but the outlines of a few pieces of burning furniture were visible on the lower floor. The wall next to her was completely gone, and while the ceiling above her was also lit, she could see tiny pieces of the night sky through the billowing smoke.

Focus, she told herself, re-centering her vision on her roommate.

Vanessa spoke a few more words, looking Arica in the eye. As she held out an open hand, Arica realized she was probably trying to encourage her. To help make up the gap, her feet sidled closer into the fiery room, moving around a steady beam on her toes with ballet dancer precision.

Arica reached out her own hand and let Vanessa take a firm grip around her wrist. At Vanessa's beckon, she took a deep breath.

She was getting out of this. But she had to jump first. There was no asking for advice, no thinking twice, no giving into her fears. Vanessa was there, waiting to help her.

"Jump," she imagined Vanessa saying, her eyes brimming with fake confidence and hope. Arica took a sooty breath, tensed her legs and flung herself across the gap.

For a brief second, she fell. But before gravity could completely take her over, Vanessa's uncanny strength pulled her the last foot to safety. Safety relative to standing in the middle of a collapsing room.

She fell into Vanessa's arms, the picture of a perfect romantic moment if one ignored the immediate danger.

The second her feet touched the ground, however, she was being dragged away. Smoke congealed around them, making her wonder how much further into the building they had to go. Even though she trained her eyes on the floor, she couldn't see it. But assuming that Vanessa wasn't walking on air, it felt safe to walk closely behind her.

Inhuman screeching filled her ears, making her free hand fly to one as her muscles clenched in pain.

Vanessa didn't seem to have heard it, but she noticed that Arica had stopped running. Vanessa's hands grabbed Arica's cheeks, enunciating whatever she was saying.

Then it stopped. Fire still rose on either side of her, Vanessa still yelled, smoke still made her eyes water. But it was all silent. Not a bird, not a crackle, not even her own breath.

She screamed, the air tearing at her throat. Tears soaked her eyelashes as she squeezed her eyes shut. "I can't do it!" she yelled, terrified that nobody could hear her at all. This had to be a dream. There was no way the fire had deafened her, or that she was standing in the middle of an inferno without burning alive.

Vanessa continued mouthing words, using her hands in subtle gestures. But she didn't wait long. She finally took Arica's arm and continued to pull her along.

Under their weight, Arica could feel how precarious the structure was becoming. She watched the fire parting for them effortlessly. She wondered if the wave was leading Vanessa, or if she was leading it, but whatever it was, she was clearly the queen of those flames.

A good part of the library looked intact, the floor especially. It gave her hope that they'd be able to escape without much more effort. Looking behind her made her a little dizzy. It was unrecognizable as a building. An out-of-control bonfire.

They arrived at the stairwell and another problem presented itself. Vanessa covered her face with an arm as the blaze flared up and spat at her. As it died again, she craned her neck, peeking over the edge of the intact flooring. Even Arica could tell it was too far of a drop straight into fire.

"What now?" she tried to say.

Vanessa backed up a few steps, looking around. The smoke receded further from her, almost drawing from her sight.

The floor shook under them.

Arica froze in terror, knowing what was happening but unsure which way to run until Vanessa launched back across the floor, but she didn't have time to reach a safe place before it bucked again.

Boards broke loose, cracking onto the floor below as they caught fire. Arica fell to her knees, grabbing an exposed pipe near her face. It should've been scalding; she could feel the heat but it was only uncomfortable in her palm.

Her knee broke through the feeble sub-flooring as she tried to get her feet back under her. The angle increased. Her sweaty palm slipped from the pipe, so she scrambled up before gravity could pull the floor down further. Her foot slipped, making her lose all her progress and then some.

I'm okay, I'm okay, she repeated in her head over and over. The ground shook one last time, sending her legs over the edge. She scrambled to pull herself back up, but she lost grip.

Five feet later, fire split away from the burning hardwood to catch her in a cushion of ash. She choked, the air bitter.

Vanessa was suddenly there, dragging her to her feet. She staggered her way through the ash before finding sturdy footing. Her eyes watered so badly she'd given up trying to see and instead blindly followed Vanessa's lead.

They jogged for maybe another minute, before finally, Arica felt cold air on her skin and let out a sigh of relief. She scrubbed her eyes for a moment, hoping it would be easier to see. Her foot slipped, pitching her to the rough asphalt and scraping her knee. Her head swam and her skin shivered.

There were hands holding her steady. Then they wrapped around her waist and lifted her up.

Vanessa held up almost all of her weight effortlessly. Her vision cleared enough to see bright red, blue, and orange lights reflected in the chrome surface of a nearby vehicle. But the lights were a little way off. Why wasn't she being taken to an ambulance, or a cop, or something?

Vanessa readjusted and hauled her a little faster.

There was still nothing to hear. Not a siren, no yelling, not even her pulse or breathing.

Haze took over the edges of her vision, distorting the light as her head started floating away. *Is this what losing consciousness feels like?* she wondered as she lost track of her own weight. But nothing went black yet. Maybe it was out of pure will. The last thing she wanted was to be deaf and blind—especially after experiencing something so supernatural—while she was in the care of a practical stranger.

She felt two entire hands massaging her temples and cheekbones. It only lasted a few moments, but it left her skin tingling. In fact, it was a very familiar feeling.

"Get her ears. I think the heater deafened her when it blew."

Arica gasped so sharply that she might as well have inhaled glass.

"Got 'em already," a male voice said nonchalantly. It wasn't one she recognized off the bat and sounded slightly more southern. "She's responding to us."

"Where's Jake, anyway?"

Arica opened her eyes, realizing that she didn't know how long she'd been lying face up on the backseat of the unfamiliar vehicle. It was clean and smelled like it was brand new. Not like her, and the bitter smoky stench clinging to her.

"You can hear fine, yeah?"

She looked down at the blond guy leaning in through the backseat door, not touching her anymore but still uncomfortably close. *Okay, this one has to be Zak.* "Yeah, I... Now I can."

Zak smiled brightly and held out a hand that she didn't hesitate to take. But as soon as she was upright, she grabbed her throbbing head and moaned.

"Headache?"

She tried to nod, but just the tiny attempt to move made more pain surge to her brain.

"Here," he gently tapped her forehead, and like the sun coming out from behind a dark cloud, the pain faded to a happy warmth, leaving her feeling a little high.

"Thanks," she twittered breathlessly, closing her eyes so she could savor the feeling for a moment.

"Did you find Jake?" Zak asked casually.

Vanessa's tone was patient, but anything besides friendly. "I'm sure he'll catch up."

"He has," said a low voice that had Arica cringing. She finally opened her eyes, convinced she wasn't dreaming anymore. Time to deal with the situation.

Vanessa lounged in the front seat of the car, her legs jutting under the open driver's door where Zak leaned. Arica's hulking assailant walked up to them but stopped a few feet away from the car.

In front of them towered the ashy skeleton of the building still standing, patches bright with flames. Black smoke billowed from the base, through which she could barely make out the lights of at least two different fire engines.

They were quite a ways away from it, in an emptier back parking lot.

Arica noticed the smell again, a little more sharp than your average campfire. And since her clothes were singed, she was probably the source.

"Where have you been?" Vanessa leapt out of her seat flawlessly, startling Arica a little.

"You asked me to watch her; I was watching her," Jake reasoned as he stuffed his hands in his jeans pockets.

"Until she started the building on fire," Vanessa growled, crossing her arms.

He theatrically pulled his shoulders up. "She ran away."

Arica furiously jumped to her feet, throwing a finger out at Jake. "I didn't do anything. It was him!"

Vanessa sent him a sharp glare, receiving an awkward smile in return.

"I... *may* have activated her powers trying to heal her..." he said through his teeth.

Then she whipped towards Zak. "Where did you get the healing anyway, and why are you giving it out?"

He shrank a bit, but his voice remained strong. "I wanted to make sure we'd be okay without Derrick."

Vanessa then placed her hands on her hips, her feet spread out. "Well, I hope you're all happy with this disaster."

Jake argued, "I mean, it's not really a..."

Vanessa grabbed him by the front of his jacket despite being over a foot shorter than him and spun him to face the burning apartment.

He folded his arms and looked at her, smirking. "As if we've never blown up a building before."

Vanessa's anger melted from her expression as she threw her hands out. "Fine. I have to clean it up now though. You go get Arica packed, and—"

"Packed?" Arica interrupted, her voice cracking a little. She stood up, an unexpected weakness slowing her.

Both of them turned to her. Then Vanessa held a hand out. "You didn't think we were going to let you stay here and make more messes, did you?"

Arica's heartbeat sped up as she steadied herself with both hands on the car's door. "But I don't even know any of you! I don't understand what happened up there..."

"You'll be a lot safer with us," Jake agreed.

She stared at him a moment before screaming, "No! This is ridiculous!" The world spun, pitching her to her feet. Zak was right there next to her in a second.

"That magic took a lot out of her," she heard Vanessa say, a lot closer than she'd been only moments before. Then she heard one word before dozing off in a stranger's arms.

"*Sleep.*"

Her eyes shot open, jolting from sleep as if something had electrocuted her. Haze clung to her memory, but she didn't feel lethargic because of it. In fact, she felt good. Refreshed.

She sat up as confusion set in, along with a bit of vertigo, but it quickly passed. She was in her room, on her bed, with her every trinket and belonging exactly where they were supposed to be.

But how did I get here? She turned out the tiny pockets in her jacket. Only a bit of lint.

Her hands rested on the edge of the mattress. Nobody had bothered covering her, just plopped her on top of the haphazardly made bedspread. But who had done it, anyway?

"Vanessa," she mumbled aloud. It seemed right, after all. Hers was the last face she could remember. And she'd pulled her out of a burning building.

Arica raised her hands, palms towards her. They were spotless, not the tiniest hint of an injury or burn. Her sleeves were untouched.

Time for answers.

She got up, mildly annoyed that she'd slept with her shoes on the bed. Opening the door into the hall, she nearly ran into Sera.

"Ew," the girl immediately squeaked, her button nose wrinkling. "Hun, I'm glad you survived, but you smell like you were toasted over a bonfire of plastic. You should get those clothes professionally cleaned."

"Shower imminent, I got it," Arica agreed quickly.

"Sera, leave the girl alone," someone else called from the living room, only to be revealed as her desperate friend, Mindy. "Are you alright, Arica?"

She quickly made her way into the living room to join her and a couple of others, Sera's best friend, Jordan, and a long-haired man who had his arms around her on the couch.

"I'm okay," Arica added, remembering why Mindy was still staring her down.

"Thank God, I wasn't sure how you'd feel. Some of us are taking it harder than others."

They both looked over at Jordan, who stared vacantly at the cheap coffee table letting her boyfriend coddle her.

"Then, naturally, Sera's resilient as they come," Mindy added as an afterthought.

"So, you all got out of the building in time, I see. Was anyone really hurt?" Arica couldn't think of any other way to pry for information. She leaned on the couch, not feeling quite as refreshed as a few moments before.

"No fatalities as far as we've heard. A few burns and mild panic."

Arica let out an inaudible sigh. She felt Mindy's hand touch her shoulder.

"Are you sure you're alright?"

She nodded, getting a whiff of perfume through the roasted smell as Mindy flipped her long blonde locks out of her face.

"How did it even start?"

Arica looked up. What a good question. How *did* it start? She had such a vivid nightmare of hiding, of handprints of flame, and the burning carcass of a small room. But it couldn't have been real.

Across the room, still cuddling Jordan, Bryant finally piped up. "Jason Mills said he thought it came from the third floor. Police are speculating about a drunk pyro. Fireworks, a cigarette, maybe someone screwing with a lighter."

A pang of guilt waved through her. The professor had worked so hard to bring that building back into something beautiful. Had she really ruined it so easily? She tried not to let the vivid memories continue to clarify in her mind. Then she glanced down the hall towards the other two bedrooms. "Where's Vanessa?"

Mindy's brow lowered. "Who?"

"Vanessa?" Arica clarified snappishly. "You know, the older chick, our room-mate." She looked around at the three confused pairs of eyes drilling into her. "In the back right bedroom," she added just as impatiently. More stares.

Rolling her eyes, Arica lifted her weight off of the couch's arm and made her way into the furthest bedroom. No light shone out from under the flimsy door, but she knocked anyway, worrying too late that she was disturbing something important. But there was no answer.

"Arica, nobody's been in that bedroom in months," Mindy called, chasing her down the hallway. Her forehead creased in concern.

Arica grabbed the door handle, twisting it open with ease. "Don't be ridicu—"

It was empty. The closet hung open; the mattress was stripped. All the walls and the one bookshelf were bare, all of it looking as if it had been weeks since someone had been in there. The few times she'd gotten a glance inside the room, it had seemed bare, but still obviously inhabited with clothes and bedding.

"That's not..."

Mindy took Arica's shoulders. "Sweetie, I think you need to take a hot bath and maybe get a little more sleep."

Her face warmed as she let go of the door, and let Mindy take her back to the main room.

"Sera, go whip up something calming for her. I'm going to call the nurse, just to make sure she isn't concussed."

She barely heard Mindy speaking, only one thought making sense amidst everything else.

What happened?

"No, no, sorry," Arica gasped, setting a hand against her racing heart. "I'm fine. It's been a crazy couple of days. Getting like no sleep, trying to catch up on assignments."

Mindy set her hands on either shoulder. "We're all a little stressed, but you need to keep it together. Self care is important."

"Right. I think I'll go sleep some more. Maybe I'm sleepwalking, anyway." Her last sentence may have been laying it on a little thick, judging solely by Mindy's fake smile, but it was done.

All she knew was that she needed out of there.

"I'll bring you something to eat in a little while, okay?" Mindy asked as if talking to a child, but she steered her back towards her room.

"Great. Thanks."

Her door swung shut, closing out any more conversation.

I am not crazy.

She took a few slow steps into the room, glancing around for inconsistencies. Something that felt off.

Her door opened sooner than she expected, but it wasn't *who* she expected. It wasn't someone she recognized at all. A small girl with a dark bob and soft features, her brown eyes wide as she slammed the door closed.

"Um, excuse me?" Arica asked.

"Arica. I don't have much time, I don't have time," she squeaked, her voice twinkly and small. Her eyebrows creased with concern, her gaze darting about the room. The strangest part besides her intrusion was the fact she wore a basic black tube top and workout shorts, but no shoes at all.

"Do I know you?"

Her worried gaze stayed on Arica for only a few moments. "I know you. We've never met. Trust me, I know you," she blurted.

Arica balked as she came towards her, but the girl didn't touch her, instead knelt to look under the bed like something was hiding there.

"You're with the weirdos, aren't you? You know Vanessa."

"Vanessa. I know Vanessa." Her voice was fairy-like and faint as she rambled off. "Yes, I'm one of—No, I'm here to... There's something wrong. Yes, and no. There's something wrong here. I have to fix it."

"Are you... having a stroke? Can I help?" Arica asked as she pulled a suitcase out from under the bed.

"No, no, that's fine there," she whispered, pushing it back.

Arica stood frozen in place as the girl leaned a hand on the bed and jerked her blankets away from the wall.

"You—" The words stuck in her throat. The glinting gold of a long weapon lay on the edge of the bed against the wall, but she only got a glimpse before the girl threw the blanket back over it.

"No, that's supposed to be—should be there."

"What—No it's not, why is Vanessa's sword in my bed?" Arica demanded, her own voice threatening to squeak too.

"You won't remember. It's okay. Something is—but I don't know. I don't know what," she mumbled, small hands open in quiet frustration as she scanned the room.

"Okay, calm down," Arica insisted, holding her hands out, not quite touching her in case it would trigger a meltdown or worse. "Let's just talk for a minute. You're with Vanessa, right? Where is she?"

"Vanessa? Oh, I don't know. Vanessa's not here. I don't know."

"I know, but I think we should probably find her." It was the only logical thing to do because even before anything weird went down, Vanessa was the kind of person who could solve weird problems.

For a long pause, the girl stared at her hands as if there was something gross dripping from them.

Without warning, she went to the desk and started pulling items from it, starting with the largest potted plant.

"Let's not make a mess, now—"

"This is important," she mumbled, setting the leather satchel to the side. Then she pulled Vanessa's book from where Arica had hidden it behind a purple stuffed deer, and let it fall open on the desk.

"That's not mine, you probably shouldn't—"

She ripped a handful of pages from the spine and held them up. "This is it. The wrong thing, this is—I found the problem."

"What is that?" She didn't recognize the pages before she crumpled them into a ball, but she got the briefest look at a drawn picture of a scary-looking man.

The girl quickly put everything back into place. "It's okay. You won't remember I was here. I fixed the problem. I found the problem."

"Wh-why wouldn't I remember you here? This is pretty unforgettable if we're being honest. And that sword—"

Cradling her prize like a greedy gargoyle, the girl took one more look at her, then grabbed her shoulder. "This is important. Follow the path, okay? Follow the path and you'll be okay. You'll know. You don't need me to tell you."

Arica's mouth opened, but no response made it past the mess of thoughts piling up in her brain.

Then the strange girl left the room, closing the door securely behind her.

Arica stared at it for a long minute, then looked around the room. Everything was in place, as it should've been.

Putting her hands in her pockets, she mumbled to herself, "Why am I standing here? Man, I'm tired."

4

THE GOLD COMPLICATION

The moment had arrived. Other students were filing out of the classroom, some in a hurry, some meandering as if they had nothing else to do with themselves.

Arica stayed in her seat in the healthy middle of the room, close enough to hear the professor well, but not so close that attention would be on her. She always arrived in time to choose her seat. After those punctual kids who wanted to have a perfect record or didn't want to miss a word, but before the slackers and kids that were so busy that they ate, slept, and studied all at the same time.

She took a deep breath, shouldering her weighty bag. Her world history textbook was the heaviest one she owned.

There were a couple of kids gossiping in one corner. She didn't know any of their names but knew they were the kind of kids that got bullied throughout grade school, only to be popular for their intelligence later. Other than them, there was only one other student that had remained, but he'd stretched out over several seats at the back of the room, face buried in a book.

Arica turned back to the front, where a burly man with terrible posture leaned over a wooden red-stained desk. Her lips pressed tight again, nauseous from nervousness, but she had to talk.

"Professor Lannert. Are you okay?"

He looked up, pale eyes dull and dark with tiredness.

He tossed aside his phone, still open to his calculator app, then set his meaty hands on the desk in front of him. They weren't the hands you'd expect to see anywhere near the sleeves of a suit, not even a casual one.

"I suppose so," he sighed. "I expected some mess, some youngster-related destruction, but..."

Arica forced a sad smile as a weight settled in her chest. "I'm sorry."

He lazily waved his braced hand. "We fall and rebuild. It's the human way. I didn't see you again that night."

"You weren't in your office." She lightly rubbed her cheek, trying her best to keep eye contact, but he wasn't trying too hard either.

"I didn't make it," Lannert admitted with a soft chuckle. "I was redirected."

She lifted her chin a little higher. "Was it Vanessa? The woman you wrecked into?"

Lannert nodded an affirmative, then shrugged. "I apologize."

"You remember meeting her?"

"Yes. She is quite the interesting character." He chuckled warmly. "Arica, I'm not concussed, if that's what you're suggesting."

"No, no, I just... She left without saying anything and I don't... understand why," she said, staring at his old wooden desk. "Before she did, I saw some stuff... Can I ask you a question?"

"Of course," he approved with a small smile. Professor Lannert patiently waited for her to continue, even though the time had passed for awkwardness.

Idiot. Spit it out. This self-pep-talk seemed to be a step in the right direction. "I just wanted to ask, for conversation's sake, what would you do, as a scholar, when you... see or learn something that doesn't make obvious sense to you."

The professor's eyes narrowed softly. "As a general rule," he started slowly, opening his hands to gesture at her. "A good way to *make* it clearer is to study whatever it is. I suspect that's... not exactly what you're looking for, though. Do you... perhaps, have an example of what's confusing you?"

She stood, trying not to let her leg shake out of anxiousness. This was already going terribly. "Well, no. My mind is playing tricks on me. I'm trying to make sense of it all."

His hands opened as a sympathetic, understanding look crossed his face. "It's not uncommon, unfortunately. The number of people getting a good night's sleep around here is minimal at best." Then he leaned forward over his desk. "But that's not what you wanted to hear, either."

Arica forced a small smile, eyeing the wrist brace. "I just thought I was crazy for a minute there."

"Miss Tanson, a part of growing up is realizing that those things you do—that you've always done—are often different from person to person. Life isn't what it looked like it would be; it's a constant feeling of uncertainty as you learn. There are people who do things you can't understand, people who know things you couldn't learn, and do things you've never even thought of doing. Trying to keep up with it can sometimes seem daunting, but sometimes you may find *yourself* while doing so. Maybe you'll find out that you could do things you never thought were possibilities."

Her smile grew slightly pained, her body instinctively leaning away from the professor.

He flashed white teeth, letting out a quick sigh. "That's *really* not what you wanted."

This observation broke some of the tension in Arica's shoulders, and she let her lips curl into an actual smile. "Well, no, not really. I don't know what kind of answer I was looking for. I guess that's why I asked."

"Never a bad time to ask a question," Lannert concluded loudly, then shook a hand at her. "Out, though. You look like you need some rest and food. Why don't you come by my office on Thursday? I won't have a stack of papers to read, so I'll make us some coffee and we can talk about the whys and therefores of life. Since we didn't have time to speak Friday."

"Thanks. I will," she said with a small smile. She shifted the bag on her shoulder as quickly as she could and hurried away while she had the ability.

What did any of that even mean? She asked herself this, eyes trained on the newly glazed hardwood floor under her feet. *Is he trying to confuse me? Does he* actually *know what he's saying? Maybe he's in cahoots with the rest of the weirdos?*

As if summoned by her thoughts, one of said weirdos was walking down the hall in the opposite direction. But she didn't notice until she nearly collided with him; turning her body gracelessly to the left to keep from making contact.

"You!" she shouted, louder than she'd intended.

The tall, dark-haired fellow shifted the imbalanced books in his arms. "Do I know you?" Jake mumbled with a lazy glance of annoyance.

"From the party last night," she insisted, astonished that he didn't recognize her. "You touched me, and... everything kind of blew up."

"Look, sweetheart, I barely remember anything past chugging a few—"

"You were drinking ice water!" she interrupted, turning as he attempted to shoulder past her, resolute.

"—but whatever happened after I 'touched you', I swear it meant nothing," he mumbled passively.

"Are you serious? You're just gonna stand there like nothing happened? " she demanded, searching his face for the joke. "I have no idea what's going on except I burnt down a *library*. If the book nerds find out, they're gonna hunt me down and turn me into themed bookmarks. I need *help*."

Jake's deadpan gaze wore on her resolve and her stomach turned. "You're right. You do need help."

Her mouth hung open as he turned his back and continued on his original route; no attention paid to her claims. He was getting away, and she was panicking too much to come up with much else. Except for a simplistic question.

"Well?" she called after him. "Where's Vanessa?"

Jake turned back, a touch of a smile forming on scarred lips. "Now you're asking the right questions."

She expected some sort of elaboration but was severely disappointed as she watched him retreat.

Shoulders hurting, Arica dropped the bag next to her bed and collapsed. *I don't like change. And this is just painful.*

What was any of that supposed to mean? Something weird was going on, this was for sure.

She grabbed the pillow above her and pressed it over her face, pretending to let out a real scream. Her arms slacked, and she lay there for a little while. She could hear a noise outside her room, proof the rest of the apartment was still alive. Though the more expressive of the voices was definitely Sera's.

Eventually, Arica placed her pillow back into its spot against her headboard, but she wasn't about to be any less lazy. Her arm draped heavily across the rest of the bed.

Her elbow hit something heavy.

"Ouch," she chirped, snapping her arm back to her body to nurse the limb as it buzzed with pain.

She threw the blanket to the end of the bed, wondering why she was so disorganized and what she could've left there this time. Her jaw dropped.

Shining in the dull light of her cheap light bulbs, there lay a mass of gold and steel formed into a long, molded weapon long dictated obsolete.

She reached out, unsure that her fingers would actually touch the golden hilt of the sword, even though her arm still ached from slamming into it.

It was cool to the touch, smooth even over the detailed swirling design of the crossguard, though the leather straps wrapped around the handle were worn and dirty. She touched the gem in the middle just to see if it felt instantly fake, but she couldn't tell. It was polished well and seemed to be set securely. Her skin itched to hold it even as she rationalized why she needed to leave it there. Ultimately, the unpleasant thought of trying to sleep with it won her over.

At first, she only gripped the black dyed straps around the sword's handle with one hand, but the smallest tug made it obvious that she'd need the strength of both. She pulled it out from the rest of her bedding, revealing the blade, longer than expected despite her glances when it still rested in Vanessa's truck. Shame it didn't have the same scabbard protecting it.

"Why is this here?" she mumbled, letting it sit in flat palms. It had to have been seven or eight pounds, an excessive weight to be any good in real life, or swinging around on a stage.

And the gold; it was such a perfect, smooth metal. If it had been actual gold, plated or not, it would've been worth more than her car, and her mom's house, probably her brother's house too. This also begged whether it had a purpose past decoration, as gold didn't seem like a good metal to make weapons out of.

She set the padded tip in the carpet, standing it up vertically to her body. It matched her generous five feet six inches with a bit extra, which meant the sword was ridiculously disproportionate. That included Vanessa, who had several inches on her, or even Jake, who probably hit seven feet and then some.

So what was it for? And why was it in her room?

She felt a pang of greed. It had to be worth something, and if they'd left it here, it couldn't've been important. She didn't know what else to do with it, so back it went, regaining its blanket covering.

As she sat down at her desk intending to unpack her backpack, she spied the old leather book she'd left splayed out, and picked it up. There had been one passage she'd read the night before, over and over. Maybe this was why she hadn't slept so well.

What can one know about magic? What can one know about the miracle and energy of life? Are they any different? Life is a label for something we know but don't understand. A babe's first heartbeat, or the last spark escaping an old man. This is what we call life, for otherwise we couldn't understand anything. Magic is a label reserved for the energy we don't know, and few understand. The forces that keep the flame warm. The rules that up is not down, oxygen is transparent, and time cannot stop. So what happens when these two things we don't understand marry into a force of their own? Could one control both?

Said book full of creatures was still there, sitting in her hands, so even if the sword and Professor Lannert's information weren't proof enough, Vanessa *had* been around, despite the empty room and clueless roommates. She wasn't going crazy just yet, though her sleeplessness would push her there much faster.

"That's it…" Arica mumbled, shutting the book. "I have to return it. Maybe she left it accidentally, maybe she wanted me to have it. Either way, I don't want it."

She felt nervous, even saying this out loud. She didn't want to deal with it, but she couldn't imagine just throwing something so beautiful away, and selling it seemed like trouble that could lead back to her.

Pulling the blanket back, she once again exposed the gorgeous gold plating of the sword.

Now, how do I sneak it out of here? This question brought up the next one of how it had gotten there in the first place, even assuming it had been early morning when they'd placed her in bed.

She took some canvas straps from one of her backpacks and used them to wrap an old shirt reserved for painting around the upper exposed part of the blade. It was extremely sharp, as she quickly learned. So sharp that the cut on her arm was dry for an entire minute before bleeding.

She was probably going to cut up the shirt, but better that than herself, and the leather straps crossed over the blade barely covered half of it.

It was heavy enough that she had to cradle it in her arms like a baby, her hands alone barely able to take the awkward weight.

Hopefully, it was just some ostentatious decoration.

Arica worked a hand free to get the door open, hoping everyone had dispersed. She couldn't hear any more talking, and it wasn't unusual for people to come and go.

The hallway was narrower than the sword was long, so Arica sidled down it at an angle into the living room.

"Whoa, where'd you get that?"

She jumped at the brunette's voice, almost unbalanced enough to drop the sword, but somehow kept it safe.

"Sera," she sighed, spying her across the room over a boiling pot.

Sera wiped her hands on the frilly towel over her shoulder, staring at the weapon with a strange hunger. "It's beautiful," she awed.

"And heavier than it looks. I gotta go," Arica dismissed, taking long steps towards the door, prepared to open it and scoot.

"Where are you going?" Sera called as she jogged after her.

Arica stopped for a second. That was a good question. "Uh… I'm supposed to hand this prop over to the theater group, I'm gonna meet someone. Just realized, though, I don't think I ever got the address. Hey… do you still have access to the database?"

Sera hesitated, folding her arms across her chest. "I mean… not technically."

Arica turned back to the room and gently laid her burden across the back of the couch. "I'd just need a phone number, or an address. Something simple."

She waited, her breath all but frozen as Sera glanced at the food on the stove. Then her stance broke, and she swiped her laptop from the kitchen table. "Fine. I know you aren't cut out for full-time stalking. Just don't tell anyone."

"Thanks so much," Arica said with a deep exhale, then followed Sera to the coffee table.

"What's the name?"

Arica knelt on the floor next to her, giving herself a break for just a moment. "Vanessa."

Sera's hands hovered over the keyboard. "And?"

Her cheeks flushed as she realized she didn't know it. How could she not know it? "Well... try Vanessa... Damage."

Sera's lips pressed together, but after a click of the keyboard, she shook her head. "Nothing even close."

"That's probably her stage name then. You know how theater geeks are. Are there any Vanessas in there?"

"Uh... There's seven of them," Sera recited, her eyes waving back and forth as she read. "Only two are current. Claire and Johnson."

Arica's shoulder fell a little. Of course she wouldn't leave a trace so obvious. However, Sera's face darkened with a look of confusion, giving her a glimmer of hope.

"This one, though... There's nothing. I don't know what she's in here for if she's never been here. No school history, no work history, no applications, not even any contacts. Just an address."

Arica let out a dramatic sigh. "That's the one."

Sera pulled a sticky pad and a pen out of her computer bag. "Vanessa Stanton, 172 Meadowdown."

"Thank you," Arica chirped, taking the piece of paper from her, then jumped to her feet. "I'll be back in a little while. You're my hero, Sera."

A tight-lipped smile was her only response as she watched Arica gather up the strange weapon, and drag it outside to her small car.

Normally, she walked everywhere she went. She wasn't a fan of other exercises, gasoline wasn't comfortably affordable, and most of her destinations, even work, were within a reasonable distance. But she owned a little red four-banger that was three decades old, usually used for trips to see her brothers. Hauling around an old, super heavy weapon seemed to be a good reason as well.

It barely fit in the backseat at an angle, and was anything but hidden, but it got the job done.

She pulled out her phone and typed the address into her map, instantly glad she'd opted for the car. "It's out in the hills..." she mumbled aloud, climbing into the driver's seat. "Uhg. I've got a drive ahead of me..."

5

GAMBLING

The fuel gauge on Arica's dash read dangerously low so far out, but this was not the worry on her mind. Winding hills stretched out for acres in all directions. She was already at least an hour in. And she was being followed. A little black sedan coasted the roads behind her, far enough for a few dozen cars to be between them, never opening or closing the gap.

Reason was trying to convince her to calm herself. There weren't many turnoffs, and this was a way through to the valley.

About twenty minutes later, she approached a tiny gas station with two single pumps and a little sandwich shop out the back of it. Her gauge beeped, begging her to fill it back up. Unfortunately, the black sedan had the same intentions.

She ignored it and pulled up to an empty pump. She hadn't filled up the tank in a long while but decided this time it was necessary. There went her going-out money, but she rarely *enjoyed* it with Mindy or Sera and their consistently growing array of plans. At least she'd actually have an excuse not to.

She glanced up from the pump. The black sedan's driver closed the door and jogged into the store.

Her heart dropped. *I knew it.* Arica anxiously finished her task, her mind racing as she planned out this encounter.

A smiling older gentleman toting a mop around held the door for her.

"Thank you," she expressed, and hurried further into the little store. She glanced over the snack shelves and the simple auto parts and fluids. It wasn't hard to find Jake at the back wall, looking at drinks.

She waltzed right up to him, ignoring the tug of anxiety in her stomach.

"Hey, so, I guess this means you've come to take that stupid sword from me, right?" she blurted quietly enough that she hoped the cashier couldn't hear her.

Jake pulled a bottle of juice from the fridge and leaned his arm on the top of the door. "What's this?"

Arica froze for a second. This was not at all how it was supposed to go. He should've asked if she was sure, or sighed and agreed. What did it have to do with drinks? She took the offered bottle anyway and glanced at the label. It was some fancy artisan juice in a glass bottle. "Pineapple juice."

Light-colored eyes glanced at her, his expression calm and curious. "Is it good?"

"How have you never had pineapple before?" She shook her head. "That's not what I wanted. You were following me."

"I was," he agreed, voice low in volume and tone, then crouched and pulled a cola from a lower shelf. He was barely shorter than her in this position, but it made eye contact easier. "Does that mean you're ready to accept help?"

Normally, she would avert her gaze when anyone stared her down. But something told her she couldn't show him any limitations. His thick jaw jutted only because he was almost glaring at her. He had thin lips and sad, more tired eyes than a twenty-something-year-old should've had. The color of them, however, was amazing. A crystalline blue, almost indigo... *No,* she realized. Purple. He had flat-out violet irises. She wanted to stare at them until they lost their luster, but it was already feeling odd.

"If that means you're taking the sword off my hands," she finally responded in a whisper. "I don't want it. And I'm sure you know exactly where Vanessa is."

He sucked on his tongue as he looked back into the drink cooler. A scar ran from underneath the collar of his jacket to just underneath his ear, thin but white on fair skin. "The thing is..." he began under his breath. Then he stood all the way up and closed the fridge. "I'm not supposed to touch it. But I *can* take you to Vanessa."

"What is she, your mom?" Arica mocked, trying to mask her indecision. Really, she just wanted the whole thing over with.

"I've been ordered not to. It's your job to take it back," he explained rather kindly.

"So now she's your overlord."

He leaned on the cooler, folding thick arms. He paused a moment before finally answering her. "Maybe, but you're the one who needs her help right now."

"What? Why would I..."

He pointed at her.

Arica noticed the bottle of juice in her hand and how it had gone from its natural, sunny yellow color to a nasty green and felt surprisingly warm. Her grip loosened out of shock and sent the bottle to the floor, where it shattered and splashed over both of their shoes.

"How did you do that?" she gasped, stepping backward out of the gross puddle.

"I didn't," he whispered, looking around the store with suspicion. "I'm virtually powerless here."

She grabbed onto a cooler handle, feeling lightheaded. She pushed out an apology when the crashing sound attracted an employee.

She insisted upon paying for it but quickly grabbed some citrus soda on the way to the register. Jake followed, taking a turn to pay. It was only after they both exited the store that their conversation resumed.

"So would you like help?" Jake asked as casually as any older person would when passing someone struggling to change a tire.

"If I have to bring it myself... then I think I'm okay. I know where I'm going," she explained as confidently as she could muster.

He nodded once, stopping in front of his own car. "Alright, then."

Arica stopped as a thought occurred to her. Then she looked over her shoulder. "You're going to follow me, aren't you?"

Jake stuck his hand in the pocket of his jeans. "Yes, ma'am."

"You lead."

Arica heeled the black sedan for a while. It followed the same path the GPS on her phone attempted to bring her, all the way up to the marker. This was where Jake led her differently than she would've gone on her own.

The address was for a small, run-down cabin backed into the woods just like the ones used along trails as shelter for the public. Nothing spectacular.

Jake turned his vehicle into the barely existent driveway, but instead of stopping, he drove to the side, then towards the back of the house. Arica stopped, her engine rumbling as she faced the little cabin. She didn't want to follow him. None of this was making sense at all. She didn't even know if her car would make it through those weeds and underbrush.

Just as she was about to stop the vehicle and walk, Jake's car disappeared entirely, giving her a spurt of bravery. She tossed her phone onto the seat next to her and chased after him.

The initial drive into the weeds was bumpy and terrifying, but soon her vehicle found the tracks of a few previous off-roading daredevils, and it smoothed. Still, she sat entirely upright on the edge of her seat, looking for rocks or dips. She crawled at less than five miles an hour, cringing every time something scraped her fragile car's body.

Their makeshift path wound out behind the cabin and into the trees away from it, at least assuming the little black car ahead of her followed it. She hoped it wasn't far from their destination at the pace they were going.

She lurched in a painfully deep hollow in the ground as she passed between the first two trees. They wound to the right, where they came out into a more open area. She confidently assumed this was the destination because of the jacked-up truck parked in the middle of it. Jake drove his vehicle to the right, giving Arica plenty of room to park between the two of them, as much as she detested the idea.

The pickup's tinted windows rolled down as soon as she opened the door, but the woman inside wasn't looking at *her*.

"You weren't supposed to find her," Vanessa barked across Arica's roof.

On the other side, Jake closed his own door and stood up to his full height. "I let her get most of the way. Just didn't want to wait the next few days before she found us here."

Vanessa glared. Arica could see the athletic blond on the other seat, looking non-confrontationally forward, neither seeing nor hearing.

Shaking her head, Arica pulled open her back door and hauled the gigantic sword out of the car.

"Here, this is yours," she puffed, letting the end of it *plunk* into the dirt.

Both Vanessa and Zak opened their doors and jumped down. Then Vanessa took a few long, elegant strides to her.

"Did you leave it with me, just so I'd have to return it and show up in the middle of the woods? Where nobody can hear me scream?"

"Indeed I did," Vanessa admitted coldly, then held out her empty hand.

Arica ignored the hand and let the blade fall into the dirt with a much harder *clunk* than she'd anticipated. She nodded a few times, then threw her arms across her chest. "Cool. Well, I'll see you."

She turned and walked the few feet to her driver's door, but the woman didn't stop her like she'd expected. She abandoned her fake attempt at leaving without gathering more information and whirled back to Vanessa. Her arms were limp, hands interlaced in front of her like a waiting queen in jeans and a leather jacket.

"Okay, fine, I give. What on earth is going on here?"

"First," Vanessa barked. She scooped up the sword with surprising ease and marched to the bed of the pickup. "Here. I gathered your things on my last trip through the apartment." She caught a large backpack over her shoulder, then tossed it at Arica.

Stumbling to catch the heavy thing, she corrected herself, but pretended it hadn't smashed her nose. "This isn't all of it," she puffed.

"No, only what I could fit or thought you would need. Before it was too dangerous," Vanessa told her tersely, then gestured at Jake to come closer. "Your brother will likely end up with the rest."

Arica glared at her, a mixture of fear and frustration boiling up in her throat. "How do you even know where Travis is? And what was so dangerous about the apartment?"

"A government organization was crawling all over the place before I left. I couldn't stay any longer," she said, as if this would explain everything perfectly.

She climbed into the truck, then handed two more bags to Jake, who silently hauled off with them.

Arica mouthed her first two words in awe. "The... the government? *What?*" *What have I stumbled into? There was nobody at the apartment, I was just there!*

"Don't worry about it, dear," she replied, handing another bag to Zak. "They're always trying to corner us. It became a little too close this time. I had concerns about introducing you. But we'll slip away and disappear before they find us, as we always do."

"What does any of that mean? I have school. That doesn't tell me why they're there or if I can go back," she tried, her desperation slipping into her voice.

Vanessa jumped down, landing in the soft dirt with perfect grace. Arica noticed the boys in the background, piling their bags on the ground in front of a pair of close-standing trees with thick trunks. They seemed to be normal spruce trees, yet their needles flaunted an odd color. The tinge, she realized... was actually a soft glow. She remembered back to the guy that had approached her a few nights before. His boots had glowed the same almost lavender color.

She quickly averted her eyes.

For the first time since she'd arrived, they made strict eye contact, but Vanessa's face remained expressionless. "I assume that by now you're aware that none of this was chance." Then she looked away with a hint of a frown. "Except for the fire, of course."

"I'm not really aware of anything that has to do with you people, honestly." Arica folded her arms defiantly across her chest. "Every time someone explains things, it makes even less sense. You have answered none of my questions, not even remotely."

Vanessa picked up one last backpack and slung it over an athletic shoulder. "And I apologize for it, but we haven't time. I hadn't anticipated problems."

To emphasize her hurry, she tilted her head, then followed the guys' lead.

"Problems?" Arica squeaked, chasing after her. "No, wait, just..." she sighed, letting her brain settle some of the random things she'd heard, but let her legs obediently follow. "What are we doing? What's the plan?"

There wasn't yet any answer as they approached the trees where Zak leaned, one hand on the left tree in front of them.

Vanessa looked back at Arica, her mouth open, but took her time before she actually started speaking. "For the sake of perception... It's been overdue for us to find you, bring you where you belong. Overdue enough that some people have caught on. It won't be any trouble once we can disappear, but it gives us little time to explain, to break you into the truth more gently."

"Disappear where? And what would they do to me?" Her voice rose in pitch.

"We've yet to find out, but I doubt it would be pleasant, and I'm positive that your life would not be the same after. As for our destination, it would be much easier to show you. But I promise you, it will be dangerous." She smiled a little as if this prospect was pleasant. "You obviously have the talent of someone special. So why not test it out? Train it a little."

Arica was staring at the ground, trying to figure out what this all meant. "I have a big test tomorrow, and I didn't study for it because I'm here. Mindy's birthday is this weekend. I was supposed to have coffee with Lannert."

"Lannert? Ah, so my suspicions are warranted. I've no doubt said coffee wouldn't be as casual as you think."

"Are you still trying to tell me my history professor is a spy?" Arica demanded, following up with a short, mirthless laugh.

"I suppose you'll find out if you stay here," she offered slyly.

"It's ready for you, sir," Zak called softly as if he didn't want to interrupt but urgency was going to force him.

Arica's breathing got a little more desperate as things settled on her. She couldn't go back to her apartment? What about her degree? What would Travis think? And her mom, if she just disappeared? "Wait," she gasped, pressing a hand over her jackrabbit heartbeat. "So, you're kidnapping me."

Vanessa reached out and took Zak's hand, before glancing back at her. "No." Then she turned back, and also touched the tree, almost ritualistically. Both of the guys looked antsy, but none of them broke the silence.

Eventually, Vanessa backed up, losing her grip on Zak's hand. "It's ready."

Then she turned back to Arica as if this was her last problem. "I'm giving you a choice. If I really wanted, I might be able to get them off your tail and curb your magic so they can't find you again. You could go back to school, end up working long hours to get by, and filing taxes for the rest of your life. Or," she suggested so enthusiastically that it was almost sarcastic. "You could follow us, go on an adventure, and uncover secrets that most people would die for."

She tried not to flinch back and show her sudden nervousness. "This seems like a trap. Like, a human trafficking level trap."

Vanessa tilted her head but seemed to catch that she was joking. "I'll make you a special offer. Give it a few days. If you can't handle it, I'll bring you back. You can spend the rest of your life selling little plants and eating hot dogs."

Arica continued wondering as Jake and Zak gathered the bags they'd rested on the ground. Then she stared at the faint glow of the trees, and the woman silhouetted in front of it. Why was she even contemplating this?

"Go ahead," Vanessa guided, almost softly, as she looked up at Jake.

They all watched him throw a leg into the space between the trees, then squeeze his body the rest of the way, only to disappear into the trees. Like magic.

It was obviously a ruse, all of it. Just a little more complicated than your average 'white ice cream van' plan. So why did she feel such a compulsion to follow them wherever they led? It was insane, and Travis would shake his head, telling her she always was too impulsive and whimsical. But she couldn't help herself.

I don't even like hot dogs.

SPARKS FLY

The smell washed over Arica faster than her eyes could adjust to the darkness. It was light and crisp, like a spring morning in the mountains, but much stronger and sweeter. Leafy camouflage shrouded her sight in near darkness as she braced herself on a rough tree trunk.

"The fresh air," Jake said, then let out a loud sigh.

"Watch out," Vanessa called, but didn't say what to watch out for.

A wave of nausea hit Arica as a cool breeze washed over her arms, bringing goosebumps to the surface of her skin. It was the middle of summer; she hadn't been so cold in quite a while. She stumbled over the crunchy undergrowth as Vanessa's presence crowded her forward. The silhouette of a leafy tree was suddenly in her face, embracing her with chilly dew-dusted leaves.

"Ouch," she whined as her hand caught a sharp branch. She stopped trying to move in such little light and sat down on the cold, spongy ground to close her eyes for a minute.

"Finally!" Jake yelled in his deep voice, making Arica jump hard enough to startle a hundred leaves above her. "They're back."

"Who's back?" Arica called, wiping dew off her arms. She caught one of the leaves, awed when it unfurled to be as big as her face, edges curled towards the stem with an old parchment texture. The sap smelled different too, an almost sickly sweet summer apple. As cool as it was, though, she knew there was nothing like this in Montana. Nothing she'd seen.

Tears of frustration leaked down her cheeks as she settled in harder against the cold ground.

Bluish light filtered over Arica's body, the leaves creating a shadowy camouflage pattern. She shrank back. The tiny sounds of her tears hitting the foliage made her self-conscious. Her hands and face warmed with a feeling that was already too familiar.

"I don't see Zakary or Arica," said Vanessa as the light shifted.

Someone crashed through the undergrowth near Arica.

"Over here. Arica is too," Zak responded, his voice just above her.

She clenched her hands, ignoring the purplish color radiating from them. *I'm going crazy.*

Leaves parted above her and a hand gripped her upper arm to help haul her up. She complied weakly and didn't hide her hands or face from him despite the urge to.

"It's okay," Zak soothed, putting both hands on her damp shoulders. "I reckon you're just as scared as I was the first time through that gateway."

She shook her head, unable to speak through angry tears. Her fingers buzzed uncomfortably as they clenched at her sides.

"It'll be easier once we're settled in." One of his hands reached for the back of hers.

The feeling and color vanished instantly, allowing her to take a calming breath.

"See?" he said cheerfully, then clicked his tongue like he was leading a horse.

"I don't understand any of this," Arica whispered, trying not to let her voice waver too much.

"I know, but we need to get out of the forest," he urged softly, then stepped back. He let go of her as she trudged through the leaves after him.

The light grew as they shoved through low-hanging branches, eerily ghost-like as the forest painted harsh shadows over Jake and Vanessa and the gear they hauled. The light moved again, making it clearer that it rested in Jake's hand, but it was too bright to look directly at.

"Kylen's station isn't far," Vanessa said evenly. "We need to move. Dawn is almost upon us, and we should be out of the dense before it is."

"I can already see his fire," Jake said, craning his neck to look over his shoulder.

Vanessa didn't wait for anything else before heading off to carve a path through the thick foliage.

"Wasn't there a path?" Jake asked in annoyance, but he followed right on her heels.

"It's a few yards. You'll survive."

Arica felt better that Zak didn't pass her as she struggled to follow. She didn't want to be left alone, but it was all she could do to not fall behind.

It was only a few minutes before dull light radiated ahead, and the strong scent of a wood fire reached out for them. Jake's blue light was squelched under his fingers.

A pile of glowing embers sat abandoned in a tiny clearing. A trio of horses tied to a stake greeted them with quiet snorts.

"So where is he?" Zak asked, breaking the impossible silence of the forest.

Vanessa's elegant features were blank as she scanned the scene.

"Could've been something dangerous," Zak added quieter.

Jake set his hands on his waist, his stance completely straight and even. "Hopefully it's nothing. Seeing as we're weaponless."

"I can fix that for you," Vanessa said lightly. Then to Arica's surprise, she unshouldered the strap supporting the gigantic sword, lifted it in one hand and gave it a slow heave towards Jake. He easily caught it by the protective straps, but its weight, even for him, appeared significant.

Then Vanessa glanced once more at the scene. "Get everything strapped. We'll leave our gear here for now and follow him."

Arica felt both heavier with worry and physically lighter as Zak gently took her backpack from her.

Her skin and brain numbed as she watched them strap their things onto the two unsaddled horses. Vanessa took a bundle from a horse and set it on the ground. It clanked lightly as she rolled out a few iron swords, simple and only a few feet long, much more practical than her golden monstrosity. As practical as a sword could be.

"There. Do you feel better now?" Vanessa demanded, distracting Jake from his tying. "Everyone grab something."

Arica fidgeted in place. She wouldn't be a part of "everyone" this time. Luckily, Vanessa didn't seem to mind because as soon as she, Zak, and even Jake had grabbed one of the plain weapons, she re-secured the rest of them.

"You've a plan now, aye?" Jake asked as he walked a few steps closer to the fire. Zak finished up the last of their chore and joined them.

"He's not far. Bialsa is com—"

"Hey buddy!" Zak cheered as a fluffy orange-brown fox bounced into the firelight. It leapt at him, caught in readied arms.

"You... have a pet fox?" Arica squeaked, resisting the urge to pet the fluffy little paws.

"This is Rune," Zak introduced, scrubbing the fox's head and ears affectionately. "I missed you, bud."

Rune squirmed in his arms, rubbing against his palm and nuzzling his chest with unbridled energy. He looked bigger than a regular fox, but Arica had never actually seen one so close.

It looked in Vanessa's direction, then jumped from his arms and scampered past the horses into the forest. Zak looked at her too, as if for permission to follow.

Vanessa bowed her head a touch. "Come on. Kylen hasn't strayed far."

Arica followed with an uneasiness settling in her stomach. It eased as they walked, but only because of the silence that fell over them. They followed what could barely be called a path through the thick trees, but it wound and snaked aimlessly.

Fifteen minutes later the thickness hadn't changed, but someone called them over with a quick greeting.

As they emerged, Arica saw a hooded man kneeling on the edge of a cliff, carefully watching below him. The leafy trees huddled together right up to the sheer drop, so Arica worried if she strayed even a few feet from the path Vanessa walked, she'd find herself slipping off of it.

Luckily, none of the rest of them got as close as the scout was. Arica edged just close enough to get a better view of the landscape in front of her. Stars blazed on a dark blue canvas, a million more of them than she could see from her apartment. Black mountains faded into the distance, the hills underneath them soft and expansive.

It was the tall squared castle glowing with moonlight that really caught her off guard, almost directly below them with sharp, light-colored towers reaching fruitlessly towards them in the middle of a vast courtyard. A large town spread out in front of it, hundreds of pinpricks of yellow light backlighting tall buildings and narrow streets. It eventually disappeared into one of the larger hills, whole buildings nestled into the forest at the base and even reached up the natural slope of thick trees like the ones surrounding them.

What city is this?

Arica startled when she caught movement in the corner of her eye, but it was just Jake propping a foot up on a gnarled, exposed tree root hanging on the very edge of the soft cliff. Her jaw shut as she realized he wasn't looking out over the intense view. He was watching *her*.

His lips pulled into a mischievous grin as she met his gaze. "Welcome to DeRael."

Her eyes tore back to the scenery as if worried it would disappear before her. Or maybe she was more worried that it would still be there. Her lips pressed tightly together, her heart rate increasing as confusion set in. She glanced behind her but only saw the dark silhouettes of dense trees.

"I... I... How..." She might've continued, but she couldn't spare the breath.

Jake removed his foot and reached into a back pocket. He unfolded the thick piece of cloth before offering it to her.

She took it in shaky hands, tilting it so the moonlight hit the black ink and would light it up without reflecting it. It was a map. A continent she didn't recognize, and despite only getting a C in high school geography, she was pretty sure she hadn't forgotten about any floating islands in backwoods Montana.

"How..."

"So, we're right here above Neva, the city you see below you. Most of what you can see to the horizon is one of eight regions, Nevaria, one of the smaller ones too." He used his pinky finger to poke a spot near the middle of the map. "If you look to your left, some of what you see may be part of Khantaria, but only a small part of it."

Arica nodded as if this made any sense, but it quickly turned into a brain-jolting shake. "*What?* How did we leave..."

"I suppose the gist of it would be..." Jake trailed off as he stepped from the map. "Magic."

"Right..." she murmured, unable to tear her gaze from the map.

"I'll try again." He cleared his throat. "*Magic...*" This time he twirled his fingers in a circle, drawing her gaze as a dozen tiny lavender sparks followed the pattern he drew. They suspended in the air for mere moments before sputtering out.

Arica blinked.

"Jrasko!" Vanessa snapped. She knelt next to the scout—Kylen, Arica remembered—but glared pointedly at the tall man. "Are you overwhelming her?"

"Rather hard not to," Jake excused loudly as he threw an arm out towards the view. Then he gestured at her, immediately changing the subject. "What have you found out?"

Vanessa bowed her head at her companion in the dated cloak.

The shadows gave him the appearance of age, but when he pulled down his hood and allowed the moonlight on his tanned skin, Arica decided he couldn't've been more than thirty. He had deep eyes and easy features, and most of his light hair was short, except for a long skinny braid down the middle of his head and draped over his shoulder.

"I don't know what's happened exactly, just that I got a distress signal about eight minutes ago," he said.

Vanessa stood, dusting off her hands. "Their barrier is down. We have to see what's happened."

"Winter's Staircase is only about fifteen minutes south." Kylen gave a quick point past Arica.

Something brushed Arica's foot. Not crazy considering how much stuff reached past her calves, but when she glanced down to be sure, she caught sight of a white, scaly rope writhing with muscle and thicker than her arms.

She jumped at least a foot to the side, letting out a scream of terror. Jake's large arm caught her before she careened off the edge of the cliff, then gently guided her back like a toddler about to walk off a curb.

A dozen white coils piled in the grass near where she'd stood moments before, all of them shifting and moving like a long sock filled with insects. Her skin felt just as insect-infested as a triangular head of solid white scales popped out of the grass, staring at her.

"She's just curious," Vanessa soothed, holding a hand out towards the giant snake.

Arica froze in place, hypnotized by either the narrow blue eyes or pure fear. A black tongue whipped out, sampling the air between them.

She finally found her voice, but it was weak and strained. "I don't care if it's the reptile of immortality and ultimate power. I can't do snakes."

"Bialsa," Vanessa snapped, breaking their stare-down. The snake obediently turned to her, its thick neck lowering its head to the ground. "You're scaring her. We're here now. You can choose something smaller."

The snake looked at Arica, making her jump again. She might've been able to deny that one had Jake not shifted to stop her.

Its skin roiled as if it had eaten something not so happy about being swallowed whole. Within moments, the snake's white coils convulsed together and folded in on themselves. Long white fur sprouted underneath small scales until it was only a pile of white fluff. The animal unrolled, stretching four little paws in opposite directions as a downy tail unfurled itself and flicked in the air. A quick yawn revealed some little pointed teeth and blue feline eyes batted from under a cloud of fluff.

"Holy..." Arica groaned as the cat, now barely any bigger than Rune, pranced up to her and continued the interrupted sniff of her ankles. "It's like you guys are *trying* to make me pass out."

Jake must've felt like she could stand on her own because he let his arm fall from her back. She took a few long steps away from the steep edge, but the fluffy cat gently flicked her with its feather-duster tail as it sashayed through the weeds after her.

"I'd rather you didn't just yet," Vanessa sighed, setting her hands on her narrow waist. "Anyway, this is Bialsa, my—"

"Familiar?" Arica asked, then glanced at Rune where he obediently sat at Zak's feet, watching.

"Andromae," Vanessa countered stiffly. "Very unlike a witch's familiar, as I understand it. A race of small creatures. They exist very much on their own, with incredible abilities, as you can see, allowing them to camouflage in many situations. Some time ago, they decided we as a group needed their protection. Mostly, they bond with those of us in higher positions, though it's been proven possible to coerce their protection." Her gaze bore into Zak for a moment, making him avert his gaze to the forest floor.

"I didn't steal nothin'," he grumbled, then bent to pet the fox.

Arica rubbed her brow for a minute, clutching the confusing map in only one hand. "I don't... a group? Who..."

Vanessa interrupted with a quick sweep of the arm. "We'll have time for questions as we go. It seems I have, once more, underestimated our timeline."

Arica's questions were not, in fact, answered as they went. The brief trip to Winter's Staircase was as quiet as possible, with Arica doing her best not to fall behind. She felt like a video game character, running desperately through the jungle despite only moving at a hurried walk.

She wasn't able to ask questions when they began the descent, either. While in most places, the steep path did have the appearance of a stone staircase long abandoned and overgrown, there were also difficult patches. Sloppy mud threatened to spill them down the slope, ledges dropped far enough to buckle braced knees, even trees crowded onto the path in some places, forcing them to take small paths around.

Part of the danger may have been the darkness. It wasn't as easy to judge how far a drop was, or how steady her footing was in the patchy moonlight.

Kylen returned to his little campsite with instructions to take the long way back with his horses and their gear, so at least she didn't have to lug her things too. Arica's legs ached, her breath heavy, but as they neared the last stretch, she told herself once more to be grateful they were going down and not up.

Ivory towers rose above them step after step, sometimes hidden behind leafy trees, but always there lording over them.

The path met with a shallow, dry canal stretching straight across a mossy wall framing the castle's courtyard. They followed it until they reached a large iron gate and climbed the edge. Vanessa used an iron key to allow them into a blooming garden.

The stones underfoot were smooth and fit together with cut precision, and while most of the flowers were closed up in the fading moonlight, they were still big and brightly colored.

"Shall we scout?" Jake asked, the first vocal noise in a long time.

"No." Vanessa didn't continue until she tore her attentive gaze from their surroundings. "We'll stick together until we know for sure we don't have enemies lurking."

"Enemies?" Arica repeated weakly, but they all started again. Even Zak passed her without saying anything else. "But... this was just supposed to be..."

"Quiet. Come," Vanessa beckoned softly.

She didn't feel like she had a choice.

They reached the wall of the castle in silence, and Arica fought back and forth between boredom and awe. She wanted to go exploring through the flower bushes and trees in the daylight, not be sneaking around in the shadows as the grounds grew darker.

Vanessa threw an arm across the path, stopping the group.

Low voices murmured close, too quiet to make out what they said. A hedge along their path shook, a few heavy but slow footsteps on stone.

A man grunted in pain a moment before something heavy thudded to the ground.

Jake slipped his weapon out of its leather sheath silently, then looked at Vanessa. She barely gave a nod before he sprinted forward and shoved through the hedge as if it were a beaded curtain.

Low, alarmed screaming broke the night's calm. A large section of the hedge exploded into a cloud of leaves and sawdust moments before a pair of cloaked figures darted out, one considerably bigger than the other.

Vanessa was in front of Arica faster than she could blink, driving her backwards and out of reach. Then she interrupted Zak's second step in his attempt at a sprint by grabbing his arm. "No. Let them go."

Zak did stop, even turned around, but his jaw was tight.

Jake returned through the broken chunk of foliage, but gripped the upper arm of a young man; shorter than even Arica, but quite stocky. Blood smeared the right side of his face and into his buzzed scalp from a shallow, swelling cut in his temple.

"Banen," Zak said with alarm, then trotted to his side.

"I don't know if you saw, but it was Nian Netosi and Siddek Helim," Jake said with a jerk of his head.

"They ran," Vanessa replied evenly. "They were only supposed to scout, I assume. Where was your partner, Lord Sraota?"

Banen barely shook his head, making Zak mumble an objection as he prodded at the wound with a newly donned glove. "They dazed me. I think Elvy ran for help."

"Why... Who were they?" Arica forced out.

"Dovevians," Vanessa said, hand to her hip. She scanned the perimeter, expressionless. "Though they aren't usually so brash."

"They weren't asking me anything," Banen grunted as Zak finished taping up the cut. "Just took my weapon and argued about whether to drag me off."

Vanessa nodded. "They're just testing us out. We'll find Commander Rapier before we plan an offense."

Arica flinched when Jake slammed his sword back in the sheath on his belt, but she was the first to follow his measured walk down the path.

They made it around to the front of the castle without any more incidents, but it wasn't as quiet here.

A pair of men walked the path in front of them, one holding out a pale flame-drenched hand to light their path. He walked straight and looked Jake in the eye as they approached. His hardened expression was only relieved by a touch of a smile on thin lips. He'd pushed a tan cloak behind his shoulders, his left hip supporting a long, slender sheath with a protruding gold hand grip. The other man wore a sleeveless tunic with long gloves up amber skin. Most of his dark hair was back in a short ponytail, allowing the irritation on his sharp features to be apparent.

Apparently, they were really going with the medieval theme.

"Master Damage," called the tall, pale one with mild surprise. "You've returned."

"In the nick of time, it seems," Vanessa said, stopping in front of them.

Arica would've stayed in the back, but a pair of large hands rested on her shoulders and steered her to stand at Vanessa's side with him.

"Don't be shy," Jake said cheerily, then reached out and gave the flame-wielder's forearm a quick, mutual squeeze. "Arica Tanson, new tyro. This is Steen Callovoi and Ricken Kisok." He gave the irritated man, Ricken, the same greeting. "Both knights."

"Knights? Like… of the queen?" Arica asked, eyeing the row of sharp, chipped daggers on Ricken's belt.

"Close. Of The Zenian Court. Welcome," Steen said, extending his hand. She did her best to repeat the gesture Jake had performed and lightly grabbed his brawny forearm as he gripped hers. His scarred and calloused hand felt like a pumice stone on her skin. Luckily, the awkwardness was over quickly.

"The Zenian Court?" Arica asked curiously.

Steen's thick eyebrows rose as he glanced at Vanessa.

"Someone decided we were there for personal amusement and started a commotion. I haven't had time to explain."

Jake set his hands on his hips, head back for a long second. "I was doing as you asked. You wanted to be out of there before Lannert got more information on you."

"Here we are again with 'Lannert's secret evil society'." Arica tried to chuckle, but it came out sarcastic.

Vanessa's lips were in a tight frown as she glanced between the new boys. "Where's Commander Rapier? I want to know why we had to chase Dovevians out of our courtyard."

Ricken jerked his head in the direction he'd come, his voice low and grumbly when he said, "The portcullis. We're grid scouting."

"Thank you. Back to it, men." Vanessa gave them a dismissive wave, then checked once more on Banen.

He still clutched his torn arm, but he wasn't breathing as heavily.

"So... Zenian Court?" Arica asked, forcing herself into a gimpy jog in order to keep up with Vanessa's brisk walk.

"A group of magic wielders with the sole job of protecting DeRael. You're a Zenian. Or you could be, if you wanted to."

"I'm halfway convinced to jog back up that mountain and take my chances with house fires," Arica admitted, blindly following Vanessa's confident steps.

"It's not normally so entertaining around here. Don't worry, if you still want, we'll have you back home before you know it."

Arica froze in place. Vines reached around thick columns and webbed across decorative benches and fountains on either side of the path. Lush hedges lined a towering portico, broken in the middle with a giant gate of metal open only enough for an average-sized man to pass under. The hall beyond was dark but led straight into the jowls of the towering building in front of them.

Jake passed her, bringing attention to a small group of people standing near the gate at the edge of a worn-down section in the path.

A few armed people shot off, leaving only two. The young redheaded woman in a long-sleeved top and tight pants had a rather large crossbow strapped over her shoulder. Her pale eyes were wide with worry, soft lips in a concentrated frown.

The man was only about Vanessa's height but had huge, bulky arms and shoulders obvious even under loose clothing. His expression and features weren't aggressive, his blue puppy-dog eyes sad and his sandy hair sweeping. His squarish jaw dropped a few millimeters when he finally noticed the approaching crew. He turned to watch her as she walked right past him to a spigot camouflaged in one of the tall hedges. "Vanessa."

"Banen, you're okay," the redheaded girl said as Banen reached out to grab her arm.

"Catch me up, Commander. What's going on?" Vanessa let water splash onto her hands, then used it to wipe her face and dirty arms.

Rapier's voice remained soft and calm as he explained. "In the middle of the night, scouts watched the barrier disappear in a moment. Both layers, without any indication, but we couldn't figure out how they did it."

"That's not good," Jake murmured as he stretched his long arms.

"Far as we've seen, it was just a couple of low-level scouts, but we're sweeping the entire estate."

Vanessa shook water from her hands. "We found Siddek and Nian poking around near the crypt, but I'm confident they've left the property. Do you think it was an accident?"

"What are the chances they just happened upon the barrier's weakness?"

"What are the chances they have something strong enough to break it in a snap?"

The commander shrugged a shoulder with consideration.

Arica swayed on her feet, some mix of exhaustion and overwhelming confusion.

"You've returned faster than I expected," Rapier said, his calm voice lowering as Vanessa returned to stand at his side. She looked like the director of an Arthurian movie, interrupting the set in her jeans and leather jacket, but something about the way she held herself fit right in.

"We had to get out of there rather suddenly. I'll tell you more once we've cleaned up this mess. Finish up your scout, then we'll get the barriers back up."

"Of course, sir," Rapier said with a slight bow of the head.

Arica's heart rate picked up when the imposing woman turned to her. "We did bring Miss Tanson back, if only temporarily."

Her eyebrows narrowed. *Was I targeted?*

"This is Commander Jadrion Rapier," Vanessa then continued, glancing at the muscular commander. "My second. You can ask him for anything you need."

Rapier bowed his head again. "At your service. Welcome."

"However, Jake will be in charge of your training, so you'll see more of him than any of us."

Arica craned her neck to his see face, but he looked indifferent even when he caught her eye.

"And I'm going to send Bialsa with you."

The white cat, kitten-sized now, leapt onto Vanessa's shoulder as if from thin air.

"She'll keep an eye on you when I can't spare one, and answer your questions when needed."

Bialsa crouched on feline haunches, then jumped the incredible dozen feet or more between them.

Arica reached out, catching the cat by no skill of her own. "She... can talk?"

"She can, often choosing not to." Vanessa jerked her chin in Jake's direction. "Get Miss Tanson a room. We'll pack down as soon as Kylen has returned and we've gotten a few hours of earned rest."

Jake nodded, and Arica felt an encouraging hand on her shoulder. "This way now."

7

Hidden in Plain Sight

A rica could hear voices.

At first she thought she was going crazy, then it crossed her mind she was dreaming. Except she couldn't remember what she'd dreamt about. Her hazy brain forced her eyes open a little, but painful light flooded them. Eventually, everything came into focus. Including Jake and Zak, standing at the foot of the large wooden bed.

Arica shrieked in surprise. "What the heck are you doing in here?" She frantically covered herself with the blanket before realizing she'd never taken off the clothes from the night before. Then she set a hand on her chest, trying to let her brain and heart discern they'd awakened and weren't in danger. "Do the two of you make a habit of stalking into girls' rooms?" she finally panted in a much more calm tone.

"Not as far as I remember," Jake said, looking at Zak for clarification.

"Well, there was that one gal in Veyber."

"Still," he droned, leaning lazily on the bedpost. "We knocked. We had to make sure you were still here and not kidnapped."

"That probably would've been a record," Zak agreed with a haunted gaze at the floor.

Arica threw the blankets off and climbed out of bed, stifling a yawn. "Sorry. What time is it, anyway?"

"Mmm... near noon, I suppose," Jake said, squinting through one of the narrow windows framing the bed.

Her stomach grumbled its agreement as she combed out her hair with her fingers. "I don't even know how long ago I got up. It was only like one when we left Montana."

Jake nodded. "Our realms don't always match times."

Our realms.

Arica didn't know how to respond to that, so she tied her shoes in silence. She felt rested, but a deeper tiredness still clung to her. The carved stone floor and tall ceiling of the room wowed her even more in the sunlight. Two comfortable couches sat against opposite walls with the entrance between them. Next to one of them, a bookshelf sat empty, and next to the other, a tall dresser held only the couple of hygiene things Jake had handed her. A dormant fireplace sat to her right near a large steel bowl half full of water.

"Here." Jake picked up a folded navy garment from the end of her bed and tossed it at her. "You don't have to wear it, but parts of the castle can get chilly. Kylen's brought our things, so we'll go to the supply room to pack down."

She took an edge and let the fabric flutter to the floor. The top was cinched carefully around a large hood, a simple silver pin stuck in the hem waiting to be used. She carefully flipped it around her shoulders and let it settle before pinning it closed near her collarbone.

"This feels amazing," she awed, letting her hands run over the soft lining. It was a little long on her, about an inch from dragging on the ground, but she didn't mind. It felt a little weird over the denim jacket, though.

Then she noticed the boys fit in better, too. Jake's button-up and watch were swapped for a long shirt with a V-neck and elbow-length sleeves, while Zak wore a loose tank, showing off a surprising amount of natural muscle. Both of them wore dark, buttoned pants suspiciously similar to her jeans, and big hiking boots.

"You guys changed," she said if only to excuse her staring.

"You'll have to too," Jake said, oddly serious. "We can't keep anything from Ellteria on us. It has to be packed away."

"Ellteria?" Arica balked a little.

"The word we use for your world. Few know we're crossing plains, and it needs to stay so. If Garal found out, it wouldn't be just our world in danger."

She gestured forward, indicating she was ready, then stuck her hands in her pockets. "Okay, so who's Garal, then? Leader of the... Dovevian guys?"

"And High King of DeRael."

"He's the king? Then haven't you guys already lost?" Arica stopped when she noticed Bialsa curled up on a couch. She must've understood they were leaving because she immediately jumped to the floor and pranced to the door where the boys waited for Arica.

It still hadn't talked to anyone.

"We exist to protect the people," Jake answered, staring into space as he held open the door. "We do our best to counter the Dovevians' grip, but our ultimate intention is to drag Garal from his throne once and for all."

Arica's eyebrows went up. "That's... pretty intense."

Her stomach continued its wail of hunger, but she was too shy to complain about it. Luckily, those few good hours of sleep had given her a boost of clarity, subduing the consistent breathless sensation she'd felt before going to bed.

The night before, she hadn't noticed that the wall across from her door wasn't actually a wall. It was the row of thick marble columns open towards the front courtyard they'd entered from. The thick vines and hedges filtered the high sunlight until it was patchy, sparkling across the polished marble floor.

It all felt so surreal. The echo of their boots and the soft twitter of a few birds hiding in the nearby bushes were the only sounds to focus on. And like the night before, they barely passed anyone as they made their way down the long corridor.

"This whole thing is... so weird," she mumbled, trying to peek through a cracked door. She saw nothing but empty furniture.

"I'm always a little out of it the first few days after crossing," Jake agreed with sympathy.

"It's more chaotic going to America from DeRael," Zak stated. "Feels like you can't get a moment's peace, like your heart won't stop racing."

"I can only imagine."

"But are you *excited?*" Zak asked with a cheerful grin and a quick bounce in his step that brought to attention the slight limp in his normal gait.

She lifted her eyebrows. "For?"

"Everything." He gestured vaguely around the hall. "You're in a new place, learning new things, meeting new people. Eventually, anyway."

"I think you guys still fall into the 'new people' category," Arica pointed out. She followed them away from the colonnaded hall into a much darker tall corridor lined with braziers in deep alcoves. A long, worn carpet led down the middle of it. "But yes... In a less 'happy' excited and more an 'I'm-gonna-throw-up' excited."

Zak chuckled. "I was pretty freaked out when I was new too."

Arica glanced up at Jake, expecting him to add something, but he was quiet for a minute. She would've goaded him on, but they stopped in front of a rounded iron door. Jake flipped out a key on a leather cord and unlocked it before forcing the heavy door open.

Shelves lined walls reaching towards the high ceiling. Assorted clothing filled them, all of it folded neatly, with wooden boxes on many of the lower ones. Boots, linens, bags, different little shiny boxes, small glass bottles and other small things covered the middle shelves and several low tables against the walls. A few saddles leaned in one corner, and two comfy couches sat back to back in the middle of the wood floor.

Arica wanted to explore and touch everything, but she restrained herself. "Okay, this is pretty cool."

The guys went for the pile of dirty bags against the end of the couches.

"You're welcome to anything you need," Jake offered. He snuck past Arica as she wandered further, only to ignore any of the items and open one of the two satisfyingly symmetrical doors on the opposite side of the large room. The room beyond it looked small and much darker. Jake searched for something against the walls.

Arica picked up a small vial from one of the waist-high shelves and swished the congealed fluid.

"Well, here's yours, Zak," Jake called, heaving a large chest off a shelf, and setting it on the floor.

Zak paced over, already pulling things left and right from the bag, including what looked like the outfit he'd worn in Montana.

Jake set another chest next to Zak's and went for another. "I don't know if there are any empty ones in here."

"Do you even have Vanessa's key?" Zak's chest opened with a quick turn of a key.

"Nah. I'll throw her things in mine for now. Ah-ha, here's one." He pulled a third one from the perfectly shaped cubbies lining the small room. It was obviously lighter than the other two had been as he jumped over them and set it on the couch. "This is for you, Arica."

She walked over to inspect it. Thin steel bones secured thick, solid wood planks together, a dark oiled finish completing it. A little brass key sat in the keyhole, so she turned it and opened it.

"All belongings that'll be suspicious go in there. Anything with print on it, anything plastic. Most jewelry is acceptable, most clothes as long as they've no tags. Some things we can work with. Nothing that could betray access to another world."

He tossed a bag at Zak, then placed one next to Arica.

"I suppose it makes sense," Arica murmured, pulling open the simple drawstring backpack she'd lost track of before. She pulled out her old hiking jacket. It might as well have been the first thing to go in the sturdy chest.

She glanced up as another chest snapped shut. Jake also glanced at Zak.

"I'm gonna run. I still gotta stop by my room before meeting Mistress Damage," Zak said.

Jake gave a dismissive wave of the hand, earning only a quick nod in response before the blond worked around the crowded room and left.

Arica felt a sudden rush to get through her things.

Nestled between the jacket and a navy skirt rested a little rose jewelry box filled with shiny earrings, a few thin necklaces, and an emerald bracelet. Just for its safety, she set it in the chest and re-cushioned it with the clothes. Underneath that, a figurine of a growling tiger cuddled with a magenta plush lynx. "I'm surprised she grabbed some of this, and not more clothes, honestly." She set it all in the chest and pulled out two books. One was a decorative bound sketchbook full of drawings and notes, and the other was her favorite novel in a custom dust cover.

"As crass and aggressive as she is, Vanessa can be very sentimental about home-themed trinkets," Jake admitted lightly. "Besides, there's plenty for you to wear here."

They were mostly things more prominently displayed in her room. Things that a stranger would assume meant the most to her. At least, besides her fragile plants. She pulled the leather satchel out next. It was odd to be reminded of it, but it was less mysterious knowing where it originated. It fit in with the chests and general feel of the entire building much more than even she did. This was the first thing she kept with her.

Except... who was that guy?

She eyed Jake as he haphazardly tossed things into his chest. He was abnormally tall, like the mysterious person, though maybe too tall. But she was sure he was stockier than the intruder, held himself more confidently, and his voice didn't have the same raspy mischief.

The intruder had mentioned he knew Vanessa, and that they maybe weren't the best of friends.

Jake pulled out a few things she recognized; Vanessa's small tool kit and a pair of tall leather boots, and tossed them with the rest of it.

"So are you and Vanessa close?" Arica dared in a strong tone.

"What ground makes you suspect so?" Jake asked without looking at her.

"I dunno... You just seem like you know each other well." She paused upon finding her wallet. Her money was useless. Not that she had that much of it.

"Then it may surprise you once you notice how well many of us get along. War and survival often connect people." He said this lightly enough.

Her arms settled at her sides as she gazed at the intimidating man in front of her. A question slipped out before she could think. "Are you really a warrior? Do you fight like last night a lot?"

Jake got up, and after returning his chest to the closet, started grabbing things from the shelves. His voice was careful when he finally answered her. "Yes. We have to. We can do things not everyone can, and we owe it to the world to do as much good as we can, just like everyone else."

"And these bad guys... they're... like us?" she asked tentatively.

"We're the same. But unlike us, they believe—King Garal believes that with our extra, immense power, we should control the lands. Vanessa's position has always been one that guides mortal government, but doesn't control it. We fight to give control back to the majority of DeRael's population because nothing else is powerful enough to oppose the Dovevians and the absolutism of their magic."

He cleared his throat, setting a pair of bottles in Arica's newly empty backpack. One was pink, the other a matte white.

"That's... pretty cool," she whispered without looking up at him. "Except the power struggle part, I guess."

He shrugged, then set a pair of jeans and a shirt on her lap. She took an extra minute to inspect them, surprised at how well sewn the denim was. "Jeans? Seems to break the whole medieval feel here."

"I don't remember what medieval refers to, but you'll be surprised how mixed DeRael's cultures and even eras are. That, and Vanessa is occasionally inspired by Ellterian pieces." He pulled a second pair from a different place.

"So... is it common to bring people from there to here?"

Jake paused, his hands over something made of a thick, gray fabric. "No," he said firmly. "I don't know why you're ours, but Vanessa's done it, anyway. You're only the fourth, Zak the third. And it's been... around three hundred years since we started going over there. The rest of us are native to DeRael and her surroundings."

"Zak is from..." *That's actually not surprising.*

"I can't remember the spot exactly. Big state. Hot and dry. He has this hat..." He grabbed the air at the top of his head as if he wore an invisible hat.

"You don't mean Texas?" Now that she'd mentioned it, she remembered the touch of a southern lilt.

Jake looked up, squinting his eyes a little. "It sounds about right."

Arica's shoulders fell as she looked back at the mess of stuff. *Wow... that's all... scary.* Without being able to vocalize anything else, she shut her chest and closed the bag over its new contents.

Jake added a few things to the pile on her lap. "Keep the key with you. See which size fits you better and, as I said, you're welcome to whatever you need in here. There are weapons and armor behind that second door, but I doubt you'll need any of either while you're here."

"I'll be honest, that's comforting," she admitted, grabbing her own arm for security.

"You've no reason to worry," he reassured again. "Go in there and change. You'll probably need to throw the clothes you have on in the trunk."

She fumbled with the things she had, trying to figure out what to wear, but just brought it all with her into the open closet. As she closed the door, she realized that there were no windows to let in light like in the main room. It was still plenty of light to see, not that she ever couldn't, so she dealt with the dimness. There were two shirts, but she chose the long-sleeved one. It was a dark red color and laced up the front. It was unusually long, though, halfway to her knees. She tucked it into her jeans for now, the second pair, as the first had been a tad baggy. All the fabric felt strange. She couldn't pinpoint why, but at least it was soft.

She opened the door to exit the room but stopped to take a peek at the rest of the chests. They all snuggled in their deep cubbies the long way, each of them with carvings under their thick rope or iron handles. Some of them had carefully carved names, but some had more rune-like lettering that made little sense to Arica's brain.

Zak's was there on the bottom shelf. She picked out a few more, labeled Elvy, Jerim, and Steen.

"What are these weird letters?" she asked, pointing at one such chest. She looked up as Jake spoke. He'd changed his shirt again, similar, but in a dark red.

"You'll find characters from multiple languages in there."

She touched one at eye level, six letters in a single line. "What's it say?"

"It's my name," he mumbled, leaning on the doorframe so he could see inside.

"It's too long."

"It's Jrasko. Jake is a nickname."

She gently touched underneath the letters, leading her hand along. They were unevenly engraved in the wood like it was done freehand with a hot metal rod. "Okay, so that's a D? And R-A-I-S-O. Right?"

"Nope," Jake dismissed, a gentle smile on amused lips.

"D-R-E-Y-S-O. Dreyso."

"Not even close," he chuckled.

"D—"

"It's a J," he interrupted. "J-R-A-S-K-O."

Her eyebrows creased, then she shook her head. "Your mother just threw a random K in there to screw with people, huh? Weird sense of humor," she murmured.

"Aye, I'd like to see you tell her that... But it's a Malsydon name."

She stabbed her finger at the offending letter, but it unexpectedly shifted under the weight like a loose puzzle piece. She pushed it harder on instinct alone, and something clicked. A piece of wood popped open at the bottom of the chest. A hidden compartment.

"Oh, sorry, I didn't—"

"What did you do?" His wide shoulders filled the doorway.

She hooked a finger in the cubby and pried out a cold chunk of metal heavy enough she had to catch it in her other hand.

It was almost the size of her hand, the gold face carved with a decorative design focused around an old skull wearing a spiked crown. Bars jutted from the top and bottom for a belt or sash, but it weighed several pounds; probably not the most comfortable decoration to wear. It felt good in her hand.

"It's not yours?" Arica asked as Jake took it.

"No... It's a hero's crest. They're not all that common." He glanced over it with low eyebrows. Then he looked over his box, shoehorning Arica into the corner.

"I wonder how long it was there. Guess it pays to be a snoop," she joked, but he looked too concerned to care.

After a minute, he left, pocketing the heavy item.

Arica frowned but stepped back out and tossed the rejected jeans on the couch. "These didn't fit well."

He nodded and traded for another pair of the right size. "Well, we'll head to talk to Vanessa and probably spend the rest of the day exploring the castle. We'll wait until tomorrow to start training you."

Trading a few more things he'd given her for those in her hands, she finalized what was to put in the chest and what to keep out. Jake grabbed the old trunk off the couch and took it back to its place.

Arica didn't know how she'd find it again, but she had bigger things to worry about.

"Ready?"

She tied her bag up neatly and slung it over her shoulder, then gave the room one last sweep with her eyes. "Yep."

Jake opened the door and let her back into the hall.

Arica controlled a shaky sigh as it tried to escape. "What exactly will training entail?"

"Mostly, it'll be giving you a safe place to mess around until you know how to control your magic. Usually we sword train in tandem, but I doubt it'll be of much use in Ellteria."

She was quiet, looking over the vaulted ceilings and the careful carvings in the pillars and artwork lining the corridor. Most of the paintings were too detailed to understand what they depicted with a quick glance as they passed, but they had an intense feel to them, with deep colors and harsh lines.

They saw very few people as they passed, most simply clothed people who kept their eyes down as they passed.

"You know... My brain still thinks I'm gonna wake up in my room eventually, and I'll forget ninety percent of this."

Jake stuck his hands in his pockets now that they were empty. His posture was incredible, no slouching or hunching as they walked, just his head high and spine straight to display his full height. She should've noticed he was different in the beginning.

Maybe she could've gotten away from all of them in time.

"I understand," he murmured. "I remember the first time I went to America. It was similar. Such a different place, so much to learn, it's overwhelming. Although I didn't have the new sense of power."

"So you weren't just suddenly thrown into this kind of thing?"

He gave her a tiny, serious smile. "I grew up knowing more than likely I'd have the same power my parents did, if that's what you mean. But it's run in my family for many, *many* generations."

"Then why do I have it? None of my family is special." She cringed a little. "Well, not in a good way."

"Not *everyone* inherits it from their ancestors, though I'm sure you have some, even if it's further back."

Arica tried to come up with something to say but came up short.

"We're taking a detour," Jake said, just as she grew confident that they headed back out to the courtyard the same as the night before.

"Okay..." Arica murmured but jogged after him as he picked up speed.

In full daylight, the garden was even more beautiful, the flowers and greenery bright and colorful. The warmth of the sun had brought out a delicious sweet scent, and the same heat was welcoming on her skin.

She followed quietly as they worked along the cobbled path back around the castle. Mostly to listen to the songbirds twittering and dashing from hedge to tree and back.

Eventually, they came upon a small, unimpressive square building, a shack of stone with a few steps up to it. Probably storage for watering cans and shovels. Jake pulled himself under the low awning and set a shoulder against what she had to assume was a door, despite the absence of hinges or handles.

"Since I know I'll likely end up the one who has to do this, I'll get it done preemptively," he said passively as he set a hand on the smooth, tan stone. A silent puff of dust erupted from the edge nearest his hand.

A simple click quickly quieted a sharp ringing, so Arica scrambled forward to check out what he was doing without getting in the way. He wedged a few fingers into the new crevice. With his shoulder and arm muscles all tense, Jake inched the large slab of stone away from him. Tiny metallic pings went off with every other centimeter, making Arica wonder what had happened to the mechanism that had once opened it.

"I don't know... who closed it again..." Jake puffed, using a foot to get better leverage.

Dust rained into the slowly appearing hole, the slab retracting until slowly but surely a steep passage into darkness revealed itself. Jake let go and brushed his hands off.

Arica just pointed. "Maybe you should fix it."

"There's no point anymore," he sighed, waving a hand. "There's nothing important down here anymore."

She glanced down the steep steps. The bottom was within sight, but it was dark enough she couldn't tell how far it was. "It's okay," she cooed, glancing back up and giving Jake a sympathetic pat on the shoulder. "I still need you to protect me from the scary spiders in the basement." She hopped down the first one, curiosity getting the better of her.

"Mocking me is brave," he growled, but followed her down the steps.

Until she froze, staring into a black, empty abyss as the large man almost knocked her down. *What am I doing?* "Wait, there aren't any huge wolf-sized arachnids down there, spitting venom and clamping their giant pincers... are there?"

Jake reached a hand over her shoulder, letting an all too familiar glow take over it. "Not so sarcastic now, are we?"

Her heart fluttered a little, a bubbling in the pit of her stomach. It only worsened as a single tiny flame licked up his palm and spread over his hand as if it were drenched in fuel. It gave off the faintest purple tinge.

"You'll have to start learning sometime," Jake said, way closer than she'd realized.

"I can't do that again," Arica whispered, trying to swallow past the lump in her throat. How did he know the idea terrified her?

"You will not survive long if you refuse to mess with a little blaze once in a while." His fingers fully spread out, blasting the flame to brighten the passage, and temporarily blinding Arica.

She ignored the urge to cringe back, and took another steep, jolting step down, trusting her instincts and Jake's light to guide her.

The deeper they went, the closer in the walls pressed and the worse the musty stench invaded her nostrils. The walls all the way down were solid stone, but a thick, dark brown substance that Arica was much too squeamish to touch covered them. Luckily, Jake stayed only about a step behind her the entire way down.

It abruptly opened into a long room, sectioned off by square pillars. Dozens of matching alcoves lined the walls, floor to ceiling. There were wooden boxes in some of them, but more had only pieces of the boxes. Only a few had slabs of stone blocking them off entirely. With the broken boxes, there were many bleached white human skulls. Most of them were in pieces but carefully arranged, and there were a few other skeletal parts, a few hands and maybe a part of a rib cage, but most of the skeletons were missing completely.

A soft, dark red glow took over the walls at regular intervals by reddish gems set into the trim between the alcoves, probably powered by Jake somehow.

"What is this...?" Arica asked in awe.

"Once, it was a respected tomb for Zenian families," Jake whispered, his deep voice reverent. "Many of the most prestigious family members, especially. Teres, Marc, Leadd, Damage, Valkosce, Bonds, Kisok..."

"Why is it such a mess?" she mumbled, inspecting an alcove with no box. A large skull with only half of a jaw sat carefully upright. The dark, hollow eyes stared at her until a sharp tickle ran up her spine.

"There have been a variety of different rituals to contend with the remains over the last thirty or forty hundred years, but a common one for this area comprises cremation in a special funeral pyre that leaves behind one piece of their remains. As you can see, usually their skull, but hands, feet, and rib cages aren't uncommon either. They sealed these pieces here with a talisman from their life. They're said to contain the Zenian's powers, though that usually isn't the case."

Arica pulled out a box too askew to be pushed into place and inspected the steel lining and the tiny gold plaque on the front. But it was missing its label.

"Respect and a fear of the ancient magic protecting the tomb kept it undisturbed for many millennia. Until King Garal took control of Nevah for a short time, in which he broke the protections and ransacked the tomb. Every one of them had family here, and still, they tore it apart for every small scrap of magic. We did what we could to put things as they were, but..."

There were no body parts in the box, but she found a tiny gold chain wedged into a crack in the wood, a small, crude stone carving of a bird looped onto it.

"They wanted the talismans," Arica whispered as she unhooked the chain and offered it to Jake.

He took it with calm reverence. "Yes. That would've been one, but the power in it is gone. The reason they left it behind. There's no way to tell who's it was." Letting it fall back into Arica's hand, he gave no instructions on what to do with it, leaving her floundering to decide.

She watched as Jake pulled the gold hero seal from his pocket. With a firm grip, he held it next to a collection of boxes high on the wall. This brought attention to burnt carvings on the front of a few.

"Are you trying to find a match?" Arica asked quietly.

"Mmm-hmm. These things are rare. If I can pinpoint whose crest it is, I may figure out how it got in my chest. We've a record of family crests, but I'd recognize it, at least I'd think, and I don't." Jake passed through a narrow archway separating the two sections. His small light lit up the markers as it bobbed along behind him.

Arica pocketed the necklace. It wasn't doing any good there, so maybe she could find a good place for it.

She followed to the second section even as Jake passed back into the first. She just wanted a quick glance around. An empty pedestal stood at the end of the room, another wall of deep alcoves, but the other one had shallow shelves instead, lined with a few decorated urns.

In the corner, she noticed one of the alcoves had a cover, but it was slightly askew. *Why would someone close it but not bother to make sure it was sealed?*

She crept another foot or so closer, hoping for a peek of a full skeleton or a mummy. However, as she reached it, she realized it was fuller, a colorless arm and shoulder in a short-sleeved shirt. Then the side of a head with dark, close-shaved hair. Intact, but not alive, not by the coloring and sheen. But where was the smell?

She jumped a touch, Jake's voice tearing her out of her focus.

"Are you coming?"

"Yeah," she squeaked, then scrambled after him. She hadn't realized how fast her heart raced.

Jake shook his head, turning to the stairs. "I don't see it."

"So; to Vanessa?" Arica asked, forcing a quick swallow. She hadn't seen the strange woman since they'd arrived, and she didn't want to admit she needed a friendly face.

"Yes indeed. Lead on up, Miss Tanson."

8

THE ZENIAN COURT

What should I be expecting?

Arica stared ahead, following the worn red carpet lining the middle of the castle floor. Her hands wrung together, her arms rough with goosebumps. She never was good at new things. Her first job, her first class, her first driving lesson. Even her first concert had been a mess of nerves, just because she didn't know what to expect.

Jake nudged her to a turn, forcing her to focus a little more. They turned the wide corner to an open hall horizontal to theirs, but directly in front of them stood a pair of giant iron-wrapped doors. The left was open to a bright, inviting room, but as Arica felt an urge to get closer, a low, accusing voice cut through her enthusiasm.

"So you're admitting you've been spying on me?"

Down the hall, closer towards the front of the castle, Vanessa stood chest to chest with her commander, Rapier, holding him against the wall. She held a long, slender knife, the tip digging into his beefy shoulder.

"To make sure you're safe," Rapier murmured, his soft features blank. He glanced over her shoulder, noticing Arica and her companion.

"Shall I intervene?" Jake called, voice loud but his tone soft.

She stood her ground without acknowledging him. Then she lifted her unarmed hand, revealing a ball of gray fluff. It leapt from her palm, sprouted tiny wings, then grabbed onto Rapier's collar.

"I'd better not find her again," Vanessa warned coldly. She flipped the knife away from Rapier's body, and it disappeared near her waist. Then she turned, stalking towards the door in work boots. She wore a dress of deep red, light and fluttery with slits to allow her long, athletic legs full motion, a high neckline but no sleeves. Her long hair was down against her back but stayed mostly in place.

"You're late," Vanessa snapped, then held an arm out towards the open door.

"I'll explain why later," Jake answered, tapping Arica's boot with his.

Sweat beaded on her hairline, but putting it off wasn't going to get her out of it. Instead of following her instincts, and high-tailing it back to bed, she jumped forward and charged through the door before anyone could decide they wanted to go first.

Bluish light flooded the large room from the blue and purple tinted windows lining the west wall. A huge natural oak table filled most of the floor space, circled by tall chairs. About twenty people crowded to the nearer half, several of them not even sitting.

A quiet fell over the small crowd, most eyes turning on her. She froze in the doorway and had to be pushed forward again.

She recognized a few of the people though, Zak, sitting next to Kylen, and the pale guy from the courtyard. Steen? There was Ricken, too, sitting next to a girl that had the same black hair and serious features.

The rest were a bunch of strangers in casual clothing and a few small, inconspicuous weapons. Most of them were men. In fact, Ricken's relative, and the redhead from the courtyard the night before, were the only other women. All of them looked to be on the younger side, nobody over fifty, at least at first glance; all athletic, even the generously pudgy fellow with a lazy smile.

Jake guided her to the side of the room against one wall like a parent corralling a shy little kid. This didn't help Arica's confidence.

Luckily, she quickly noticed that they weren't looking at *her*. They were waiting patiently for Vanessa as she stole a few more words with the commander.

"Are these *all* the Zenians?" Arica asked under her breath.

"We're quite rare," Jake said with a nod. "But this is only one of three similar groups."

Arica's curious gaze met eyes so black and empty that she froze in fear. Only after gaining sanity did she wonder how she hadn't noticed him the moment she'd stepped in. He didn't match the others and their humble normality; how they could've blended into her world like Jake, Vanessa, and Zak had. His skin wasn't a pale ivory or deathly gray but somewhere in between, deeply contrasted by his short raven hair and a pair of incredibly black tattoos running around one of the arms crossed across his broad chest. His clothes were black and plain on his stout frame, and he didn't quite reach the commander in height.

He broke her stare, but she didn't feel any better. Those eyes remained just as vacant, his expression so emotionless that Arica would've thought he was a badly painted statue if not for an occasional blink or turn of the head as people spoke.

"Jake," she whispered, lightly kicking him as her eyes stayed on the strange man.

She couldn't believe the question she was about to ask, but with his soft, "hmm?" as he crouched closer to her height, she'd committed.

"That man on the left of Ricken... He's not a... vampire, is he?"

"Oh, him, no, that's just Derrick," he dismissed with a little wave of the hand.

Her face warmed a little, unsure how to feel. "Well... what's wrong with him?"

Jake took a deep breath like he was about to launch into a rapid-fire explanation, then shut his mouth again and caught her eye. "You should ask him. He's not aggressive. Though it may take some talent to get him to talk. And you should go about it more judiciously than 'What's wrong with you?'."

Her eyebrows went up. "Can't you just..."

He lazily scratched at a scar on the back of his hand. "Some tales should be told only by those who carried them. Besides, you won't learn much if you only ever talk to me."

Vanessa stopped at the head of the table, hands gracefully clasped in front of her. Arica couldn't help but stare, too. It was obvious why Vanessa had given off such an odd vibe, as if she didn't belong in a little college campus living with some average girls. She belonged there.

Rapier slipped into the room last and mostly closed the heavy door.

Vanessa continued in silence until she stood at the head of the table, near a stocky brunet staring at the old wood. Her hands hung in front of her as she looked around. The silence oozed respect.

"As all of you should be aware by now, we were attacked last night," Vanessa announced. "A few low-ranking Dovevians. We're still investigating how they broke through our barriers so easily, but for now, it looks to be a mistake. An accident. I want to assure you that it had nothing to do with our return. We did lose track of one of ours, Lord Moor, and will do our best to find or recover him. Did anyone have anything to add about the incident?"

"We had what we needed to succeed, but the barriers..." Steen let a hand open on the table, his rounded jaw offset.

"I understand, and I have some of you looking into it."

The man to Steen's right, a bulky guy with a long yellow braid and tan skin, leaned over and whispered something that didn't affect their expressions. A scar ran across his eyelid, preventing him from opening the eye more than halfway, even when he looked back up at Vanessa.

"That is Master Damad," said a piercing, melodic voice out of nowhere. "An oddity brought to the Zenians from a hidden elven city."

Arica's quick, darting looks were probably suspicious, but she finally glanced down. A long-haired cat flourished a floof of tail across her ankles like a performer's ribbons. A triangular face turned to her, crystalline eyes staring.

Arica crouched and gave Bialsa a quick scratch on the head. "Can you... read my mind?"

"In a way." The feline's mouth didn't move, the tiny voice disjointed but not internal, as if she could hear the andromae with a hidden set of ears. A soft purr tickled her fingers.

Arica's name drew her attention, and she shot back to standing as if guilty of something. Bialsa sat on her foot, licking her tail.

Vanessa glanced away from her. "Jrasko will be training her, but she may only be with us for a few weeks."

A red flush spread over her cheeks as a few light scoffs and chuckles came from the group. Luckily Vanessa launched right into the next thing about defenses, but Arica chanced leaning towards her future teacher to ask a question. "What's so special about these barriers? What are they? Like a force field?"

"When we're not in a siege, it acts more like an alarm," Jake said softly enough to not draw attention. He set his fingers together, but she wasn't sure if he was demonstrating or just gathering his thoughts with a gesture. "It's not very strong, but it stands alright on its own. The way impenetrable magic works is that it either has to have a continuous source of magic or a place to focus all vulnerability. That place often manifests as a weakness. We usually have two of them with weaknesses, so we aren't expelling so much magic. If the first barrier shatters, we have time to change the inside one and supply it heavily. Make it nearly impregnable."

Her eyebrows stitched together as he jerked his head towards the table, but she wasn't totally lost.

"Whatever they used to get into the castle broke both barriers simultaneously. The chances of them finding the weakness of the second without breaking the first are slim, but the chances of them just stumbling upon both are less."

"But that's what Vanessa thinks happened," Arica pointed out.

"Hmm. And so we'll assume until we find evidence otherwise."

Arica nodded, trying not to let her mind go blank as she tuned back into Vanessa's voice.

"Had they intended to fight, they never would've sent in their newer blood. I'm sure you all wonder what I have planned in retaliation, and the answer is, for now, nothing."

The crowd didn't sound super thrilled about this.

"An accident like this isn't something to brush aside, though. We'll be taking extra measures to dissuade more curiosity, and I've already sent out messages to confirm the status of our other strongholds. We'll also be looking into the Dovevian outpost outside Raven. Supposedly, Anraquella and Ransom are only there to monitor Raven's lord, who's been threatening Khantaria's reign, but this morning we received word that Navin was undeniably in the area, and Drake and Lise may have been there as well."

A murmur came over the crowd, but the only one to speak up to their obvious leader was a young, slender man with orangy hair and a spray of dark freckles. "So, with Nian and Siddek close, we could be looking at half the Dovevians less than a week from us. That we *know* about."

"That is Jerim Enileny," Bialsa squeaked in a bored tone.

Vanessa nodded assuredly but didn't answer before Rapier stepped forward, hand resting on the pommel of his sheathed sword. "We will defend first, as is our strength in this position. I'm sure you're all anxious to be toe-to-toe."

Low murmurs of approval supported his suggestion, but Arica had her hands on her face, trying not to let her stomach twist any tighter.

"But we won't get to that point until we can relinquish them of any more tricks," Vanessa warned.

"Master Damage," said Ricken's brusque voice. "What exactly was in the notes sent to the other bases?"

"You've met Master Ricken," Bialsa quickly whispered in her tiny voice. "His sister is Malon. They come from Veyber, a harsh farming community in Utor-Kassic's wetlands, and hail from a long line of Zenians."

Vanessa regarded Ricken with what seemed to be suspicion. "I asked them to keep a greater watch and ready their barriers as we will in light of this. Commander Herak's unit, especially."

"And Commander Vanne's? His is okay?" Zak asked, eyebrows low in concern.

"Have you conceded yet that we should *know* where these other bases are?" Ricken demanded.

Vanessa leaned both hands on the table, glaring evenly. "I have not, Lord Kisok," she spat through her teeth. "And do not ask again."

Rapier said nothing, but set a hand on her bare shoulder in a show of support, or maybe to soothe. Her glare switched to him, but her stance lost tension immediately.

"Unless you've more brazen questions, Lord Kisok, or anyone else, I'm going to allow Commander Rapier to hand out assignments now. You shouldn't have questions about them."

Arica let her arms fall from the awkward cross-armed stance she'd held, then faced Jake. "I'm starting to get the impression that she's, like, important..."

He lifted his proud chin even further but still glanced down his nose. "High Master von et Vanessa Damage of the Zenian Court. There is no one ranked between Vanessa and the gods. At least there shouldn't be."

"That king dude," Arica guessed, then let out a soft sigh.

Jake nodded slowly, his lips pressed into a thin line. "That king dude. Garal."

They both looked over Arica's shoulder, watching as Rapier sorted out a pile of thick square pages to a low-energy crowd. Vanessa watched for a moment, then hands again clasped in a peaceful manner, she walked around the commander and joined the newbie and her chaperone.

"I'm sure this must be a lot for you," Vanessa said, but her voice was void of empathy or concern. She was just stating a fact. "But it isn't complicated. You'll learn how to control your magic, what to do to temper it, how to use it to your aid, and how to feel what your deeper self is trying to do with it."

"Tomorrow," Jake grunted.

She gave a soft nod. "Agreed. Take a day to explore your new home for the next few weeks."

"A few *weeks*?" Arica squeaked. "I don't even…"

"I'll rearrange things when we bring you back," Vanessa assured, a stray inkling of warmth in her tone. "By the time we're satisfied, Lannert—or whatever manner of suspicious individuals and their concerns will have abated enough to continue your life. I'll take care of the rest."

Arica's voice wasn't even strong enough to get through a "Yeah."

Warmth spread across the Zenian Master's lips in a subtle smile. "Then you two have the rest of the night off. Enjoy."

She bowed her head as she stepped away. Arica bounced on her feet and right out the door before Jake could boss her or push her.

"So, a tour of a giant building, some food, and call me a resident of an actual castle?" Arica asked cheerfully, swinging her arms extra far as she walked. "Or is it going to be so bad that I wake up tomorrow and go into full panic mode when I can't leave?" She stopped in the bright hallway as the white cat sashayed past her.

"Do you want me to carry you?" she blurted, holding out a hand.

Bialsa turned, silent, then in a graceful leap pounced onto Arica's shoulder. She was lighter than expected, with no claws digging into her skin, and kept her balance perfectly as she settled against Arica's neck.

"Don't worry," Jake murmured as he gave the cat a quick scratch between the ears. "We'll get you settled in. A good night's sleep did no one that much harm."

"What do you mean by that much harm?" Her voice rose a few octaves.

He slowed for a moment, casting his gaze over her. Then he shook his head dismissively. "Forget I said anything. It rarely happens."

Arica stopped in her tracks and glared at him. "Did you really think that I wanted to hear that, especially if you want me to get a 'good night's sleep'? Is something going to come crawling out to eat me?"

"Oh, dear, no," he purred, a tinge of amusement in his features. "I was talking about the Dovevians. But if we're being honest, I'll give you three weeks before you're dead, anyway. To make it more interesting, I predict it won't be by blade in the middle of the night. It'll probably be your own clumsy accident."

Her eyebrows went up with his candidness. "Is that the pep talk you usually give the newbies?"

He shrugged his large shoulders nonchalantly. "There's no use sugarcoating. You're a Zenian now. You gotta be tough or you won't make it long. Besides, you're the one who asked."

"Well, all your talk of nighttime assassins has failed, anyway," she announced, skipping past him. "Because all you've done is make me wonder where your room is. You're a heavy sleeper, right?"

He smirked, sticking a finger out at her. "Quite the jester you are. But no, I'll wake up if you so much as breathe in my room."

Arica didn't know where she was going, since she was ahead, but the corridor went straight for a little length. So, she turned towards him, walking backwards a few steps and smiling just a little. "Scared of me now?"

"Uh... no. As far as I remember, you haven't a single weapon to your name."

She shrugged, letting him catch back up. "Best not to think about it too hard."

He gave her a half-glaring, half-challenging look, then shook his head. "We've arrived, Miss Tanson. And I'll be generous. Maybe you'll live a whole month."

DIFFERENT STRENGTHS

"Well?" Jake demanded impatiently.

Arica fidgeted, staring at the row of shiny blades that he'd ever so carefully arranged on the wooden planks in front of her. "I... can't just pick one."

Sitting cross-legged on the floor across from her, Jake rubbed his temple and gestured out at them. "Pick any of them. You can always change later if you decide you don't like it. Or I can get out the heavier stuff if you want it."

He'd arranged them by blade length. The longest one was about the length of her forearm, including the crude steel hilt. It had a rough texture except half an inch around the shiny edge. The smallest one was a tiny blade about the length of her thumb, a mean little razor blade poking out of a thick handle. In the middle, there was one with a thin, evilly curved blade and a gold-plated handle, a few plain steel ones, and a skinny one stained black.

"How am I even going to learn to sword fight with any of these?"

"Kid, this is just for protection. You're training with this..." He jumped to his feet, then stalked across the large, brightly lit room to the benches along the wall. Earlier, he'd brought in a large piece of furry hide wrapped around a heavy-looking pile of weapons, out of which he'd pulled all the daggers.

The first sword he pulled out had a flat blade. The second was considerably bigger and much more beat up.

Arica followed, curious.

He turned to her, holding the larger one correctly, but the other he held out to her, handle first, the blade parallel to his arm.

She was hesitant to take it from him but did.

It was smooth on her palm, a simple polished steel handle that twisted around the blade. She loved how sturdy it felt. Until Jake let all of its weight go. She barely kept the tip from slamming to the ground.

"How am I supposed to swing this around?" she asked, heaving it upright. Both of her hands squeezed onto it, allowing a little more control of the weight.

"You'll get used to it."

Feet spread and arms clenched, Arica weakly swung the weapon through the air, almost unbalancing herself.

"So, there are a few rules for magic," Jake said as he watched her stumble around like a drunk kitten, indifferent.

"I thought this was sword practice." She raised it up to about shoulder height and kept it steady. As long as she wasn't swinging it around, it wasn't too heavy.

"It is, well, it's both. I thought the whole reason you came here was to learn control?"

She looked around, wondering if he'd allow her to hack at the overstuffed dummies on the opposite wall. The sunlight cast over the wooden planks shone from the huge glass panes, but it was reaching farther and farther into the room. It had to be past lunch time already.

"You said sword practice was okay," she managed, focusing on balancing the weapon in her hands.

"I'm not going to force you into magic, but that will have to stay our focus even if you want to play around."

"Hey, maybe I'll never need to throw a knife around in defense—Well, so I hope—But it'll be *great* for impressing my brothers." She didn't mind distracting from the fact that doing anything magic related terrified her.

She looked at him after a few moments, wondering if he was going to answer at all.

Jake stood, giving her an amused stare. "You're the one who says you're going home. The rest of us... well, the rest of us don't believe it so much."

She let one hand let go of the handle just so she could put it on her hip. "Oh, yeah?"

He held his hands out. "DeRael is too irresistible. You're staying by your own will, whether or not you know it now."

She turned her whole body towards him, much more ready than he was in his lazy lean against the wall. "Because what's more irresistible than no indoor toilets and bad guys cutting you in your sleep?"

Then she took a step forward, throwing as much force as she could into a side swipe.

"Hey," Jake objected abruptly, but faster than lightning, he had his steel between himself and Arica's blade.

A harsh, metallic screech emitted from the swords as they clashed, but there was no chance for another strike as Jake pushed their blades harder together and forced Arica off balance. She crashed to the ground.

Pain shot up her shoulder, taking most of the impact while her weapon skittered across the wood with an abrasive scraping noise.

"Not a bad hit," Jake chuckled above her, but he made no move to help her up.

"Ow..." was the most she could manage. Her hands pushed her off the floor and onto her knees, where she could reach back out for the sword.

As she stood, Jake spread his feet and pointed his sword at her. "Rule one. Bring your gloves."

Arica threw the sword up, both hands gripping the hilt. She let the tip of it touch Jake's with a tiny *clink*.

"They're in my stuff in my room," she explained quietly.

"Well, from now on, they need to be on your hands."

She noticed that he himself was wearing a thin pair of black ones underneath generously long sleeves.

"Why?"

Jake lightly swung the weapon at her side, making her jump back, but the flat of his blade connected with her hip anyway, just hard enough to sting. "Metal is a weakness. If much of it touches your skin, it can cap your power, make it so your magical energy can't escape."

"Just metal in general?" She backed up a step so it wasn't so easy for him, her muscles already quivering with the heavy item.

"Silver and gold are safe to touch, in fact they work well to enhance and direct more magic, like that seal you found. It's also why you'll see some of the older Zenian weapons made from it, but most of us don't get that luxury. We just cover our hands so we don't have to constantly sheathe our swords to perform the tiniest task."

"So I'm powerless right now?" Arica asked, shifting her sweaty palms before easing the sword around to get used to her balance.

"Yes. Another weakness is skin contact. Especially if both people have the energy." He relaxed his weapon, but not as much as he had before she'd struck at him.

She zoned out for only a moment as she spoke. "After we came here, I was sitting on the ground and I... I felt like I was losing control again. Then Zak... he just touched my hands, and it stopped. I thought he used his magic to stop it..."

Jake shook his head. "He didn't need to, and if it'll make you feel better until you're fully trained, you can keep the gloves off. Touching your sword will have nearly the same effect if you feel you're getting out of hand."

She blushed a little, looking at the heavy thing. "That's comforting, honestly. Do I really have to haul this thing around, though?"

"We'll get you used to it," he assured.

Arica's fingers worked around the handle, trying to adjust it to be more comfortable. It slipped out of her grip and clattered to the ground. She skipped away before she sliced her feet open.

"This is dangerous..." she whispered in fear, staring at the shiny blade.

Jake let out a warm laugh, then gave her a quick nod. "Hang on. I've got someone coming over here to help."

"Another one of your many friends?" Arica inquired.

Uncharacteristically quietly, Jake explained, "He's more like a brother..."

"I love how close you are to everyone."

"Happens when you spend so much time fighting for your life with them. You turn into a family."

"Vanessa is the mommy, Rapier is the daddy..." Arica teased. "You can be the big brother that's kind of mean but protective."

Jake shook his head in skepticism but smiled. "Then *you're* the new baby that everyone might like but doesn't know what to do with."

"I suppose that's fair," she shrugged a little. "Are you actually related to anyone here?"

He bent over and picked up her abandoned sword. "Quite a few of them, actually. One of those old families, most of which are connected in one way or another."

"What's your last name, then?" It felt strange to her that she didn't know. But she'd only known him for a few days.

"Damage," he mumbled distractedly. His gaze fell across the room to where two plain plank doors stood propped open to the cool outside air.

A woman in red stepped softly and deliberately into the room but gave an acknowledging nod.

"Vanessa," Jake called, pointing at her with his sword. "Come watch. She's rather funny to see."

"Hey," Arica snapped, jerking her head around to glare at him. "Just teach me a little better."

"You'll have to get used to his style of teaching, I'm afraid. He will continue after we leave in the morning," Vanessa said as she approached.

"What do you mean?" Jake asked, swinging his sword in a circle as he wandered towards her. "You're scouting tomorrow? Am I not joining?"

"I need someone I trust here. You might as well train with her."

His mouth closed into a grimace for a few moments. "I've no surprise I'm left again to *babysit*."

Arica let out a little puff of air, folding her arms crossly.

"Don't argue," Vanessa said carefully, giving him a bit of a stare down. "I suppose it's been too long since I gave you a new tyro, yes? What are we without our young?"

"Fine," he spat back. "But I'll not clean it up when things go rotten."

"I don't expect you to be able to, not on your own," she countered coldly. Then she shifted her feet and crossed her arms. "Well? You offered a show, so show."

Arica had to stifle a laugh at the sour look on his face as he turned back. But it was also a relief. "So... I don't have any painful assignments, right?"

"You're not fit for one, not at all," he reasoned. He switched his weapon to his left hand with a showy flourish. "Forget being unskilled. Look at you."

Her mouth dropped open in surprise, ignoring Vanessa's scoff and whatever that could've meant. "Are you saying I'm *fat?*"

He twirled the light sword in a circle, his feet close together in a stance more cocky than defensive. "No. I'm saying you're weak. And probably rather slow in the feet."

As true as his words may have been, her hands tightened on the burdensome weight in her hands.

"Well, you're rather muscular and really rude."

He smirked, then pointed at her. "But not a liar."

She straightened her stance, lifting the weapon. "Fine. At arms, or whatever. Come at me."

She had to take a step as he did just that, amusement melting off his expression, easiness disappearing from his stance.

There was no avoiding the swipe, so she held out her own weapon, trying her best to duck behind it. The vibrations that sprung from Jake's sword as it hit hers blew through her hands, instantly painful.

She let the point fall to the ground before realizing he wasn't done. The flat of his blade whacked her on the same shoulder she'd fallen on minutes before.

She stumbled backwards, clutching the shoulder. She tried to lift the weapon, but it was so heavy she couldn't get the tip of it higher than the hilt, and Jake carelessly smacked it away.

Her other hand went back to help haul up the unbalanced weight, her feet dragging her backwards as Jake approached, slow and slinky like a stalking mountain cat.

Arica recoiled as he lightly shifted the sword into his hand more. She didn't want to admit the terror creeping into her chest.

Then he struck out again. She jumped to the side, then swung at an angle. It was weak, and he deflected it before it was even halfway through, but she was pretty proud of her quick thinking, anyway.

Then Jake twisted the sword around, turning her offense into his, throwing her sword and her arms to the side, then unnecessarily thunked his blade across her hand.

She dropped the sword and grabbed her white fingers. "What are you even trying to teach me?" she demanded as tears edged into her eyelashes.

"As of yet? Nothing. I'm trying to judge just what I need to teach," he said without sympathy.

She knelt on the ground and pressed her hand between her knees. The initial shock had faded into a sharp ache that ran up her arm. She squeezed a few tears out, focusing on the wooden planks making up the floor.

"Well... how am I doing?" she groaned quietly.

"Your instincts are relatively sharp. Your strength is... average. For a woman."

"For a woman?" she demanded, glaring at him from the floor. "Isn't that a little sexist?"

Vanessa was the one who spoke up, stepping up next to Arica's attacker. "You're smaller and built differently. If you fight like Jake, if you fight with muscle and strength, you will always lose."

"Because I'm weak."

"Seven, it's because your *muscles* aren't the same," Jake droned impatiently.

"Because you've different strengths," Vanessa added with a sideways glance. "You have to play to *your* strengths, not anyone else's. Maybe in the future you will pull off a more strong-armed approach, but that's another thing we're watching for. Not just what we should teach you, but how."

Arica let her hand go to look at it. It was stiff and hurt a lot, but her fingers had turned pink instead of white. Was that a good thing? "Why do you swear in numbers? It's distracting..." she panted.

Jake let out a frustrated grunt. "Our gods are the Seven Severed—Look, if you don't accept your limits, you might as well lie down and die right now."

"How are you going to teach me to fight like a girl when you fight like a man?" she asked, wondering if he'd let her start the first part of lying down to die. "Or whatever excuse you used to not differentiate."

"Because *I* can do any style," he paraded, leaning an arm on the newly sheathed weapon hanging from his belt. "Well, I can teach any style. I haven't quite the skills to master everything, and I'm *far* from Vanessa's skill in certain aspects, but I can teach the basics, and have frequently."

"At least you're aware," Vanessa murmured, giving him a soft smile.

Jake held a hand out to her. "Would you prefer to take over?"

"No, you're doing fine, my dear," she answered almost mockingly.

"Not that it matters," Arica groaned quietly. She decided she had to straighten out, or they were going to think she was a complete loser. But as she reached across the floor for the sword she'd dropped, she couldn't help but *loathe* the idea of touching it again.

"Two seconds," he called as she reached out towards it.

The edge of his sword met her neck, but she didn't try to deflect it.

"Pick it up, or you're going to die," he goaded, the blade flawlessly still.

She let her arm go slack, bowing her head slightly. "Go ahead," she panted. "I'm good at this point. I'm satisfied with my life. It was a short time, but a good time. Don't put that on my headstone, though. Put something like... 'She tried, but there are no donuts in DeRael.'"

"Pathetic," her contender growled.

"You *cannot* underestimate my survival instincts..." she announced with frustrated exhaustion. She was sure he was moments from forcing her back to her feet. Instead, he sheathed his sword.

"To magic then."

She groaned loudly, then got to her feet, pulling the weapon parallel to her body. "Fine, I'll do it."

She barely saw the flash of his weapon before it struck hers, pushing her a few unbalanced steps back. Her arms shifted to start a strike, but he went once more, nearly throwing it out of her grip.

"I... I can't do this..." she gasped, letting the tip of her sword hit the floor.

Jake gave her that troublesome smirk. He hadn't even broken a sweat, let alone started weakening.

"Well? You're the one who gave up on magic five minutes in. You want to sword fight. So fight," he said with amusement.

Focusing on how heavily her chest rose and fell, she shook her hair out a little, annoyed when it stuck to her forehead. She wouldn't admit the churning going on in her stomach.

"You really should attempt it again, dear," Vanessa recommended from the slow circle she paced a safe distance from them.

"How long is it gonna take to get control of them?" Arica asked, almost fearing the answer.

"Maybe a year or two to fully control. Usually a few decades to master to your fullest extent."

She couldn't keep her face from falling into apparent disappointment. "A year or two? I can't even stand a few minutes of this. I can't do it for years."

She screamed and held up her weapon as Jake jumped at her, but he wasn't even holding his up. Her muscles all trembled, but he just looked amused.

"The first week is the hardest," he chuckled. He tossed the blade up in the air, where it twirled a few times before he caught it again. "A few weeks to ensure you won't hurt anyone or anything again."

"That doesn't make me feel better either," she panted, her heart erratically pounding against her rib cage.

"You need an actual challenge, child," Vanessa taunted, brushing her hands off.

Arica's mouth dropped open to object when Vanessa unsheathed her sword with a *schlinc* and struck at Jake quicker than lightning. He barely countered her but was hesitant about striking back.

Arica collapsed to her knees in relief. The boss lady wasn't challenging her, instead distracting Jake. Maybe she could have a moment's break. She stared at the couple as they attacked again, metal ringing through the air.

Vanessa's sword wasn't the decorated one that Arica had spent so much time returning. This one was smaller and much more plain compared, yet still silver at least at the hilt. In her hands, it seemed to be just as deadly, probably more so.

Jake did more than counter. In fact, he threw his weapon at her with alarming savagery. Every swipe seemed like it would be a fatal blow to the smaller fighter, but at the last second, she would twist out of the way or counter with blazing, impeding angles, only to respond with her own lightning-fast slash. It was surprising just how elegant Jake was dodging her strikes, feet dancing around hers back and forth.

"You've gotten lazy," she goaded lightheartedly.

"Then why are you pulling out all the good moves?" he chuckled, feigning to the right then throwing in an extra hard blow towards her head. Despite his insistence that they had to fight differently, there wasn't that much of a difference in fighting styles. Vanessa still blocked and bashed, muscles tightening and sword swooshing, but she used more complicated flicks, twists, and twirls.

Jake threw his weapon straight downwards towards her, which Vanessa caught with the middle of her blade, redirecting them both up and over her head as she twirled in a half circle and out of harm's way.

Sparks scattered as their blades slid across each other, creating an echoing ring. Jake sidestepped, swinging his sword in an effortless circle.

Arica wondered if he was always so cocky with a sword, or if it was just to impress the females in the room.

They both moved rather slowly when dormant, casual and playful, then blindingly fast to attack or defend. It seemed an excellent tactic to save energy, at least.

Jake lashed out sideways, but Vanessa blocked with the flat of her blade, using the palm of her off-hand to reinforce the block, somehow without injury. He still threw her back, not quite stumbling.

I suppose this is what he means. He's just stronger.

Vanessa threw out a strike that barely touched Jake's defensive swing before cutting towards his side. The tip of his sword only just deflected hers from slitting his shirt. He lunged forward, even as their swords crossed, both being thrown to one side between them.

Vanessa pulled her elbow back as if to punch, but still held her weapon.

Jake spun to one side, avoiding her thrust, then attacked her other side, but she'd thrown herself also out of the way. They both turned on a dime, loudly crossing weapons again.

Then Vanessa kicked out booted feet with a precision that instantly buckled his knee. He let out a small grunt when it hit the ground, but there was no hesitation blocking another of Vanessa's light strikes.

"That was pathetically neglectful, boy," she chided with honesty.

He countered with his sword, then almost as quickly lashed out with his offhand, grabbed her by the knee and pulled her onto her back hard enough she let out a winded grunt.

"I just wanted to go easy," he chuckled. Then his sword turned in his hand, pointing downwards, but checked just above her stomach, freezing in what Arica could only guess was a kill strike.

She bantered back with, "That's what I was accusing you of."

Arica raised her eyebrows. "Do I need to leave?"

Vanessa batted Jake's sword away with hers, leaping to her feet in a swirl of skirt. Jake much less elegantly returned both feet under him as well. Then, taken by surprise, just barely deflected a swipe to the head.

A sharp whistle suddenly caught Arica's attention, like a badly played flute. It was distant to begin with, originating outside. It slowly rose in volume, getting more annoying with every passing second.

It wasn't until Vanessa and Jake noticed the sound that the clanging ceased again.

"That isn't what I think it is, is it?" Jake asked with worry creasing his face.

Red flying behind her, Vanessa sprinted towards the huge bay windows and peered out. "Seven's sake," she sighed, barely audible. Then, as fast as she'd gone to the window, she headed out the door, her last words whipping out in Jake's direction. "Keep her safe."

Arica ran to the window to spot what her mentor had seen, but as she looked out into a sunlit garden full of bright flowers and vines, she couldn't see anything out of the ordinary.

Then a wavering in the air caught her eye, slightly off-colored, shifting like sunlight reflected on calm water. Purple erupted on the edges of her vision. She'd been blind beforehand. The color saturated her vision and made the barrier as obvious as a sheet of brightly dyed plastic.

"That's what's protecting us?" she demanded, surprised that it looked so thin and brittle. It wasn't even smooth. There were little ridges and cracks snaked throughout the surface of it.

She jumped away from the window, instinctively shielding herself as the metallic sheen exploded into a million insubstantial pieces. Arica had been expecting the sound of glass shattering, or even a boom as the air inside the field released, or anything, but there wasn't a sound except for that of her own scared whimper.

"Jake!" she called, standing back up and leaning on the windowsill. She couldn't see any unusual activity, even with the barrier completely dispersed. The gardens enjoyed the nice weather, no matter the danger that could be growing. "That couldn't have been a good thing, could it?"

She looked back as he reached the window, but said nothing.

Her feet got antsy, watching him look so intently, so she made her way around him to pick up her long discarded sword. There was no way she could use it in defense, but maybe just bringing it with her would be enough. Assuming Jake wasn't planning on staying at his superior's request.

She silently hoped they stayed, and that nothing was going sour. It could've just been a precaution, right?

"Bialsa," she called lightly, unsure where the little cat had snuck off to sleep.

"I'm here," she responded musically.

Arica looked around, unable to sense what direction she was answering from when a tiny albino hummingbird flitted out of her pocket and perched on her shoulder. She didn't know when Bialsa had prowled in there but didn't bother asking.

"I wouldn't miss something like this," the animal giggled in Arica's mind.

"Like this?"

"What?" Jake asked, looking over his shoulder.

Arica blushed, rubbing her arm with her free hand. "Oh, I was talking to Bialsa."

He nodded and resumed as if she hadn't interrupted.

"Why, a battle over the castle! I'm sure we're being attacked. Although, I hope they've snuck inside and aren't planning a siege. I haven't the patience to sit through another siege."

Arica herself was hoping for nothing of the sort, but she tried not to think about it too hard.

There was a call from outside, deep and loud, like a war horn. It lasted about fifteen seconds before abruptly cutting off, and silence settled again.

"There's a lot of them," Jake mumbled, looking even antsier now. The look that crossed his face told her the second he decided. "Come on, we're not staying here."

She wasn't about to argue with him, even though she wasn't sure this was a safer choice.

10

UNCONVENTIONAL SPY

Steen, after expressing similar concern and confusion, walked with Arica and Jake nearer the front of Neva's castle. They followed the sound of the commander barking orders, all anxious to find some answers.

"I've already sent men to secure the king and queen," Rapier stated as Arica and her entourage turned the corner. "What I need right now are soldiers holding the perimeter beyond the castle walls. Do *not* let Endré's army in, no matter the cost."

Standing near the sandy-haired commander was a man dressed in metal armor painted forest green from neck to toe, his head only protected by a gray hood. He had dark, leathery skin and a neatly trimmed beard the color of tar. The intricate carvings and details on his armor gave him an air of importance. On either side of him stood two indistinguishable soldiers with silver armor and masks crudely carved with rough, screaming faces.

"General Fredsan, and part of his special unit," Bialsa introduced in Arica's mind.

"I understand, Commander," the general said with a stiff, brief bow.

Rapier turned, taking a step before he saw Jake, and stopped short. Arica didn't want to notice, but he did have a fresh, pink scratch along his neck where Vanessa's knife had touched him.

"Where's Vanessa gotten to?"

"She left when the barrier broke. Probably to support the king."

He nodded once as if this was expected. "I sent a few to protect him the instant things shifted. They'll have gotten to him long ago. Hopefully, all is well. Nobody's reported any evidence of Dovevians yet."

"So, it's just that the barrier is down?" Steen asked, his face wrinkling with distaste. "Is it possible it wasn't set up correctly?"

Rapier pointed his arm down the brighter corridor, towards the courtyard and the front of the castle. "We've seen an army of six hundred waving Endré's colors marching across the plains from Raven. There's little chance the barrier was an accident. The rulers are their first targets, I'm sure, but if there's a single Dovevian behind this, it'll be our prisoners next. I'm now heading to secure them."

As he spoke, a pair of Zenians sprinted towards them, Ricken ahead of Kylen, though the latter had a bloody scratch across his exposed forearm and looked a little pale and winded.

"Dovevians have breached the castle," Kylen gasped. He set the hand with his short sword against his side, wincing.

"The king and queen are dead," Ricken added with respectful grief. "As is Forien, we think. His injuries were great, and they're hoarding him. Drake has Master Damage. We couldn't fight against so many of them, though Anraquella fell injured. They killed the queen's entire guard and holed up in her quarters."

A man appeared at Arica's shoulder, silent, startling her enough to take a long, jumpy step towards Jake. The gray skin under black clothing was instantly recognizable, and as he made eye contact with her for a moment, she got the chance to look into irises almost as dark as his tattoos. He must've come from the direction the army general had disappeared, out towards the inner courtyard, walking silently enough that nobody noticed.

She shrunk back behind Jake a bit more, weary.

Rapier continued without even noticing Arica's behavior. "Master Damage can hold her own. I assume they are being suppressed effectively?"

"They are," Ricken agreed. "For now."

Then Rapier looked at the dark newcomer, Derrick. "Report?"

"We didn't find the spot they broke the barrier. Anyone wanting entrance has already gotten it," he answered with an even tone, a tiny touch of roughness to it.

"Are *all* the Dovevians hiding in the queen's rooms?" Rapier demanded impatiently, his head swinging to face the first two.

Kylen squinted a little. "Three or four I think. We didn't see Lise or Patryk. I'm not sure about Navin."

"They're headed to the dungeons," Steen concluded loudly.

"Callovoi, follow Ricken and Kylen back to reinforce the others. Don't let them down into the lower levels. We'll intercept whoever's headed to the dungeon. Find out where Vanessa's gone. I'm sure she's free of that bastard already."

Steen was the one to hesitate as if hoping for a different order, but his hand stuck to his sword.

Rapier was after him just as fast. "I'm not your *recommender*, GO!"

This time, the reaction was instantaneous; Steen chased after the Kisoks. Then Jake and Derrick followed Rapier. Arica wasn't about to be left behind.

"Do you know where Vanessa is, Bialsa?" Arica puffed as quietly as she could. She wasn't sure, but she thought the little andromae still hunkered in her higher cloak pocket.

"I do not."

It was worth a shot.

"I'll keep my mind out for her," Bialsa reassured.

There was a growl, low and vicious, so close to her ears that she jumped back into Jake, actually causing him to falter.

Above them, empty alcoves lined both sides of the ceiling, big enough for the head of an elk. From one of these dropped a man in a tattered cloak, skin bleached white and eyes a blazing red.

Derrick wasted no time in assaulting him with his clean silver blade as Jake roughly grabbed Arica's arm and dragged her to his other side, out of the line or reach of either of them.

"Now *there's* your vampire," Jake called as they ran away from the fight.

"Wait, really?" she looked over her shoulder, trying to believe such a thing.

Derrick easily forced the man back. It didn't have a weapon in its hands, but it didn't seem to restrict him. Every blindingly quick swipe lithely avoided with steps even more elegant than Vanessa's had been. The vampire struck back about a quarter of the time, using only his hands.

"Patryk," Jake continued. "Luckily, he's the only vampire dumb enough to be under the king's thumb. Not that it matters. An army of vampires would be easier to take down than the Dovevians *any* day."

The stone halls darkened as they turned once more, each hall and room examined closely by the commander before he'd actually turn. Finally, they came into a dead end. One cream stained-glass window took up the wall facing them from about two feet above the floor to the ceiling. A large metal door to the right hung on only one hinge, the top corner digging into the wood wall behind it. Wide open to a dim, dusty room. Part of the wall was black and charred, lining up with the door's warped edge.

"I can't imagine this is a good sign," Arica whispered, unsure if anyone could even hear her.

Rapier held an empty hand towards the stairs for a moment. "Well, they're gone now. Though the doors are all still armed, so unless they got around the rest of the doors, Corrin and Reganold are still detained."

There was an awkward pause as if he expected someone else to say something, but Jake just stood impatiently with arms crossed.

Finally, Rapier gave a command. "Stand guard. I'll do a sweep." He didn't even wait for an answer before launching down the steep steps, leaving Jake and Arica alone once again.

Jake looked annoyed, but effortlessly stood guard until Arica couldn't stand the unnatural silence anymore.

"We aren't in a lot of danger, are we?" she asked, the memory of the red-eyed man refreshing itself.

Jake finally moved, swishing his sword in a distracted circle. "I can't say for sure."

Once again, the sudden appearance of the mysteriously dark man startled her. He walked up, emotionless, a glint of watery blood on the tip of his short sword.

Neither of the men uttered a word. Arica thought about stealing one of their swords and killing herself just to ease the tension.

"They're warriors, Arica," Bialsa whispered in response to her emotions. "Both trained mentally as well. I highly doubt that they are as anxious as you are at the moment."

Still, she held herself awkwardly until, finally, she could hear Rapier's heavy steps as he returned.

"They're still down there. I put up a few more protections. But the safest bet will be to keep their allies away from here," he explained.

"Well, let's drive these morons back then," Jake suggested with enthusiasm.

As if on cue, a rumble rolled through the ground around them, enough to shake dust free and create a void in Arica's stomach.

Jake didn't wait for an order, but Derrick stayed put until the commander started.

Arica had to practically sprint to keep up with Jake's long legs until one of the commander's thick arms abruptly cut him off. "You should stay back with the tyro," he said with authority.

Jake let out an annoyed growl, looking back at her like he'd forgotten about her.

Rapier didn't give him another chance to argue; he left him behind and expected him to stay like an obedient puppy.

Arica said nothing as Jake's hand grew white on his sword's grip. She was too scared to.

He looked at her again, teeth clenched, but didn't glare or look all that angry.

"I'm sorry?" she tried, sincerely.

"It's not your fault," he murmured. "I'm often chosen to train, but usually we don't have assaults on a tyro's second day."

She grabbed her elbow, still tasting guilt. "Guess I'm just unlucky like that."

He sheathed his sword and pointed down the hallway opposite where the others had left. "It wouldn't hurt to go scout out the upper floors."

Arica followed but was skeptical. "Nobody will know where we are."

Jake answered, but Arica was too distracted to hear him. She caught sight of a dark hallway leading a sharp right and further into the heart of the castle. The few sconces lining the walls were cold, but it lit up with a bright color.

"You can see that, right?"

"What?" Jake asked, following her gaze.

"Yes. Through your eyes," said a twinkly voice.

She glanced up at Jake but wasn't speaking to him. "I've seen it before, just this colorful light in random places. Is it... normal?"

His expression sobered.

"No," Bialsa said flatly.

A visual tint she was growing used to, but this time it was a much more solid, unwavering color, like a purple lens over her eye.

Bialsa didn't need any provoking to direct her. "Follow it!"

Arica shot down the hall, deaf to Jake's sudden objections. Bialsa climbed out of her pocket with tiny claws and latched onto the shoulder of her shirt.

"Seriously, what are you doing, kid?" Jake called, right on her tail.

She could tell it was dark, and maybe she wasn't supposed to see, but the purple kept just barely light enough in the shadows to make her comfortable.

"You can't just run around with Dovevians on the loose!" came a deep roar behind her.

She stopped in front of a short iron door. Without knowing why her heart raced, or where the sense of urgency came from, she searched for a door handle with her hands. "What's behind this door?" she asked breathlessly as Jake approached, spreading light across the shiny iron with his glowing hand.

"It's... ah, just an old storage room, I think."

"Then why's it locked?"

Jake reached around her into a crevice about waist high and pulled a flat-surfaced lever that immediately reminded her of her car's handle back home. There was a powerful click, but the door didn't move.

He silently pulled Arica back, then threw a heavy kick at the door. It only slid open about two inches, but upon the second kick, it opened enough to enter.

The purple receded from her vision as she entered the dark room, but there weren't many directions she could go, anyway.

Light filtered in from the middle of the floor, a square metal grate several feet across. Jake bent to avoid the low ceiling, his head occasionally brushing some of the many hooks dangling from metal rods against it.

Jake suddenly grabbed her from behind, clapping a hand over her mouth, and pulled her into the closest corner. His boots barely made a noise even as hers squeaked as she struggled.

"I didn't ASK for your opinion," roared a voice so close that Arica froze against her kidnapper. "Take out the door, kill the Zenians. Is that not clear enough for you?" It was an aggressive, rough voice, like every word abraded his throat, almost nails on a chalkboard for her.

Arica looked around, but she could clearly see each wall in the small, empty room. Jake let her go, confident she was aware of the danger. But he crouched down closer to the ground, placing a hand against his sheathed weapon to silence any clinking.

"We're *trying*," a firm female voice argued in annoyance. "They're using something to strengthen it."

Arica got on her hands and knees, and with excruciating slowness, started crawling to the grate.

"What about the soldiers?" the male asked irritably.

"Rounding, per instruction. Navin says they're cutting through Fredsan's army with ease. Though their protections wore off much earlier than predicted."

She reached the edge and peeked over, just enough to see below them. There wasn't much *to* see. A large open brazier positioned directly under her, filled with black and gray coal visible by a smaller flickering fire out of sight. A thin layer of grease and dust caked the floor, leaving her hands sticky.

"Have they gotten to Drake yet?" the man asked, much calmer. The voices were fading.

The firelight came from the right, so she carefully inched left in order to get a peek at them. She wasn't sure why she was so curious about it, but at least Jake wasn't interfering.

"Ransom left him. He decided Miss Damage wasn't a priority if we could break the door. Drake was defending himself well enough, but I doubt he was able to long enough in such a small room."

Arica finally caught sight of a long curtain of shiny hair, maroon in the firelight, her already pale skin washed out by a modest black gown. She carefully stepped around the cold stone room, observing everything within reach. As she turned in Arica's direction, she revealed her face. A sharp nose, and slim, dark eyes. A small part of her bottom lip twisted unnaturally, following a small scar down her chin.

Arica backed up, realizing all she had to do was breathe too heavily, and they'd catch her.

The woman whirled back in the other direction, dropping a small carved block she'd removed from the fireplace. "Are you really sure it's in here?"

"The king seemed to believe it would be," said the man from even further away. "Though I've only so much patience. If we can get rid of most of these pests, we'll have time to tear the castle apart."

The echo of his voice made Arica wonder how long the room below really was. From the little she saw, it had to be a kitchen. She looked over her shoulder at Jake, who met her eyes for a moment. His expression was blank in concentration.

"If you hadn't blocked the passage entrance, we could just drive them out," she bitterly argued, now moving out of Arica's line of sight. "Instead of trying to overpower them."

He got after her, already agitated again. "We'd have a better chance if you'd help bring down that damned door!"

She said nothing else to him.

Out of the corner of her eye, Arica saw Jake hold out a hand to her; a sign that it was time to go. She worked her way around the edge back to him, when she noticed that the man was standing much closer. She stopped in case he heard her shuffling. All she could see was a large man in a black cloak, not unusual compared to the rest of the people she'd met recently.

The air caught in his cloak unsettled the dusty ashes under her. She felt the knife in her belt loosen, but a second before it fell, she grabbed it and saved herself a lot of noise. Then she sneezed.

The cloaked man turned abruptly, but just as fast, Jake grabbed Arica's arm and hauled her to her feet, breaking their attempt at silence.

"I can run by myself!" Arica yelled as they bolted back down the hall, almost too fast for her own feet.

He surrendered her arm, but forced her to keep up the pace by sheer fear of being left behind.

"That was Lise and Anraquella," Jake announced, his feet skidding unnaturally as he tried to slow around the corner.

"What were they looking for?" Arica asked, sure that this was a much better question to be answered.

Her feet stopped as she passed a window, the brief glance of the view startling her enough to take another look.

The window was alone in an alcove that could've stored a suit of armor, though none were present. It looked out over the front of the castle, mostly over the inner courtyard and out towards the city itself. Hundreds of tiny houses clumped together, all bordered by a thick line of trees. To one side of these, in some fields, she could see some kind of animal walking in circles, paws up and down as if crushing ants. There was little to compare size to, but it looked easily bigger than a house, black as tar with two huge wings fanned to the sides but unused, and a long tail that whipped in circles.

"What on earth? Is that.... a dragon?" She looked up, noticing Jake had leaned one arm on the windowsill above her, also studying the landscape.

"No, a solzetair," he mumbled.

"What?"

He glanced down at her, eyebrows low. "How do you know what a dragon is, but not a solzetair?" He looked back out, jaw setting for a second. "Either way, it's Drake. Out there trying to help Endré's army and probably trying to urge some of us to go out after him and leave the castle more vulnerable."

Arica stared at the faraway beast, trying to see if the tiny specks in the distance were actually little soldiers swarming the monster's feet. Then Jake tapped her shoulder, signaling the time to work their way back to their destination.

"So Drake isn't a Dovevian, either. Like the vampire," Arica summarized out loud.

"No, he is. It's just one of the—"

The rest of his answer cut short as they neared the main hall. She could hear a hundred battle cries, and a rhythmic pounding similar to but a hundred times as powerful as a child pounding on her parent's bedroom door.

Gigantic doors in a pair stood open, defenseless to the main hall. Most of the Zenians worked against a matching pair opposite them, one partially cracked unlike what the woman had told Lise, swarmed with warriors in close combat.

"The hall blocks the castle in half perfectly," Jake explained, gesturing with his sword. "In case of a siege, half of a castle can be easier to hold than an entire one. The only way to the other side without going through here is from the courtyard, but that's just as impossible with the portcullis down. Stay back!"

Even though Jake was yelling, the ring and clatter of dozens of swords striking metal and wood nearly drowned out everything else. Arica witnessed the primary group of Zenians all furiously fighting off both plainly armored soldiers, and several obviously different people in the opposite doorway, but most were too swarmed to recognize friend from enemy.

Jake charged in, realizing before Arica that they were trying to fight them back enough to re-close the doors while they secured a few of their friends from the Dovevian side.

Kylen was there, trading huge, almost slow blows with a smoky-skinned man with a short beard, arms and torso bare except for a cape pinned against his thick neck.

Then a Zenian woman, Elvy, crashed into a pair of soldiers, thrown back by a bald man with two curved sabers, who started sparring with Jake even before his previous opponent was all the way down.

Steen was the first to be rescued from the mob, finally able to retreat enough to not have to block with his sword to save himself. The doors closed a little more every time someone backed up, slowly thinning out the onslaught as more people shoved against this side than the other.

"Don't let them close it!" came a booming order from the other side as Zak ran back into the room. He dragged Vanessa's gigantic sword ahead of Vanessa herself, who struggled arm-in-arm with Aaris.

"Back, get it shut!" Rapier countered as the crowd in front of them thinned out. Finally, it slammed closed with a completing *bang* that shook Arica's insides.

"Seal it up," someone yelled, but there was already a sparkly sheen growing over the incredibly sturdy oak doors. The sudden cut-off of noise felt eerie as some worked to seal the doors, and others went about collapsing or nursing their wounds.

Arica raced to Jake. She'd spotted him helping Malon to her feet. Blood dripped off his shoulder, but she couldn't tell if it was his or not.

"Are you okay?" she asked, more worried than she'd intended.

"Enough," Jake said, looking around for everyone else.

Rapier shoved through a few people on his way to where Vanessa limped, followed soon by Jake and Arica. "Are you hurt?" Rapier demanded, shouldering her arm to help her stand.

"Stop. A little bruised is all," she mumbled, a hand staying over a cut against her rib cage as she lazily pushed Rapier away.

Steen and Zak stood close. Zak still held Vanessa's sword, and Steen had blood caked into the hair around his ear.

"And Drake won't be walking right for a little while," Steen announced proudly, throwing his dirty sword over his shoulder and grinning.

"Good man," Jake hissed in triumph, offering his arm out for Steen to take in their happy greeting. "No wonder he yielded to play with the armies instead of stand here."

Vanessa leaned a steadying hand on Rapier's arm, both still serious. "They've taken the north towers. We're cut off from the stables and the king's army. They've secured most of the residents upstairs."

Arica looked up as the rhythmic pounding resumed. Huge circles of power erupted over the surface of the door like ripples in a still pool. They distorted the coloring and clarity of the barrier, turning it a rainbow of colors, only for it to smooth back over seamlessly.

"We're blocked off from the armory and the augment room as well," Rapier continued. "There's no way we'll be able to drive them away without it. Shall we force our way through them?"

"What's an augment room?" Arica whispered, leaning over to Jake.

"A room with a table that can amplify our magic. We can use it to drive back the Dovevian's source of power, forcing them to retreat. It's usually a last resort because it takes a *lot* of power. Not always survivable, even for our own," Jake whispered back.

She barely caught the end of Vanessa's explanation of why forcing their way through the Dovevians wasn't plausible.

"Besides, they've probably tried to break, or seal it," Zak agreed.

"Why did they know where it was in the first place?" Steen asked with genuine, quiet curiosity.

Vanessa held herself up a little taller. "The same way they knew exactly what we were doing. The same way they knew exactly where the king and queen were. Someone's telling them."

"Shall we retreat to the track, then?" Rapier asked, distaste clear in his expression.

"That's how they got in," Jake piped up. "We overheard Lise and Anraquella, thanks to this one." He bumped Arica's shoulder almost affectionately.

Her face grew pink even though it felt like a compliment.

"They sealed it up behind them."

Vanessa shook her head, then took a deep breath.

"We don't have anywhere to retreat to anyway," Zak reasoned.

"Maramore," Vanessa whispered under her breath quietly enough that Arica wasn't sure she'd heard quite right. Then louder, she said, "We have Maramore still. I've been preparing it. It's not quite where I wanted it, but it'll be sufficient for the situation. We *could* attempt to stand our ground here, maybe let them drive us further into the city where we'd have a better chance with them one-on-one, but I'm afraid they wouldn't be very kind about leaving the place intact on the way. For Neva, at least, this may be our optimal decision."

"We'd still have to push to the passage, but they don't seem to be guarding it. It shouldn't be difficult to break their blocks," Rapier agreed, though the grimace on his face suggested he wasn't exactly thrilled.

"They're after the book," Jake added.

"I'm not surprised, but it's safe, yes?" As Vanessa looked at the commander, he bowed his head like he couldn't look her in the eye.

"I haven't had time to get it, and you were both otherwise distracted," Rapier defended softly.

"Understood. We'll push them back," Vanessa announced with a finality that none of them were brave enough to dispute. "We'll attempt to push to the augment table, but when it becomes apparent that they're catching the upper hand again, we'll retreat."

"When, huh?" Steen remarked quietly, nervously biting one of his knuckles.

She shot him a threatening look. "Yes, Lord Callovoi, when. We haven't the resources—" She looked at the commander. "—or the raw power to be the victor, assuming they do indeed have Endré's army under magical protection. As for priority..."

Her gaze shifted to Jake, and like cats so did everyone else's. He frowned, looked at Arica for a moment, and sighed. "Dirty job."

"In this case, the opposite. Get the book before they find it. Take the rune in the west tower. There should be enough for you to slip to Maramore. And of course, take her. She'll be much safer, assuming you sneak through any problems."

Instead of arguing, he inclined his head slightly. "Understood."

"Decided," Rapier announced, turning to address the rest of the crowd obediently awaiting instruction. "Master Damage has spoken!" he yelled with enthusiasm. "We're to fight off these blaggards with the same craze as they. It'll be a challenge, absolutely..."

Most of the Zenians watched him, still and quiet.

"But are we to cower in front of a bunch of cursed daisies?"

"NO!" came the roar back at him.

"No! So let's get out there and give them something to—"

A warm hand touched Arica's shoulder, startling her.

"Are you ready?" Jake asked above the noise.

She nodded, and took his offered hand, scared enough that she couldn't force words through the lump in her throat.

Looking back, she wondered if any of it was even real anymore, if there was any chance for it to end well. Vanessa leaned against a sturdy oak chair, and Rapier shouted encouragement. An entire group of people she'd just met and didn't know. And she didn't have any idea how difficult the battle before them would be.

"Jrasko, wait," Vanessa called suddenly, causing Jake to stop in the doorway and turn back to her.

Neither one of them moved, but there was a long moment where they looked into each other's eyes as if the rest of the world had stopped.

Then she lifted her chin and smiled ever so slightly.

Her compassionate episode ended almost as quickly as it began, and she was joining her companions' side, strong despite her injury.

With eyes widened, Jake stared after her a moment before looking at Arica. "They're going to be... fine..."

11

MARAMORE MANSION

Despite her lack of oxygen, Arica gracelessly trotted after Jake, her heart racing. Fear of being left behind was the only thing keeping her from falling behind as he slipped in and out of small hallways.

Backtracking a step or two, he grabbed her by the arm and jerked her against the wall, hurting both her arm with his grip and her shoulder as she crashed into the unrelenting wood. She made an involuntary squeak on impact.

A layer of magic grew over them, shielding them as a group of people rounded the corner. Arica froze in terror, realizing she'd gasped all too loudly.

"Don't worry, as long as they don't notice the energy field, we'll be fine," Jake said softly.

A bulky man led, face covered in a black silk mask underneath his already concealing hood, so Arica could only assume that he was the man from the kitchens, Lise. Behind him pranced a petite girl with shiny black streaks through her blonde hair, her grin wide. Out of all the Dovevians Arica had seen, her skin had the most color at a grayed peach. The man towering at her side wore the same type of dirty smock and a rattish scowl, but even if he'd had pleasant features, his easy nine feet of height intimidated plenty.

Jake made an unsatisfied *tsk* with his tongue. "They were locked in the dungeon. Rapier's protections failed."

"Is he... a giant?" Arica whispered, still unconvinced that they couldn't hear her barely fifteen feet away.

"Madellian, actually. They're just large people. Though Reganold's still tall for them."

She glanced at him over her shoulder. "Do you have any in you?"

"Some," he mumbled passively.

The Dovevians passed by and left far enough away for some tension to melt from her shoulders, but she waited for Jake to signal by letting down the field of magic before moving again.

"Hey, do you still have Bialsa with you?" Jake suddenly asked with curiosity.

He stopped mid-stride as Arica dug through pockets without hesitation until the small white fox jumped out of her hood and into Jake's open hand on her own.

"Three Dovevians are coming to flank you from behind. Reganold and Sutlie have been released from captivity," Jake told her monotonously.

Bialsa's paws playfully batted at his wrist as if she hadn't heard him at all. Then she looked up at him, blue eyes sparkling. "We'll set a trap for them. Do not return to us," she informed him, giggling, not in the manner Arica guessed Vanessa or the commander had spoken the original words.

Jake quickly tucked the andromae back into Arica's hood and dragged her into a jog again.

"So... telepathy, I guess?" Arica speculated.

"It's the only form of long distance communication we've found that our enemies can't home in on. Though it has its disadvantages. The andromaes don't always feel like talking to each other."

She nodded, but he was too far ahead to see her.

After her feet were so sore she barely wanted to move another step, they finally made it to a small, flimsy wood door which Jake had no hesitation opening.

A musty scent accompanied the warm humidity, a surprise for a low basement room. Jake left her in the doorway to scan through a low bookshelf. There weren't many books on them, and the ones unfortunate enough to be there had swelled with moisture. Several other bookshelves lined the stone walls, illuminated by Jake's hand, but only the middle one had a single shelf on it still usable.

Jake pulled a loose stone tile away from the wall. Laid in the middle of the perfectly cut alcove was a huge red leather-bound book with thick pages and a small lock in the center.

He let out a calming breath of air. "I don't know why the king thought it would be in the kitchens." His hands were barely big enough to grip the binding, and he had to work to haul it up at chest height.

"What's so special about this book?" Arica asked as he set most of the weight on his shoulder.

He grunted and carefully lowered it to the ground before answering. "It's an aid, enchanted to keep records of... well, anything magical, really. The Dovevians have a forged copy, but they haven't been able to enchant it to keep up by itself; they have to add the information manually. Which sort of defeats the purpose when you don't have all the information. We had to recover it after the king stole off with it and announced himself the ruler. We lost a lot of lives, but that's just what it's worth."

"Wow," Arica whispered, reverently touching the cover. The dark red leather felt sturdy, despite its worn appearance, and had a simple carving under the lock, a five-pointed star with the lower left point missing. "How old is it?"

"Extremely. Almost as old as magic itself. Some of these records are rumored to be written in the language of the gods, which we can't confirm because we can't read it, but..." He set both hands on it, almost like he was bracing on top of it.

"Do we really have to haul it out of here?"

He glanced at her. "Not like this."

She realized his hands were ever so slightly glowing. The book began shrinking, pulling in on itself. Arica's brain felt tricked, trying to focus on it, but within a minute it was barely bigger than his hand and apparently much lighter.

"There," Jake mumbled as he tucked it into a small pouch he'd pulled from a pocket in his cloak. He slid it back in, where it disappeared entirely. Then he held a hand out for her.

This time they went faster, maybe more confident they wouldn't run into any threats, but he kept a comfortable pace.

Arica followed him into an empty vaulted room, footsteps disturbing silence. Dark blue paint peeled from the walls, most of it already worn away from the stone floor. There were barely any furnishings, though the sun shone through a beautiful cyan-stained glass skylight, casting colored light across the upper half of the room. A dozen or more banners averaging about six feet hung along the single circular wall most of the way around. All were faded and dusty.

"Yeah, she's got another few sparks left in her," Jake mumbled, hands in pockets as he kicked at dust caked into a huge carved symbol taking up most of the floor, round and symmetrical. He peered back at the painted door they'd entered from, and with barely a twitch of a finger, it slid back into its frame obediently.

"What's the point of this?" Arica asked, following him into the middle of the floor. A circle five feet in diameter waited in the exact center of the room, completely untouched for all but its paint job.

"They're plyways. Elven magic that can fold the space between two points. They were used a lot in the... 2200s, I think? They called it the Brutal Age. Maybe that was after, though. I forget."

Arica gave him a look of complete bewilderment. "2200s?"

"Right, your years are a little off to ours." He shrugged a little, then barely pointed a finger before purple sparks splashed across the ground like spilled glitter.

She jumped out of the way, but before she could even put both feet down they soaked into the dusty stone. A faint vibration tickled her feet.

"Point being, we don't make them anymore," Jake said casually. "Don't have the means. Vanessa's hoping the Maramore one is still working just enough." He jerked his head, then jogged to the edge of the room. He pulled back the thick banner closest to him, but all that was behind it was an empty doorframe made of stone. He moved onto the next one before she was ready to stop looking, but she said nothing.

"Is it working though?" Arica asked softly.

"The reservoir took the magic just fine, that's a good sign," Jake said with a point at the rune under her feet. The fourth or fifth curtain gave them a jolt of hope.

The door looked into a pile of flat, gray hay, with a dark horse stall just beyond it.

"Come," Jake said with a quick nod. "Before it closes. Or it might kill us.

"Sounds pleasant," Arica whispered, following his beckoning wave. His hand wrapped around hers, tugging her the last few feet until she stood directly in front of the doorway. A cool breeze encouraged a few goosebumps.

He gripped her hand harder. "It's okay. I was joking about it killing us."

She hoped he wouldn't notice how much she was shaking, but it was bad enough to be obvious from across the room. She fought the urge to pull back as he stepped into the barn and dragged her behind him. She expected a whoosh, or a buzz of electricity, but it was as if the two rooms were naturally joined like this.

When she looked back after keeping Jake anchored in one spot for several long seconds, she saw only the wooden wall of the rickety barn.

Jake tugged her into a walk.

"So... Are you polytheistic? I heard you mention something about gods." She tried to keep her voice even. Pressure constricted her chest, but not from her own emotion. Her breath came a little harder.

"Yeah. There's seven of them."

It wasn't hard to find a ruined doorway and step outside. She took a deep breath, soaking in musty air that smelled of rain. Dark storm clouds brimming with moisture blanketed them from the sky, giving the area a dull gray aura. They stood at the edge of a field, with more low buildings stretching out behind it into the distance.

"Not kept as it should've been," Jake mused as he began trudging through soft soil, disrupting some of the young crops underfoot. "But this area isn't wildly populated."

Arica freed her hands from him to balance her steps on the rutted ground, glad her boots protected her ankles.

"How many gods do you have?" Jake asked.

"Oh, just one. A lot of us are Christian, and we believe that there's only one God," Arica said positively, glad for a distraction from the mud sucking at her boots. It was a little surprising to hear someone ask *her* a question

"I don't know how only one could take care of everything. Sometimes I wonder how ours deal with things even split between them. Though... for some of them, it's a miracle they're still alive."

Arica gave him a confused look. "Are we even talking about the same kinds of deities?"

"I don't know. Protectors of the world? Unearthly beings of immense power?"

"I mean... that's not exactly how I'd describe it, but yeah, in a sense..."

A hut sat to the side of their straight path, and just beyond it was a strip of darker, packed dirt; a barely distinguishable road leading into the distant town.

"Gods can still die, Arica," Jake told her darkly.

"Maybe yours..."

Jake shrugged, bringing back his casual demeanor. "As you say."

The houses of the small town spread out, never touching each other, and often had a plot of land between them. Even the stable grounds and the building with a huge forge in front of it. What was odder was the lack of life. Not a single soul anywhere. The streets, the yards, even the small market stalls situated into a tight circle in the middle of the road were vacant.

"There's, like, no people here," Arica whispered, looking over her shoulder in case they were all following in a zombie hoard fashion.

"Not an active populace, honestly. They're probably just hiding from the storm," Jake calmed.

"It is freezing..." she added quietly, tightening her cloak around her arms. Her feet ached enough that the pain leeched into her legs.

"We'll make a fire soon, be patient."

She regarded him for a moment, the calm in his face and ease in his walk. He almost seemed serene in the dark atmosphere. But would he seem otherwise, anywhere at all? She tried to copy, not wanting to ruin his mood with her nerves.

After an entire hour of achy-feet trudging up slope after slope through the abandoned town, and the even less active houses clustered in the middle, it became clearer where they were headed.

A large black formation sat on top of the last upward slope in front of them, mostly shrouded in a thick fog. Rounded towers eventually jutted out towards them, made of a dark stone. The front section boasted a huge carved door, still the lowest part of the roof. It gradually ascended to the back, where it cut upwards to the bottom of a grand terrace wrapped around the skinnier midsection of the building.

"Naturally, we're going up to the creepy mansion," Arica mumbled under her breath, yet still he heard her.

"Yes."

She couldn't control a shiver that drained her remaining energy even faster. "Can't we just find a cute hotel or something?"

He looked at her sideways.

"Uh... An inn?" she tried with a bit too much condescension.

"Oh, that's right," he said with a wave of a hand. "Don't worry, we're not going inside. We're set up out back."

Arica kept the rest of her complaining to herself. The last few feet to the dark metal fence running around the grounds was the worst, a steep enough incline that when paired with soft and moist dirt under foot was extremely hard on her feet and calves.

Arica wondered if pure force had opened the gate because of the way it bent inwards, already hung halfway open. The corner dug into dirt long settled and the hinges were mostly rust. The dirt was dark in the courtyard, and while there were a few trees, they all had dark trunks and leafless limbs, gnarled together like corpses reaching out for each other. Loose cobble took up the middle of the garden, leading to the enormous front doors of the mansion.

Like the castle over Neva, it seemed to share a backyard with the entire deciduous forest they'd entered from. Unlike Neva, however, these trees shared the same dark, diseased appearance in varying depth to both sides. Sad, dark foliage barely peeked through the naked branches.

Arica wondered exactly how there was an "out back". The trees seemed to grow right up the sides of the dark stone mansion.

"So," she started before realizing that her companion was behind her a little way, tiredly leaning on the cold gate as he stared up at the mansion's taller tower.

She narrowed her eyes, sure he was plotting something.

"You know..." he mused slowly. "There haven't been vampires in Maramore for hundreds of years." Then he shot her a smirk. "Or say the tales."

Oh god, don't say it. "Yeah, or something like that," she agreed cheerfully. "Well, let's go find that place Vanessa wants us to go to right now. How's that sound?"

"The others should be only a bit behind us if they're taking the plyway over," he said with a quick gesture behind him. "And it's cold out here. There's sure to be a fireplace." He took his weight off the gate, brushed off his hands, and walked down the path past her. "Just a peek, hun. Promise."

"Oh man," she squeaked as she followed.

Jake pulled on a circular handle. The towering door acted like it was going to stick at first, inching open gravelly, but broke free under minor force. Dust rained on them, sticking to their wet hair and jackets. Old gears ground and screeched, painfully shrill.

Arica grabbed the thick edge, knowing she wouldn't be much help but was willing to try. A layer of frost stuck to her fingers. A metallic clang vibrated the metal door as it stopped its slow progress.

"Damn," Jake muttered, shifting one of his feet underneath Arica and against the other door to get better traction.

He dragged the door open a few more inches; enough space for them to squeeze through.

Jake went first, hopefully so he could check for threats and not just because he wanted to leave her behind. He stayed halfway in, looking back, forth, and everywhere else before pulling himself all the way through.

"We've got good airflow from somewhere," he commented as she slipped through, still against her better judgment.

Dull light filtered through small windows near the ceiling on either side of the spacious front hall. Jake had his light out again, but it spread out further than usual, casting long shadows of a chandelier hanging unnaturally low over an elegant set of stairs curving on the second floor to meet in the middle. Polished wood peeked through worn-out pieces of a once vibrant carpet. In some places, it looked like age had not only stolen the carpet but also sections of the floor itself, making Arica doubt it was even safe to walk on. To either side of them, an arched doorway waited, identical, from what she could see using Jake's light.

"If I remember correctly..." Jake stepped further into the middle of the foyer. His finger lazily pointed to the right, toward a closed door of normal size, completely unremarkable. "That leads to the library, and eventually the kitchens." He pointed forward to a lower hall leading into darkness between the staircases, saying, "That leads to the ballroom and mess hall." Last, he pointed to a darker room cast in shadow. "And that is the reception rooms, and maybe the sitting room too."

Arica didn't respond because she didn't know what any of that had to do with a quick peek.

Then he turned to her, clapping his hands. "Let's go get a fire going for a few minutes; we'll warm up before we get to sleep in the rain."

Can I just go home? "If you think it's okay..." she mumbled, wrapping her arms around her shoulders.

"Don't worry, we're alone."

She followed him all the way to the left, the way he'd guessed to be the reception rooms and maybe the sitting room too.

It was dark in the room they entered, Jake's light their only source. The rugs covering the space felt thicker than the foyer's, though just as faded. Jake approached a circle of sofas open to the room's entrance, but Arica stopped as her boots crunched.

Sparkling, shattered glass covered the carpet, once installed within four window panes completely boarded shut. A once adorable little window seat with saggy pillows ran the length of the window, also covered in shards of glass.

More light suddenly flooded over the room, flickering orange. Jake had found the fireplace.

The room was even more depressing in the light. The wallpaper was falling off the walls in long, damp strips, nonexistent in many places, which just added to the dirt and junk piled up in the edges of the room. Opposite from where they'd entered, a wall boasted a gaping hole leading into a dusty closet space, but the cobweb hanging over it was way too huge for Arica to even consider being curious about it. Bookshelves lined the wall opposite the window, all but the one closest to the fireplace empty and in disorder. The exception looked newer, almost shinier, and had quite the selection of preserved books residing on it.

Arica nearly tripped over a broken furniture leg trying to get to Jake.

"This is a mess," she mumbled, shifting things with a foot and steadying herself against the wall. Her thumb hit a raised piece of plastic with a satisfying click, but nothing happened. Upon further inspection, she found it was just a little on-and-off switch on a panel made of a hardened resin. It fell away from the wall with her interference, swinging by a few wires protruding from the back.

"A light switch?" she muttered under her breath.

It made little sense, but she quit messing with it to continue her journey around the rest of the stuff.

"That fire. Does it even need the wood?" she asked with curiosity. At least she was finally getting the questions that would help her learn magic.

"If it didn't have it, it would need a constant source of magic to stay going. This way, I just needed to provide the spark."

"I guess it makes sense, like the force field thingies."

"Thingies," Jake repeated in amusement.

She stopped climbing over a dirty pile of linen to pick up a small square box.

"What is this..." One hammered metal side was missing entirely, leaving a pile of spewing wires and connectors, so she pulled a few of them. They crumbled away. She pulled out a few more, revealing a more complicated circuit than her beginner-level tech classes back home had ever taught her to understand. She bent to pick up a translucent piece framed by a metal similar to the box itself.

"Some sort of... computer?" she guessed aloud. The box fell out of her hands, cracking as it hit the floor. She pressed a hand over her suddenly quick heart, trying to understand. "There was electricity here once. Some sort of power, a..." Her eyes caught something else she thought she recognized. She leapt over a pile of junk just to get to it.

It was a thin metal cuff that could've covered about half of her forearm. A screen spanned the inner space, about the size of her phone back home, and near the palm was a strange plug-in she didn't recognize.

She brushed the screen in awe, waking it up to shine into her darkness-adjusted eyes. She blinked, squinting slightly. Nothing but static showed up on the screen; gray and black lines, and a wavy white at the top. It only lasted a moment before going black again.

"But at the castle... And this is all so ancient..." She looked up at Jake, eyes saddened. "What happened?"

His expression was dark as he leaned on a poker against the mantle, motionless. "Magic happened."

She reached out to give the small computer to him, which he took with a calm blankness.

"Jake... do you live in some sort of... post-apocalyptic society, formed from radioactive survivors of scientific warfare started around the fabrication of this so-called magic?"

He paused a moment, tossing the item to the side, and set both hands on his poker as he visibly tried to decide how to respond. "Well... Most of the words you just said are not in my vocabulary—"

"I thought it was pretty clever..."

"—but I'm going to assume you're blowing it out of proportion."

Arica sat back on her heels, staring at the place the box had landed. "Was DeRael once socially—technologically—advanced, like my world?"

"More so," Jake agreed quietly. "Twice, actually."

She gave him a questioning glance.

"Tens of hundreds of years ago," Jake started with a theatrical wave of the hand.

Arica stood on shaky legs and moved to sit closer to him.

"Well, thirty-two hundred some odd to be more precise... I don't know where my map's gone to, but just picture this." He held his hands in front of him, gesturing gently.

"We are in the upper northern quarter of DeRael. The west side of the continent is mostly desert and swamplands, a lot of swampland. This is where Tuaria once was. Towers built hundreds of feet into the sky, railways running every which way, and even though the swamps have taken over most of it, you can still feel the history there. Enormous buildings crumbling to the water, an entire language that nobody understands, these huge machines for all sorts of tasks. I can't even explain it, it's... incredible, what you can see there even now. But it was beautiful, and great what they'd achieved. They had magic, even then. It powered so much, it allowed them many achievements."

He stopped for a moment, gaze vacant. His fingers rubbed together absently as he started again.

"We don't know what happened exactly, it was so long ago, and records only last so long, stories don't stay true, but as I understand it... One of Vanessa's predecessors, a high master, was a man named Tolstolryn Dohvevna. He was said to be great, until... until—so it's said—one day he tired of the humans, and how they thrived without the magic he so thoroughly prized. There's so many versions, so many reasons a war began, so many ways he could've lost it; we really don't know. Except that a recurring theme is power. Magic became a lesser power. So... he destroyed everything that made it so. Everything, not just Tauria, but all of DeRael. A handful of people survived his armageddon. Most were his fellow Zenians, but nothing stood a chance against him. We don't even know how he did it single-handedly. Maybe he took the powers of the gods, as some stories say, maybe he built a machine of destruction. But there had to be something. So much of Tuaria was just obliterated out of existence, so we believe."

Arica was finally able to stop shivering and sat still.

"Including Dohvevna. Maybe he'd wanted to destroy everything to where even he ceased to exist. Maybe it was just a minor err in his power frenzy, but it took his life along with countless others. This event was decided to be the last of an era. They declared the year after his death the first. The leftover Zenians were the monarchs of most of the current Zenian families. Damage, mine," he said with a shrug. "I'm sure you've heard others before. They did the only thing they could. The only thing humans ever want to do. They rebuilt. None of DeRael's current cities were here before Dohvevna's death. Not a single one. And Tuaria is the only ruin we have left, the only proof we have that the whole thing isn't just a story to caution children."

"None of this is left over from that, though," Arica observed.

Jake shook his head. "No, much more recently, there was another rise in technology. Humankind finally caught back up and started into an age of advancement. They had a few good years. But history repeats, as they say. The king, Garal Leadd, the same man we fight against to this day, one day put an order out to his Dovevians that the modern world was too advanced. That he didn't want a repeat of Dohvevna's destruction. That they had to stop the humans before they became independent."

"How old is this man?" Arica asked with disgust.

"Very." Jake shrugged unhelpfully. "Immortality isn't reserved for demons and the like in our world."

This was obviously a much touchier subject for the man. He'd spoken of Dohvevna's treachery like a schoolteacher in a lesson with fifth graders, but this... His eyes grew hollow and dark like he was living it himself.

"His home city, Endré, was the first to be 'cleansed'. It didn't take long for the others to follow suit. Tens of hundreds slaughtered, mostly by affiliation, while he forced everyone else into the streets as their buildings came down around them, and their tools and resources were taken away. It's been almost four hundred years, but if you speak to the residents of the cities, you can sometimes sense the trauma resounding through generations. I suppose we should all be grateful that he held himself in a more sophisticated regard than his idol, the 'great' Dohvevna, otherwise, he may have destroyed and weeded out a lot more people than he did. Then came his apocalypse..."

"Apocalypse? That's not a light word in my world," Arica murmured.

Jake let out a mirthless chuckle. "No. DeRael died under Garal's apocalypse and she was only revived under the stubbornness of mankind." Then he threw a hand out towards some of the stuff she'd been sorting through. "Most of this was already trashed, and Maramore abandoned, during the peak of society's advance. The king must've decided that it wasn't a threat leaving it, maybe just didn't think of it."

"So this dude just killed a bunch of people and forced the rest back into the dark ages... because he was worried magic would become obsolete?"

Jake took a deep breath and stood up straight, holding out a hand to her. "Welcome to the Zenian cause, Miss Tanson."

"Boy, you guys couldn't pick a worse person to join you though," she argued, disregarding the hand.

"I suppose we'll see," he sighed, picking up the shiny silver poker again.

Arica stared into the fire for a moment, glad that the smoke from it filled her nose rather than the smell of whatever mold infected the baseboards.

She ran her fingers through her hair, loosening mud and dirt, only to realize how wet it had been outside. What she wouldn't give for a hot shower. And yet it seemed she was getting further and further from home.

12

BLOOD SCENT

The intact bookshelf in the otherwise abandoned room caught Arica's attention again, so she settled onto the hard ground to dig through the books on it.

As variegated as the colors of the bindings were, the sizes were even more varying. One near the bottom in brown leather was nearly as large as the book Jake had rescued. Then there was one barely bigger than her palm squished between a pair of more normally sized books. This one she pulled out just because she liked miniature items. Little sketches of everyday objects filled the pages. Several of the books had titles down their spines and sometimes thick protective covers.

"How are these still alright, with everything else so decayed?" she asked, touching a soft, almost furry binding.

"They're preserved," Jake mumbled, still guarding the fire with vigilance.

"But how?"

He lazily turned to her, raising an eyebrow.

"Okay, but how was I supposed to know that there was ever a reason for a Zenian to put a spell on a bookcase?" she argued, annoyed that she'd once again asked a stupid question.

"It's not a spell. But you'd be hard-pressed to find a place we *haven't* hidden out during the last thirty hundred years. At some point, it was probably a woman's favorite place to put a plant she kept killing, or the place a lord kept his great-grandfather's watch and cane to keep them from rusting. Who knows? But it ended up here to guard the books, a regular shelf. And so it will stay another thirty hundred, even as the room deteriorates around it." He finished his statement with a little shrug.

Arica glared, sensing that he was mocking her just a little bit. She doubted it was regular for him to give such emotion to a bookshelf. "Wait, but doesn't it need a source of magic to stay working, to keep from decaying?"

Jake threw her a cocky grin. "Careful there, you might start learning."

"Just answer the stupid question," she huffed, almost embarrassed.

"I tease. No, what you see here is one way we can use our magic. Basically, taking an inanimate object, filling it with magic, and giving it instructions on what to do with it. It does fade, but depending on what the magic is doing, it can take many, many years to do so. Takes quite a lot of power, and you have to be well disciplined, but it can be useful. Make a weightless bag, a rock that can tell you about the weather, a wardrobe that sorts your clothes by color. You understand."

She nodded affirmation. "So... enchantments. You put enchantments on stuff."

"No. After it's done, the object possesses the magic put there."

Her eyes narrowed, studying his face to figure out whether he was being a tease or a stickler.

His face was unreadable, so she returned her attention to the books, pulling a few forwards to look at more thoroughly. A dark green velvet one caught her attention. The pages were all well-handled and jagged, some dirty. *A Simple Guide of Botanical Benefit.* Maybe someone else wouldn't have been quite as fascinated with it as she was, but there was a reason she was trying to major in botany. She scanned through the first page, but it started off in an arrangement of characters unreadable to her.

Deciding she'd just flip through it a moment, she opened up to one of the middle pages. Instead of information on what to use to counteract poison ivy or the benefits of taking yarrow, she found sloppy handwriting in thick black ink, splattered all over the pages with no regard to the print inside. A few more pages revealed that much of the thin book was defaced in this manner. In fact, some pages had white or yellow ink painted over them for clearer handwriting. The worst part was that it didn't even seem important. Huge underlined words, tiny scribbles next to complicated diagrams, small samples of colors in places, writing in every which way and direction, some scribbled out or replaced in a way that made her wonder what kind of lab work the owner had been doing.

She came to a few words that were in English and was suddenly more intrigued. Just a couple mixed in with the foreign ones, simple words describing the differences of a clay crucible and an iron one. It only made sense if this person was bilingual, but something about them bothered Arica even still.

Then another page caught her eye with a thick red line painted over the edge, big handwriting scribbled along it.

You belong here now. You aren't leaving.

It seemed like an odd thing to write down the spine of a book, but clearly, whoever had owned it first was not entirely stable.

"Want to hear another story?" Jake offered out of the blue.

Without taking her eyes off the book, she turned and answered, "Sure."

"Vampires?"

She gently shut out the bothersome letters and smiled, but most of his face hid in shadow. "Naturally," she chuckled.

"Back in the... 2600s, I believe," he began with a slightly more upbeat, fairy-tale feel to his voice. "This mansion was home to the cousin of the king of Nevah. Wasn't a nice guy, in fact, he was pretty hated and often simply avoided. He had a tendency to go through slaves and help unrealistically quickly, and any man under the service of his commander went insane with little provocation. Maramore was never a central trading point anyway, so as the problems got worse and his soldiers and commanders started disappearing, the king cut it all off. The town below took the blow, but most of the residents noticed nothing off, as they were all used to the random night raids and dark clouds taking over the sky. A young lady was the one to change all apathy..." He suddenly trailed off, so Arica looked up from her book to watch.

His head cocked to the side as if listening. But for what, she was unsure.

Arica's heartbeat picked up. It was unnaturally quiet without Jake's powerful voice. Not even the fire crackled as loudly as it should have. *How long will it take to get to him?* she wondered as she stared at the junk and the large piece of furniture between them. Terrified, she kept her eyes in Jake's direction. If she couldn't see anything sinister, then it wasn't there, right? Just to be safe, she dragged her feet in his direction.

A few more bated seconds passed before Jake relaxed again. "I'll admit, I'm a bit antsy, but I'm sure there's—"

With an evil hiss, the dull light from the fire died, plunging them into darkness. A darkness she'd never experienced.

He was too far away.

"Jake," she gasped.

"Come here, but be quiet," he calmly directed.

Both of her hands stretched out as she walked forward, but a familiar hand wrapped around her wrist a moment before she slammed her toe on something sturdy.

"Ow," she complained, but Jake was already pulling her to the wall.

"Shush," he hissed. He pressed her up against a surface, and maybe she would've felt embarrassed about it and how his arm crossed against her chest, but fear and confusion kept her quiet and still.

She heard metal chafing leather as he pulled out his weapon, left arm still against her.

Jake's presence left. Only the sound of his calm breathing confirmed the blackness hadn't sucked him up.

Darkness. With nothing to hear, nothing to see, and nothing but a damp wall touching her, Arica's brain started rejecting that there could be anything there at all. Who knew what was going on right in front of her eyes? Finally, she heard something, maybe voices from a long distance. Yes, voices shouting.

Then an icy hand touched her mouth, stifling the following squeal of surprise. The matching hand clasped her upper arm tight enough to keep her in place.

"Calm down, you're just going to attract them," a low voice mumbled near her ear.

His hands stayed where they were, but he started moving away. It took her a minute and nearly falling to realize she was supposed to follow. Instead, she pulled back, trying to break away, but his grip was strong.

"Let me go," she whispered through her teeth. "Where's Jake?"

He jerked her in his direction but kept her between him and the wall. She didn't trip over anything going backwards, but the wall felt soft.

"Let me go," she growled, more angry than she'd intended.

"The moment I do, it'll attack you."

Her eyes still hadn't adjusted enough to see anything but blackness. She couldn't recall a moment it had ever been so dark, not even behind her own eyelids. She could hear something though, just light hissing like a tiny kitten trying to be ferocious.

"What is it? Where is it?" she breathed, shaking more out of lack of personal space than fear.

"A shadow creature. A vampire," he clearly told her, evidently not worried about being quiet anymore. His cool hands shifted grip near her elbows, but he kept them firmly on her. "It's staring at us."

"Derrick?" She'd only heard his voice a time or two, but was sure nobody else would've been able to match the complete monotone to every word, or the casual evenness even talking about danger.

"Yes?"

Her heartbeat picked up again as he began sidling along the wall, dragging her with. Their feet quietly crunched through old debris piled against the walls. She was sure she was making most of the noise.

"Why isn't it attacking?" she whispered, looking around and begging her eyes to see anything.

"It can smell me."

Arica jumped further into the confusing man at the sound of horrific, angry hissing only feet away from them.

Derrick's grip slackened only moments before a heavy, muffled thud interrupted the silence, followed by a crunch of paper and wood.

"One down," Jake jeered loudly, but she couldn't tell how close he was.

The familiar clamor of metallic weapons came from the same direction as another animalistic growl. At least one other being started trudging through trash just as Derrick abandoned her as quickly as he'd come.

Arica slammed her body against the wall, trying to stay out of the way. Only her heartbeat was recognizable among the shuffling, beating, and crunching noises as they overlapped and echoed quietly. There was a growl, more human than the hissing and snarling from before.

"Teres!" Jake scolded in anger, his voice strained from physical movement.

There was a loud, shattering crash as if someone had just thrown an entire bookshelf full of porcelain dishes and glass goblets down off of a balcony, silencing all other noise as it settled.

Someone moaned.

Arica knew she had to do something. Standing there like a target without helping was ridiculously cowardly. Of course, they were warriors, and she was anything but. She made her mind up as her vision wavered in and out, shadows and colors fading in and shifting.

"Focus," she heard in her mind, maybe Bialsa, maybe herself.

Things became clearer, but only barely. There were a few outlines, displacement of the darkness. There were two, maybe a third further off, that were similar, a pair wrestling around on the floor. Then there was one across the room on the floor, different, lighter almost, easier to spot.

I have to help.

The poker by the fireplace. Jake had been handling it like a weapon. Maybe it could help her.

Hands in front of her, she jogged forward, finding the back of the couch by a faint outline. She leapt over it less than gracefully and reached forward to touch the old stone fireplace. Praying she didn't accidentally touch a still scalding stone or ember, she found the poker untouched.

She leapt back over the couch.

Her vision had wavered nearly out again, but still, there was a struggle on the ground in the junk.

"Right in front of you!" Bialsa squealed almost happily.

Arica jumped back, feeling a displacement of air against her jeans.

I can't do this.

The poker grew warm in her hands. She shifted her grip, staring at the black space where there should've been a struggle.

"You don't have to pierce its heart, just distract it," Bialsa soothed patiently.

That didn't seem like a simple task in any way.

Her heart raced as she tried her best to see again, but she didn't know how to do it. She cringed away from another animalistic hiss.

"Now!" Bialsa sang with urgency.

Arica flipped the poker around, holding it more like a shovel than a sword, and plunged it towards the ground. She felt the resistance, like it should've stopped a moment after touching skin but it slid all the way to the handle in seconds.

Her hands left the weapon as she fell backwards off balance. Her stomach churned at the sound of thick, wet choking.

Everything went quiet and still, except for her heavy breathing and possibly someone else's.

Did I just kill it?

"Jake? Derrick?" she called quietly, unable to stop a few tears from leaking down her cheeks. "Did I kill it?"

"It's just unconscious. Let out some light if you'd need it," Derrick suggested calmly. "I could use some over here."

I don't know how...

"There's an old torch there near the fire," Bialsa directed in her mind. "I have a touch of magic myself. I'll light it."

Arica ignored the sick feeling in her stomach and ran to do as she was told. There was a heavy thump behind her, but she didn't turn back until she'd retrieved a thick wood stick from the exact place Bialsa suggested.

It flared up with barely a sound, and she replaced it in the sconce it had roomed in for so many years.

"Oh my god," Arica gasped, regretting the scene in front of her.

A pale face with inhuman teeth bared even in unconsciousness faced her on the ground not two feet to her left, though it didn't have any open wounds. Derrick was on his side, facing a second pale-skinned monster wearing a tight, revealing dress, a silver handle jutting from her back. Jake was across the room, picking himself out of a pile of glass from the broken window.

She ran to Derrick's side, worried the vampire had bitten him, but realized the problem was her own doing. He'd been wrestling underneath the vampire when she'd struck. The poker had pierced all the way through the vampire's thin waist... and into Derrick's stomach.

"Oh my god," she repeated in horror, reaching out a shaking hand but unable to help.

Derrick shoved a hand against the limp vampire, barely showing the bloody poker between them. Watery red liquid leaked out from the blackened puncture in the vampire's chest and Arica had to cover her face as her stomach clenched, barely suppressing a gag.

"I am so, so sorry," she whispered after a second, amazed that not only did he stay conscious, but his features were painless. He had a few long, raised scratches over his cheek and chin, but no bite.

He shoved a little harder on the vamp, making the handle sink into her pliable skin with a sickening, wet sucking. Finally, he gripped the silver between them and it heated under his hand, melting and freeing him from the vampire.

"Don't be," he told her bluntly. "Normally I wouldn't have needed the help."

She couldn't tell whether to take that sarcastically, or what made this an abnormal fight for him, but she didn't bother trying to respond correctly.

Derrick looked upward and reached for a dull gray blade a foot or so above his head. Once in his possession, he carefully dipped the tip into the liquefied silver that had puddled on the wood floor between them.

Then, without even getting up, he drove the weapon straight into the vampire's heart.

Arica looked away, seeing a moment too long of a rapidly decaying body.

"There," he mumbled as if there wasn't a rod puncturing his liver.

Arica looked at him in time to see him struggle upright, mostly shaking in his hands. He gripped the silver in his torso and carefully pulled it out.

At least it hadn't been as far in him as she'd first thought.

"I really don't know how I did that..." she whispered as he tossed the broken piece to the side.

She had a bit of practice nursing, so she went to put pressure against the wound as it dripped thick, congealing blood that in the light almost looked deep black.

"Don't," Derrick snapped, grabbing the offending hand before she'd even gotten close to the wound. "It'll burn you."

She pulled her hand back, his gruffness making a few more tears escape. She sniffled with resentment and got up to take care of Jake, unconcerned with Derrick's health anymore.

He didn't look too bad, mostly dazed, but the leg of his wet jeans sported new tears, and tiny cuts littered his arms.

"Are you okay?" Arica asked as he leaned over the leg, wiping dribbling blood away from a minor wound.

"Sore for a few days. Nothing worse," he murmured, but swayed a little.

Derrick approached, glancing over him. "You've a bite."

He must've felt it because Jake immediately clasped a hand over the circular marks near his elbow.

Arica's hands covered a gasp. "That won't turn him, will it?"

"Of course not."

She glared at the pale man. "I'm sorry. I don't know anything about 'real' vampires."

Jake waved a hand, then took the helping hand Derrick offered. "They're venomous, but it's mostly a narcotic. I'll just get a nap in and I'll be fine."

"Everyone else has congregated behind the mansion," Derrick reported without any promptings.

Jake leaned on the wall near him, trying to get back full use of his leg. "Probably smart," he growled.

Derrick caught Arica's eye for a moment, still expressionless, so she didn't know why nor what he was telling her. Then he turned in the foyer's direction, only stopping long enough to spread some of the thick blood on his hands against the door frame as if an animal marking his turf.

Arica stayed with Jake, ready to help if she could, but sure he just needed a minute to recover. "I feel bad for stabbing him. But I don't think I like him…"

"You'd be in the minority if you did," Jake mumbled back, shoving himself off of the wall and stooping to pick up his sword. "You stabbed him?"

She pointed back at the mess they'd made, a pile of bones in a dress, a tiny puddle of silver and a larger puddle of blood of varying colors. "I don't know how, but I stabbed the vampire all the way through into him."

"*I* know how," Jake teased. He carefully started over the glass mess, apparently oblivious that a good portion of it was stuck into his skin. He didn't limp, but he was slow and careful.

"I didn't use magic," Arica argued stubbornly. For once, she wasn't struggling to keep up with him. They made it into the foyer without any more adventures.

"Maybe you didn't *mean* to."

She stopped, partly to glare and partly to let him get ahead of her. She didn't want him to see how shaky she still felt. "You didn't do this on purpose, did you? Endangering my life so I'd have to use magic?"

"I'll never tell." He made the trip back to the front much easier.

"Maybe I don't like you either," she grumbled.

"Once again. Minority if you did."

She stopped in the doorway outside, letting him squeeze through and drench himself first. "I don't believe that. Everyone seems to like you."

They said nothing else as hundreds of tiny drops of water assaulted them. Neither of them bothered trying to close the door again.

Arica pulled the hood of her cloak up over her already-soaked hair, struggling to see through the rain. Luckily, it didn't matter, as Jake was there, leading. "Don't think I forgot this was your fault," she called over the pattering rain.

"The Zenians' approach drove them in there," he grumbled.

She stepped into a puddle by accident, soaking her pant leg. "We didn't have to go at all. Your fault."

"I'll take credit for adventure."

She stifled a giggle, keeping her eyes on his back so she didn't fall behind.

13

WHISPERS

Behind the mansion rested a stone barn, cracked and worn with weather, and covered in soggy, blackened vines. The inside was huge and empty; plenty of room for the large fire someone had started in the middle.

Arica woke up stiff and groggy, the thin bedroll wrapped around her, neither cushioning her from the stone floor nor keeping her warm. Next time she'd keep her cloak wrapped around her.

The rest of the company was already up, all of their belongings piled in a corner opposite the small medic tent they'd rigged up. Jake had gone to it to patch up after nearly collapsing in the barn's entrance. Someone had mentioned Vanessa's absence, but not much more.

Arica gathered up the bed and the hefty backpack full of things someone recovered for her and gingerly set it in the pile. She was happy to join the beaten group and get some of whatever was cooking in the pot that smelled so delicious.

"It was when Drake broke open the queen's dorm I knew we were screwed," Kylen explained across the fire with an odd enthusiasm. "I mean, we just barely got to her before they did, then her entire guard was struck down by Drake and Ransom within two seconds, naturally, and everything just kind of blew up. Vanessa showed up out of nowhere, but I think they were expecting reinforcements to rescue the queen. Drake took her down and pretty much held her hostage when Anraquella and Ransom set off some kind of... firevolt, but it was like..."

"It blew up normally," volunteered an only slightly older-looking fellow with a yellow braid down the middle of his head, sides shaved, and an unusual scar that kept his right eye from fully opening. Damad, she wanted to call him. "But then it reversed, sucked the force and pressure back in on the device, just leaving the destroyed room and Forien in awful shape."

Arica realized she didn't know where her furry companion was. There were no names or facts or instructions whispered in her mind. She looked around, also noticing Jake wasn't around, but other than the tent, there wasn't really anywhere he could've hidden.

Her eyes caught Derrick a few people away. After barely helping Jake to the tent, he'd forced her to let Elvy treat the few minuscule cuts she'd gotten in the mansion. But when she'd asked Elvy just how badly she'd hurt Derrick, she'd confusingly stated that Derrick hadn't had any injuries to heal.

Arica continued eating the thick, creamy potato and bacon soup to herself, only half paying attention to Kylen and his tag-team story about fighting the Dovevians all the way down to the foyer, while looking out the huge open side of the barn. Rain still drizzled upon them, the sky only slightly lighter than the day before.

It took her a moment to notice the small group standing in the darker corner of the barn near the entrance, quietly talking. Rapier seemed to talk the most, with Aaris standing next to him across the two strangers, a hand resting on the sword at his hip. One stranger was an average-built man wearing a large hood over his head, with plain features and longer fawn hair. He was someone who she could've had as a substitute professor back home and not even batted an eye.

But the other was obviously not human. Slightly shorter than the first, he had bleached, almost translucent skin, dark hair, and even with the distance, palpably shining red pupils.

"Don't worry," said a voice so close to her that she couldn't control a jump.

Jake stood above her, looking a mile tall from her place on the floor. Then he held out a hand for her.

"I noticed you staring. But in a room like this, he's no threat."

She smiled a little, letting him help her to her feet.

"I hope you're done eating. We're going to go play a game." He had a slight smirk on his lips, so she wondered just what kind of game he wanted to play. He was standing straight, the cuts in his neck almost fully healed over already. At least from where she could see.

"Are you going to endanger our lives again?" she asked, only half joking.

"I'll try not to," agreed Jake indifferently.

Arica looked over at the small group again. What were they even talking about?

Rapier caught Jake's eye. Arica wasn't sure if they had some sort of code or silent language, but they obviously traded some orders.

"Come on, Miss Tanson, let's introduce you to a pair of vampires."

Eyes wide, she tried to come up with some excuse, but he dragged her forward too quickly.

Rapier seemed all too eager to introduce someone else into the conversation. "Good. I'd like you to meet two of Mistress Damage's close companions. Miss Arica Tanson, and Jrasko Damage." Then he held a hand out to the hooded man. "This is Tektemnksiklý, leader of the nearby undead tribe, and his advisor, Kasper Valkosce."

"I've met Valkosce before," Jake said formally. "I've no love for the details."

The vampire seemed to agree, staring him down with blood-red pupils, though she wasn't sure why Jake personally knew such a creature. From this distance, Arica could see red veins lethargically pulsing under his translucent skin. She tried to keep from shivering, but it was almost like just with his eyes he was able to prick the nerves along her spine, a centimeter at a time.

"We were just discussing the manner of our lady's arrival," Rapier informed him with distaste. "It may be several days before she's able to join us. Don't you agree?"

"Most likely," Jake agreed with confidence. "And as I'm sure my companion here has already gone over, we're not permitted to discuss the status of our company, so wait you must. Now, if you don't mind, I've young ones to teach dangerous things to."

Rapier glared at him as he slipped away with Arica on his heels, not even giving the strangers time to respond. Jake blew a sigh of relief, briefly glancing back.

"What was that?" Arica asked quietly.

"It's standard procedure. We don't discuss plans, especially while Vanessa is gone."

"No... I meant you seemed to know him already, maybe kind of hate him. What are the chances of that?"

"I'll admit, I find it less than a coincidence that he would be the one to show up here," Jake agreed with distaste. "He was a Zenian commander in his life. But it wasn't vampirism that caused him to be a distrustful, sleazy, greedy villain, no—he was already so. That's why this fate is so fitting. In any case, Vanessa may have pinpointed this area for his help."

Arica nodded slightly, not sure how to respond. She tried to imagine the creature as a man. His carob hair was short except for a longer patch brushed over his eyes. But other than that... the red light in his eyes was more reptilian than human. Was that even possible? If magic could mutate a human to that extent, did it even have any business existing?

Moisture hung in the air so thick Arica's lungs weren't working quite as well as they should've, and she could barely see two feet in front of her. Jake consistently breached past those two feet as she tried to keep up with him. Dark, dead trees sprouted up from the ground, eerily showing up out of nowhere before fading out of her vision as she passed them.

She felt the thick air tickle up her arms and neck, causing her to shiver a bit more violently. How was it so dark, yet so white out? And where had Jake gone?

Her feet stopped so suddenly that her cloak fell forward over her shoulders, shrouding her body. At least this way she was warmer. She twisted her body around in a circle, looking in each direction without moving her feet from the one she'd originally faced.

"Jake?" she called out with growing terror. Her voice barely carried, as if she was standing in a tiny closet.

Her hands trembled. Part of her wanted to sit down and panic, but she tried to rationalize. Maybe she could see his bootprints.

The ground was certainly soft enough, though it was stringy, coarse soil, obviously not something that could support much life at all. There were no prints but her own. But this meant she could follow them back to where Jake's left off. Or go back to the camp and leave him by himself, as he deserved.

"Bialsa," she tried confidently, but there was no answer.

She started to follow her footprints back.

The movement of her legs caused tiny tornadoes along the ground as she trudged, dirt sticking to her feet while her lungs fatigued from the moisture she inhaled.

A whisper passed over her shoulder, incomprehensible yet enough to once again stop her dead. She suddenly didn't feel so alone, though the fog kept her wrapped up tight.

Maybe it was just the wind through the trees, she told herself. But what wind?

Her new pace quickened just a touch.

"Can you smell it?"

This time she was sure she wasn't hearing things, though the voice sounded low, and from a distance. She didn't feel like she was making a lot of noise, but there was enough.

She heard another voice, but it sounded from the opposite side, and she wasn't sure if it had spoken words, or just made a low, hiss-like growl. Again, this time a word but not one she recognized, *"Ersiasevaer."*

Then she noticed the fog breaking. No, not breaking. There were shadows forming in it, small, and possibly far away.

There was one in front of her, though it moved rapidly upwards. Her head whipped to the right to follow more whispers. There stood a few of the shadows, humanoid in this direction that seemed slightly bigger than the first.

She turned behind her, stepping backwards upon hearing a soft call, like an old man calling in his cat for the night. This shadow was about a foot tall. Did that mean it was closer?

"Ersiasevaer," the fog whispered.

Her foot caught on something jutting from the ground as she took a step backwards. It crumbled with little provocation, though part of it still erupted from the ground, broken off and jagged.

Arica swore aloud.

It was a headstone, much too old to withstand the weather and her tampering. But as far as she could tell, there had been no recent unearthing or re-earthing of the headstone's owner.

Something caught her eye in the rubble, shiny and different from the white and black flecked material. She bent down and brushed back some powder. It was a dirty gold coin, about the size of a silver dollar, embedded into the middle of the headstone until her meddling. It wasn't difficult to pry it out the rest of the way.

She had to squint and hold it close to her face in order to see the inscription, but there was enough light to do it. It was flat, but for four embossed words.

He's to your right.

"No way," Arica breathed, looking in the direction it prodded, then back down at the old coin. "Well, I guess there's nobody here to tell me helpful little brownies don't cohabit with vampires, so…"

She followed the little coin's directions, not because she thought it would work. Because in her twisting and turning, she'd lost sight of any clear footprints, and she could still hear whispering here and there.

She ran, just in case the owners of those voices were closer than she'd seen. Her arms worked free of her cloak as the sticky dirt threatened to pull her off-balance.

As long as she could get out of the living fog.

She jumped violently as a shadow appeared dead ahead. It sat casually on a large boulder as if she hadn't been panicking and lost for the last ten minutes.

"You have a good sense of direction, I'll give you that," Jake commended, his words distant in the thick air.

"Where did you go?" she demanded, her intended anger translucent against the upset in her tone.

"You're going to have to learn to survive on your own as well," he said in his even, instructional way. "We're a team, but sometimes we have to be alone. Planned or not."

Her previous mini experience was unpleasant enough, but the thought of being left alone in the wilderness of a foreign world for who knew how long brought her to tears. "Doesn't mean you need to leave me out here in the middle of a cold, gross forest teeming with vampires," she whispered into her sleeve, both hands against her face.

"The closest vampire is almost a mile away. And I could hear you the whole time. I just needed to know how you would react."

She took a long, nasally inhale, trying to pull herself together. "I saw a bunch of them further that way, though. You really think it would take them that long to get to me?" She pointed back over her shoulder but wasn't sure she was pointing even close to the right direction.

"I was watching out for you, okay? However... You saw them?"

She let her hands drop, nodding gently.

Jake leaned both arms on his knees, expression one of approval. "I suppose I shouldn't be surprised. It's a bit of a higher skill, but then you're also a little older than most of the tyros we bring in. Or, maybe you're just stronger."

"So... seeing things like that? It's normal?" she asked timidly.

"Seeing the darker creatures, yes," he agreed happily. "Sometimes strong magical ones, if you hone your sight enough."

She relaxed just a little. Knowing she'd never been in any danger was a bit soothing, but the knowledge that he'd do such things to her was anything but.

Jake didn't give her time to dwell on it, though, and started into a lecture. "Seeing as we're in a much more desperate situation now, there's a pressing need to get your basic training done." He shifted, fingering a small object against his palm. "Since you're struggling anyway, we're going to do this the faster, more entertaining way."

The way he had one eyebrow cocked was suspicious, but she didn't know how to keep him from exploiting his seniority.

"What's the funner way?"

He held up one finger, signaling just a moment.

Arica jumped as a stone hit her arm, hard enough to sting. "Ow," she complained, rubbing the spot. A second one hit her shin, once again, only hard enough to hurt.

She glared at Jake, sure it was him, but he reclined back, casually covering his mouth with a hand.

"Is this *your* doing?"

In response, three more hit her in various places and she desperately tried to deflect them with her damp cloak.

Dozens of relentless little pebbles pelted her. She let out an ugly screech and ran in a circle, trying to cover her face and arms with her cloak. They came from all directions, but she couldn't see where she was going through the thick fabric.

"Jake, stop," she demanded, crouching down, but they only increased.

They started hitting places that were already sore, and the odd one would get through the cloak and hit her neck or face.

"Just throw them back, hun," he called.

She reached out a hand, trying to figure out where they were going to land next, and after getting hit several times, kept one in her fingers. She weakly threw it in Jake's direction, but didn't need to see to know she'd missed by a long shot.

Then a few hit her harder.

"Ow, please," she begged, trying to come up with a way to make him stop. There was no way she could catch any more. So she waited until he spoke again to get her bearings.

"Use your—"

She barreled into him with more force than she'd intended. They both toppled over the small boulder and onto the ground. Rocks and pebbles dropped around them, motionless once more.

"That was not what I meant, Arica," Jake growled, dragging himself out from under her.

"It stopped, didn't it?" She rolled onto her back and pulled her hood over her face.

Jake sat up with a low groan. "So you're just going to hug your enemies to death?"

She pulled the hood back and looked up at his stupid grin. "They wouldn't expect it."

There was a pause as he shrugged. "Well, there's that."

She covered her face with her sleeves, half ashamed, half frustrated with her achy body. "I can't just use magic, Jake. You haven't even told me how."

"Let us put it so you may understand," he suggested, leaning back on his palms. "When you want an infant to walk, you stand them up and help them walk. You don't explain to them how their muscles pull, and the exact angles their joints need to be in at any given moment; you don't give them an in-depth lecture on what it is to walk. You coax them until they do."

"But you don't just set them on a bridge six inches wide over boiling lava and tell them to do it," Arica argued, trying to keep her voice from cracking.

There was a long pause. She was almost happy she'd silenced him.

"I am sorry I upset you, Arica. I know you're frightened. Would you like a little boost?"

She uncovered her eyes, faced away enough that she wasn't able to see him. "Would it be anything like the building that I burned down?" she asked.

"I would do that same thing nearly. But you probably won't burn anything else down."

There was a longer silence this time, just two people getting steadily more soaked in the wet fog. Finally, she heard Jake shifting around. "Get up, child. We need to do something."

Arica did as ordered, but was resentful about it. Jake sat back down on his boulder, then held out his gloved hands. Frowning, she took them.

"Now, normally we don't worry about this until you're being readied for your first true combat situation, but again, this is a different circumstance. Most of us, both The Zenian Court and the Dovevians, have a withstanding personal barrier that can reflect points of highly concentrated force from entering our personal space. It feeds on your own power, but not enough to kill you or weaken you." He gestured with their hands for a moment.

"If you'll allow it, I'll help you create the pattern. I'd still be able to throw rocks at you, but not hard enough for them to do permanent damage." His eyebrows rose slightly. He was teasing her, at least a little.

"If that's the case, then have at it," she encouraged lightly.

He made a quiet agreeing noise and held her hands still for a moment.

At first, Arica just stood awkwardly, but after a minute warmth and a fuzzy static washed over her skin. It rose out of her chest and suddenly her mind was hazy. In fact, she couldn't see the person sitting in front of her. Then, in a beautiful streak of violet, her vision cleared over and she stopped swaying.

"Well done," Jake stated proudly. "You took it over just fine."

Arica took her hands and stepped back, rubbing her own arms, and looked around. She hadn't consciously done a thing. "I don't feel more protected. If it was working, wouldn't it make it so nobody could touch me?"

Jake shook his head. "It only works at a certain velocity and force. Magic shot at you, stronger projectiles. But people and creatures can't move quick or hard enough to be deflected, and most natural situations won't be affected. You can still breathe poison and suffer a stab wound."

She glared at him for no real reason.

Then he stood back up, pulling a pair of swords from his invisible sheaths.

"So, since you're so magically incompetent—"

She grabbed her arms in annoyance.

"—we'll do a little more physical training."

She was so sore and cold and damp, the last thing she wanted was to get a whole new bunch of bruises. But at least this was something she could *try*. She took the weapon.

They crossed iron. Arica's was shaking despite her resolve. Jake's was effortlessly steady. She backed up a step, letting the blade slide along his with a satisfying ring. If neither of them ever struck, would they just stand there forever?

Then he swiped at her leg underhanded, an incredible move just because he was so much taller. She jumped to avoid it, but the sword heavily connected with the side of her shin, nearly throwing her to the ground already.

She threw him a rather spastic swipe that didn't even make it near his body but threw her stumbling to the side.

"Keep your feet further apart. And your arms closer to your core. Don't just use the strength of your arms," he instructed, not even trying to hide his smile. His hand shifted the handle in his palm, but both of hers could barely keep her sword up.

"Are you left-handed?" she asked before running at him. She was viciously repelled in the other direction.

"No, I'm actually heavily right-handed, unlike most of us. Two swords can be useful. But I'm rarely one to go for usefulness." He once more blocked a weak strike she brought from the side. "I just thought it might give you more of a chance."

She stopped a moment, dropping her mouth open to be dramatic. "How dare you! I'm amazing at this." Then she brought the weapon up as fast as she could, forcing him to back up a jump.

"What kind of attack was that?" he demanded, his voice a few octaves higher.

Arica looked at her sword, repeating the motion slower. With the tip of her sword towards the ground, she heaved her strength into flipping it up towards the sky.

"No, no, no, never do that again," Jake growled, grabbing the tip of her weapon, despite it being relatively sharp. "You're going to pull a muscle or break your arms."

She tilted her head. "Why?"

"Do it again," he commanded.

She thought he was going to point out the flaws, but as soon as she repeated the movement, he brought his own weapon down onto hers with the extra force gravity gave him. The collision was not only incredibly loud but instantly painful, the reverberations shooting pain through her arms. She fell to her knees, dropping the sword and clutching her arms to her sides as she blinked tears of pain away.

"Ow... why did you do that?" she moaned, rocking until the initial pain faded.

He chuckled a little, saying, "You learn better this way."

"I hate you so much..." Arica mumbled into the dirt.

"Grab your sword," he ordered apathetically. "Come on, let's warm up inside."

There were no different words that could've made her happier in that moment.

14

THE REVENANT

Arica looked at the pile of things in her lap. It wasn't a lot of stuff, but it was almost everything from the backpack someone else had packed for her. Some of it had been in her chest. The rest Jake used magic to pull from thin air. He'd explained that most of the containers they used, they'd enchant in a way that they could retrieve the contents from short distances. She was just glad she'd kept all the important things in the bag and not strewn about her room.

Most of it she placed back in the backpack, but some of it she decided should go in the little leather satchel the stranger had given her. The book from the mansion, the gloves she should've been wearing, a few bottles of various hygienic and medicinal liquids, and a small dagger all went in. It didn't take long for her to realize that although it only had so much space, when it was closed, it kept a flat shape and weighed no more than it did empty. Maybe she shouldn't have been surprised over a satchel that kept her things weightless and shapeless in a world of impossible magic.

Before she set it into her backpack with the rest of her things, she pulled the book back out.

It was getting darker outside, and with it, colder. Colder than it had been the night before. She naturally felt herself drawn to the fire, but as she noticed Jake standing on the open side of the barn, she decided to deal with the cold and join him.

The unfamiliarity surrounding her eased only in the presence of the three she'd met at home. Vanessa was first since they'd lived together for several months, but she was pretty busy with boss-type things, and while Zak was nicer, warmer, and apparently from her world, he was also much more social, forcing her to be closer to strangers. This made social loner Jake an obvious choice.

His hands were moving close together, his fingers waving, but his gaze never tore from the darkening woods around them. She realized he was on his shift of watch duty.

There was something hovering between his hands, a bundle of small, dark flowers moving in slow circles as tiny particles of dirt ambled upwards from the ground to stick to their surface.

"Wow. I can learn to do that?"

He looked down, finally beholding his creation, only to pluck it out of the air.

"You could do it right now if you wanted to," he mumbled, then held it out.

She reached out to the detailed sprig, the individual petals that, while were the color of dirt, still had beautiful details. As she pulled it from his grasp, it crumbled, covering her hand in soft soil.

"I... I can't..."

Jake turned back to watch their surroundings, his talented hands going into his jeans pockets. "The difference between destruction and creation is impulse versus intent. You've used your magic on impulse. Now you need to do it intentionally."

Arica sighed through her nose, staring into the dark trees back-dropped by twilight. It looked like once there had been a type of pasture, the remains of a stone wall reaching out into the sun-deserted forest.

"So, what's the plan now?" Arica asked quietly. "Like, we aren't going to just keep camping out in this Aztec barn, are we?"

"I don't know which one, but we'll likely head for one of the other bases. The Dovevians were quick to hit us; they can't be far from the others. I haven't spoken with Vanessa yet, so..."

They both glanced inwards.

Vanessa had set herself up in the darkest corner as soon as she'd returned from her scout and retrieval, and while several other Zenians had approached her, the conversations were brief. For several hours she'd paced, gone through her things, and scribbled on paper alone. Arica hoped this meant they'd be leaving the area soon.

"At least she's—" As she turned back, she spied a figure standing within the trees. "What... What's that?" she whispered, squinting to see better.

She wasn't sure if it was moving, but it wasn't far away, about thirty feet from the tree line, barely outlined as a tall humanoid.

"What do you see?" Jake asked, peering in the same direction.

She waited a few moments, stifling her breath as if the creature wouldn't easily notice them. It seemed to meander towards them. The harder she concentrated, the clearer it became, and soon she could make out ragged clothes on a skeletal body.

Then, like headlights flicking on against a moonless night, a pair of white eyes lit up. Warmth spread across her face.

She couldn't see the figure beyond the light anymore, but she wasn't so worried. It was nice, whatever it was. The warmth spread into her arms and legs, expelling a chill she'd hadn't managed to shake since arriving. She didn't want to let go of that. Maybe it was time to invite whatever it was inside to meet her friends.

Arica blinked, and black was the only thing left.

Her knees buckled, sending her onto them as her chest chilled like her heart had turned to ice. Air filled her lungs again, reminding her how to breathe, but it didn't soothe the cold, empty feeling vibrating through her body.

The dirt at her feet was clear in the flickering firelight, but as she looked up again, all she could see in front of her was blackness. She looked further to see Jake with one hand pressed to the darkness as if it was a tangible wall.

"What was that?" she asked breathlessly.

He answered much more calmly than she felt the words deserved. "A revenant. If you'd looked much longer, you'd have died."

"Huh. That..." She was too shocked to even finish.

"Jrasko."

Rapier jogged towards them, looking concerned, but as he spoke, it didn't seem to be for the reason Arica had assumed. "You need to lower your barrier."

"There's a revenant outside," Jake argued softly.

"I know. We agreed to meet with it."

Jake's eyes scrunched as he glared down upon the commander.

"The vampires warned us we're on his territory, so we called for him to come to terms," Rapier continued to convince him.

Looking as if he'd tasted something rancid, Jake looked at his barrier. "At least warn everyone..."

"I did. I was working my way to warn you, I've Master Damage's permission, so you can—"

Someone yelled for help within the camp, drawing pretty much everyone's attention. Vanessa was on the ground in her corner, unresponsive to Elvy's shaking.

Rapier looked conflicted on whether he should make sure Jake was in line, or run to her. The latter won out, so Arica followed behind to see what was happening.

Elvy dug through her bag set on the ground as fast as she could search.

"Give them space," Rapier growled, using his wide body to push through curious Zenians.

"What... what's wrong with her?" Arica asked meekly, her fists both close to her face in worry.

Rapier glanced up only briefly. "That *snake* poisoned her."

She tried to remember names and faces. "Drake, right?"

Nobody confirmed it, but they didn't need to. Arica jumped at the voice practically at her shoulder.

"The revenant." Derrick moved past her, his black, soulless eyes barely having to sweep over the woman on the ground. "Damage's sword created her injury to flare up with the first bit of darkness that touched her. I'll have her fixed up in a few moments."

Rapier seemed to be satisfied with this because he stood back up. "I'll go explain; try to keep it at bay until she's ready."

Elvy knelt next to Derrick, holding whatever she'd retrieved from her bag. "It didn't look to be poisoned at all," the girl mumbled.

"Don't blame yourself, it would've been impossible for you to tell," Derrick murmured flatly.

Arica looked over her shoulder, jumping as her eyes passed over the ragged trousers she would've guessed belonged to someone long buried. She kept her eyes lowered, but a shiver still made its way up her spine.

Rapier was only a few feet away from it, keeping his face lowered to the ground even as he spoke. She wondered if the creature would even understand a word he said.

"Up." Jake smacked her boot with his, distracting her from the odd scene, though he seemed to monitor them as well.

She didn't want to leave, but it didn't look like he'd give her a choice. He herded her to the enclosed side of the barn to be with the gist of the company.

It was eerily quiet for so many people in such a closed space. It was unusual to see anyone doing nothing. There was always cooking, cleaning, repairs, and practice going on at least, but most of the company huddled up along the wall as they did when sleeping.

The pair of fires were down to embers, giving very little light to see by.

Jake steered her into the open space with her things between Zak and Malon. She sat down when he put a bit of pressure on her shoulder.

"Stay put. You'll know when it's safe to get up," he murmured before leaving her there.

She huddled against the wall in the shivery dimness, facing a monster.

Zak lifted a hand, offering it to her, so she wrapped her forearm around his and slipped her fingers into his warm grip.

"Why is everyone so quiet?" she whispered, shivering again.

She looked at Zak's face when he was quiet for so long, worried they were all under a spell. He met her eyes, his thin face serious. "We can't fight this evil. We just have to wait and see..."

Arica lifted her blanket up over her shoulder, unsure if the cold was natural or supernatural. Either way, she kept shivering and held fast to Zak.

"Jake said it was a revenant. Is it really so dangerous? Aren't they supposed to be some kind of zombie?"

She chanced a glance at it again. It looked towards Jake, who'd anchored himself next to Rapier and stared at something in his own hand. It looked hauntingly human, nearly as tall as Jake, but bone skinny. The gaunt skin on its cheeks and the visible ear was pale, but unblemished. It even had a raggedy sweep of dark hair.

One hand rested inside a pant pocket, the sleeve of a matching suit jacket covering any more skin, if he even had it. It was a ridiculously casual stance for something supposedly evil.

"They're manifestations of loose magic, often created from horrific tragedies or the deaths of extremely powerful beings, unkillable by sword like many immortal creatures of the god, Solyve. They can take energy, even kill, with only eye contact. Luckily, they aren't inherently bloodthirsty. We must've just wandered into its territory."

"Jake said something horrible happened in that mansion with vampires," Arica admitted.

Zak nodded slightly. "I wouldn't be surprised if that had something to do with it."

"You believe in their gods, too?" she asked softly.

"Maybe I believe things here aren't the way they are back home," he reasoned, voice reverent. "Solyve is one of their gods, the Seven Severed. They say each of them took part in the creation of life, though Solyve's creatures are the only ones that life does not rule. They are dark, evil. Demons and like." He jerked his chin towards the creature.

She shrank down further against the stone. "What's the plan, then?"

"Vanessa will have to bargain with it."

She checked on the medics that knelt over the high master. She sat upright, her face pale.

"Zak?"

"Yes?"

"I'm cold."

He gave her a tight smile. "Come here; I am too."

Arica was glad to be warmer, and although she still couldn't tell what time it was for lack of sun, the few hours of sleep she'd gotten had refreshed her. Zak, however, was still leaning on her shoulder, passed out.

She held the book stolen from the mansion in her hands, taking glances at the dome taking up the center of the room. It was a blue and purple mound of crackling energy shining pale blue light over everything. She could only catch glances of the spindly demon and the high-ranking woman speaking within it.

Jake paced slowly around the barricade, arms crossed and gaze alert. He, the commander, and Aaris had taken hourly turns watching it, but only them. He'd relieved Rapier a few minutes before, giving the commander a chance to retrieve some food. While Rapier had taken the dinner, he still paced near Arica, alert.

Flipping to the last few pages of her book, Arica searched for something to cure her boredom. There were so many pages of random scribblings but they served little purpose since she didn't understand them. She noticed that the very last page and the one before bragged only handwriting, but these were spaced even and straight, more like a journal entry than the rest of the book.

"What is this?" Zak asked groggily.

She hadn't realized he was waking up but lifted the page a little closer, then flipped back to some scribbles.

"I found it in the mansion, but I can't read it," she admitted.

He looked at it for a moment, then touched his finger to some of the writing.

"I can't read it, but it looks like Raellic. Go back to the end."

Arica obliged and watched him squint at it.

"I don't know what that is. Hey, Rapier?" He summoned the muscle-bound commander with a hand. "Do you recognize this?"

Rapier crouched in front of them as Arica turned the book around, a little embarrassed to be drawing even more attention to herself.

Still shoveling food into his mouth, he looked over the symbols for a minute.

"It looks like it's in Raellic," he finally told her, standing back up. "An older language that virtually nobody speaks anymore, let alone reads."

She looked back at Zak for a moment, who shrugged, an excuse for not recognizing it. "Well, do you?" she asked back at Rapier.

He shook his head, taking another bite of his dinner. He quickly finished chewing before saying, "No, I don't. You should show it to Master Damage. She can."

Arica frowned and glanced again to where she stood behind the sparkles. "Will she ever finish talking to it?"

"Just be patient," Rapier shrugged. "It'll be over, eventually."

He was more right than he might've guessed because it was then Vanessa emerged through the sparkling barrier. She looked pale and tired. She said something to Jake, who immediately began working the barrier.

It thinned, and darkened, then followed the revenant to the edge of the barn, only sparkling out of existence once the demon's back had shrunk with distance.

Voices murmured excitement at the return of leadership, and perhaps the increasing absence of danger, but Vanessa didn't look quite ready to address the gist of them as she hurriedly spoke with Jake.

A small cat pranced towards Arica's feet, the first time she'd seen the little creature since the battle.

Bialsa giggled a terse request. "Come join us in the tent."

15

THOSE OF SOLYVE

Debating the entire time on whether she'd gotten the message right, Arica went to the small tent in the room's corner, joining not only Vanessa and the commander, but Jake as well.

"Good, thank you for coming," Vanessa said, holding a palm out to the girl for a moment.

"You appear unscathed. I hope your training has continued."

"M-me?" Arica muttered, looking around for a moment. After everything that had happened since they'd last spoken, she was almost surprised the woman even remembered who she was. "Yeah, it's... it's all good." She added an awkward smile for reassurance.

Two cots took up most of the room, angled apart in a V, with a few bagged belongings scattered around.

Vanessa lowered herself onto a cot and pulled a bowl of water onto her lap. She quickly washed her face with her hands.

"We have much to discuss now. This, uh, unideal situation may put a slight damper on your plans of returning home, dear," she expressed as she pulled a cloth from a nearby bag to dry her face and hands.

"Oh. Oh, I wasn't... Too worried about that, honestly. Rather not die, first." She forced a little laugh, glancing up at Jake as if he'd rescue her. His face was blank.

"Well, I want you to know that I have much use for you, but I will not put you in harm's way deliberately."

"Me?"

"You're one of the few I can trust at the moment. And now, I *know* there is a traitor among us. There was no reason for the Dovevians to attack when they did."

Instead of coming up with some answer, Arica just held herself awkwardly. Everyone else spoke to this woman with so much respect; treated her like a queen. It made her eager to impress, to not embarrass herself or sound naïve, even more than she already did.

Jake broke the formality. "Are you really going to force me to ask if you're all right?"

The high master tilted her head, jerked up the knee of her skirt, and, like a dancer, displayed a calf with a short horizontal slice through the muscle. Considering it was a wound of war, it didn't look all that bad.

"And I've no physical marks from our undead companion. I am absolutely fine," she reassured.

"You're lucky Drake went so gentle on you. If he'd been anyone else, you'd be dead already," Rapier told her in a low voice. "Or missing some limbs."

Vanessa shot him a look that obviously wasn't agreement or approval. "If he'd been anyone else, he would've been dead before he touched me."

Arica couldn't help pick up. "Why...?"

She replaced the things on her lap and stood up, slowly, even taking Rapier's offered arm for more balance. "Because he's my husband," she breathed, growing paler now.

"Maybe you should lie down," Jake mumbled.

"In time. I've sent for the vampires. The sooner I can settle this, the better."

"Are... are you really married... to a bad guy?" Arica asked, hoping she wasn't disturbing her.

"It's a long and rather grim story, but in short, yes," said Vanessa as she let go of the commander, steady on her feet. "He wasn't a Dovevian when we married. We can't seem to harm each other all that effectively despite intending to. It's always been a problem. Though, this poisoning ambition is new."

"What else did you need?" Jake asked softly.

Arica felt strange standing there. With a big, muscly commander on one side, and a skilled, athletic, apparently wise warrior on the other, with nothing in the middle. A college kid who didn't like summer and was weary of men in general. A twenty-year-old interested in books and plants.

She didn't belong there.

Vanessa, after taking her sweet time, finally answered, but it was a quiet, serious response. "The words we say next must not leave this tent."

Arica just wondered how a tent could become soundproof.

"Magic," Bialsa giggled.

No more questions...

"This is dangerous," Vanessa said with a tight smile. "And by now, the only one I can fully trust is Arica."

Rapier shifted uncomfortably, his expression pained, but Jake blankly let her continue.

"Within a few days, even that may be difficult. But without some sort of structure, we as a group will be impossible to control. We have to have *some* trust, even if it is misplaced."

Arica tried to stand as still and professional as the other two but knew she looked more like she was eager to leave.

"We have to go to Santsin Val and make sure Colten and his still stand," Vanessa explained patiently. "Their victory in Neva will have made the Dovevians cocky, and I haven't been able to contact either master commander or their subordinates. I believe Santsin Val is secure. Kopion, less so, but I'm sure if the king finds out or knows where it is, they won't hold back. So, we will take the track. It's the fastest, surest way to get there, despite the Dovevians that explore the routes. Because of that, we'll march in three groups."

Then she pointed at Jake. "Jrasko, you will take Kylen and Aaris ahead to scout. I'll lead the first half of the company. Then only two hours behind, Rapier will lead with those remaining. There are good chances of running into guards, scouts, or an ambush while under there, but in close confines and split as we are, we'll have a much better chance of overtaking them."

She took a longer breath than usual before continuing. "Meanwhile, I will search for more clues to find out who is betraying information. I'll not give you details, but I may come to any of you with simple tasks, if I need. Do you have questions?"

Rapier seemed to be almost bursting with one, so they all looked towards him. "What of the revenant? How did you send him away satisfied?"

Vanessa paused, then gave him a nod. "I..." She looked up with a hint of a smile. "I threatened him."

Jake let out a sharp laugh, and Rapier just looked dumbfounded.

Vanessa surrendered her hands, still smiling slightly. "Now, it wasn't easy. In the beginning, I was sure he'd outsmart me, and towards the middle, I was making offers I was not ready to fulfill. But as he continued to decline my steep offers like they were table scraps, it became apparent that it would *not* go smoothly. Once I ran out of ideas, I had one choice: to threaten him, or risk offending him."

"Wait," Arica interrupted softly. "Is there a difference, though?"

"Revenants gain little from being of the earth, so even though death is their sustenance, they'll humor bargains for passage through their domains. Refusing to negotiate with one is one of the highest forms of vanity, and will ensure instantaneous death. The only choice is to come to terms. So, I threatened him not only with our force but with his own vampires." She smirked in Jake's direction with a hidden meaning. "Valkosce will back me up. But this gave him a chance to compromise."

Rapier made a face of disgust. "What do we have to do?"

"He wants a Dovevian," Vanessa said, lifting her chin slightly.

"That's not a big deal, right?" Arica asked, trying not to sound awkward.

"Death by any of Solyve's soulless creatures is not ideal for anyone, and normally I refrain from sending anyone, even enemies, to any terrible fate. We shall do our best and hope that since the Dovevians are also of Solyve, their fate isn't so serious. I won't hesitate if the consequence otherwise is losing my entire crew."

This seemed reasonable. Arica wanted to continue asking questions, but the high master set a finger to her lips before she could.

The tent parted behind her and Jake, allowing a translucent-skinned vampire into the small space.

"Valkosce," Vanessa greeted without hesitation. "I think a warning is overdue. When you agreed to allow me to scout out the area, you failed to mention someone already claimed it."

He gave her a fanged grin, his voice cool and even. "I figured you could handle it. You aren't dead, so I suppose I wasn't wrong."

"Surprise me again, and I'll fill my cup with *your* blood. You'll be happy to know your companion has volunteered your services to ensure I gather his payment."

He's coming with us? The idea gave Arica a sour taste.

"Does that make you nervous, Mistress?" he hissed mischievously, and even though he addressed Vanessa, it was the fresh meat in the room his serpentesque eyes wandered to.

Vanessa chuckled lightly. "I can't find immediate harm in allowing it. A single Zenian can easily fend off a vampire, or even a group of them."

Her stare in Jake's direction was an undeniable accusation.

"In my defense," he started immediately. "You know as well as I do that cursed castle was dampening my magic, and frankly, I was more worried about them grabbing Arica than killing them. Teres is the one who threw my plans into the physical and metaphorical window."

"That mansion has *always* been a duller of magic, and I thought you'd avoid it for that reason. Though, I had concerns when Rapier mentioned sending Teres in after you. He tends to complicate such a situation."

What on earth are they talking about? Were they being vague on purpose? Or were they just so used to talking in code that it was a permanent switch for them?

"Miss Tanson," Bialsa reported femininely from who-knew-where. "I've alerted Mistress Damage of your curiosity, and she permitted me to translate their words so you could understand. The story itself is Derrick's to tell, but there's no reason not to warn you."

Arica looked at Vanessa, who listed which Zenian was going where. She made no indication that she'd been talking to the andromae, or that she knew Bialsa was translating information.

"Derrick Teres is different. He has talents that aren't known to Zenians. In the mansion, Jrasko changed his vision in a way to see the damned, the demons and monsters of the god Solyve. He saw Derrick in the same way, because of his... talents."

"His talents?" *Of the god Solyve.* Then she caught on.

Derrick's a Dovevian.

"I have another question, though, about the Dovevians," she whispered carefully.

"What of them?"

She looked up at Vanessa, forgetting that while Bialsa was in her mind, her words were vocal, and all of them, commander, high master, vampire, and her mentor, could hear her.

She must've stared too long because after a minute, the vampire swiveled his head towards Vanessa, sticking one hand in the pockets of his pants.

"What's with Junior?"

"I can trust a tyro more than I can you, as is clearer by the hour," Vanessa replied haughtily, then let her body rest on the cot in a more casual position. "What did you want to know, Arica?"

She felt her cheeks warm but didn't want to waste their time. "I was just gonna ask Bialsa why they seemed so... different. Their skin was weird. And... I don't know exactly."

Jake was the one who answered. "You are observant. Though it wouldn't take a magician to notice their differences."

"So, they aren't just some named faction of super-soldier?" she asked with a bit more confidence.

"It's considered more of a religion," Vanessa explained. "Our patron is Areun, the god of magic and power. He's the one who watches us, takes care of us, and gives us our power. The Dovevians, however, honor Solyve."

"The evil one," Arica remembered aloud.

"Not evil necessarily. Darkness, heroism, vain magic, strength, and hunger. When the king came into power, he gained many followers, promising many things, power, consistently. They take Solyve's curse with no heed of their own god nor their own souls. But they believe they are doing it for good. They believe in Garal's ridiculous fantasies of control. They believe humans need a mortal god's rule to keep them safe, even if it's in servitude. The ritual they perform gives them different, darker magic. It does often leave them discolored, but not always."

"So…" Arica mumbled, trying to sum it all up in her head. "They're Zenians… cursed by a dark god for bonus powers… who think they need to be in charge?" Then she looked up, giving each of them a few moment's stare. "But what is you guys' plan for the humans? What do you fight for, against him?"

Vanessa smiled slightly but gave someone else the podium.

Jake shifted a little, shrugging. "It's Vanessa's dream, and many others', to restore The Zenian Court to what it once was. To put mortals in charge again. We belong beside the kings and queens, giving guidance and wisdom. We always had a powerful presence in the hierarchy of DeRael. But we were not dictators or rulers. We don't deserve to be. As proven, we already have too much power."

"Perfectly put," the high master complimented softly.

"I admire that," Arica said thoughtfully. "And I think I agree. It's hard sometimes to see who's right and wrong. And I'm not saying that you guys are all saints, but it seems like you're working for a better cause. Even if you're slowly losing ground over him."

"I didn't doubt you'd see correctly," Jake smirked, giving her an innocent wink.

Valkosce sighed softly, a dramatism to his otherwise breathless body. "Ah, the self-appointed righteousness of the Zenian cause. I miss it as much as one misses a cancerous tumor."

"You've died for our cause already, Kasper. I don't think I can ask much more of you." Vanessa forced a smile of reassurance as she held a dismissing hand towards the tent's opening.

Arica wasn't sure if everyone was being kicked out, but Jake's large hand rested on her shoulder, steering her out anyway.

"Don't get me wrong, though, I still don't want to fight anyone," she said over her shoulder. "I'll probably leave that to you and all the other guerrillas in the area."

"We'll change your mind yet, Miss Tanson," Jake chuckled sweetly.

16

KILLER STRESS

Blackness rolled around her in notable contrast to the figure made of light. Cold, revealing light. The first time she'd looked into the revenant's, she'd felt a fictitious warmth, but this time she knew what lay beyond the baiting glow.

"Stay away from me," she tried to say. Her arms moved as if in a pool of cool honey.

The darkness responded, the voice a familiar whistle of the wind and rumble of the earth.

"Ersiasevaer."

"What? Did you say something?"

She could see movement beyond the light if she didn't focus, but she still couldn't completely tear her eyes from the revenant's eyes.

"Ersiasevaer."

"What does that mean!" she screamed, but no words reached her ears as if she was deaf again.

"Arica."

This voice was different. Her shoulder jerked back and forth.

"Arica, wake up."

Her wake-up wasn't violent. In fact, the images just faded out as the noise faded in. Still, she kept her eyes closed to the real world.

"It's time to pack up. Get up."

Her body turned in her blanket, her arm shoving Zak's away.

"And here I was gonna help you," he chuckled.

Arica moaned, but forced her shaky muscles to sit her up. She was tired of sleeping on the ground but didn't know if it was going to change soon. "We're getting ready to go?" she asked groggily. Vanessa had mentioned the plan, just not how soon it was going to be.

"Yep. So if you could stop sleep-talking..." he teased lightheartedly.

"Ersiasevaer," the voice repeated, the whisper clinging even in reality.

She blushed, shaking it off as she began piling her bedding up for storage. "I was dreaming about that revenant. Is that normal?"

"I dunno. I've never seen one before. None of this is 'normal' in my book."

She nodded, wanting to continue with questions, but his job was done, so he went to help the last of the stragglers. Luckily, she'd already had most of her things picked up in anticipation of leaving. At least the few things she'd actually pulled out of her bag. She was almost too scared to go through the rest of it.

Then she noticed a small white kitten curled up on her big backpack, the tip of its tail twitching slightly.

"Ersiasevaer," the andromae murmured in the quietest corners of her mind.

A wave of relief crashed over her. So she wasn't crazy, dreaming in a language she didn't know. She just had a crazy animal buried in her head.

Bialsa stretched out fluffy paws as Arica gently stroked her soft head, and like the first drops of a warm shower, all ethereal murmurs evaporated completely.

A smile crossed Arica's lips as she urged the cat onto her shoulder.

Vanessa, Rapier, and Malon all exited the small tent as Arica picked up the last of her few things. There was a sharp whistle, drawing nearly everyone's attention to the refreshed woman in leather as she slowly picked her way to the middle of the room and the dying fire.

The kitten scampered across the stone away from Arica, tiny paws stepping much too elegant for a real kitten.

"Thank you for your patience," Vanessa announced with authority. A calm settled over the rest of them. "I'm going to be brief with you. We will head out soon. Based on the events at the castle, I know well that someone is contacting either a Dovevian or the king himself."

There was a little murmuring, but nobody sounded shocked.

Arica's face flushed a little. Obviously, it wasn't her, but even being accused of it as a group made her feel nervous and guilty.

"Regardless of your intentions," said their leader, slightly quieter, more serious. "I'll act upon you fully as a traitor and a Dovevian spy. Measures to find out who is crossing us will begin immediately."

She crossed her arms, looking over the scattered crowd with an emotionless expression. "If you turn yourself in, your sentence will be less brutal. If it was accidental, as ridiculous as that may be, then I may work to pardon you. You're all much more anxious to know our next move, I'm sure. There's a significant chance treason has reached another base. Our plan is to march on that base and provide our help as needed. I've already set about alerting them. I will release very few details until I can decide what isn't sensitive. For now, the revenant has been taken care of and we can leave."

Then she reached out a finger and pointed it in Jake's general direction. "Damage and Rapier are the only ones that need to know of any specifics for this very reason. Don't take this as mistrust, just a precaution."

Zak was standing near Elvy, arms crossed over his chest. "What are we doing about the new girl?"

Arica felt a pang of betrayal, maybe because he was drawing attention to her, or maybe because the words felt dismissive.

"I'll continue her training as I can, and, if possible, use her to sniff out those who wish us ill. Nothing, nor anyone, can fake her tyro's blaze, and she's never had the slightest Dovevian interaction."

Or less than formally, should you find yourself in the wrong company. The memory came back, along with a bit of sharp guilt. It wasn't her fault she was being stalked by evil even at home, even though nothing had signaled that this person was actually one of their bad guys.

"But I'll leave it to you to finish preparations. We'll be leaving shortly," Vanessa finalized.

"Zak," Arica called, gesturing for him.

"What's up?"

Lowering her voice as he approached, she asked, "Is the whole... Earth... portal thing common knowledge?"

He shook his head gently, leaning in closer. "No, only a few of us know. The rest of them think we're just trekking to other regions just outside of DeRael."

"Who else does then?" she whispered, matching his quietness. Then she glanced around to see if she could guess.

"Well, me, Jake and Vanessa, obviously, then Rapier and Aaris as well. The two leaders of one of our bases, Herak and Marc, also know. But I don't know if anyone from the third stronghold actually does."

"What about the Dovevians?" This was it, wasn't it? She was going to find out that a bad guy had approached her and she was keeping it from Vanessa.

Zak shook his head without hesitation. "None of them know. It's why we keep it so shush. We can't let them, either. It could be disastrous."

Her shoulders loosened in relief. So, who was it? One of these commanders, maybe? Someone Zak didn't know? Maybe that's why they didn't notice him hanging around Montana if they didn't know who he was. Was that any safer, though?

Zak smiled reassuringly and went back to helping pack up.

Arica checked her surroundings. Some boys had brought an entire herd of horses from somewhere close, all geared to the teeth.

The absence of her more familiar instructor compelled her outside.

One wouldn't guess from the light that it was already past dawn, but the fog was visible, instead of the world being black all around, so this was probably the closest sign of daylight.

She found Jake near the entrance, long legs crossed on the moist ground, elbows leaned on them. He was still, as he usually was, strangely reverent.

She was worried about interrupting some personal reflection, or a prayer, but his head turned to the sound of her boots crunching through dead branches.

"Hey," she began, so it didn't seem like she'd failed to spy. "What are you doing out here alone?"

"Resting," he breathed.

She almost turned around and left him alone, but settled against a leaning tree stump in front of him. His eyes were low like he was tired. A book lay in his lap, loosely covered by the edge of his cloak.

She laced her fingers between her hands and rested her elbows on her knees. She couldn't bring herself to interrupt his quiet for a bit, so she watched the progress of the camp behind him. They were being remarkably thorough in leaving no trace.

Jake finally moved, tugging his cloak off of the book, then opened it to a seemingly random page.

"So, part of understanding magic is understanding how the world is classified," he began in his strong, instructive voice. "Heat, as you've experienced, is the easiest, most uncontrollable natural component."

Arica gave him a quizzical look. "I didn't know I was coming out here for a lecture."

Jake shook the book a little. "But I knew you'd come after me, so I prepared accordingly."

Her arms crossed in front of her chest. "How on earth could you know that?" she demanded childishly.

"I've noticed the way you stick to what you know the best. I may be nigh a stranger, but I'm still what you know better than all else. You fear what you *don't* know." He raised an eyebrow as if daring her to object, only continuing when she didn't. "I'd guess you had a lot of unknown, a lot of instability in your childhood, and you clung to that person you knew better than anyone else."

Arica tried to stop her face from warming but had no control. *How dare he make assumptions like that!* "You know what?" she announced defensively. "I'm in a foreign world entirely. I think I'm entitled to fear everything."

"Except for myself, which was the entirety of my point."

She glared at his smug look, then gestured at the book in his lap. "Just give me the book to study. You can train me in these settings instead."

"I would, but it's in Raellic. I'm translating as we go," he admitted, letting the top fall forward enough to let her glimpse the foreign letters. "Zak ruined the Endreyan version."

"I'd need an English version, anyway." Arica shrugged.

Jake looked at her, giving her a brief look. "You speak it fine, you should be able to read Endreyan as easily."

She returned the confused look just as convincingly. "This is English. We're speaking English. Derived from English. Established in England. Home of the English language."

"Actually..." he sighed, leaning back slightly. "*I'm* speaking Endreyan. Established in Endré. They're the same thing."

"You don't actually believe that English, and 'Endreyan' just *happen* to be the same language?" Arica demanded, wondering if she was even awake anymore.

"It's unclear exactly what happened, but we do think someone, maybe some-*thing*, introduced English to DeRael. It's much newer here than Ellteria for certain. It's not likely just a coincidence, but we've no proof of what happened, so..."

Arica nodded, but it wasn't out of understanding. "Right. That seems cheap."

"You should be happy about it, otherwise we wouldn't know what the other was saying." Jake shrugged with a little smile.

"Sometimes that's the case anyway," she sighed. "But I didn't mean to get you off track. Go ahead, pick up your book, and—"

A large bug touched her shoulder suddenly enough that she jumped, letting out a little squeal.

It had long, fluttery wings, about the size of her fist, black as night, but shimmery with moisture. It hovered in the air for a moment, then was startled off by her movement.

She froze, heart pumping fast. She wasn't afraid of butterflies, but this one was gigantic and really seemed to want to land on her. It dove without fear, then perched on her knee.

A couple more fluttered into view through the fog surrounding the first.

Arica slowly lifted a hand to avoid spooking them. With her luck, they'd turn out to be vampire butterflies, and try to kill her, but Jake watched carefully and made no move to shoo them away.

One perched on the heel of her hand, its legs tickling her skin lightly. She got a better view of it and was shocked to find it wasn't a butterfly, but the tiniest of humanoids with huge wings. It wobbled on two toothpick legs, tiny black hairs covering all but its head, hands, and feet.

"They're fairies," she breathed, watching the tiny thing dancing in a dainty circle, wings fluttering in and out. She looked up at Jake. "Are they dangerous?"

"Not at all. They love Zenians. Especially women," he responded quietly.

She watched it bend down and touch her skin with fingers so tiny she could barely make them out. Sparks surged from the contact, and the hair along her arm stood up, but it didn't hurt.

"They like playing with our magic," Jake continued as the little fairy jumped into the air, throwing strands of purple light into the fog.

One of them fluttered closer to Jake, but he shooed it away with a hand. The other three hovered closer. One dared to dart in and touch Arica's cheek for a second. The onyx butterfly wings fluttered back, leaving behind a trail of light that imprinted on her retinas.

She couldn't help but smile.

A small one with lighter hair sat on the exposed skin of her ankle, hands on its fuzzy face.

Unlike this one, most of them were chipper, dipping down to touch her, then throwing sparks into the air. She noticed a bigger bluish one land on the collar of Jake's shirt, but he didn't seem to notice. She said nothing to him in case he tried to shoo it away.

"I kind of like this. There's something of DeRael that won't kill me," Arica said, smiling.

Of course, he had to take that down a few notches. "They could if they wanted to."

She noticed the fairy on her ankle slouch, then slide onto the ground, limp.

"Whoa," she whispered, carefully scooping up the creature. Her wings felt delicate, like just a fingertip could tear a giant hole. The fairy hopped up, shaking off her sudden droopiness.

"They can feed off of your emotion as well," said Jake.

She didn't think she'd been that depressed, but the little creature certainly disagreed.

He shooed another that strayed too close to his face, but barely disturbed the one lying on his neck. "They've been used to determine mental issues occasionally."

"Ah. Well, that makes a bit more sense. I have plenty of those."

The temporarily sad fairy flew off of her hand and joined the others, perfectly fine. They shared the little sparks with each other, taking turns to make patterns.

"Ersiasevaer," she whispered as the memory of the nightmare came flooding back. Part of her expected some kind of magic to happen, time to stop or the sky to change color, but everything stayed still and cool. Maybe the fairy had picked up on that confusion.

"I am here for you."

She looked up from a blueish fairy to Jake's calm face. "I know. I appreciate that," she mumbled.

"No... 'Ersiasevaer'. It's Raellic for 'I am here for you'," he said, just as factual as the first time. "Where did you hear it?"

Arica blushed. Of course, he wasn't being sensitive, just putting up facts as usual. "Oh. Well, I think the revenant said it to me and I just didn't remember until I dreamed about it last night. Or, Bialsa said it to me. Or maybe I made it up. If it's an actual word, though..."

This seemed to be enough of an explanation for him because he didn't question her further. Then she added, "And I remember Bonds, for some reason. He, or Bialsa, or whatever, also said Bonds. I didn't know what that meant."

"Bonds, and ersiasevaer?" he repeated. "That's it?"

"Yeah. Does it mean anything to you?"

His mouth scrunched into an unsympathetic smile. "Not at all."

"You... It does, doesn't it?"

He shrugged, something about his searching eyes telling her he was withholding information. Then, as his shoulders went down, Jake felt the one on his neck and brushed at it dismissively. But instead of flying away, it tipped over. He caught it in his hand before it slid all the way down his shirt.

But Arica knew something was wrong because it didn't move, even laying in his hand. She leaned forward, grabbing the hand. The fairy lay with one leg twisted out at an angle, one wing crushed.

"You... you killed it," she whispered.

Jake tipped the tiny body into her hand. "That's why I was trying to keep them off," he explained calmly.

She cupped it in her hand as the other fairies fluttered closer around her, then began a frenzied dance in a circle before scattering into the fog completely, a darting line of light where they'd been.

"You should've felt it," she accused softly.

"I'm not overly sensitive to touch."

"How stressed out are you that it could kill a little... bug? Animal? In a few seconds?"

He was silent as she tried to decide what to do with it. She used a couple of fingers to test out the dirt in front of her. It was packed, but moist enough that it wasn't difficult to dig a little out.

"You know... You've saved me enough times that even though I've known you for like a week, I consider you a friend. You can talk to me if you need to."

She looked him in the face, trying to challenge him, but he looked back blankly. Even just sitting, their height difference was intimidating.

The dirt came up in her hands easier after a few inches, and she continued to put the extra into a little pile. "I guess I can imagine how hard it is to be driven out of your home again. You're probably missing a bed and clean water and closed rooms. I can see how someone would be upset."

"It's not that," Jake argued.

Arica pushed back a smile. That tactic always worked on them.

"I'm tired, that's all. I'm tired of fighting."

"It's something that would wear on anyone," Arica agreed.

She laid the fairy in the wrist-deep hole, trying to fix the crumpled wing but only made the delicate membrane wrinkle more.

"You know... at a glance, you look a lot like any one of the guys I've talked to in my age range. But when I look into your face, like, *really* look... I understand a little more than you think I do. I won't ever understand the things you've been through, but that's never meant you can't talk to people who don't."

She ignored the grunt he gave her, just to spare her feelings. Her hands sifted through the loose dirt, then carefully piled it on top of the dead fairy.

"Or, I can just say screw you and ignore you like the rest of your 'friends'," she spat back.

"Wow. And here I thought you appreciated being saved at every other moment."

She flipped her hair back over her shoulder and folded her arms on her knees, wondering if he was going to teach her again. Then she cast her eyes on the tiny grave in front of her.

"You mentioned once that the king was immortal. Is that, like, a thing?"

"Your eloquence is exceeded only by your grace."

She mumbled a quick, "Thank you" while twisting her hand into a theatrical bow.

"It is true, though."

She blushed a little, briefly wondering why she'd brought such a topic to life. "I've always been confused. It seems to mean different things for different people. I mean, obviously, Zenians can die. So does that mean they can be, like, really old?"

Jake didn't move a ton but did a little shrug that may have also been a nod.

"I already know the king is way older than he should be," she whispered, following suit and staring at the ground almost dejectedly. "So, what about the rest of you?"

"It depends, Arica," he said with less patience.

She tried not to glare at his stupid smirk. It was like he knew exactly what to say to annoy her most. Only andromaes could read minds, and, as far as she was aware, he didn't have one.

Then she took a big breath and let it out before looking up at him under her eyelashes. "How old are you, Jake?"

He let out a breath of disbelief as he smiled, still messing with his hands. "I don't know if that's necessary information, Miss Arica," he said with a sly glance.

She folded her arms across her chest proudly, knowing she was onto something. "*Rapier* couldn't read Raellic. *Rapier* wasn't old enough to read a dead language," she accused.

He raised an eyebrow. "Just because he's twice as big as me, doesn't mean I have to be younger than him."

She smiled, trying not to jump up. "So?"

He shrugged, lips locked, but that smile still peeked through.

"Hmm. What about... seventy?" She looked him up and down, trying to imagine a man looking like him and being old enough to be her grandfather.

"Zak and Kylen were the youngest before you came into the picture. And they're about eighty and thirty-nine."

Arica's eyes widened, looking for either of them but unsure where they'd snuck off to. "That... that's crazy. I can't imagine... No wonder there aren't any old veterans still trying to cling to youth and strength."

"Well, not that you can instantly see." Jake shrugged.

"What about Vanessa?" Arica asked reverently. "She's probably older than a lot of you."

"Mmm, well, yes," he agreed, looking thoughtful. "She's just over ten hundred. Comparatively, the king is barely older than her. "

"NO WAY!" Arica clapped her hand over her mouth, realizing she'd spoken almost loud enough to draw the attention of the building behind him. She leaned over to catch a look at the beautiful young woman bossing around the occupants of the barn, trying to imagine her being older than forty. Let alone older than her hometown. Older than a lot of civilizations. How was that even possible?

"No way," she mouthed, finally looking back at him wide-eyed.

He smiled crookedly, shrugging. "Believe it."

Arica leaned her head on her hand. "What about you?"

He let out an exaggerated sigh. "If you *must* know, I'm just shy of the same."

Her skin felt weird on her body as she lifted her head, unable to look at him. She raised her eyebrows several times, then just sat there across from him for a few minutes in silence, her head slightly tilted to the side.

And he let her, probably used to having people surprised at his age. *For a damned thousand years!*

"This war..." he finally said, breaking the weird silence. "It's been going on a lot longer than you may have realized."

"*How* long?" she whispered, unable to shake the chill settling on her.

She let her shoulders relax as Jake took in a deep breath, his stare at the ground between them vacant. "Nine hundred and eighty-two years," he sighed.

"In the autumn. Garal was High Master of The Zenian Court at the time. After a few long years of discord, he drew together the legions of our kind and simultaneously built them up and obliterated them."

"You remember that?" Her voice still barely broke through the heavy air.

"No. I was to be born that same turn of summer. But like everyone who's ever heard the account from one of its subjects, it bears the same weight."

"Vanessa?" Arica guessed softly.

He gave her a short nod, his lips pulled into a tight frown. "Garal expected most of his vassals to fall in line to his new title. Many did. The surprising pair to stand against him in the wreckage were his two children, Asriel and Vanessa."

"The king's her *dad?*" she squeaked aloud.

"The young siblings, with the help of a tiny fraction of the seasoned Zenians Garal had failed to turn to Solyve, brought order and structure back to DeRael, despite the war of control with the Dovevians. After some time, Asriel caved to the king's pressure, betrayed Vanessa, and became his father's right hand. They say he still expects Vanessa to cave to him, but..."

"Yeah, no, that's not happening," Arica agreed softly. She swallowed hard then took a cleansing breath. "Wow."

"Another history lesson." Jake's light words were accompanied by a slap as he closed the book in his lap.

"So... I don't suppose you're my great, great, great, great, great, great, great, great, great, great, great, great, great, great... long-lost grandpa?"

He snorted in amusement before saying, "Yeah, I've no kids that old, so no."

Arica let out a little scoff. "Don't tell me you're a thousand-year-old virgin," she toyed, trying to mask how weird she still felt over being dumped with all that information.

His eyes narrowed. "No, of course not. I've married twice. And once before those. Then once after. Sort of."

Arica's chest fell even more as she sensed she'd found her way into forbidden waters. "Oh. I never would've taken you for a widower, let alone... several times over. Now I feel bad."

He shrugged without acting like he wanted to cry or beat on things.

Either way, she didn't want to press the issue. There was enough tension and awkwardness in the air.

She let out a sigh. "Immortality. Is it... hard?" she asked softly.

Jake cringed, then turned his head to the side. "Yes," he finally whispered. "It's easy to lose track of time. You see generations live and die around you." He looked back in her direction, but wouldn't look her in the eye. "It's easy to forget who you are. Sometimes you can... sink into a state where you don't even exist." His eyes shut. "Nothing does. It's like dying, but in the back of your mind, you know you still have to wake up. You have to leave the peace and quiet."

Arica wrapped her cloak tighter around herself. "Has it ever happened to you?"

"A few times," he mumbled.

She frowned but glanced behind him at the approaching person instead of responding. He was on the heftier side of bodily strength, but his big eyes and soft face matched his quiet, almost shy demeanor. He carried not only his bag but a bigger, slightly familiar pack as well.

"Here," he said as he approached, tossing the bag into Jake's lap. "We're headed out first, yes?"

Jake took the offered hand to pull him to his feet, then glanced down at Arica. "Indeed we are."

Arica forced a smile as Jake offered a hand to help her stand.

"You mentioned Bonds," Jake then stated clearly. He turned to the quiet man, a hand outstretched. "I don't know if you've met him yet, but this is Aaris Bonds. You probably heard someone call his name while you were sleeping."

Aaris gave him a look of confusion, but Arica nodded.

"Oh. That makes sense."

"He's like my little brother so don't be a stranger, you can trust him."

"Hi," was all Aaris said in a soft, unthreatening tone.

She forced a smile.

"Wow," Jake sighed, then shouldered past his friend. "Let's get outta here before you loudmouths kill any more fairies."

17

THAT MIGHT WORK

"We'll be a few hours ahead of you. Make sure you're ready to go because no one will wait for you," Jake instructed, shouldering his pack.

Arica stared into the giant hole in the shed's floor. Even though it was nearly noon, the thick clouds and mist clung to the sad trees and filtered most of the light before it reached the ground. Luckily, even in the darkness, she could tell that it was only about a six-foot drop, but it was still daunting. The endless stretch she could only imagine beyond didn't help.

"So, this is a plyway, right?" Arica repeated loudly.

Jake leaned heavily on the old door, but the already worn wood was threatening to tear itself apart under his weight.

"Yes. This one will lead through an ancient passage to the other side of the country."

Arica looked over her shoulder. Quiet Aaris and small Kylen waited not far, both ready to go like their large companion. She turned back to Jake.

"And you really won't take me with you?" she pleaded softly. Waiting around was the last thing she wanted to do. She never thought the constant stimulation from her home world would ever bite her in the ass so hard, but her patience for such things was just shot.

With a shake of the head, his stance remained casual. "It'll be too dangerous. There's a very good chance we'll run into a Dovevian or two. Maybe something worse. I don't even know if I feel good about bringing Junior over there."

He pointed lazily at Kylen, who folded his arms, glaring. "Psht."

Arica glanced around their feet where thick fog swirled in lazy circles as if alive on its own.

"Okay," she muttered with disappointment.

"You'll be on the road before you know it. Take the time to work on using your magic," Jake encouraged lightly.

He stood upright, towering over the door, and waved a dismissive hand. "Back up the hill. Behind the mansion. I'll watch before we leave to make sure you get back."

She threw a hand in his direction and began trudging back as if obeying was a defiance.

"This fog has gotten very thick," Aaris murmured behind her.

"The revenant is likely close by," Jake responded.

Arica swiveled back around, hands in her pockets. "It's not dangerous?"

Jake's expression was calm. "Vanessa came to terms with it."

"So reassuring," she said under her breath. Her steps caused chaotic whirlwinds through the dark mist clinging to the cold ground as she moved, nearly shrouding her boots altogether.

"Arica."

Normally, she wasn't one to go on alert when she heard her name, but the tone with which he said it instantly had her on edge.

"Come, you two," Jake said nearly as quickly.

Then, before she could even turn to them, blackness rolled over the ground like a waterless wave crashing down on her. Within a foot of her, it parted, rolling harmlessly above and around her, roiling in a whoosh of anger.

Jake stood almost above her, Aaris and Kylen sliding to a stop just behind him as the smoke caved in around their small, defined pocket of safety. The disturbed air tore at their clothes and hair.

Jake growled, his hands thrown forward as the darkness surged in on them, forcing the four of them closer together.

One of Aaris's outstretched arms jerked back, sending him staggering, but his look of concentration only deepened.

"How do I help?" Arica yelled over the roaring wind. She didn't know what they were doing.

She turned all the way around and caught Kylen's eyes. His braid whipped back and forth, slapping his cheek. He looked just as lost.

"Jake!" she continued. She touched his arm above her head, but he barely seemed to notice, his violet eyes slit. His hands glowed a faint purple, but whatever he was doing kept the tornado of black smoke at bay.

His coat fluttered about him, and her eye caught a flash of gold. She slithered in front of him to get a quick look.

A heavy chunk of stamped gold was strapped snugly to his waist with a sash. The hero's crest. It glowed an inviting faint purple.

A hand grabbed her forearm as she tried to snatch it up, strained eyes glowering at her.

"What's it made of?" she asked, close enough that maybe he had a chance of hearing her.

The fireless inferno raged, threatening at any moment to consume them, but he still hadn't let go of her.

"I know what I'm doing," she said with a false confidence. She had no idea.

As he let go, she felt a powerful surge in her chest, not displacing her but throwing her off a little. She steadied her feet, then grabbed the crest a little tighter, undoing a tight knot as fast as she could to free it.

The weight felt good in her hands, but the pressure from outside was increasing.

She chucked it as hard as she could. It clanked against the barrier staving off the darkness and plonked to the ground.

Jake turned to her, hands out in surprise. "What was *that* for?"

"I don't know! I thought it would do SOMETHING!"

Another clank, but this time, the piece of ostentatious decor looked possessed, sliding up the invisible surface as if dragged by fishing line.

"What is it..." Arica mumbled. Her breath caught for a moment. "Put down your magic!"

"Why would—"

"Put DOWN the magic," she ordered, but she didn't wait for compliance. She lurched forward, grabbing Aaris and Jake by their wrists.

Wind roared over them in a wave of chaos. It didn't hurt, but she may have screamed. Muscle pulled against her hand, giving her no choice but to let go of both of them. Why didn't it hurt?

She chanced a glance upward. Her ponytail stung her face.

The crest spun in a lazy circle a dozen feet above them, its sash of a tail twirling behind it like a dancer's ribbon. It wasn't nearly as dark around them as it should've been.

"What is it doing?" Kylen shouted above the wind.

"The same thing we were. Trying to keep back a deadly haze," Jake answered, staring at it solemnly.

"That's it?" Arica demanded with disappointment. "It won't do anything else?"

"Hypothetically, it could dispel the revenant, but it doesn't have enough magic. It'll run out too soon."

Her heart fell. So much for being impulsive.

"So, can we do anything?" Kylen asked, his arms tight around himself to stave off the wind.

Jake looked at Aaris instead. "We can. We can give it all we've got."

The quiet Zenian gave him a firm nod.

Arica jumped in her skin as a powerful pulse ran through her chest in time with a tone just barely high enough to hear. Nothing visibly changed, but both guys were stiller, concentrated.

"I don't even know how to do that!" she yelled, fear rising in her throat.

Jake's eyes slit, barely moving to glance at her.

"Just throw it up," Kylen shouted, drawing her attention. He shook out his hands, pointedly staring at the swirling badge. "Find the—whatever thing that is, make it your god and just throw up everything inside of you. Puke it up all over the place."

His mischievous eyebrows rose, challenging her before he turned to the task at hand.

She inhaled sharply as another, albeit weaker, pressure passed through her tight chest. Then she looked at the thing. She'd already done this. She engulfed practically an entire building in flame. This wasn't that different. There didn't need to be any precision or control, just raw, impulsive…

Magic.

This time the pressure left *her*, giving her a strong, fulfilling lightness like her body was suddenly ethereal. She didn't know where anything was, but it didn't feel like it mattered that much. She just threw it all out.

She could still feel her arms outstretched like a depth-perception-deficient toddler reaching for a cookie. The strong, disturbed air still whirled around her, the cold of Maramore's sunless sky eating at her skin, but the sensations felt distant.

Then it stopped.

Her weight fell upon her so hard her head spun, her feet barely balanced as she was crushed. Her knees wobbled.

The golden crest struck the blackened dirt in front of her.

She gave in, allowing her weight to fall to her hands and knees. A single drop of sweat clung to her nose, then dripped onto the seal.

"You're so dramatic," Jake sighed as he snatched up the item.

"You guys are the ones making magic just blast all over the place," she mumbled, pushing herself upright with shaky arms. Then her lunch escaped her possession in a heave more violent than any gust from the wind of death.

"When *waves* crash upon you or the *earth* topples down, do you not cave underneath the weight? When the *winds* bear upon you or *fire* roars over you, is it not chaotic? If someone is taken from this plain, or born into it, do you not cry?"

She swiped her sleeve across her face but felt better already. "I feel like that last one is stretching it."

Jake smirked. "Those are the five. So why would *magic* be any different?"

"Jrasko!"

Arica forced herself to sit up and search for the yeller. The air was still foggy and thick but no longer felt mystical or aggressive. Despite Jake's teasing, it was obvious she wasn't the only one affected by what they'd achieved. Aaris slouched, hands to his knees, breathing deeply. His forearms glowed the softest purple. Kylen's too, and he held a stitch in his side, face creased with frustration or pain.

Like fire from the maw of a dragon, the fog parted away from them until it revealed a woman in red and leather, her strides long and precise as she crested the hill above them.

"We're fine," Jake responded, throwing a dismissive hand.

Vanessa slowed, picking her way towards them. When she stopped only feet away from them, she bent and took a sample of the earth in her fingers. They rubbed the dark soil into her palm, displaying more than just soil. A silvery sparkle like crushed glass was mixed in. Her gaze flicked over some of them.

"Reapers were here," she murmured with an unusual curiosity. "The revenant has been dispelled. Was that *your* hand?"

Instead of answering, Jake tossed the seal at her. She caught it in her clean hand, letting its weight pull her arm back another few inches before she lifted it for inspection. "The hero's crest you asked about," she narrated, twisting it around. "You didn't mention it had a Khantarian design."

"I didn't recognize it," he excused. She stepped close enough to hand it back to him, but his gaze was sullen. "*She* knew to use it."

Arica's face flushed under Vanessa's gaze. "I-I-I didn't... *know*. I just saw it and was like, 'Hey, that might work.'"

Vanessa's gaze didn't waver until she stepped past Arica to the other two men. She gave them each a once over, then held out her arms. Both of them calmed in contact with her skin. She returned to Arica and offered the same courtesy.

With it, her mind settled like a heavy rock into a pillow and the lavender glow faded.

"Dare I stand impressed," Vanessa murmured before releasing her.

"Is anyone hurt?" Jake asked.

"Not so far," Vanessa said, following his calm walk back toward camp. Arica scrambled to follow, checking to make sure the other two mimicked her.

"We noticed soon enough to cover ourselves, but Teres and Ann Ent were hitching up the animals. Rapier went to check on them."

"So, what happened?" Arica asked, feeling it was the appropriate time to ask questions. Her hands were still shivering, but the walk was helping. "Why did... Just, *why?*"

"I'm not entirely sure why our new friend decided we were too much of a liability, but that appears to be the case," Vanessa explained over her shoulder. "I've a hunch our resident vampire tribe might have something to do with it. If it weren't for quick thinking and the luck of possessing such a powerful artifact, it would not have ended as well."

They reached the edge of the camp, the barn in sight, but there was more of a commotion to the side than anything else. Steen jogged from the stable further towards the forest behind the mansion's gate.

Elvy was limp in Rapier's bulky arms, her head resting on his shoulder and her eyes closed. But it wasn't her the crowd had their attention on. It was the dark, shifting patch of space crackling with purple electricity in front of them.

"Atork nigh, not Elvy," Kylen gasped, jogging past Arica.

"Where is Lord Teres?" Vanessa demanded. Rapier didn't answer, his gaze following the strange disturbance of pitch black.

She looked for a moment before turning her attention to Elvy.

At Vanessa's touch, the pale young woman gasped sharply, not as dead as she'd appeared, but her trembling, even from a distance, was obvious.

Arica was among many that jumped as a deafening *crack* whipped across the valley as if the very sky took discipline from angry gods. The darkness faded in mere moments, leaving only Derrick's ample darkness in the middle of the spot. He held a worn-down weapon; a scythe of wood and pocked metal. Well used.

The crowd parted for him. His expression was as blank as it ever was. "Do you want this, sir?"

Vanessa made a small sound of interest as he offered the weapon. She took it cautiously, then Derrick offered a hand to Elvy and helped her stand on her own. She looked pale and shaky, but not completely hurt.

"You'll be okay," he reassured, though his tone was flat. He turned back to Vanessa. "I didn't realize soon enough that extra darkness was rising. It touched her, put her down, but only for a moment."

"I'm okay," Elvy agreed, nodding.

"Sit her by a fire at least," Rapier encouraged.

"And the reaper?" Vanessa gestured with the odd weapon.

"I sent it back to Naornagosau. I don't think it would've taken her, but that wasn't my chance to take."

Vanessa gave Derrick a curt nod, then turned to the gist of the group.

"Is it done?" someone asked. "Is the revenant dead?"

"Gone, it seems, yes," Vanessa said with another nod. "Our plans will remain, though. We've pressing reasons to move on. An hour or two and we must be back on track."

18

TOUCHES

Arica quickly found out that their path did not always stay underground. Sometimes they'd break out into an open stretch with trees growing up and around an unseen barrier, and while the sun shone down on them, it was just as cold as if they were underground.

Those patches didn't last long enough, though, as only hours later they descended on a seemingly unending slope into stronger darkness.

Little fireballs appeared around her one by one until there was at least one per person sitting in a hand. The closeness of the cave walls and ceiling shifted back and forth with the light of the Zenians' fire. It grew to be spacious, and every footstep echoed nearly deafeningly and a tiny drop of water would ring as clear as a bell.

Arica was losing her sense of time. Her feet ached even though her new shoes had thick, comfy soles, and no matter how tightly she wrapped up in the cloak, cold reached her bones and she couldn't shake a damp feeling on her skin.

Even though she'd heard them discussed several times over the course of the day, she couldn't remember the names of more cities that held gateways near them. She was too focused on sorting through the many names and places she'd heard in the last while.

"You're doing well."

Arica jumped so hard she bumped into a silent Steen, who'd innocently walked next to her for the last stretch. Hand over her erratic heartbeat, she stared up at Jake, still leaning away from him. "What the heck? Where did you come from? I thought you were scouting. You scared me."

"I was. You just caught up," he soothed, prodding her back into a walk before people could pass. "We're almost done for the day. We're about to hit Akvelia."

She unconsciously began walking much closer to him. "I thought Akvelia was on the other side of the country. We're supposed to pass through a portal."

A smile wrinkled his cheeks. "We did," he chuckled. "Didn't you feel it?"

Her shoulders rose as she wracked her brain, but all she could remember was mind-numbing marching for what felt like days.

"It's okay," Jake quickly said with a reassuring nod. "It's strong, ancient magic, barely discernible from the very essence of the world around us."

"So they're safe from the Dovevians tampering."

Another nod. "The worst they could do is set traps or blockades for us if they could even guess our path. We'll be able to detect them."

Arica nodded thoughtfully, staring ahead at the dull orange light growing in familiarity. "So we'll have the rest of our guys soon? And we can move on to base number three?"

"Let's not get ahead of ourselves. The walk through Akvelia itself is nearly four days."

"I guess it's not part of this whole folded tunnel—or portal, thing, business?"

"Correct. Here, we're nearly there."

Arica couldn't immediately see what he was talking about, but slowly noticed more natural light filling up the surrounding space. "We're still pretty deep, aren't we?"

"So it feels."

Arica's curiosity caught up with her and she found her feet egging her forward to where Vanessa led a tall horse pulling a small two-wheeled wagon heavy with belongings. She knew the rest of the horses were bringing up the rear.

The cave expanded the further they walked, and soon a mist hung in the air, making it even chillier. It was when they stepped out of the mouth of the tunnel Arica got an idea why, and she stopped to awe.

Water rained from sunlit fissures miles above them onto old, chiseled slabs of stone overgrown with verdant mosses and vines. Rivers carved through the stone fed from these waterfalls for so far she couldn't even see the end; only carved rocks leading into the distance. Hollows were cut into the rock walls in all

directions, shaped into large houses. They were the only buildings that had survived decay, though some of the scattered remnants suggested that free-standing
structures had graced the space once. A good portion of the city to the left had
fallen victim to the waterfalls, but to the right, darkness shrouded the ruins.

"It's... beautiful," Arica whispered. A feeling of tininess in such an enormous
world washed over her.

"We'll make camp," Vanessa called from behind her. "Kylen, Damad, we'll
find a way up to the surface, at least a place to grow some food. A few of you can
look around for something to hunt. Jrasko, wait for the commander's group
before moving forward." Then she pointed deeper into the open cave system in
front of them. "I think over there will be the driest, safest place to camp, even if
it's a little open."

"Understood," said Jake.

Vanessa waved an arm at Kylen, and the guy with long braided hair, Damad,
motioning them forward.

Arica stood alone in the middle of the cave as Vanessa left. She only felt safe
again after Jake called orders for them to take a break, and the group marched
further into the cavern to rest.

Leading Vanessa's abandoned cart horse, Jake walked past Arica. She followed.

"How long will it be until Rapier is here?" Arica asked as Jake found a skinny
stalagmite and tied the burdened horse to it.

"An hour or so," he said impassively.

She let out a breath of relief as she sat on the dry, flat side of a rock. She was
eager to get through the old civilization, but her feet and calves were sore.

Jake sat down on the floor next to her, barely an inch shorter, even with her
rock's extra foot or so.

The rest of them split into smaller groups, as they usually did. Jerim and Steen
sat nestled in between a pair of boulders, talking about the book they leaned
over, maybe some sort of notebook or sketchbook. On the other side of the cave
they exited, Zak reclined on the floor across the sweet girl, Elvy, and Aaris, the
formal guy that Jake was close to. Then the last guy, Parel, was by himself across
the way, carefully picking through the moss growing around trickling water.

Arica wondered where Jake would've been without her there. They sat in silence only a few minutes before Jake looked over at her, faking a slight smile.

"Oh no," she moaned, pressing her hand into her eyes.

He repeated the words exactly as she'd imagined. "Let's train."

Her arms had just stopped aching from the session the night before. The last thing she wanted was to make it worse.

"All right," he chuckled in response to her grimace. "Let's just talk for a minute."

"I can handle that," she agreed, leaning her elbows on her knees.

He reclined back on his palms, staring into space for a minute. "I think I've already told you that... I haven't trained many tyros recently."

"Like the last three hundred years?" she grumbled, setting her chin in her hand.

"Maybe a little less. Anyway, one of my favorite things to teach is about... our touches."

She gave him a weird look. "Touches?"

He smiled a little. Clearing his throat, he stretched his long legs out in front of him and crossed his ankles. "As you should know by now, magic is a general force that can be used in many, many ways. There are rules, but it can still go awry. Most of it is just at the limits of your imagination." His hand clenched the air like he was strangling an invisible cat. "Now take all of that information and throw it away. Pretend that it's the complete opposite of what it really is, the rules and grounds for it are absolutely flipped. That's how you get a touch. A specific power, unique to each of us; an inbred talent that your magic clings to and grows. Some say they're the sole reason we have any control of natural magic to begin with."

"This seems like a really important lesson."

"A touch can often remain undiscovered until the tyro has more control, and often they break all the rules set by regular magic. Some *have* to be used with skin contact. Some can be used while chained in iron. And some break the physical limitations *completely*, allowing the Zenian access to a power that would be impossible by anyone else entirely."

"How do you know what yours is supposed to be, then?" asked Arica quietly.

"It happens naturally. Over time, we realize that there may be something that nobody else can do, or someone else notices, and they practice and hone it." He shrugged casually. "Sometimes, rarely, someone won't notice anything different. Maybe they can fuel flames with less power, or can see through enchantments easier, but those are usually the most common type of touch. Which brings us to the classification."

Arica let him know she understood by nodding. "Maybe I can breathe fire," she added, then blew through puckered lips.

"That would explain the smell," he chuckled.

"Hey! I haven't seen the blunt end of a toothbrush in like a week. It's not my fault you guys live in the dirt."

"I gave you—" He interrupted himself with a quick grunt and pulled his heavy backpack off the end of the cart. He rummaged around before dragging out and unwrapping a black block that looked like clay.

He broke off a small corner like it was wet chalk, held it out for her to see for a second, then popped it into his mouth.

"Here," he said, depositing the whole thing in her hand.

She broke off a piece as he held up four fingers. It was soft and chalky but tasted like syrup.

"There are four types of touches. We call the most common an Enhancement Touch. These are the ones that are often just an enhancement on normal powers, sometimes making them more capable of certain things. They're also the most useful, usually."

Then he looked over to where their comrades all relaxed by themselves, setting his hands around his mouth.

"Hey, Bonds!"

Aaris acknowledged his friend with a simple wave of his fingers.

"Show off your touch for the new kid," Jake called.

"You asked," he chuckled warmly.

Arica watched him reach up above him, barely moving, then simply touched the wall behind him, as high as he could while staying in his seat.

The rock ground as if under immense pressure. Fractures webbed out from his fingers until a loud *crack* echoed off of the many large surfaces, and a crevice separated the wall nearly in half by an inch or two as it settled down.

"And there you go," Jake said, looking back at her, satisfied. "You or I could've done that. But not nearly as easily as Aaris's powers let him, nor as precisely."

"That's pretty cool," she gushed, still scanning the artistic destruction.

"The second, only slightly less common type of touch, is a Mental or Emotional Touch."

"I think I get where this is going." Arica leaned closer to where he sat.

Jake continued using his hands to gesture lazily. "Probably. As you should know, you can't use magic on life, or while touching it. These touches are an exception to that. These are used to give either self or others false sight, thoughts, feelings, or emotions. Sometimes used to control them. Vanessa and Rapier both have this kind of touch."

"I see," Arica said, hoping he was going to clarify.

"Vanessa can be very convincing if she's nice about it. So if you ever find her being excessively friendly or flirty, then there's a good chance she's using it to persuade someone of something."

"Jeez," Arica mumbled, trying to remember an example of such behavior.

"Rapier's is a little less... helpful in everyday situations. His is limited to skin contact, but he can control the emotions of someone, as long as the emotions are already there, at least a little. Make it more intense, calm it down. Like I said, pretty useless."

"He touches Vanessa a lot," Arica said.

Jake scowled, nodding. "He's taken it upon himself to keep her level-headed, and she lets him, even though she was just fine before he was around."

She watched him for a second, a smile creeping onto her face. "Are you... jealous? Are they, like..."

"What, *together*?" he asked, raising an eyebrow. "Yes. But no, I'm not jealous."

She rolled her eyeballs. *Sure.*

"On track," he barked, demanding attention. "Touch type three, Physical Mutation Touches. Like the emotional and mental ones, these destroy the natural rules of magic. These are used to physically change the user's appearance or body. Can be willing or controlled, but they are arguably only the second-rarest type. It's definitely the least flaunted, at least."

"Like a shapeshifter," she said with a funny hiss in her voice. She rubbed her hands together cartoonishly.

"Well, you've gotten a glimpse of one already, remember the solzetair?"

Her hands stopped, recalling the gigantic black dragon-like creature she'd spotted stomping around the fields of Neva. "Oh, yeah. Who was that supposed to be, again?"

"Drake. That's his touch, though usually metamorphens aren't so dramatically gigantic. It's just how big solzetairs are." He took a deep breath and launched right into type four. "Visionary Touches. These touches are usually the most powerful and are often the balance between battles. Many of the most famous Zenians through the years had Visionary Touches. They're usually described as a sixth sense that can gather information nobody else would be able to, but aren't really something that they can turn on and off, or control."

He stopped to think for a moment. "I don't think you've met anyone with one yet." Then he looked over in Aaris's direction again. "Hey, Bonds, are there any visionaries in our group?"

"Uh... No, I don't think so. Lyrenel's the only one that I know for sure, but obviously, he's not here."

Jake turned back to Arica without responding. "Okay, well, I'll have to give a different example. The most incredible one I've ever met was a man named McCarter Bonds. He was Aaris's father." He jerked his head in Aaris's direction. "And was like one to me. Part of the reason Aaris and I are so close. He was in Jadrion's place once, the commander at Vanessa's side..."

His tongue smacked a little as he tried to gather up the right words. He stared at the ground, silent for a long moment. "He..."

"How did he die?" Arica prodded softly, hoping she was helping.

He just smirked, eyes focusing on her. "He actually isn't dead. His famous touch, the reason he was so powerful, drove him to madness. See, he could see things nobody else could. The future. He described that even though he had long visions of it in his sleep, he also had another sense that made him see several minutes into the future, always. He was... impossible to surprise, and it made him just amazing on the battlefield. It caught up to him, though. He lost sight of what was now and what was going on years away. His mind broke down, and Vanessa had to send him away before he hurt himself. He'd been trying."

Then he exhaled sharply, smiling. "My point isn't that a visionary or someone prophetic is going to go crazy, just that they are *powerful*, and helpful, and pretty rare, too, even though McCarter was a special case all his own. Like Aaris said, the commander of one of our other bases, Lyrenel Herak, has the same type of touch. He can sense things wrong with people, automatically, as he explains. Not just injuries, but even things like deficiencies, illness, even heated emotions sometimes. It's interesting."

"It sounds cool," Arica agreed softly. "Kind of annoying for him, too, I would guess."

"It is," Jake said. Then he continued loudly enough that the rest of the group could hear. "And then you get oddities." He looked over, but Arica wasn't sure who at. "Isn't that right, Zak?"

"I know bait when I hear it, Jake, it ain't odd," Zak yelled back, sitting up from his recline.

"You probably noticed right before we left Montana, Zak gave Vanessa some of his power for a bit. That isn't a normal thing. He can take anyone's power, as much as he wants, like it's a physical substance, and give it back. As long as the other person is willing."

"I'm damn good at it, too!" Zak hollered from his place.

Jake gave her a cocky grin, probably wanting to tease Zak back. "The thing is, it doesn't classify well. It's *kind of* like a mental power because of the control. It's *kind of* a physical mutation power because our magic *is* physical. It's *kind of* a visionary power, though he's got a lot more physical control of it than most of them, and it's kind of an enhanced power because when it comes down to it, all we're really doing is moving and commanding natural forces anyway."

Arica sat still for a minute, nodding her head. "I think that makes you an oddity, Zak," she concluded loudly.

"Y'all are just jealous," he grumbled, folding his arms.

Elvy giggled, reaching over to pat his arm and speak to him.

Arica assumed Jake had plenty more to teach her, but as she turned back, he was standing.

"Take some time to rest and try your magic if you can. I've to make a round now."

It was nearly two hours before the commander showed up with the rest of their company, and all of them were antsy for something constructive to do. Luckily, the newcomers didn't want to stop and rest long before moving on.

Jake and Rapier briefly argued about the spot they should camp, but in the end the commander conceded, saying Vanessa's orders were best.

Arica couldn't get over the way the cave had formed. It was spacious, a natural, protective ceiling so high that it almost could've been its own world, the real one peeking through to the sky in small places, draping with green life, vines and mosses hanging down towards the cool floor. The river roared to the left, carved so deep into the ground that it had created a dangerous cliff side that occasionally they strayed much too close for comfort. The air was cool and damp from the mist, and the roar of the rapids was more than distracting when they attempted any conversation. So many boulders and variants in the ground's level existed that it was impossible to decide what had once been carved into something beautiful, and what only nature had touched. They passed under arches, trekked around dips, climbed over jagged pieces, and sidled between boulders into cracks.

She thought the walk to the specific flat place would be short, but she was exhausted by the time they arrived. It felt like they'd crossed a lot further, but the picture in her head of the overall area might've been inaccurate.

She did her best to help set things up, but there was so much activity that she got lost and distracted easily. A small group of them had gone to gather up firewood. They put the tents up in a few minutes, the protective barriers even before that and supplies were being replenished as they worked.

Three tents went up to face the designated camp middle by the largest of three encouraged fires. The way they'd situated them, there were higher boulders all around them wherever there wasn't a fire or tent, creating more of a physical barrier than they usually had. Arica found it cozy.

It was only after they were settling down in the dimming light that Vanessa, Kylen, and Damad returned. Vanessa hauled a bloody, skinned hunk of meat with four legs over her shoulder. Her arms were smeared red nearly to her elbows in her sleeveless leather with some of it even across her cheek. Rapier caught sight of her and stopped giving Arica suggestions to stare after her.

Ricken and Parel began cutting it as soon as Vanessa threw her prize down to the stone nearest the campfires. The bulging bag over her shoulder was the only thing she discarded before jogging over to the nearest little waterfall and drenched herself in it.

Arica smiled as Rapier got up from his seat next to her to greet the high master.

Her attention was then focused on figuring out where Jake had disappeared to. She'd been trying to follow him when she could, but he'd made no effort to let her keep up.

"I'm here."

Arica jumped, twisting around to find her target. His hands slipped into his pockets, one eyebrow raised as he stood above her.

"How'd you know?" she chuckled nervously.

"You looked lost. I've been here for a bit." He stepped over the knee-high rock she used as a seat, crowding her back towards a fire. "I need around you, hun."

She slid out of the way, blushing when he touched her shoulder to steady her.

Like a puppy, she followed him around a few people and close enough to a fire that her legs started burning, only for Jake to find a spot closer to the fire to relax. He lowered himself to the floor, dropping his bag to recline on.

Arica settled in close, pulling her knees to her chest. Her heartbeat skipped as she caught a glint of red from directly across the fire. The vampire sat near, wrapped in a black cloak with a thick hood.

Kasper's cheeks were noticeably puffy, and his mouth hung halfway open like his fangs were too big to be comfortable. And he was staring right at her.

Can probably tell you're terrified, idiot, she scolded in her mind, averting her eyes immediately.

Zak was on Jake's other side, quietly talking to Steen.

Jake stretched his legs out so far they were practically in the fire.

Arica glanced up at his face as he hung his head back, rolling his neck. "I've heard that really tall people have, like, a lot of back problems, maybe just health problems in general."

"Not that I've noticed," he mumbled, indifferent.

"How tall are you, anyway?"

"Arica..." he snickered, giving her a playful shove with one of his large shoulders as he dragged himself into a sitting position. "You should go talk to someone else. Mingle. There's only so much you can learn from me."

Her face flushed hot. Her behavior would annoy her too, but she hadn't realized he'd noticed it. She looked around only a little, suddenly aware of how many strangers were around her. "No, I... think I'd rather stay with you."

"Suit yourself," he shrugged. "Never took you as the shy type, but if you really don't want to, fine."

Arica abruptly flung the bag off of her shoulder, staring at Jake's face in defiance as she opened it. She pulled her book out and slammed the bag to the ground.

He glanced at her but said nothing else.

Her favorite page was still one of the last ones, one with neat, even writing, though it was still in Raellic. She slowly read through it again, almost memorizing the foreign words, before flipping to a different page, another she recognized.

"So, we're in Akvelia, right?" Arica asked, glancing up from the book for a moment.

"Yep."

She traced her finger over a sketch of Maramore's mansion thoughtfully.

"Who used to live here? Before they were ruins?"

She had to look up after a minute because he still hadn't answered, but he was waiting for her to do so, so he could shrug.

"Why are you being so quiet?" she softly accused.

Jake's lips cracked into a grin and he shrugged again, probably to annoy her. "You need to go talk to someone else, Miss Tanson," he enunciated as if worried she didn't understand.

She let the book lay open on her lap. "Am I... annoying you?"

"Arica, I want you to get to know everyone. If you stay, this is your family. Your life is going to be in the hands of these people, over and over and over, and theirs in yours. So, for tonight's lesson, I'm assigning you to talk to at least two people that you haven't yet spoken with." He ended his statement with a sweet smile.

"If I do, will you stop being a jerk?" she mumbled in annoyance.

Jake nodded, then tilted his head in Zak's direction. "Zak doesn't count. Neither does Vanessa nor Rapier. But anyone else, yes?"

Lightly biting her tongue, she looked around a little, trying to come up with a reason not to.

"Look, there are plenty of choices," said Jake as he sat up straighter and looked around. "You could go talk to Parel and Elvy, over there cooking. I think you'll like Elvy. Or you could hang out with the Kisoks. Bialsa probably told you Ricken and Malon are siblings. Kylen is their cousin of some sort. Or Damad, he's got story after story to tell. Uh... Oh, you could ask Teres the questions you had about him. Or Aaris and Banen over there; neither of them are much for talkers, but they don't mind questions, and Aaris has some experience under his belt."

Then he looked at her expectantly.

Setting her book to the side first, she stood up and brushed her knees off. "Fine. See ya later."

He smiled but said nothing else as she carelessly stepped over him.

She'd wanted to go to the major fire where they were cooking. But as soon as she caught sight of the pale, dark-haired Derrick, she turned around and headed for the third campfire. She was just not that brave yet, and she wasn't going back to the vampire near Jake. Maybe it would be nice getting to talk to another woman, anyway. One that wasn't busy with battle plans.

"Hello," Arica called nervously as she approached the fire and the four people around it. Kylen once more had his brown hood covering his head, only the end of his braid falling out of it as he scrubbed a gross brown substance over the surface of a worn crossbow.

Across from him, Malon sat doing her own thing with a little bowl. Her thick umber hair was loose, shrouding most of her face. The heavier man whom Arica couldn't recall the name of stopped watching Malon to turn to Arica as she approached. He held a strip of something dark to his mouth, chewing as he eyed her threateningly.

On his other side sat the sibling, Ricken. "Welcome," he greeted passively. He was the only one not doing anything busy with his hands.

"Do you mind if I sit with you guys?" Arica asked nervously. She got close enough that if nobody said anything right away, she'd be standing awkwardly to the side.

But Kylen nodded to the large empty place next to him as permission.

The large, rough-faced man stared at her like she was intruding as she settled in place, crossing her arms over herself as a defense. Nobody said anything, as if they'd all been sitting in silence all along.

Arica tried glaring back at him, knowing that just ignoring it didn't always work. But it was only a second or two after this that Malon elbowed him in the side.

"Stop," she scolded, chuckling quietly. "You don't need to be rude. She's one of us."

He obliged, lowering his gaze to the fire as Malon stopped mixing her bowl's contents to look at Arica.

"I'm sorry, he's just like that," she apologized, giving him a brief glare even as the corners of her lips smiled. "Anyway, we've never been properly introduced. I'm Malon. This is my brother, Ricken," she jerked her chin in his direction. "The nice one is Kylen." She leaned forward, setting an elbow on her knee, smiling nicer than Arica expected. "And this freak is Garrin, but we just call him Skah."

He just grunted a greeting.

"Hey guys," Arica said with a general wave of her hand. "I'm Arica."

Malon nodded once, brushing her hair out of the way so she wasn't catching it in her bowl. "I heard you're from Ellteria."

"No," she started, but realized her mistake. "I mean... yeah, uh... yeah." *Remember to use the cover-up.*

"What's it like? We've never been," Malon continued with casual interest.

"It's... nice. Y'know, when people aren't trying to kill you."

Malon nodded like this was reasonable, so Arica prided herself but decided it would be best to change the subject. "Where are you guys from?"

"Ricken and I are from Veyber. Skah here is from Kyrgan." Then she held up both hands, thumbs pointing to either side of her. "Complete opposite directions from here. And, well, Kylen..."

"I was rescued from my Dovevian mum when I was an infant," he obliged, pausing his scrubbing. "So, I've run around with the Zenians for as long as I can remember."

"Wow," Arica whispered. "From your mom? Are you upset about it?"

He smirked, trading a look with Ricken. "Nah. My dad raised me. I met her a time or two before she was killed. No regrets, she was awful."

"Tell her the story," Malon prodded with a little smile. "The whole thing."

Kylen's smile was slightly nervy, staring at his hands a moment before looking Arica in the face. "All right... I don't know how much of this is true, but it's how he always told me. So, a few years ago, my father ended up wounded during a battle or a raid or something against the Dovevians, and next thing he knows, he's in the dungeon at the castle of Endré." Simple hand gestures accompanied his words, more calming than distracting.

"Anyway, so he's there, and my mother was a sly, kind of... mischievous person, I guess, and liked to just mildly tease their prisoners. Not torture necessarily, but punished and interrogated. My dad just took it. Eventually—and this is how he tells it—his stamina and resilience against her torture impresses her and she begs him to sleep with her and as a gentleman he obliges..."

Arica broke out in a grin when he paused just to roll his eyes. "Oh, sure, sure," she giggled.

"Then sometime, a few months later, he hears from one of the Dovevians passing his cell that she's in labor." He shrugged, taking a breath so he could continue. Then he grinned. "So, he just goes crazy. When the Dovevian brings him a meal, he completely fights the idiot out with his bare hands. Finds the keys after he's unconscious, then sneaks upstairs. Takes out a *bunch* of guards on the way up."

"Understand, too," Malon quickly interjected before Kylen could continue. "It wasn't just Histor's paternal instincts gone savage. Garal is a monster with aunseyant children. None of them have turned out okay, and while we're not sure why exactly, we know he's doing something evil and unnatural to them."

"Oh," Arica breathed solemnly.

"So, anyway," Kylen continued. "He works his way upstairs, avoiding the Dovevians and fighting off anyone he has to with his magic and stolen weapons, and manages to find my mother's room. He fights off the Dovevian taking care of her. She's obviously in no condition to overpower him. So he pins her down. Grabs one of his new knives, then just cuts me straight out of her womb."

Arica's lips split open.

"He wraps the baby up, tucks it in his cloak, and runs. The Dovevians try to grab him, but he works his way up to the higher towers. They didn't expect him to go upwards, so he had an advantage. Then he climbs onto the roof and carefully works his way to the ground below. Vanessa and these guys show up just outside the city, and the rest is history."

"Wow," Arica breathed. "That's... crazy. I'm so sorry. And... impressed."

He shrugged. "Just how it is around here."

"Just one of the... disadvantages of power," Ricken agreed in a low voice.

"What do you mean, exactly?" asked Arica, hoping she wasn't annoying any of them.

Malon took a deep breath, rolling her eyes in her brother's direction. "Seven's sake; It's nothing."

"We're cursed," Ricken argued, giving her a stern look.

"It's not a—"

"If there isn't a curse," Ricken snapped viciously enough that even Arica balked sightly. "Then WHEN will you and Skah finally ADMIT you're in love with each other?"

Even Arica scrunched in her seat as his gaze blared over the pair. Neither moved, but Arica could've sworn they'd leaned slightly further from each other.

Malon cleared her throat. "Ricken..."

"Family just doesn't work for Zenians," he continued in a much softer voice. His gaze switched to the fire, sharp jawline tight. "It never has. So much terrible death."

Malon leaned forward, getting after him loudly. "When you can't die of old age and can cure sickness easily, the likelihood of a peaceful death decreases dramatically, brother. So yes, we all die terribly. Otherwise, nobody would ever die. Then where would we be?"

"Probably in Endré, under control of DeRael."

They all looked at Kylen, the seriousness in his tone heavy.

"What?" the young one defended quickly. "I was just saying, we probably could've overthrown Garal by now."

Malon rolled her eyes again. "If we couldn't die, I think it would be safe to assume that the Dovevians wouldn't be able to, either."

"So, we'd just have to overpower them and force them into a dungeon. It wouldn't be hard, there's like five times as many of us already."

Arica didn't think that sounded too outlandish, but the other three stared at him like he was speaking some alien dialect.

Then Malon set her bowl of thick black paste down, leaning closer to him. "You fought them at Neva, right, Kylen?"

"He did well enough," Ricken approved.

She looked around them a bit, then carefully stepped over her brother to sit next to Kylen. At her bidding, Arica slid in closer to the two of them.

"It was way too easy for us," Malon whispered, leaning closer to Arica. "They have something cooking."

"But we lost," Arica reasoned.

"We got away. With everything of importance. I may be wrong. Maybe they counted on Drake Damage's poison to work better, but even without Vanessa, we would've been all right. I think we're walking straight where they want us to."

"It's not like we haven't evaded traps before," Ricken growled.

"What if they have something huge? We already know they won over a few of the dragons from Bkian's Peak. And even Mistress Damage admitted it's strange that they're taking so many prisoners instead of just killing. We don't know whether they found a way to force the Dovevian curse on us yet or not. And if they take Castle Kopion, if they capture Commander Herak and Commander Marc, they'll have an incredible ambushing location. What if we're walking into a massacre?"

Her words settled around all of them heavily enough that it was another minute or two until someone else spoke.

"Vanessa hasn't trained a successor yet," Ricken finally calmed in his low voice. "So we know they won't kill off everyone. It won't be a massacre."

Her voice lowered again. "We don't know that. Jrasko and Commander Rapier are with her *constantly*. Either could be at the side, already ready for it."

Ricken pointed in Arica and Kylen's direction then. "I don't know how much you were told, Kylen, but I can tell that Arica doesn't understand."

"The high master can sense the end of their reign," Malon continued in his stead. "It gives them time to train a successor, ready the next one to take the power and control that they have."

"They say that this is why King Garal took over for the humans." Ricken traded a quick look with Malon that Arica didn't understand. "That he sensed his end but feared it. So, he overthrew the king of Endré, making a deal with death's god, and fulfilled his sense by surrendering his title as High Master. The problem was he didn't appoint anyone else the power before he left."

"Gave the Zenians a tremendous disadvantage to begin with," Malon agreed solemnly. "But that was long before any of us were here. The ones who remember seem to choose not to."

Arica looked over at Skah for a moment, realizing that he still hadn't said a word, just huddled in his cloak, staring at the rest of them without blinking much. The firelight was so good at making everyone look so much creepier than they really looked, anyway.

Malon got back up, going to him before gathering up her few things. "That's enough. Let's go see if dinner's close."

19

COME AT ME, BRO

Soft light filtered across the surrounding rocks, giving Arica the impression of rain with no evidence that it actually was raining on the surface. Behind her, everyone packed up, readying to move on. As she tried to help, she'd noticed a spot to the side that she hadn't seen before. It was a little copse of nature in the direct light from the broken forest floor far above them. The trees had thick, dark trunks, and the foliage grew dense, all of it huddled in one spot to gather the light.

Arica decided it was close enough that she'd be able to hear if anyone called her.

She found herself on a large boulder, crouching above some greens. She couldn't quite see the floor through giant leafy plants but estimated it was only about three feet down.

She jumped, a little off on the distance, but only barely missed a perfect landing and rolled her foot.

"I'm gonna be feeling that all day," she grouched, massaging the side of her foot against the nearest tree.

The foliage dragged against her as she took a few steps into it, most of it almost to her waist. She'd have to be careful not to fall into a hole, or find any deep water. In order to reinforce her balance, she kept a hand on whatever tree was nearest. They were thick enough that it was pretty easy to do. She didn't get very far before she couldn't find an easy way around the tree trunks and had to back up a few feet.

The obvious trail of broken weeds and bushes would make returning easy.

Most of the plants were a tropical variety, the kind found in wetter, swampy places, or more humid climates. She noticed a colorful flower with long skinny petals clinging to the trunk of a tree, then reached out and touched a tan, thick vine wrapped around another one. She avoided a sharp, spiny blue flower that she didn't recognize and started working her way back.

Her hand brushed a different vine, this one thin green, so she looked up to see what kind of plant it belonged to.

"Hey, that's a vanilla orchid." She climbed onto a protruding root and closer to the tall white flower sprawled up the tree. She looked up and down the long green vines, but couldn't find any beans.

"Man, I wish I had a place to plant one... See if I could keep it alive." She carefully picked her way back down the tree. At the last second, she decided it wouldn't hurt to take a piece of the vine with her.

She'd helped Zak and Parel grow some potatoes that morning. A common Zenian provision was a variety of seeds they could use to grow food, assuming they had enough soil and water. Using magic, they could coax them to grow in an easy fifteen minutes, depending on the seeds. And while it reduced the nutrition and flavor using this method, Parel's touch helped him keep as much of it as possible. So if anyone could do something with the vanilla vine, he could.

Using a small knife, she cut a long piece of the vine away from the tree, making sure it had enough roots with it. She used a hair tie to secure it to her belt, pinning her cloak to one side to keep it unbroken.

In much less time than she expected, Arica was back at the boulder she'd jumped from and made her way up the most gradual side. Her calves were burning as she got to the top, so she sat down to rest a moment.

She was higher than she thought she was; from her vantage, she could see the camp relatively well. Beyond that, where the river rushed against the rock, some of the old sculpted buildings waited on the other side. A tall, slender one jutted out from the rock wall further than the rest of them. It looked like it may have had steps up to it at one point, but she couldn't tell whether the entrance had always been so gaping. The style reminded her of the old Greek creations she'd seen in movies and documentaries at home. Only these were more modest, natural, and flowing into the formations around them like they didn't need to be noticed.

One fire in their little camp still flickered, maybe providing extra light for the tiny people walking around. Vanessa's tent was the last standing, but most of the people gathered around the lacking fire. Maybe breakfast was over.

Then she noticed one person broken off from the rest. This wasn't that odd. People weren't sticking together like they feared bears or something, but he was further away than usual, his cloak shrouding his face. He was positioned suspiciously on the other side of a dip in the wall before it met up with the forest that Arica had just escaped from.

She was about to look away, as he was probably just relieving himself when she noticed him fling his hand out, not unlike throwing a Frisbee. Her vision lit up purple, somehow able to see a trail of whatever he'd just done like smoke from a jet.

What kind of magic was it, though? What had he done?

She followed it all the way to the other side of a cave. Maybe some kind of quick little bird he'd released.

Then, as she looked back at the man, he turned towards her, also looking in the object's direction. It was Rapier.

Arica ducked down into a small depression, just in case he saw her watching him.

She waited an extra minute after she guessed it was clear, just to make sure he wasn't there anymore.

She was quick descending the rock and on her way back towards the camp. Her hands looked abused, covered in scrapes and cuts.

They'd nearly finished packing up. The fire was cool, but Vanessa's tent still stood. Arica looked around for the commander, trying to decide what to do. She avoided getting run over by Zak and his armfuls of gear.

"Arica. Catch."

She turned just in time to gracelessly catch a package against her chest, then looked up to see who was throwing things at her.

"Oh, hey Parel." The cloth was warm and smelled like fresh-baked bread. "Thanks." She flipped a corner open, breaking a piece of the soft potato-based bread in her mouth. Then, before he could leave, she called him back. "Hey, by the way."

Arica untied the vine as Parel turned back and smiled, then held it out. "I don't know if it'll do you any good, but I found some vanilla in the trees over there. Who knows?"

He took it in his meaty hand, looking it over. "Good eye. I'll certainly try," he said enthusiastically.

"Are we leaving soon?" Arica asked.

"In a few minutes. Once Mistress Damage is done."

She followed the line of his gaze to Vanessa's tent and politely excused herself. Her fist was in the air before she realized she didn't know the courtesy in entering tents. There was no point in knocking, and it stood unzipped, so she just split the weighted flaps and entered.

An underwhelming amount of things were in the room. Just a pair of bags in one corner, and a flimsy-looking table with a few things on it. The owner sorted through it with her back to the entrance.

"What do you need?" Vanessa asked hastily.

"Um... I just wanted to... tell you about some suspicious activity."

She turned to look at her, suddenly a little less stern. "Oh, lovely, what can you tell me?"

Most of Arica's confidence drained under the high master's gaze. What if she didn't believe her, and even later wouldn't believe her when it really mattered? Or even worse, what if the commander got undeserved punishment because of her tale-telling?

"It probably isn't anything, but I saw—"

"We're all but strapped now, sir," Rapier called as he stepped into the room behind Arica.

"I'm nearly done here," Vanessa agreed, folding her hands together. "But, continue, Miss Tanson."

She grabbed her shoulder, sidling away from Rapier.

"I... saw Rapier sending out messages. I think."

Vanessa smiled, cocking her head and looking up at Rapier. "Did you now?" Then she nodded at Arica once. "Good work, Arica. Luckily, he was just working under my orders. Although, if she caught you…" Her gaze flicked to the blond.

"I was certain I wasn't being watched. I apologize, sir," he expressed quickly.

She went back to her table and started rearranging and sorting the few things. "I suppose there's no harm in letting you know. We've a plan in motion to sabotage the Dovevians, and maybe the traitor as well. Jadrion caught onto some notes back and forth, nothing too incriminating, mandatory reports mostly. But the theme of all of our evidence points to the fact that they're getting desperate. We found Skah snooping around yesterday."

"You think it's him?" Arica asked thoughtfully. He was pretty quiet; but a Dovevian?

"No. Jake noticed Elvy suddenly understood more Raellic than she'd learned. And Jerim gave us a skelt report that nearly got Steen killed this morning."

Arica pulled on her fingers nervously. "Do you think there's more than one?"

"Also no. There's no way the king could corrupt so many with no evidence."

She was about to ask another question, but Vanessa just continued.

"Fresh evidence did suggest that recently there was some commotion involving Dovevian black magic and the failure of such an attempt."

"I thought we already knew that it was the Dovevians screwing with things," Arica stated, unable to hold back a little smile. She was catching on to things, even if only slowly.

"Fortunately for us, the Dovevians aren't grayed and marked as a fashion statement. It's a symptom of the rite they go through to get those powers. It's involuntary."

So, if they were using the dark magic stuff, they'd have to look like a Dovevian too. "So what's happening, then? You don't think it's Derrick, do you?"

Vanessa took a deep breath, giving Rapier a questioning glance that Arica didn't understand. "I've thoroughly thought that through. But I am confident that he is neither contacting our enemies, nor our problem."

She traded another look with Rapier, a sly, proud one. "So, no. I think we're dealing with a shapeshifter."

Arica's eyebrows raised as her hands set against her hips. "Wow. Okay. That sounds impossible."

"Now, normally you would be correct," Vanessa admitted. "But, as I've been informed, Jake explained to you the use of our touches. In this way, it is possible, even if rare."

She bit back her arguments and suspended her disbelief for a moment. "Didn't... Drake, that guy you're married to, is one, right? Yeah, like the dragon thing he does."

"Technically," Vanessa explained leniently, showing her teeth for a moment. "But not in the sense we're talking about. Drake is limited to his solzetair form. I'm speaking of someone who could look like anyone."

Arica tried processing this. "So... they could just about hide indefinitely."

"Herein lies our problem. If my brother once again isn't as dead as I thought, I think there's a significant possibility that he's infiltrated us. He had this exact power. Luckily, he's probably masquerading as someone long-term; killed a member and took his place without any of us even looking twice. From here on out, trust no one. Including Jake."

Her shoulders slouched a little. How on earth was that going to happen? He was the only one that wasn't crazy or cold.

"But... what about you two?" she tried insecurely. "He'd be able to look like anyone, right?"

"There are a few ways to tell," Vanessa nodded once, folding her arms across her chest. "Memories, for obvious reasons, though they can be faked with general knowledge and manipulation. And touches. He may mimic appearances and voices, but there's no way for him to mimic most of our touches."

"How do you know *I'm* not a bad guy in disguise?"

"Another thing he wouldn't be able to fake is a tyro's blaze. One of the high master's abilities is to sense the untrained magic of a youngster, making it much easier to find them. I can still see yours, likely for a while, at least until you develop a touch." She forced a small smile for a moment. "I certainly hope he tries to mimic you. Because I'll notice within a moment and we'll have him."

Her eyes then shifted to the commander and her features grew more serious. "We're going to force a slip up. Shouldn't be completely impossible. He's likely relying on our ignorance."

"Why isn't Jake in on this?" Arica asked, hoping she didn't sound whiny. She wasn't sure she'd be able to keep everything from him.

"Because it would quickly become tedious—dangerous—to make him use his touch every time he's been out of sight for over two seconds. I've already spoken with him, and he agreed to take this one out."

He never showed me his. "Jerk," Arica whispered under her breath.

"In this, your help may be tantamount to his. Can I count on it when it's time?" she asked, steadily staring her down.

"Yeah... I guess so," Arica agreed with hesitation. "But... I don't think I signed up for this. Could I just go home? At least until all the... fighty-danger stuff is over."

She caught a flicker of amusement on the high master's face, but Vanessa set a hand on her hip, looking at the commander calmly. "I've been keeping an eye out for an area to tear into, but we haven't found any, and the only ones I know of are far from our path."

"T-tear?"

"My magic is only so strong. I have to find somewhere where the veil between your world and mine is at its thinnest. Pockets of strong magic anchoring them together. I can't just pop back and forth whenever and wherever I choose."

This was not what she was hoping to hear. It must've shown on her face, because Vanessa beckoned with two fingers, drawing her gaze back up.

"Trust me. I'll get you home in one piece. *When* is the only variant."

Arica decided that was going to have to do; there wasn't much else she could do about it.

Vanessa tapped one hand on her thigh. "It's about time we start across the vale. Rapier, can you assist?"

Arica ducked out of the tent and out of the way, watching for someone to help. She walked to where the cart sat, already laden with gear. Both Aaris and Jake approached with what she hoped was the last of the gear besides Vanessa's tent, which was being broken down even as they waited.

"Are you... what's the term... strapped?" she asked, legs swinging over the edge of the wagon.

"Nearly there," Jake said with a puff of air.

"You never told me…" she started in a voice of boredom. Then she glanced around the rock encasing them.

"Where the ruins came from?" he guessed in a cheery voice, giving her a toothy smile at the end.

She gave him a stern nod.

"Well…" His arms rested on the pile of tent canvas. "They're ancient, as you may have guessed. We don't know a lot about them."

"Who lived here, though?" she asked more outright.

"The Sceztiak."

She tapped her lips with a finger. "Let me guess… elves."

"We don't know." Jake shrugged his large shoulders. "Could've been elves. Could've been human. Maybe even Zenian. Could've been any number of intelligent creatures. The few records you can find of them are nigh impossible to read."

Arica looked around again. "I say, definitely elves."

She was suddenly pushed off of the wagon, hard enough that even though her feet hit the ground correctly, her knees buckled.

Then Jake kicked the tip of the sword strapped to her hip, throwing it forward and out of the sheath. The sword was on the ground before she even jumped in surprise.

"Atvotshio fengra."

"Ought… vashi… what?" Arica demanded, turning her knees in the dirt to face him.

"It's Raellic for 'pick up your damn sword and fight me'," Jake goaded, making his own long sword scoot hers closer to her.

"So like… en garde?" She reached out and gripped the leather-wrapped handle, but didn't pick it up just yet. Her heart still raced.

"If en garde means 'pick up your damn sword and fight me'," he said, walking a slow half-circle around her away from the cart.

"I guess it kinda does. But I prefer… 'Come at me, bro'." She looked up, her voice teasing back, but was still in an indifferent position on her knees.

"Come at me, bro," he repeated with a serious expression.

She couldn't help snickering.

"Well?" he demanded impatiently, for she kept her sword on the ground as if her arm was an overcooked noodle. His slammed into the dirt in front of her, but she didn't flinch.

Then she looked up at him, feeling her heart sink even as it recovered. "You aren't going to—"

Like lightning, Jake whipped the sword backwards in a circle, throwing it forwards fast and accurately enough that she let out a terrified gasp when it reached her neck. The sharpest edge kissed her skin without trembling even a touch, a tool of precision in his hands.

"If you don't learn to defend at all times, your instinct and response time will fail," he spat, serious. Unnervingly aggressive, his pretty eyes darkened as they narrowed and his lips curled into an ugly sneer. "Be on your guard, *always*, or you'll be dead before you can even realize you were close. You think I won't hurt you, but maybe I'll have to. My job is to teach you."

You think I won't hurt you.

Her eyes blinked back tears, her lips frozen.

His expression softened, but only a fraction. "Well?" he demanded. "Are you going to defend yourself?"

She convinced the muscles in her neck to move just enough to shake her head, which broke the rest of her brain loose. "No, go ahead," she accepted, her voice strong and serious. She wasn't enough for this. She wouldn't become like them, no matter how hard she tried.

"You have a sense of invulnerability that I absolutely hate. It needs to be cured *now*."

She threw her sword forwards across the dirt, nearly hitting his boot. "It's not an invulnerability. I just don't *care*!" she roared in desperation. "If you don't do it now, then SOMEONE else will get the pleasure down the road, I'm sure."

She looked back up, though his sword remained alarmingly close. Confusion replaced the anger in his expression.

"Look," she huffed, gingerly touching the flat of his blade to guide it away. "I don't know what you're trying to do, but I'm no big, tough, expert badass like you, okay? I just..." She closed her eyes for a moment, then breathed deeply. "I know… you're trying to spark that… 'survival instinct' in me, or whatever, but… I just don't care."

Jake's arms folded across each other after sheathing his weapon again, but his wide stance over her was intimidating all by itself. "So you *don't* have any will for survival?" he asked.

Arica's lips parted a little, the serene calm in his tone making her honestly wonder. "I…" She noticed a few Zenians who'd gathered behind him, observing them. Zak caught her eye, raising his eyebrows in question.

"I… can't fight anyone," she finally forced out.

"Not wanting to live and not wanting to fight are two different things," Jake surmised, before holding a hand out to her. She took it, letting him drag her to her feet like a doll. "I can deal with the latter."

She would've smiled reassuringly if she hadn't then noticed that Vanessa was also standing witness, hidden from her view. The elegant woman looked on, emotionless, with her hands on either hip. She gave Arica a nod of acknowledgment, then moved on to help.

Arica had no idea what the lady had seen, what she could've been thinking, but the damage was done.

She definitely didn't belong there.

20

SANTSIN VAL

Dragons had been a passion of Arica's in her younger days; but then again, who wasn't fascinated by beautiful shiny lizards with gigantic wings and rumbling voices, carefully guarding over their exhaustive treasure hoards and maybe a beautiful princess or two?

So many books she'd read featured them, some of them purely *about* the dragons and the surrounding myths. Being an adult, she'd long stopped believing in such tales, even though she still held onto the daydreaming about what it would be like to see one, or even just write about them.

Her adventures in DeRael had brought a lot of realism to the fantasy she remembered as a kid. There was a lot more grime, exhaustion, and fear than she thought there would ever be. Where were the dragons, the mermaids, the wonder? Since she'd fallen asleep thinking about these things, they filled her dreams for the rest of the night. Glinting golden scales, gigantic gossamer wings, sparkling tails, and fields of pink flowers.

But naturally, a tall, grumpy man in tight clothing had to ruin it by rudely shaking her awake, dispersing the images of an elegant, towering dragon with fur and feathers the color of a raven's.

"Ack, stop, Jacob, stop," Arica whined. She pulled her blanket over her face.

"It's not *Jacob*," he playfully growled, jerking her bag out from under her head.

She slapped his hands away, hanging onto the last tendrils of sleep. "I couldn't remember the other name; just go away."

"Don't you want to hear my news, though?"

Arica froze for a moment, the mischief in his voice urging her curiosity. She flung the blanket back down, glancing at the other two sleeping women to confirm that he was awakening her at an ungodly hour, and not after letting her sleep in. The fact it was dark outside the small tent meant nothing anymore.

"Fine, I'll bite. What news?" she asked quietly.

He shifted from his kneeling position to sit cross-legged next to her. "Rapier and Aaris left to scout out our base before we go in. They should be back soon."

Her eyebrows rose slightly. "I didn't realize we were so close already."

"It's a short walk. It's out in the middle of the wetland. But they aren't going all the way, just enough to make sure there's no active sieges or Dovevian ambushes."

One of the other girls stirred.

"Why wake me up for that, though?"

"Because you need some ground experience, so unless Rapier reports something dangerous, you're going."

She looked away from him, holding her blanket tight.

"You have everything we've already taught you," he soothed.

"But I haven't been successful at any of it."

He smirked a little, then reached for his belt. "Here. I got you one of these."

Arica took the offered item, a simple pouch wide enough to put her head in but pretty shallow. Jake unhooked a dagger she usually used for food from her bag and slipped it inside. It disappeared, the bag unburdened by its weight and mass. She'd seen other people carry bags that did similar magic.

"Keep secondary weapons and supplies in it, but don't lose it. It isn't easy to retrieve things without it."

"Oh my gosh, thank you," Arica whispered with excitement. She scrambled to put a few things into it.

The tent opened behind Jake, allowing Vanessa in. She wore a sleeveless coat that swung around her ankles more like a skirt over a red long-sleeved blouse and a pair of her thick leather pants.

Against what Arica expected, she casually knelt down near them.

"Don't worry. I think you're ready for a little reconnaissance work, dear," she whispered. "Jadrion reports there aren't any traps left on the way. But they didn't get far enough to tell who's left at the base itself."

"This still seems dangerous. But I'll go," Arica agreed nervously.

Vanessa looked up at Jake for a moment. "Once everyone is up, get everything ready to move and stand by in case the need arises."

He nodded obediently as a tiny white snake slithered over Vanessa's shoulder and lithely slipped into the collar of her coat.

"Let's go, he's ready," Vanessa ordered calmly.

Arica began scrambling to straighten out her things.

But Jake pulled the blanket out of her hands before she could get out of it. "I can take care of your things; just bring what you need."

What exactly would she need, though? She ended up just bringing her cloak and the sword they forced her to haul around.

Leaving Jake in the tent to do her chores, the women met with the commander standing near the cold remains of a fire with two other guys, one dressed in an almost formal blazer, and the other holding a small, packed bag. Aaris and Steen.

"We're ready, Commander," Vanessa called, strong but quiet.

At Rapier's command, Aaris left the opposite direction the other four of them started in.

The plane of gravel and dust they'd found to camp on top of was much more enclosed and darker, and the cave system had reduced around them the afternoon before. Stone carvings weren't as prevalent there, but formed many crevices and tunnels. There weren't as many directions they could've gone, making it slightly easier to guess where they were going. It wasn't long over the uneven floor that the cave closed in around them in the same fashion as the cave they'd left on the other side of Akvelia.

Arica was nervous about the way Rapier kept the longsword in his hand, but neither Vanessa nor Steen had a weapon drawn.

All of them were annoyingly silent through the boring stone cave, but it was only about twenty minutes before they got to a strange split off. The cave was the same forward, but the firelight cast over the branch off showed that it was a lot darker, the stone more mangled, like it wasn't a natural formation.

Naturally, this was the one Rapier chose.

Within about fifteen feet, it widened again. A crude but thick wooden gate guarded one side of the cave entrance to the other, the door itself hanging off its hinges and splintered into several pieces. Above it, a natural platform jutted about five feet from the ceiling, with a small blind covering the most exposed side.

Inside, she could see a dead fire pit and some random litter in the corners of the room. A pile of large logs were stacked to the side of the gate.

"So, as you can see, someone forced past the gate," Rapier started, using his sword to gesture about. "Over there, there are traces of blood, not Dovevian, though."

Vanessa made the flame in her hand follow along with his point.

"And over in that corner, we have a bit of Dovevian stain."

"I hope that the absence of any more scouts means that this was just recent enough that they haven't attempted to recover this area yet," Vanessa mused.

"Or that the Dovevians aren't in the middle of breaking in still," Steen suggested coolly.

Rapier shook his head. "There isn't anyone outside of the base's barrier, I'm sure of it."

"Regardless, the quicker we get there, the better," Vanessa pressed. With a wave, she led further into the darkness.

Arica complained mentally, her feet and calves already sore. She still hadn't gotten used to this level of physical strain, and she wasn't sure if it would ever get easier.

Soon enough, the cave brightened with more natural light, but before she could even see it, warmth soaked into her bones.

Arica trudged behind Vanessa and Rapier, trying to keep up with their long-legged pace, but no matter how far behind she fell, Steen stayed behind her a pace or two. Probably by order. Luckily, she never got too far behind, finding an extra boost here and there during which she'd close the gap. If nothing else, it was fear of being left behind.

They could see the end of the tunnel. Mossy green blocked everything, the musty scent of stagnant water and rotted plants permeating the air.

It was early enough that there wasn't any direct sunlight, just a dull blue glow over everything. A few birds chattered above, but no frogs or crickets made any noise.

As they came out of the cave, Arica realized they'd reached a high ground, even having come up from an underground tunnel system. Dark ponds lay still under a hovering damp fog in any direction, thick-trunked trees reaching up out of the muddy edges, their leaves soggy and limp. The mud underfoot was dark and sticky, an ugly sage-colored moss covering a good portion of it.

"This is kinda gross," Arica reported, dragging a foot up with a wet sucking sound.

"Enough of a place to hide a base, though," Vanessa said with only a glance backward.

All of them were relatively slow, but Vanessa confidently led the way through the trees, following an unseen path.

Arica quickly wished she'd left her cloak behind like Steen had. Though it might've been because he had a sword strapped to his back, and not because he'd planned ahead.

She learned that the drier spots had less moss, so she kept her feet more on those places like a child in a grocery store jumping on only specific colored tiles. Steen walked next to her most of the time, Vanessa and Rapier only just ahead of them.

The slope of the miry land bar they stuck to steepened, but Arica still couldn't see the tiniest hint of a Zenian base anywhere, even if their path was straight.

She nervously watched the land dip closer and closer to a dark pond. She wasn't the strongest swimmer, and hated the thought of that cold, mucky water.

"Single file," Rapier called from ahead, just past a particularly narrow piece of land that dipped down on either side right into the water. Steen stopped, allowing her to go first.

She was shaky but crossed with only a little resistance from the mud underfoot. Steen came across after her but went a little faster than he should've and slipped just enough that his foot went out from under him, pitching him to his knees.

"Here," Arica quickly offered, grabbing his hand. She used her weight to counter his lack of balance and dragged him back to his feet.

"Thank you," he expressed as soon as she let go. He brushed mud away.

"I don't see how anyone could take over this base," Arica called over her shoulder, staying close to Steen in case one of them slipped again. "You can barely even get to it."

"Turi's swamps are terrible. This is a much easier walk than it could be," Vanessa explained calmly. "Besides, it's camouflaged. There would be no point in having a hidden base if the gardening could give it away from five miles off."

Rapier piped up then. "It would be ridiculously hard to find either way. It's far enough from any proper cities."

They got low enough that water lapped at Arica's boot. She moved a step or two away, nearly running into Rapier.

Everything went silent.

Arica looked at Vanessa with bated breath, who looked at Steen, then Rapier. What was that feeling in the air that was prickling at her spine?

"There aren't any alligators here, are there?" Arica asked, voice slow as she skimmed the surface of the water with her eyes.

Steen's careful gaze broke from their other side to stare at her. "What?"

"Inalbaents," Vanessa clarified, grabbing her arms across her chest as if she was cold.

"She said alligators," Rapier countered softly.

"We're not in Ellteria, my love, they're inalbaents."

Arica jumped as something moved close to her right, but it was just more water.

"There's one there," Steen breathed, pointing across the small pond. "But there might be some closer."

Arica strained her eyes to see it, but everything was the same dark brown or forest green color in the fog.

"Let's move on. We'll dissuade them if need be, but we're nearly at the entrance," Vanessa guided softly.

Rapier turned to follow her orders, only barely slower than before.

Watching around her as thoroughly as possible, Arica followed, glad that Vanessa had been correct about 'nearly'. It was only a few more yards before she froze in place, holding up a hand to signal them to stop.

Her hand reached out into empty air but stopped halfway outreached. She looked satisfied. All Arica could see beyond were more trees, the land bar gradually curving to the right. The water level in the area in front of them was lower. They all waited silently, watching Vanessa frozen in her position.

Vanessa pulled her hand back, looking over her palm. "Well... This should be working..." She replaced it against the invisible barrier. "This isn't good."

"Maybe you should try to unseal it here since it's not responding," Rapier suggested.

Vanessa frowned, retracting her hand again. "I suppose."

With barely a wave of her hand, a nearly ear-splitting crack resonated from the barrier instantly, disturbing a few nested birds nearby and making Arica brace herself on the soft ground.

In front of their eyes, the mirage melted to show a giant dome made of a dark stone sunk deep into the ground, encrusted with leafy vines and moss. A sturdy section of dirt led around it like a dangerous pathway, but to the right a few yards, it dipped down into the dome and the ground.

"Oh," Steen mumbled behind her.

"Did you just break their barrier?" Arica asked quietly.

Vanessa set a hand on her hip. "It should've opened to my touch, but only mine, my commanders, and their subordinates. The way it shattered under a light touch of magic means they breached it somewhere else."

"We're entering a dead base, aren't we?" Rapier asked with distaste.

She glanced up at him, moving her hand to her sword. "I fear so. But we won't know standing here. The entrance is there."

On solid ground, finally, they made quick work of the distance and before long, Rapier was breaking open a sealed iron door at an awkward slant in the dome.

He cracked it, peeking in before pulling it all the way open. "Welcome to Santsin Val," he mumbled as if this was the last place he wanted to be entering.

Vanessa jumped down first, followed by Arica and Steen.

They dropped into a dim, low hall. The curved walls stood carved every few feet with swirly pictures, most of which with runes she didn't know, but it was too dark to tell what they resembled.

"This is the hall just off the armory," Vanessa thought aloud, pointing her drawn sword to the right.

"The torches are all out, that's unusual," Rapier reported in the same tone. He strode a few feet, looking further down the curved hall.

Steen reached behind him, pulling his weapon out.

"What are we expecting?" Arica asked quietly. The walls' angle in towards the ceiling gave her a bit of claustrophobia, which normally was not a problem for her.

"By now it's obvious that they've all but abandoned this place," Vanessa started, waiting another few moments before following Rapier. "We've got to figure out what happened. Maybe they felt threatened, so abandoned it, or were overpowered and left as we did. It's a possibility they were surprised, and the Dovevians killed off or captured most of them. Whatever it is, we'll find out. We will also gather up anything of importance they may have left, assuming the Dovevians didn't steal all of it. We may find some survivors, and we'll have to check through the dungeon and see what's left. Do you understand better what it is we're doing now?" Towards the end, she looked at the tyro expectantly.

Arica nodded, pressing her lips together in thought. "This isn't good, is it?"

"No," Vanessa admitted more solemnly. "Out of our three bases, this was supposed to be the most secure. I still can't contact our third."

"Kylen is going to be in shambles when he hears this," Arica mumbled. "His father was here."

"We all have relatives and friends here," Steen said evenly.

Vanessa added, "And we don't know yet if they're in danger."

They all turned as Rapier called from the hall. "There are signs of struggle."

Vanessa was the first to chase after him, but Steen and Arica were close behind.

The hallway curved right, only straightening out just before it opened up into a large, round room. Shallow stairs ran around the edge covered in thick worn rugs in rich greens and reds, all the way into the middle of the empty room. Three more nearly identical and perfectly symmetrical halls led out of the room, situated to each side and in front of them in a plus shape.

Rapier handed Vanessa a simple iron sword with specks of a lighter metal scattered throughout the blade. Arica was no blacksmith, but it seemed unusual.

"I found this discarded a few feet back," he reported, gesturing behind them. "There's that tipped brazier over there. And I'm sure you've noticed the traces of Dovevian stain."

Vanessa ran a finger along the wall near him, rubbing away the residue invisible to Arica's eyes.

She inhaled between her teeth and looked back into the room. "It's enough. Let's sweep for survivors, then see if they breached the ground floor."

"Probably won't find any bodies. They usually take more prisoners, or at least the bodies," Rapier grumbled out loud.

"That's why I said *survivors*, love."

Then she pointed each of them down one hall and beckoned for Arica to follow her, barking the order to meet in front of the trapped door, wherever that was.

The sweep was quick. The hall they'd chosen led to an enormous iron door before curving to the side into a neat row of doors so short that Arica worried *she'd* have to stoop.

She wasn't sure if the older woman knew where she was going or just chose a room at random, but she opened one of the large handled metallic doors and pulled it open effortlessly. Arica followed with curiosity.

As expected, the room was short, only a few inches above Vanessa's head, with both ceiling and walls made of the same dark, rough stone as outside the room. A normal-sized mattress took up the middle of it, with a squat fireplace to one side and a water closet to the other. A dresser sat with some old books stacked on top of it, a few colorful rugs giving the room a cozier feel.

Vanessa wandered the room as if she were in the house she'd grown up in, wistfully taking it all in. Her hand tugged on the disturbed bedspread before she peeked into an already open dresser drawer. Then she used the tip of her sword and dug around the cold ashes of the fireplace.

"This is Colten's room, the commander for this base," she explained quietly as she looked around the room once more. "They were disturbed during the night."

She gestured back to the door, and Arica took her cue. She expected them to search another room or two, but Vanessa apparently felt no need for it. They jogged down the middle of the hall, got halfway through, and turned back the way they'd come.

"Nothing happened up here. We need to access the bunker if we want to find anything," Vanessa said passively.

They met back at the iron door they'd passed, both Rapier and Steen showing up nearly as quickly.

"The food stores and kitchens are still intact. Very little destruction," Steen reported.

Rapier took his turn. "And, unfortunately, the backup supplies are still untouched. If anyone escaped, they brought very little."

"Let's see what's going on downstairs then," Vanessa suggested.

The door was at a tiny incline, almost as wide as it was tall, with four round handles along the middle in a horizontal line, instead of the traditional single doorknob. They had worn but bright paint in different colors.

Rapier reached out to grab the blue one, but Vanessa held a hand out. "Wait."

He did as asked, looking at her as she set a fist against her lips in thought. "If the Dovevians forced someone to open it, they could've changed the combination in case we came to investigate," she concluded.

Rapier's hand retracted a little quicker than Arica expected. What would happen if they set the wrong combination?

"Four handles, four locks," Vanessa mused as they all took a step or two back from the now foreboding door. "The original combination being blue, yellow, green, orange. But if you try to disengage the locks in the wrong order, it sounds an alarm and releases a constricting gas."

Arica backed up another step.

"Would they really bother to?" Rapier asked in disbelief.

"Someone closed it. Based on what we've seen up here, they were down there. So if they bothered to close it, they may as well have changed the lock in case of anyone snooping. You and I in particular."

They all waited as she stared at the door. Arica tried to imagine trying all twenty-four combinations in a row, and how long it would take even if they didn't have any defenses to worry about.

"By the Severed," Vanessa sighed, obviously not happy. "Stand back in the middle of the entry. I'm going to guess. If that doesn't work, the gas will hit quick enough to take me down, but you'll be able to dissipate it without struggle. Rapier, you will then try the old combination. If that is also wrong, then Steen and Arica will return to the camp, and let Jrasko know what happened. He'll know how to revive us. Understood?"

They all unintelligibly agreed in noises. Arica followed the men back down the hall into the circular carpeted room. They could still see Vanessa down the hall, fingering the hilt of her unsheathed sword.

"She's going to guess assuming the Dovevians are going to follow a pattern," Rapier whispered thoughtfully, crossing his thick arms.

Arica rubbed something in her eye that was irritating enough to blur her vision.

"Maybe, the order in which they worship the Severed. Or the level of authority the Dovevian closely related to each color is."

Or maybe the order one of them randomly came up with on the spot, she thought to herself. Once again, she tried to rub the purple fuzz out of her eye.

"In case I forget," Vanessa called loud enough for them to hear clearly. "I am going to try... green... orange... blue and yellow."

Arica held her breath as Vanessa reached out for the first one. Rapier's feet shifted under him, and Steen's fingers rubbed the hilt of his sword.

Vanessa's fingers wrapped around the worn green handle.

"Wait, that—" Arica blurted, stopping herself before she could continue.

The high master looked over her shoulder, raising an eyebrow, but said nothing. Arica grabbed her own elbow, shifting her weight. Then, before she could talk herself out of it, she jogged fifteen feet down the hall to the door again.

She was right. She hadn't been rubbing stuff out of her eye. She could see the combination.

"C-c-can I?" she stuttered, terrified she was intruding and messing everything up. Besides that, how was she supposed to explain how she knew?

"Don't worry, dear, I believe I know what it is," she soothed cheerfully.

"But…" Arica didn't come up with anything else, but Vanessa had the tiniest bit of curiosity cross her elegant features. Then, to Arica's surprise, she stepped back, inclining her head to the door.

Arica had no idea what had possessed her to volunteer for this. Or why she thought she knew better than the high master. But something… kept her staring at the yellow handle. Was it the purple glow? It was faint enough that it could've been her imagination.

Her heart pounded against her ribs. What did constricting gas do, anyway? She imagined it was extremely uncomfortable. Probably constricted her lungs. Somehow her movement. She'd have to suffocate before falling unconscious. Or maybe it just stopped her heart from beating more than enough to keep her barely alive.

She felt the weight of their eyes on her. She should've just left it to Vanessa, the woman who knew what she was doing, anyway. But when she saw her fingers on the handle…

Arica held her breath, gripping the yellow handle, farthest to the right. *I really hope it doesn't keep me awake enough to be in pain.*

It started turning left with barely any pressure, little encouragement for a lock strong enough to keep this door tight. It turned about a quarter way before it stopped, and something tiny clicked.

No clouds of poison descended on them, and Vanessa made a sound just shy of a gasp.

Arica looked behind her to make sure she wasn't dying, but her mentor just had high eyebrows, and what she could only assume was pride in the slight curve of her lips. She turned back, smiling. The next color was blue, she was sure of it. And sure enough, the blue handle turned and clicked with as little trouble as the first.

Excitement climbed in her chest. Was she really going to do this? Was she going to feel helpful? Orange turned, and she got even more excited. The last one. But even as she was ready, none of them glowed. *Which one?* Then she gritted her teeth at her own stupidity. There was only one color she hadn't turned. Green. She got it over with, turning it faster than any of the others, cringing slightly.

This click was deeper, more metallic and empty. Then all the handles turned back into their respective places, and the edge of the door popped out at her an inch or two.

She let out a squeal of delight.

Vanessa smiled the tiniest bit and respectfully inclined her head at her. It was the most approval she'd seen the woman give anyone.

She couldn't help grinning, reveling in her moment of deserved pride.

21

FORGES AND GHOSTS

The pair in charge took a lot more time and care looking over the lower level. They combed over everything from carpets to bookshelves. And for much of it, Arica struggled to be patient in the silence. The slanted door led into a low but wide hall lined with bookshelves. This had been about as expected, but what she didn't expect was the rest of the rooms, some of them huge. The base had been built down into the ground much further than it seemed from the outside.

After they worked through the short room filled with bookshelves, and several large rooms made up of mostly shelves and sitting furniture, they'd made their way across to an open doorway and a dark, shiny staircase downwards. Vanessa and Rapier both ducked down into it, not necessarily too tall.

"Ah, it's been so long since I've been here," Vanessa complained lightly, the first into another circular room, this one with a flat floor. Arica hoped it represented the middle of the giant dome above them. Rough, worn, and mismatched rugs overlapped each other. To either side, wide open entryways led into equally dark rooms, with a pair of flimsy-looking doors torn open in front of them.

Vanessa rolled her shoulders under her coat, then pointed right with the length of her sword. "Steen, Arica, go down into the foyer and take a quick look around. Jadrion and I will comb the dining halls. Meet back here and we'll all search the hearth."

Arica glanced at Steen, who said nothing even as they split ways. She just followed obediently.

They took a few shallow steps down into what felt like a wide open space, confirmed only when Steen waved his lit hand, and a metal brazier flared up to mimic the flames in his hand. Long shadows flickered over tasteful old furniture, spaced comfortably about the large room. This was the first room in Santsin Val that hadn't felt super cramped and cave-like. She purposely bumped a dark green lounge chair as she passed, letting a hand slide over the velvety upholstery.

She looked up, noticing the faintest shadow of light. The ceiling was smooth, reflecting Steen's lights, yet had a strange, random blotchy color. Then she noticed another spot, not far off, moving steadily in a waving motion. She jumped a little.

"It's glass," she blurted.

Steen paused, looking upwards. "Oh, yes. The ceiling and the furthest wall both, looking up into a pond. Though they've not been cleaned in a *long* time, it looks like."

Arica stopped craning her neck, praying that after however many years and years this dome had stood, today would *not* be the day that such hazardous architecture would fail and crush them with a thousand gallons of mucky water.

Steen held out an arm, slowly casting light across the room almost like a flashlight. There didn't seem to be much out of place. A dirty, mauled suit of armor was on a stand, leaning as if it was about to topple over. A few overstuffed chairs were against the opposite wall. Bookshelves carried a bunch of dusty souvenirs, lacking any books. Long, faded tapestries hung from the ceiling in an even row, and a gigantic fireplace boasted a huge metal grate and a stained chimney.

"Hey," Steen said lightly.

He walked towards the fireplace in the right-hand corner but stopped short. She realized he was interested in the indentation on the floor.

She followed him.

The worn, holey red carpet had torn up here, revealing a large sunken handle in the ground, surrounded by a circle.

"It's a trapdoor," Arica surmised in surprise.

Kneeling with his fingers around the handle, Steen looked at her over his shoulder. "If this is what I think it is..."

"A trapdoor," she repeated, eyebrows lowering.

He gave her a weird look, then shifted his balance and pulled up with both hands. Struggling, he shifted his feet a bit, trying to get enough leverage. The bulky muscles in his arms bulged with the effort, but there was no room for Arica to help. He let out a grunt, but the lid lifted.

Arica scampered around to the other side and wedged her fingers under the lip of the door, hoping he wouldn't suddenly lose grip and break them. She put all of her strength into lifting it up but felt like she was trying to push an entire mountain off a cliff. It went faster as soon as it fully lifted from the ground, then crashed to the other side with a painfully loud clang.

Steen stood back up, brushing his hands.

The air freed from the darkness below them smelled rank and carried a thin dust with it that wasn't pleasant to breathe.

Arica wasn't eager to descend, but as soon as Steen found the rails, he swung down.

She sighed louder than she intended. Apparently, insatiable curiosity and inattention to one's personal safety was more an immortality thing than just a trait of Jake's personality.

She followed, reasoning that it was only a few feet down. Her shoulders were narrower than Steen's, but she still worried she'd fit in the hole. Unlike his haphazard drop, she took each rough rung all the way to the bottom. She felt safer when her feet touched solid ground.

Walls built out of rough stone slabs surrounded them. They looked like someone had slapped them together, painted it black and called it good.

Steen shouldered his way through an even narrower archway, skirting the edge of a gigantic fire pit half embedded into the wall.

Arica ran a hand along the edge at waist height, then looked at the residue she'd picked up.

"I thought it was painted, but it's soot," she said, rubbing the greasy black powder between her fingers.

Steen continued around, disappearing behind some kind of pulley system along it. She followed, just in case there was something worth seeing. As she turned the corner, she was a bit more impressed.

There was a lot more room here, the walls at least eight feet high, a few dozen across, yet they mimicked the curve of the stone pit. This side boasted more contraptions.

She walked into the room, then leaned on an empty steel bench, watching Steen. He wandered in a circle, beaming as he touched several pieces in turn.

"This..." he mumbled through the grin as he shook a finger at the pit. "This... is cool."

"Some... kind of blacksmith thing," she guessed as she threw him a quizzical look.

"It's a forge. An old, old, elemental forge." He ran a hand over a long, curved handle jutting from the side of the stonework. "I do some blacksmithing. I love this sort of thing, but I didn't know this was still here. Wish I could've felt the heat from it."

Arica walked across the room, her boots dragging a bit. The firepit looked long empty, not even any trace of old coals or dirt trapped in the corners, or the layer of grease she might've expected over everything. A pile of wood wedges sat on the far side next to a pair of bellows, the only sign of where this thing might've gotten its warmth. But there was something drawing her to it.

"I... I can." She reached out with her hand, moving towards a strange warmth coming from the direction of the pit.

"What do you..." Her feet pulled her closer, and as she went, the sensation grew into an intense heat on her cheeks. Her eyes watered. It grew to a sting, forcing her to pull her hand back.

She glanced at Steen as he stared at the empty forge.

"Can you feel that?" she asked in a nervous whisper.

His gaze didn't stray even as he gave her a brief nod.

They both jumped as a sudden, striking vibration passed through them, gone as fast as it came. Her ears expected something, but there was nothing to hear over Steen's calm breath. She couldn't even hear the swamp shifting against the rock anymore.

They felt another hit, a low reverberation of something heavy and strong striking something solid.

Arica looked at several various wood and stone benches on the other side of the room. The room had been so stripped she could only imagine what kinds of tools and equipment used to sit upon them.

"What is an elemental forge, anyway? Why is it special?" she asked, taking a quiet step towards the vibrations.

Steen was as distracted by the feeling as she was, but still answered in a quiet, reverent tone. "It's special because it removes the process of forcing man-made elements together. It's more natural. The materials are pulled from the same ground that the heat is harvested from, tempered by the same rivers and rain that came from it. Those things, and the fact they're carved out by aunseyant magic."

The rhythmic beating stopped. Arica froze, carefully feeling for anything besides the still scorching fire pit. She glanced over her shoulder at Steen again.

"Do you know what weapons they made here?" she asked, her lungs breathless despite a calm pulse.

"Gyliedd, a short sword once owned by High Master Bonds; Rent, a jagged blade requested by some commander long ago; The Bausin Stones, a set of jewelry given to a Pelekan queen to protect her from magic—"

"What about Vanessa's sword?" Arica blurted without thinking first.

"Skotjretant... It's possible, but it's bloodsired, and I don't think they made those here."

Her eyes strained, trying to figure out why she couldn't feel anything anymore. "Bloodsired?"

"A weapon is imbued with the blood of its owner, and can only be wielded by those of his blood. Skotjretant is a Leadd heirloom, rumored to be requested by Raunst Leadd."

Her skin felt moist, uncomfortable, as the heat once again increased. "Commander Rapier takes the sword, though."

"He shouldn't. If he holds it too long, it'll drain him faster than a solzetair. Technically Jrasko should keep it on him, but he doesn't seem to like it."

Arica held her hands out. Her feet kept her going until she bumped into the table, but she barely felt it. Her limbs raced with numbness until something touched her outstretched hands, metal warm and smooth. Familiar. It was heavy, she could tell, yet she had more than enough muscle to control it. It didn't move, but she could feel it... alive.

"It's a sword," she whispered.

Her hands weren't in her control as they moved along the invisible blade, feeling the preciseness of the carved grooves, the sharpness of the edges, all the way to the hilt. She'd held this weapon before, but it had been with her own meager strength.

Arica unconsciously allowed it to be pulled from her grasp, but her hands reached out again. A small, icy sharpness touched her wrist. She wanted to retract, but she couldn't move even as it pierced her skin. Pain shot up her arm, the blade digging deeply into her wrist, slicing horizontally across the limb.

Shaking, she begged for whatever it was to let her go, but she couldn't struggle against her own rebellious muscles. Hot liquid gathered on her arm. It slid down her hand before dripping off of her knuckles.

A huge hand cupped the back of her intact one, then dissected this wrist as slowly and carefully as the first. Sharp, numbing pain tore up her arms.

A few tears escaped down her cheeks, her whole body tight and trembling without control. She tipped her arms to the side, letting her wrists drain more effectively. Then something tight gripped her arms, staunching the heat and pain. She shook, but this was different. It wasn't scary like she couldn't control what she was doing. Control washed over her arms again.

"Come on, come on," she heard moments before realizing that Steen stood in front of her, hands on her elbows as he shook her.

"Oh," she gasped as the rest of the pain and heat faded to a cold, wet pressure. Noise overwhelmed her.

"Are you here now?" Steen demanded, shaking her again.

"Yeah, yeah, I..." She took a step back, but knee-deep water resisted her. She looked around, grabbing Steen's arms to keep her balance.

The rushing noise wasn't an overload of her senses, but the rush of gallons of dirty swamp water pouring in from an impressive crack through the wall opposite them.

"Whoa!"

"Yeah, we gotta go," Steen ushered, letting go of just one arm, then started sloshing towards the forge's entrance.

"What happened?" asked Arica, struggling to follow.

"Magic built this place but wore it out faster. Whatever happened there with you dazed was more pressure than the weakened walls could take. It started as just a trickle a few minutes ago."

His hand slid down her arm until she could grab it. It kept them from being separated as waves shoved against them. The water level nearly reached the lip of the forge. Hopefully, it would slow as it filled the pit with water, giving them a chance to work against the drag.

She wanted to clarify a few things she'd seen with him but wasn't sure either of them could hear over the noise, even shouting.

A deep grinding stopped Arica in her tracks, despite common sense. Steen grabbed her by the arms, throwing her back as the water came crashing upon them so hard that it splashed up and over into the forge itself. They followed, throwing themselves over the edge into the pit.

It was about a foot deeper than the normal floor, but it only had a few inches of water to soak them as they landed on their backs.

"Come on," Steen ushered, stumbling to his feet.

Watery red liquid splash onto her arm, also spreading in the water where Steen's arm had been.

"Are you okay?" she asked, using the rough wall to pull her up.

"I scraped my hand, that's all," he dismissed.

They sprinted the fifteen feet across the pit a lot quicker than they would've through the deeper water above them, but as they reached the edge, the water crested the lip.

Steen vaulted up the edge with ease, strong enough to haul his own weight and then some, but Arica knew it wouldn't be as easy for her. It was about level with her chest, and she had barely any upper arm strength.

Luckily, the seasoned Zenian was ready to help her out of the fire and back into the frying pan. She stood, trying to balance in waist-deep water.

"Use the wall to pull yourself forward," Steen instructed loudly.

She struggled forward but got to the corner of the room and into the hall they'd returned from in a timely manner. They were almost to the ladder.

A fresh surge of water threw them around, shoving Arica into the corner. A much bigger splash accompanied it. Steen righted his footing, looking over his shoulder. It lapped at their armpits.

She could just barely hear the whisper of surprise under his breath. He surged past her, wide, slow-motion steps the last few meters to the remnants of the ladder.

Arica's eyebrows rose when the Zenian took one leap, one foot against the wall, and caught the second lowest rung in his hand.

"Come on," he barked, breathless.

"I... I can't do that."

He pulled himself upwards, his boots easily gripping the textured wall. With one foot on the lowest intact rung and an arm out towards her, he crouched down. He was almost inside the ring of the open hatch.

"I'm way too heavy for you to pick up like that," she argued, looking around for a better solution.

He let out an unimpressed grunt, shaking his hand out. "I doubt you're any heavier than my daughter, and we can do stuff like this. Come on."

She jumped back, splashing as something large brushed past her leg, but the sudden movement threw her off balance in the water, and she went under for a terrifying moment.

Nasty water burned her eyes and nose as she resurfaced, unstable. It was almost to her shoulders, plenty high enough to make her feel more comfortable treading water.

"It was just a fish, but hurry," Steen urged impatiently.

"How about we just wait a few minutes and I can swim out?" she yelled upwards.

"That's fine, assuming nothing *else* comes through that."

She looked behind her. The water was almost at the bottom of the crack, but it looked even bigger. Big enough for something scary to fall through it.

Arica pushed her feet against the wall and launched herself as high towards the other Zenian as she could, but she missed his hand by about a foot to the side. Her second attempt was more precise, and they grabbed each other's slimy wrists.

She did her best to pull her own weight, feet against the wall as she grabbed his arm with her other, but he pulled her up with relative ease. Her hand caught the ladder, and she pulled herself out of danger of falling.

"Thanks," she huffed, breathless.

He just climbed upwards and hopped out of the hatch. She was exhausted but followed him to shut out the mess they'd made.

"Hopefully that'll hold..." Steen grunted, shoving the handle of the door until it locked into position.

The *boom* of the heavy metal door closing still rang in her ears, but the room was silent.

The vast window spanning the walls of the common room was as they'd left it, no sign of the breakage that had affected the forge. The thick, dark water looked just as stagnant as before. Hopefully, it stayed that way.

Then she glanced at Steen and realized she probably looked like a wet, feral cat too.

"Well," he sighed, wiping stinky sludge from his arms. "Dunno what happened there."

Arica shook her head, also in awe. "I... I don't know how it happened, or how I know, but... It was Skotjretant. I felt the blade, I felt the blacksmith taking Raunst's blood to make the... whatever. To use it for the sword... It happened there."

Steen looked a little wide-eyed, but he nodded anyway. "Whatever magic remained was used to show you that. That's why the walls broke. Just... why?"

"I... I don't know the significance, yet," she admitted softly, her brain going a million miles a moment over as many of the whys and whats she could think of. "I just know... could you maybe not mention that part to Vanessa until I do?"

He shrugged. "I don't see why not."

"Thank you," she sighed. Then her attention turned to her dripping clothes.

Steen was already steaming as he dried magically, but she didn't know if she could do it on her own.

"Do you want me to help?" he offered as he used his hands to flake away the dried dirt and plant life from his arms and face.

"That... that would be nice. I'll be miserable if I stay like this much longer."

She didn't even finish her sentence before she felt her clothes warming up, stiffening with the dirt all over them. It was just a few moments before she was completely dry, left feeling crusty with the water's contents dried on her skin. She tried to wipe away the feeling the way Steen had, but her ponytail was still stiff and her socks were full of sharp, coarse dirt.

They got back to the middle room without incident, but they didn't see signs that either of their leaders had returned.

Arica had already decided that Steen was not the talkative type during moments without casual danger, but wasn't sure what conversation openers were appropriate for immortal sorcerers that looked like Olympic athletes.

She was almost ready to chance her opener being more awkward than the long-standing silence when she heard Vanessa's voice.

"They were thorough; I'll say that much," she sighed, leaning her arm on her sheathed weapon as she returned.

Rapier was barely behind her, pushing his cloak over his shoulder.

Turning to Steen, Vanessa raised her eyebrows slightly. "Anything, Callovoi?"

"Not much," he shrugged. "It all looks abandoned, quickly, but without much struggle, if any. Couldn't see any Dovevian stain, either."

Her lips pressed tightly together as all four of them looked at the last door.

"Well. Let's see if we can't at least recover some of their artifacts."

The hall past this unlocked door was so narrow that the commander's shoulders feathered both sides. It widened as they went, but Vanessa's quick gait ceased in front of a stone door that was just as if not narrower than the hall.

"They broke it on purpose," she griped. A piece of the door's handle hit the ground with a *clink*.

"Here, allow me," Rapier offered softly.

Vanessa took several long steps backwards, then set an arm across Arica's chest as if to protect her. Would she ever really stop being surprised by this woman? At least it made her feel better.

Jadrion also backed up a few steps. Then he unsheathed Vanessa's huge greatsword as if from the pockets of his cloak.

She couldn't help eyeing the long silver blade. Was it aware that it had returned to its place of creation? Aware, as if a hunk of metal could feel anything at all. And yet... magic and blood. It had more in common with them than just any steel.

Bracing his feet apart, the large warrior swung lazily in the finite space and pounded the massive sword into the door's simple locking mechanism.

Arica jumped as a loud metallic ring nearly burst her eardrums and a shower of sparks lit up the tiny room. The second time was even harder, successfully severing the edge of the door from the lock with a much heavier sound.

It crashed open under the force of Rapier's foot.

"Lovely," Vanessa stated, shouldering past him without another second spared. "There has to be a reason this was locked. There's Dovevian magic all over."

As Arica passed into the brighter room, she glanced at the buckled wood door with steel framing. If any of the Dovevians were half as strong as that man, she'd never be able to out-fight them even if it meant death.

"I don't remember what all is back here," Vanessa admitted, looking around the hall with open entryways into other rooms. It seemed like for every hall they could take, at least three more branches popped up. This one was tall, with columns that cast dark shadows by Vanessa's flames.

"I thought we'd be directed right into the lower assemblage hall, the hearth, the enchantment cache... But this..." she pointed to the right. "Is into the rooms above the forge..."

"Which... we flooded," Steen blurted, looking unsure of himself. "It was a mess anyway, but our magic triggered the wall to finish crumbling."

She gave him a little lordly look, but Arica had no idea what it meant. She continued unhindered. "The dungeon is around here somewhere, I believe..."

"Vanessa!"

They all froze, all of them hearing the distant, disjointed yell. Their small group waited in complete silence, Vanessa's expression displaying none of the alertness Arica felt.

"It's safe," she called back as loudly, but only after a few long moments.

Rapier took charge, following the tall hall all the way to the end where another second door sat, this one bigger, with a glass window over most of the surface. They could see a tan, tiled room beyond.

"Is somebody there? Help!"

"It's Vanne," Rapier announced, reaching for the door handle.

"Wait, no, Rapier!"

But Vanessa was too late warning him. The door opened halfway, and while a shiny barrier appeared almost as fast, it wasn't fast enough.

Rapier bent over, retching, and stumbled away from the door, only to puke a few feet away. Arica made a face. She wanted to help, but for all she knew he was about to turn into a zombie.

"By the Severed, you're lucky you only caught a whiff," said Vanessa as she held her hand out at her little barrier, making sure it was going to stay up.

"They really like poisons, huh?" Arica asked, frowning.

"This wasn't the Dovevians, unfortunately," she explained, waving her other hand in a little circle like she was conducting an orchestra. "We keep the more important artifacts and treasures in a room just beyond. Just as the door before, it's a defense mechanism, tripped by failed access to the room. It's something that the humans, the original owners of this place, set in. But it does us no good, as most of the Dovevians are practically immune to natural toxins. They probably didn't even realize they tripped it. But it's dissipating now."

"A lot of the creatures in this area have some variation of harmful toxins. It's easy to come by," Steen added, much to her surprise. He'd been so quiet again, hidden behind her, that she'd almost forgotten he was following.

"Are you all right?" Vanessa then directed at Jadrion, who leaned against the wall, his face pale.

"I'm fine," he dismissed, heavily dragging himself to his feet.

"It should be safe now." She lowered her hands and pulled the door back open.

"Let me, just in case," Rapier offered, shoving between her and the room.

Arica half expected him to start violently vomiting again, but he walked into the middle of the room, then turned and gave them a beckoning wave.

"Colten, are you in here?" Vanessa called.

"Mistress Damage? We're in the cellar!" The voice was much clearer now and was obviously coming from an entryway sealed with a ton of messy tan bricks and a dark substance that looked quite solid, though it hadn't always been.

"Colten, the room's been completely sealed. Are you all right?"

Arica stepped a few feet closer to hear the stranger.

"I'll live, just a little beaten up. Gent's in terrible shape, though. We've gotta get him out of here." His voice was smooth, his accent thicker than most of the Zenians'. "Don't use any magic," he quickly added with an urgency. "The air's rigged to ignite at the slightest touch."

Vanessa frowned, just looking mildly annoyed. "What about physical tampering?" she asked, setting her hand against the uneven brick alcove.

"I've been chipping at the top, it hasn't seemed to trigger it."

"I guess that's enough," she growled. With a little beckon, she got Rapier to hand over her sword. Then, biting her lip in concentration, she carefully brought it up, wedging the tip into a small crack in the bricks. Using her strength and weight both, she worked it further. Then she grabbed the huge hilt with both hands and lifted herself onto it.

"Whoa, won't that break it?" Arica blurted without thinking.

"Not unless my hands held the power of the gods," she puffed, suspending for a few minutes before dropping back to her feet. She wiggled it again, sinking it deeper into the rock.

"Who was that?" Colten asked curiously.

"My new tyro, Arica," Vanessa responded, pushing the sword back and forth.

Rapier silently went to the other side of it and tried tugging on it.

"This won't work. Colten, can you see the trap or any way to disarm it?"

"I looked earlier. It's all just some kind of gas near the ceiling, waiting for a spark."

She turned back to them, raising her eyebrows. "Well, we can't use magic to break it down. But that doesn't mean we can't use magic to make something. Commander, go back to the training room and fetch some rope."

Rapier shouldered back between Arica and Steen with a quiet excuse as Vanessa paced to the other side of the room, looking around.

Dusty shelves lined the wall opposite the bricked-up alcove between round granite columns. The column bases boasted carved leaves, roots, and flowers, making them look like they grew from the rough cobblestone floor.

"So, your sword... I guess it's the magic in it that makes it so strong, right?" Arica asked, hoping for a simple explanation.

"It's a little more complicated than your classic magic. But yes. It was made under special circumstances."

"Like the forge here?"

"No, the one here is an elemental forge. Mine was bathed in the blood of a powerful Zenian, and in some way, it kept that magic. Santsin Val's forge wasn't built until long after my sword existed."

Arica wanted to bet against that but said nothing. She still didn't completely understand what she'd seen, or why, or how.

"Who was that?" the man behind the wall asked curiously.

Vanessa's gaze flicked upwards to the alcove, fist thoughtfully resting against her lips. "Still my tyro, Arica."

Rapier waltzed back in the room, breath noticeably heavy, but he was sporting a suitable length of thick, hairy rope on one shoulder, with a thinner length of it in one hand.

"Perfect," Vanessa mumbled, prancing across the room to grab the thinner piece from him.

Arica wanted to help, but she didn't want to get in the way either. Vanessa tossed one end around the middle of the three pillars and tied it off with a few quick knots. She tossed the other end in the air, but instead of dropping back down, it raced to the ceiling as if magnetized. Then it began burrowing into the smooth stone like a worm into soil.

She took the thicker rope, wrapped the middle twice around the column, then did the same with the two ends, forcing them to burrow into the stone.

"That might work..." she said, stepping back to look at her handiwork. Three ropes held it tight in place, one in front and the other two on either side. Then she shook her head, raising her hand to the ceiling. The end of the thinner rope broke through the ceiling right above the alcove, reaching out for her hand, all too snake-like. Vanessa dragged it back around to the pillar and tied it much lower than the other end.

"So," she said, obviously about to set down some orders. "Jadrion, I'm going to break the top just above that rope towards this wall while you simultaneously break the bottom towards the alcove. Steen, you'll monitor the direction, and keep the ropes taut. Everyone, stand back and do not use magic close to the alcove, even if this goes badly. Clear?"

They all made various noises of assent, then backed up. Arica went all the way into the corner, Steen close by while Vanessa and Rapier stood as close to the shelves as they could on either side of the pillar.

"Colten! Gent! Stay as far from the entrance as possible!" Vanessa held her hands up, but Jadrion's stayed by his sides. "Ready? On my mark. Two. One. Mark."

Arica jumped at the terrible cracking noise, the damage so sudden that the stone couldn't take it quietly. The middle of it blasted away from either base, the breakage on either side angled towards the back wall. The ropes all tensed, but held as the further one dragged it forward. It tried to hang on, but ultimately was too heavy and swung out of place, guided by the ropes. It passed over the floor by a foot or two, then went crashing into the sloppy brickwork.

They waited in silence for a few heartbeats, a bit of rubble still shifting from this dramatic renovation.

Arica took a few steps closer, but it was difficult to see past all the stirred-up dust.

Jadrion followed her forward, but Vanessa was quicker.

"Wait," she insisted, setting a hand out in front of them as the dust settled. "It may still be a trap."

Both men stayed back at her bidding, and Arica paused in her place.

Vanessa carefully climbed over the debris.

They all impatiently waited, staring into the dust. A dull blue light wavered in and out, shining through the particles in the air. Arica could just make out a dirt floor a foot lower than the other rooms, but completely cluttered with rubble.

"Just as I feared..." Vanessa mumbled, stepping past the source of the light, a small ball lying in the dirt in the middle of the room.

One of the guys flicked a hand out and like fog rolling away with a sudden gust of wind, the dust swirled into a corner and Arica could see what Vanessa stood over. A pair of bodies laid against the far wall, clothing torn and skin dark gray and pockmarked, even sagging off of dull ivory bone in some places.

Arica quickly retracted behind the wall, her stomach churning. She shouldn't have been so curious. But now she couldn't banish the image of the rotting corpses.

"Colten and Gent," Vanessa sighed from inside the room. "I should've known; it was too suspicious."

The magic that had swept up the dust had whipped away the smell with it. But now it had the chance to hit her nose and did so mercilessly.

Arica crouched against the wall, holding her stomach. She'd smelled some bad things in life, but this was so much worse than she could've imagined. Sour like rotten fruit, with the same stinging potency of her older brother's neglected bedroom, a mix of drenched dog fur, and wet flowers left to decay in a filled vase for a few months.

"Quite the trap," Rapier awed quietly.

The boys backed up as Vanessa returned holding the source of light.

"Vanessa, Gent is in awful shape. You gotta get us outta here," the same voice pleaded as if the speaker stood near them.

"What... is that?" Steen inquired with disgust.

Arica was glad that for once she wasn't the only one confused.

"It's a vyte." She held it out a little more, flat on her palm. The blue faded in and out lethargically, sometimes leaving just a little imperfect rock.

"It's meant to mimic Colten's consciousness at the time of the magic."

Steen picked it up, rolling it between his fingers, but seemed unimpressed.

"Why did it know how to lie to us? Does it have, like... artificial intelligence?" Arica asked, still holding one hand against her mouth as if this would staunch her nausea.

"It neither lied nor was it thinking on its own. The most intelligent thing about it is its ability to recognize voices. Its response is limited, but it only replied based on what Colten would've said when it was done. The room really was set up. Colten actually was trapped without release. Gent was truthfully in a lot of pain. But that's why it asked who you were more than once. Colten would've asked because he didn't know you. But the vyte itself couldn't learn your voice. It only answered and stated based upon what Colten would've said or done. I should've asked a question it couldn't've answered to begin with."

Arica stared at the magic thing as Steen handed it back, feeling sick all over again. They'd been talking to a rock the entire time.

"The trick is on the Dovevians, however," Vanessa announced, climbing back over the biggest part of their battering ram. "I can use this to gather information."

She wasn't ready to keep going yet, but started trudging after them, anyway. "Wouldn't that mean they could've gotten info from him, too?"

"He never would've told them anything by will. And you can't exactly torture information out of a rock. So assuming they didn't make this, and switch straight to torture, we may find something."

They filed down the corridor into a small stairwell that curved to the right before opening up into a long, narrow room mostly filled with a giant oak table, shiny on top with little runes carved into the curvy legs of it. The opposite wall had a cold fireplace with long bookshelves above it, packed with books.

"How did the Dovevians break in?" Vanessa asked the inanimate object as if it were her old friend.

"It was rather sudden. They knew right where we were, took less than a minute for them to crack the barrier. What was worse was the troop of kinsguard on their side. I know it sounds ridiculous, but they weren't just humans, they were... almost possessed themselves. Tougher, faster. Even had their own sort of protection around them. The alarm went off. We were all sleeping. Tried to keep them upstairs, but they cracked Tova, made him open the door. We just... stood our ground. The back-out tunnels collapsed a few days ago. We thought it was just from the swamp's natural growth, but now... I'm sure they had something to do with it."

"Do you know who survived? Did anyone get out?" She stopped at the end of the room and leaned her body against the edge of the table.

Rapier sat down on the floor, and Arica copied, way too shaken up to stand more than necessary.

"I've no clue. I saw so many cut down, I couldn't tell you who lived. I hope you're helping them," Colten's voice said with such emotion that Arica couldn't understand how this was possible. "Netayin is dead, I know that for sure, and I don't think Hemer's brain could've handled the bashing it took. But if he gets the proper treatment, he may be okay. It was only about twenty minutes ago."

How long had it really been? Weeks? Long enough for this man to die and rot away like nothing. Arica didn't realize in time to catch a few tears dripping from her eyes. She stared at the glazed stone bricks under them.

"Were all the Dovevians here?"

"As far as I saw. I know Damage and Aran are upstairs making sure nobody can escape. Reganold is guarding the door right outside this room. Lise took charge of this one. He said he was going to find me a rock or something, and we'd make you a gift. I don't know what that was about."

"Is there anyone of importance locked in the dungeon?" Vanessa asked. Her questions were getting quieter as if exhaustion was taking her.

"Well, Soas Entdi was locked away, but they've likely gotten to him already. Other than that, some random creatures. I doubt they bothered with them."

"One last thing before we free you, Colten," Vanessa then announced a little louder. "Remind me how to open the downstairs hearth."

Their lady pushed herself off of the table and took a few steps to the long bookcases opposite from where they'd entered. The dusty fire pit sparked a few times before bursting into flames below her.

"The blue book about solzetairs is the key," the rock reported.

Vanessa picked out one with this description from a shelf barely within her reach, then replaced it between two in the bottom row. With a *click* the bottom shelf separated about six inches down the middle, then ground to a painful stop, as if breaking important pieces.

The older woman let out an audible sigh. "They've been into this. Colten, lead me to the vault. The hearth is empty."

"The lock is the third sconce from the right wall." The rock guided nicely.

Vanessa sidled to her right, facing the cold wooden torch obediently.

"Pressure, heat, decay, heat, curing, and moisture."

In response to this odd chosen string of words, Vanessa held out a hand, fingers barely moving for almost an entire minute before something clicked and dust puffed from the wall in front of her.

"Callovoi, Tanson, stay behind. Rapier and I will pull out anything of value still here," Vanessa directed with less sternness than usual.

As the two named pushed the wall into a recessed position, Arica glanced back at Steen, who wandered the room looking even simple things over.

"What was that? With the words, and the sconce, and..."

He looked over his shoulder at her before answering to the bookshelf in front of him. "It's a type of lock encased in layers of magic. They loosen for specific conditions."

She went back to waiting. It was only a few minutes before the pair were back, sporting nothing visibly new.

"This isn't really helpful. There was barely anything left in there," Vanessa mused aloud.

Arica instinctively raised a hand. "The Dovevians got into it?"

"No. They just didn't have much. This is a harsh place to live, even for our kind. They were running out of all magic but their own." She walked further out of the back room, then placed a few fingers on the long table as if resting.

"Did you look into the dungeons when you were up there?" she then asked over her shoulder at the commander.

He gave her a curt nod. "There was skelt. Not even a creature."

She barely even gave him the time to finish his last syllable before continuing with reserved frustration. "We'll burn the bodies before we leave, but I want to head towards Commander Herak immediately. They've gotten this one, they attacked ours. The third one has to have a target as well." Then she glanced at Arica, stabbing into her resolve. "This is why we stay in separate groups."

"You don't think they could've won with more people?" Arica murmured.

"Not likely."

Rapier came forward, grabbing her by the bare wrist. "We need to come up with a plan."

"Yes, we do."

SEVEN'S RED MOON

With aching calves and raw feet, Arica collapsed on the stone ground near her belongings. She wasn't sure she'd be able to get back up, but she knew if she didn't brush her hair now, it would be too tangled to later. Even so exhausted, she felt much more refreshed and cleaner after standing in a waterfall for a few minutes.

She found her grooming supplies and began brushing any remaining dirt or chunks of soap out of her hair. It was usually stringy, and she never would've imagined her hair being affected by the humidity, but she was being proven wrong. She carefully weaved her fingers in and out of it, creating a less-than-perfect braid that kept it out of her face. Her hand reached into the little satchel that always felt empty, searching for a little glass bottle of oil. She felt a folded piece of soft paper, something she hadn't remembered putting in there, and pulled it out.

A page, folded into quarters. She expected some ripped page of a book she'd forgotten about, or a random list or something. But for as huge as it was, it only had three words up in the top corner. *How are you?*

Her face warmed, and her thoughts raced. *Who put this here? Why were they in my stuff? What do I do with it? Why would they leave this?*

Jake had been the one to pack up her stuff for their short move from one side of Santsin Val to the other, but he wouldn't've needed to leave secret messages in her things, would he?

Well, whoever had done it wouldn't get another chance. She quickly stuffed everything back into the satchel and tucked it into her pocket. While folded, it fit nicely.

She exited the lonely tent.

Orange light danced on the walls of the bigger tent opposite her, her only reason for not immediately crashing into her bed. She could hear light talking mixed with the deep pounding of a drum and a female vocalizing in another language.

Steen stood in the open entrance, hands in pockets as he stared inside. He also looked freshly washed and in clean, more comfortable clothes, his hair fluffy. He turned his head as Arica approached.

"What's going on here?" she whispered once she was close enough.

She peeked inside, partially hiding herself behind the Zenian.

On the other side of the fire danced a girl with thick hair in a long, billowing robe sewn with strings of beads and little trinkets all over its surface. Underneath, she barely wore anything, with more decorative rocks and possibly bones tied around her and dark paint streaked in various designs. Her slim face had shiny black paint down one side and a light gray down the other. The tawny skin and dark hair made it obvious that it was Malon.

Behind her, there were a few low, rounded wooden drums. Skah was haphazardly doing his own thing on one, while Ricken carefully pounded out short little beats for Damad to copy on another.

Banen sat closest to the fire, throwing small pieces of wood and bark into it, looking annoyed.

"A red moon," Steen responded just as quietly, then used a large hand to gesture inwards. "The Kisoks and Skah are showing off a bit of Kyrgan Isle's Zenian traditions. Most of us don't practice those of its tribes, but it's cool to watch."

"Traditions for what? Just a red moon?"

He turned to catch her gaze, and she realized how refreshing it was to look someone in the eyes without feeling two feet tall.

"Well, yeah... The Seven Severed's red moon." The narrowness of his eye-brows made her realize this was probably something she was supposed to know, were she not an alien.

"Right," she whispered through her teeth. "Not as big of a deal in Ellteria."

Apparently, this was reasonable.

She shifted a little closer to Steen's shoulder to see who was giggling so loudly. Zak and Elvy laughed together, wrapped up on a pile of blankets. Kylen seemed in on it but wasn't reclined as close. Parel had his arms across his knees, staring emptily into the fire while Jerim talked softly to him, shoulder to shoulder. Kasper was telling a story, his pale hands and facial expressions changing dramatically as Aaris nodded every few words, fixated.

Arica couldn't help but smile a little. A group of friends, close and comfortable. And they'd accepted her without a word. Then she realized she was still standing outside of it with Steen.

To break the silence, and since she was genuinely curious, she gestured at a dark ink handprint haphazardly slapped on his bicep. "Whose handprint is that? It's huge."

Steen snickered lightheartedly, then pulled a hand from his pocket.

"Not like grotesque, just surprising," she quickly excused. She reached out, crossing their wrists, and set her hand against his to compare. Hers were average for her height, but the tips of her fingers just barely reached his first set of knuckles.

"I didn't notice earlier. I guess you really are supposed to be a blacksmith," she said, almost nervously. She rubbed the tips of her fingers across the rough, calloused pads, feeling just a fraction of the work he'd done with them.

"Know a thing or two," he murmured.

Her cheeks warmed as his fingers shut one at a time over hers, lightly trapping her hand against his.

"Well, um, since we're here right now..." she started, grabbing her own arm before even realizing she was nervous.

With his attention successfully drawn to her face, she hesitated. His soft eyes were bronze in the reflected firelight.

"Thanks for saving me down there." She forced her hand from her arm and slipped it into her pocket.

"I know you're new around here, but that—that's just kind of what we do," Steen explained with all sincerity.

She looked down, suddenly conscious she'd been staring too long. "Still, y'know, I kinda panicked. I'm sorry. I'm obviously not very good at this."

He was smiling when she felt it was safe enough to look back up.

"Then... You're welcome."

Before she could convince herself not to, she reached up just a touch, slowly, so he wasn't startled. As if he could read her mind, he met her lips for a short, sweet kiss. She didn't expect it to go so smoothly, so upon parting, she couldn't resist smiling.

"Well, do you want to go in before someone notices we're creeping?" he asked softly.

"Yeah, I guess that's a good idea," Arica sighed, partially relieved he'd rather join the crowd.

Steen's pale hand stayed fixed in hers as they picked their way across the fire to a clear spot. Silhouettes huddled together near the fire with familiar faces, most quiet, as if they were listening to the resonating music the boys managed with evident skill.

A foot or two behind the spot they'd bee-lined for was Jake, laying sideways against a boulder and snacking on dried fruit like some hedonistic god.

"Do you mind?" Steen asked politely.

Jake gave him a lazy gesture. "That's what it's there for."

Carefully folding her legs, Arica settled into the empty spot along the ring of bedding around the fire, letting go of Steen for a moment. As soon as they were both comfortable, shoulder to shoulder, their hands reached back out and intertwined.

"Here," Jake then offered, reaching out and bumping a little bowl into her arm before setting it next to her.

"What's this?" She picked up a small lettuce-like leaf rolled around a thick paste.

"A gift from the Severed," Jake softly announced, with a weird-looking smile.

"Just try it," Steen added with a sideways glance that she could only take as a dare.

"I don't know, guys. I feel like participating in any of this is wrong for me," she admitted softly.

"Arica, Arica," Jake whispered, leaning forward so he was much closer to her. "Listen, I know nothing of your God. But would they really hate you to learn of ours? We don't ask you to pray or to give any gifts. But the Severed may help you out in the future. Why not learn a little?"

She stared him in the face, trying to read him, but only caught slight amusement. "Well, I guess when you put it that way..."

He reached out for the rest as she eyed her piece in suspicion.

"Just one is probably plenty for you."

"Still didn't tell me what it was," she grumbled. It smelled musty, strong, like a dark spice she'd never remember the name of. The middle was thick like peanut butter but much darker. She batted her fear away and sunk her teeth into it.

"I expected more flavor," she admitted, chewing the tasteless, tacky paste. It had a tangy effect that made her mouth water.

"It's... more about the effect, really," Jake admitted with a chuckle.

Her hand flew over her mouth in surprise. "Did you people just drug me?"

Steen gave her a weird look, then smiled a little. "Don't worry. You'll feel a lot stronger in the morning. It's good for you."

She glared at the fire, shoving the rest of it in her mouth as if obeying was the ultimate defiance. "I don't like either of you," she mumbled with a full mouth. "I'm Catholic, my brother would be ashamed of me right now..."

"What's Catholic?" Steen asked, looking over with a lowered brow.

She glanced back to silently ask for Jake's help, but his only help was to cut his finger over his throat.

"It's nothing," she dismissed, trying to regain her casualness. "Hey, so, where's Vanessa and Rapier?" She looked back at Jake to reinforce she was asking him.

"Vanessa doesn't have an admirable relationship with the Severed," Jake mumbled, rolling his head on his sore neck. "And Jadrion's just a heated mutt following her about."

Arica's hand fell onto the blanket, still interlocked with Steen's. Her cheeks warmed as she wondered if anyone had noticed.

"So, like, explain this stuff. The red moon, what does it have to do with these Seven... Severed?"

"Tonight is one of the rare nights when their power is useless," Jake whispered with reverence. "Tonight, we are alone. Their offerings are given for our protection, and to ensure our further worship. Tonight, Solyve's demons and Kujra's cursed run free."

Arica sat still for a moment, processing his tone. "Sometimes I think you say things just to scare me," she whispered, giving Jake her wide-eyed look.

"He's a storyteller," Steen soothed, gripping her hand a little harder. "Truth is, we never see any of the beasts. They want to enjoy the moonlight all night. And, the plants we find probably just bloom rarely. The Severed are just a tale to explain magic. They aren't real. And even if they are, they aren't what the stories make them out to be; gods of immense power."

"Typical Pelekan," Jake scoffed under his breath. "Can't believe even in the things they see."

"You're plenty aware I'm Madellian, same as you," Steen countered with annoyance, raking a hand back through his short, black hair. "And there's never been any proof they exist."

"Vanessa has *met* them," Jake snickered in disbelief. "What more do you need?"

Hand freed, Arica let herself fall sideways onto the blanket, frowning as Steen turned to better address his taller companion.

"Just because she says so doesn't mean it's true."

Jake rubbed his eyes for a moment. "I don't see why she'd lie about it, Callovoi."

He shrugged, nonchalantly. "That's because you're mummy's little prick."

Arica suppressed an explosive laugh, covering her mouth until she felt safe again. "Way to escalate," she chuckled, turning over her shoulder so she could better see whether they were staring at each other or staring each other down.

Jake wore a scowl that wasn't a hundred percent serious but stayed far from friendly.

She quickly crawled into the space between them, hands outstretched. The sudden movement made her brain fuzzy, but she wanted to keep them apart.

Steen's glare softened as it switched to her. "I wasn't—"

"Look, we don't fight over religious stuff, we're friends," Arica said evenly, then switched her gaze to Jake. "Steen had a point, you are really amenable with Vanessa. But that's not something to throw in your face."

He looked away, smirking, and she couldn't help but feel proud that she could diffuse him so easily.

Then she looked at Steen and raised her eyebrows. "You?"

He shrugged, smiling softly, then reached out and grabbed the hand she was trying to scold him with.

"You just won't leave my hands alone, will you?" she teased thoughtlessly.

"Probably not," he mumbled, fiddling with her individual fingers as he looked at the large fire. He settled against her, on one elbow leaned against her thigh.

It was warm and comforting.

Arica then looked down, realizing that she was using her free hand to play in Steen's soft black curls. She pulled away, mouth hanging open. "This is an effect of that goo stuff you guys fed me."

"What is?" Jake asked in a grunt.

"I dunno, I'm... like, being really open, and... bold."

"Since when are honesty and bravery bad things?"

She looked up at him, not sure if that was an actual question. She felt lips touch her knuckles and forced herself to keep from shivering, avoiding looking in Steen's direction.

Jake reached out towards someone further away. "You want more, kid?"

She violently shook her head. "No, I'm kind of freaking out. Mostly because I'm not... freaking out. My brain isn't cloudy. I don't feel high."

"Just good, right?" Steen asked softly, finally drawing her gaze back to him.

"I..." she started, but one of his hands slid up her wrist, distracting her. "What... are you doing?" she whispered, letting that hand fall limp.

Steen let out a breathy chuckle, then looked up at her, leaning closer. "I've no idea, honestly. I just..." His hand brushed across her face, almost shocking her.

"Honest, and brave, and..." she breathed slowly, tracking how close he was now. Whatever he'd spritzed on after drenching himself in rainwater was pleasant, something almost homey when all she'd been smelling for the past two days was her own sun-burnt skin and foot odor.

She turned her face slightly, forcing him to brush her cheek. He let out a nervous snicker and pulled back a few inches. Her face warmed, his fingers once again in hers. Hers brushed his palm, and the sticky, hot patch along it.

"Oh, you got cut worse than I thought," she gushed suddenly, taking possession of this hand. The shiny red gash ran the total length of his palm, almost as thick as her thumb. "Why didn't you get something to wrap it?"

His lips parted as he gave her a soft shrug.

She reached for the small satchel she'd hooked to her belt, leaving his hand in her lap. She reached in, digging through items and the troublesome note.

She felt the silky material she was after and pulled out a long, thin scarf colored dark green fading into gray. Steen didn't object when she pulled the fabric taut around his hand and wrapped it a few times.

"There." She leaned on an elbow, turning her face slightly towards him. "I'm sure everyone else here has something more appropriate to dress a wound with, but it'll work for now."

His hand closed, then rested against her waist. "Thanks..."

She'd inadvertently leaned even closer. Or was it purposefully?

Then a boot hit hers, pulling her attention to a skinny blond with a cowboy accent. "Hey. Would you take a walk with me?"

"Sorry for... well, for interrupting you back there," Zak murmured, putting his hands in his pockets. It was chilly enough that she wrapped her cloak a little tighter. She was glad she'd brought it.

"It's nothing, I wasn't..." She blushed before she could get any further. "Obviously, you were more entertained than I was. I don't know what they gave me. I'm a sucker for peer pressure."

He chuckled, but his eyes narrowed. "I'm pretty sure it's just painkillers or similar."

"That makes sense," she admitted, rolling her shoulders. "I feel better than I have in days. Although, aren't you from the 1900s, when cocaine was in soda and stuff?"

"I don't remember, but that's an excellent point," Zak chuckled.

They reached the overhang and peered into the lush, wet forest. The stars were bright and tinkling. Were they the same stars from home? Zak held an arm out, so she slipped her hand into his elbow, linking them together.

"I thought, seeing as you're also from another world, maybe you'd feel better out here. I enjoy learning about their culture, and clearly I accept it often, but sometimes, like the Seven's red moon..." He used his hands to gesture theatrically. "It feels more proper to, say, sit one out. Y'know?"

"Like maybe if there are other gods out there, they don't appreciate strangers partaking in their rituals, even if they're more casual about it."

He smiled. "You get it."

They simultaneously walked out under the shiny stars and the damp grass. It was nice to get out of the cave for a minute. Then she glanced up and saw the orangy-red moon hovering low in the sky.

"You know, there's, like, scientific evidence why the moon looks like that," she mused softly.

"Lunar eclipse, shadow of the earth and sunset combined, somethin' somethin'..."

"Yeah," she agreed with a smile. "Doesn't have to be 'the blood of the innocents slaughtered in the name of Mister Sun God', or whatever."

"Yeah, but just because it has an explanation doesn't make it any less magical... Don't you think?"

She shrugged a shoulder, avoiding a tree branch. Apparently, Zak had a destination in mind, because even at a pleasant stroll he walked with purpose.

She followed happily, but in the back of her mind she wondered if it was dangerous to be out in the dark, even with the generous moonlight. She would've thought the cave was low in the ground, but like the swamps Santsin Val rested in, they went in a downward slope. Luckily, it was drier here. They reached a bubbly brook running in the direction they came from. Maybe the tiny water flow would eventually contribute to the roaring cascades in Akvelia.

"Do you like Elvy?"

Zak stopped short, glancing at her quizzically. "I mean... Yeah. Isn't that obvious?"

She blushed a little, but he'd pulled her back into a walk, so maybe he hadn't noticed. "I don't know. I'm just trying to figure everything out. I mean, living a life without the option of romance seems like an enormous sacrifice, and the more I look... The less I understand the dynamic here."

"Well, what happened at Santsin Val?"

The question struck a strange chord in her. "I... can't really talk about it."

"No, not what you found," he laughed, turning to her. "I mean, did something happen with Steen? Save each other's lives or something?"

"Oh," she chuckled, her cheeks warming as she averted her eyes. "Well, it..."

A snort of amusement accompanied Zak's smirk. "That'll do 'er."

"It's not that deep," she quickly excused. "I've said like five words to him before today."

"Well, do you like Jake?" he asked less teasingly than she would've assumed.

She rolled her eyes a little, but inside she was asking the same. "I mean, I think so. But more like if you see a pretty wolf and really want to pet it, but you know that if you do, it's probably going to bite your hand off."

He had a cheerful laugh. "That's probably the most appropriate mentality, honestly."

The foliage thickened, casting thick, dark shadows in the silvery drape of light.

"But there are many people out here more emotionally available and probably a lot nicer," he continued happily.

"You mean like Steen?"

He shrugged, taking the time to look at her. "Doesn't have to be, but he's not a bad choice."

"They're just scary."

"Get them used to you. Barriers will come down just fine. You'll find someone you connect with."

She nodded a little.

"Just don't ask Vanessa about any of this," he chuckled with some sort of sympathy. "For your own good."

"Okay, then... Where are we going?"

His eyebrows went up, smile fading into a smirk. "We scouted the area earlier while you headed to the base. Found this really cool spot I thought you might like. Since we're out here, anyway."

She was already tired, so this extra little walk was just draining her, but when asked, he assured her it wasn't very far.

They skirted a small, trickling waterfall and climbed the hill it drained from. A plateau reached out underneath them, hovering over a deep valley filled with towering trees that still couldn't reach the ground at their feet. The jungle canopied the area, giving it a simultaneously cozy and open feel as they looked out over the sea of treetops.

"Whoa," she whispered, walking out onto mossy rock.

Zak stood back, hands on his hips. "Pretty nice. See those mountains in the distance?"

Arica strained her eyes, following the point of his finger. She could mostly see greenery, but if she concentrated she could just make out a zig-zag line of sky in the distance.

"I think so."

"That's the Myser Mountains. Just the other side of it is Turrales. At least, I think."

Arica suppressed a giggle. "It's okay, you haven't been here very long." She slowly let her body shift into a crouch so she could feel the spongy, damp moss under her feet.

Zak shrugged his shoulders, looking around the dark trees as if he couldn't stop scouting for longer than a moment. Then he broke his stance and knelt next to her. "About sixty years. I know that doesn't seem like a long time when you get them boys hanging around for hundreds, but... to me it does."

A deep, calming inhale took over Arica's body before she realized she was doing it, suddenly feeling how small the situation made her. "Leaving home has to be hard. Where are you from, anyway?"

He settled down next to her, arms to his knees. "Barlowe, some miles off of Victoria."

"Never heard of it."

"You wouldn't've," he chuckled mirthlessly. "We blew it over right through. On accident, 'course. Little ranching community, fifty of us or so. There were survivors, but something tells me our exalted lady had something to do with removing the remains of our humble town from their heads, and more importantly, the unexplainable things they may or may not have seen."

"Did you leave anyone behind, then?"

He exhaled suddenly, then smiled a little. "Sister and her husband. A girlfriend too—fiance, I guess. Really thought we were gonna work. She even came here for a bit."

"Here, here? Like, stepped through a magic portal into a fantasy land?"

"Right into the magic," he chuckled, nodding with enthusiasm. "It was dangerous with the mess we made of Barlowe, thought it would be safer. Wrong, of course, and since she was—" He lowered his voice in a creepy manner. "—'mortal'... It wasn't any safer here. She went back and was gonna find my sister, who I believe was moving to Utah after everything. Haven't seen any of them since."

"Crazy," Arica sighed, playing with the laces of her boot. "I left my brothers and my mom, and I... Part of me doesn't feel any remorse, just misses them, and part of me wants to scream and cry and beg for forgiveness, but..." she trailed off.

"No, I get it," he murmured, with a reassuring smile.

She looked away from his sympathetic eyes, scared she was gonna start sobbing and force him to comfort her. "How do you stand it?" she whispered, sullen. The day's events and the emotions she'd felt came flooding back so hard she was almost dizzy.

The collapse of the forge, and how close she'd been to drowning in murky water. She'd heard the voice of a dead man as he lay there, rotting. The emptiness realizing that after everything they'd been through; they were the lucky ones.

"Why do you stay here with all these cold, empty, torn-up monsters?" she whispered as tears escaped the gravity of her eyelashes.

"I... It was hard, at first. Everything is so different. I saw firsthand what the Dovevians were doing, and how the Zenians were trying to stop them and right their wrongs. I may know better than anyone how you feel, but I think it's hitting you harder simply because..." He took her wrist and gently squeezed, smiling subtly.

"You haven't been able to see the good we do for the people. All you've gotten to see is the running, the last resorts, the desperate jabs at these so-called villains." He sounded a bit more enthusiastic now. "We exist to be guardians, not warriors. This war is as unnatural as any. It's always been a goal to take over Garal's rule, but until we can, our job, as it's always been, is to take care of DeRael, and her real, suffering people."

She let herself smile a little, if only in response to the excitement blazing in his eyes.

"I had the same mindset you do. I didn't want to turn into some cold and scared outcast. But in the end, I didn't stay because I'd made friends, or because I thought it would be fun, or even because I liked the Zenians. I stayed because DeRael needed me. A lot more than Texas ever did."

She blinked, trying to clear her eyes, and once more looked out into a sparkling sky.

"As soon as we can fight off these devils, and get to Herak's crew, I swear you'll get to see what I'm talking about, okay? We'll find ourselves a city to hide out in, Vanessa always does, and I'll show you that a Zenian isn't an unfeeling monster that hides in swamps, waiting for battle. I'll show you how we care for DeRael. How does that sound?"

She took a deep, calming breath, then smiled. "Thank you, Zak."

"Anytime," he expressed softly. "Seriously." He pulled himself out of her grip so he could give her a tight hug for a second.

It felt so familiar. He was firm under her, a real physical person. No magic, no confusion, no imagination. Solid proof she was okay. That she wasn't completely alone in her own head.

Arica broke from him only after a few long moments. Feeling refreshed, she wiped away her tears. "It is beautiful," she admitted. "And this would make a fantastic camp spot."

"You think this is nice, you should see this spot just around the corner. Come on." He lightly slapped her knee, urging her back to her feet.

They worked their way further to the edge of the plateau.

"It would've been nice, but it's so close to tonight's camp, so—" He cut himself off so suddenly that she could still hear his voice as he dragged her into thick shrubbery.

Thorns tore at her skin as she caught herself on her forearms and knees. Orange light fell over the thick bushes.

"Hey, is that you, Monrow?" called a voice not ten feet away.

Zak still held onto her upper arm, head practically on her shoulder, but neither of them moved.

The light wavered a little, growing slowly closer to their feet.

Arica turned her head as slowly as she could, a branch dragging thin, prickly leaves across her cheek. Her lips touched Zak's brow. She kept her vocal cords still. "Can't you take him?"

"I don't know how many there are," he breathed.

"Monrow?"

The voice was alarmingly closer. They'd be able to defend pretty easily, but Zak was right. How many more were lurking just around the corner? Where had he come from, anyway? Jake had made it sound like there weren't any towns for hundreds of miles.

Then she heard a familiar spine-tingling noise. The metallic click of a pistol's hammer being cocked.

"Shhh," Zak murmured, one finger tapping on Arica's forearm.

There was a shout, but it was distant. The torch was so close to them that Arica could hear the whoosh as its possessor turned to the disturbance.

Then Zak jolted out of the bush like a pouncing tiger and tackled the person to the ground.

Arica pulled herself upright as dirt the consistency of honey overtook a cloaked man, both arms pinned by the blond Zenian. He struggled, but whatever magic compelled the soil to become so carnivorous was too strong.

Zak stood, then kicked a silver gun from the man's grasp. The mud stopped sucking about neck-deep and hardened as if it had never moved. The man's head lolled on his neck.

She couldn't help staring for a long moment. "Well, that's just—"

A few loud shots drew her attention further down the plateau. She could just make out the wavering of shadows in firelight.

"Are we—?" She didn't have to go any further. Zak was already pulling himself into a jog.

They found a body not too much further, dressed in plain, unidentifying clothing. She couldn't tell immediately if he was alive or not but wasn't brave enough to check or ask. A few more slumped here or there, but as they approached the orange signal of life, the noise settled down. They rounded the corner, and it became apparent why.

Vanessa and Rapier paced the circumference of the camp, picking through a dozen still bodies, both with weapons drawn but relaxed to their sides.

Vanessa tossed her loose hair over her shoulder as she acknowledged Arica and Zak. "You're a little late," she stated.

Arica stared at her, more than a little confused, then threw her hands in a gesture behind her. "We... There w... Where did... We were almost attacked over there," she finally spewed out.

"I know. We decided to scout out this spot one more time," Vanessa said with a quick nod.

"You're lucky," Rapier said as he stood, then glanced in her direction, hinting a smile. "*I* wanted to stay in the tent."

Arica approached one body to help but instead picked up the dropped handgun as if it were a moldy piece of bread.

"This is... alarming," she murmured before looking up at her superiors. "Banging around with metal sticks is one thing in a fantasy world, but these bad guys have guns." She carefully set it back down, a growing uneasiness in her stomach. "You guys might be fast, but if someone points a gun at me, I..."

She hadn't thought much of it when Vanessa picked up one of the threatening weapons, but without even looking up from the body, she aimed for Arica.

Her blood ran cold. The bang echoed like the slam of a door in an unoccupied house.

Then both of them looked down at the discharged bullet smoking on the ground a few inches from Arica's boot. "The... y-you... Jake gave me a—"

"High-velocity barrier," Vanessa recited with her, then nodded, discarding the gun so haphazardly it would've made anyone from her hometown cringe and cry.

"Utterly harmless to Zenians and Dovevians alike," she announced, finally sheathing her sword. "Which proves that while these men were here at the beck of our good friends, they were not meant to do any harm."

"Are we sure they're here to spy on us?" Zak asked quietly.

"Is this not the exact spot you scouted this morning?" Rapier countered. "It's been mere hours."

"There isn't a town for hundreds of miles. It can't be chance," Vanessa added with reverence. "Someone has been guiding them close to us, watching. Which brings us to a point I'd hoped to keep until morning, but since we're here... I've a plan for our obvious little traitor."

Rapier was the first to respond to a rustling of bushes somewhere behind Arica, pulling his sword back into a defensive position. But she leapt away from it almost as fast, ready to scurry behind Zak and Vanessa.

A glimpse of gray skin caught in the moonlight for a moment, but it turned out to be just Derrick.

"You're too late," Vanessa called, lowering her weapon upon identifying their ally.

"So I see," the dark man murmured, glancing around at the gathered bodies.

"Next time we'll send out an alarm," Rapier grumbled, shouldering his weapon. He bent down, grabbed a soldier by the collar, and dragged it towards the middle of the small camp.

"I was already close," Derrick said as he grabbed another body.

"Mmm," Vanessa murmured as she folded her arms across her chest, then glanced up at Zak. "I'll remember, next red moon we'll have our own gathering of Ellterians, apocalypses, and god-killers."

Arica's eyebrows lowered. "Apocalypses? God-killers?" she whispered, looking at Zak.

"Don't ask," he growled, slamming his weapon into its sheath. "You don't wanna know."

23

BAIT

Arica awoke almost instantly. It wasn't shocking or confusing, simply asleep one moment, and wide awake the next. Derrick and Zak were also asleep in the tent not used for moon rituals, the only other two outcasts that weren't allowed to sleep with Vanessa. A mess of blankets and limbs made up Zak's sleeping corner, but Derrick's situation was odder. He lay on his back, hands lying on his stomach completely straight with nothing over him to keep him warm. She almost went to check on him, but didn't know if this was abnormal for him.

She rolled her head and shoulders, none of her muscles as stiff or sore as she'd gotten used to. In fact, she felt invigorated, like she could take on a Dovevian or two all by herself. She went to see what was going on during the earliest hours of the morning.

The fireplace inside the other tent was barely warm, but Parel and Aaris sat close to it, cooking on a few flat stones over coals. It seemed about half of the company had already arisen from their places of rest, though a few who hadn't looked close.

She found Jake sitting in the same place he'd been all night.

"Hey."

"What?" he asked, fingering one of the berries cupped in his other hand. The tips of his fingers were all stained a dark purplish color, a bit of the juice dripping from between them.

"Where did you get those?" she asked, her voice quiet.

His eyes flicked above her for a moment. "Parel made them. They're over there. Not the best fruit I've ever had, but I've yet to bend over sick."

She shook her head, trying to ignore how hungry she suddenly was, and how wonderful those looked.

"Wow, so that was... interesting," she mumbled, climbing to her feet.

"Sure," answered Jake passively.

Her face warmed a little, realizing that she'd left rather abruptly with a person who happened to be a man, and never came back. Hopefully, Zak's reputation for skipping rituals was known to be an Ellterian thing.

"Did you sleep on that rock?" she asked suddenly, pointing at the boulder he leaned against.

"Good spinal support," was all he said, stretching out slightly.

"Hey, where's Steen, anyway?" she asked, noticing that while his bag was still where they'd sat, he was not.

"Why would I know? You would if you hadn't just *left* him for Zak," Jake teased, but the words were harsh enough.

Her face flushed. "I-I didn't... Is that what he...? He's not upset, is he?"

"You may not've noticed, but there's a *painful*..." He let his head roll on his neck until he faced her again. "Lack of women around here, so... Well, no, that's it. There's a painful lack of women." He gave her a weird glance, then popped the last berry in his mouth and pulled his feet under him to stand.

"That doesn't mean I *owe* anyone anything," she defended. "Well... maybe an apology."

"I didn't mean to imply so." Jake's eyes may have rolled, then he pointed over at their appointed chef. "Go get something to eat from Parel, and then... maybe figure out why Vanessa is signaling for you."

Arica fingered the book in her lap without actually reading it. A soft, worked piece of paper was tucked in between two pages. The note from the night before. *How are you?* still stared at her in dark ink.

That morning, she'd discovered a small inkpot in the bag. She thought the paper was the only new thing, but must've overlooked the pot. No writing utensils had been with it, but she'd found a small dried stick and whittled it sharp enough to write with.

She grabbed the stick from where it sat by itself on the tent floor next to her.

"What should I write?" she asked aloud. Nobody could hear her because Vanessa's tent was secure and empty. Not even Bialsa was around.

She dipped the stick into the dark ink. She'd already tested it, just a tiny flower in the paper's corner. It wasn't like any ink she'd ever used: thick and almost sticky. But it left a wonderful pitch-black stain on whatever it touched.

What was the point of writing something out, though? She wasn't planning on leaving her things where someone could get to them anymore.

"What if it's the paper, though?" she repeated aloud, hoping it sounded so stupid that she'd dismiss it herself. "Magic paper. The ink appears somewhere else."

It did sound stupid, but she couldn't help feeling uneasy.

Finally, she just carefully folded the note and set it, the pot, and her makeshift pen into the satchel. "This is distracting me from my mission," she said to herself with full determination.

I gotta stop talking to myself. But this is the most boring mission I've ever been on.

Vanessa had already put away the skimpy furnishings and her belongings, only leaving a small chest that was usually loaded onto the horse last. She wasn't one for snooping, but after nearly half an hour, sitting alone was wearing on her. Maybe she could've slept, but that would've defeated the purpose of her presence there.

Bait.

"Okay, no," she repeated, closing her eyes for a moment. *Vanessa and Rapier are out of the way, scouting out our next stretch. Jake is spreading the rumor, which will push them in my direction. If anyone acts suspicious, I call for Jake with Bialsa.*

"Where is she, anyway?" she asked the barely lit tent.

She let out a breath. *Jake's rumor is that Steen thinks we found something huge, something completely game-changing in Santsin Val. Just Vanessa and I went into the vault, leaving them to stand guard. But we won't tell anyone what it was, only that Vanessa is excited about it.*

It wouldn't be so difficult for anyone to believe. Vanessa was in a rush during that morning's packing, and anytime Rapier touched her, she'd be almost bouncing, even if she never broke into a smile. It was *her* part she worried about.

Arica had never been any good at acting, and even though all she had to do was fake knowing more than anyone else about the 'treasure', she wasn't sure she could do it.

She stifled a yawn, looking around the room for something to do. Maybe she could practice magic. At least, she knew she *should*.

The tent flap opened, nearly making Arica jump. *This is it, isn't it?*

Malon stepped inside, remnants of her makeup from the night before all over her face. Her floof of dark hair bragged the effects of the humidity considerably more than Arica's. It probably felt like a wad of pillow stuffing.

"Where's Mistress Damage?" she asked.

"Oh, she already left to scout," Arica answered. Maybe this wasn't it.

"Oh."

Arica sighed as Malon turned and left without another word.

This had all been Vanessa's idea, and maybe it wasn't bad, but what were the chances someone would actually want to get information out of her? She knew nothing. Even if she was Vanessa's most trustworthy partner because of her pathetic magic skills, or whatever it was.

The tent opened again so quickly that she thought Malon had turned around, but instead, it was a face growing in familiarity. Steen.

Arica's cheeks flushed, but he didn't seem to notice or care as he approached. The door fell shut.

I don't want to be alone with anyone. Bialsa?

"I've returned," the giggly voice assured.

She felt a little better with Bialsa there. Jake was sure that the most likely person to be mimicked in order to get information from her would be Callovoi, simply because of the obvious connection they'd made the night before.

"Can't get a moment's peace, huh?" Steen joked almost awkwardly.

"Uh, yeah," she agreed.

She waited until he came and sat near her. Bialsa was nowhere to be seen, but she'd likely slithered into a hiding spot somewhere.

"Have you heard that rumor Jake's been telling? I don't know where he got it, but it wasn't me."

"Yeah, I don't..." Her face warmed, sure she was going to blow it.

"Somebody's up to something. We didn't even go in the vault. It was just Vanessa and Rapier."

She looked at him, eyebrows lifting. His fingers absentmindedly played with the laces on his boots, but he met her glance.

He's not the shifter, she told Bialsa in relief. She relaxed a little. Then Steen slid closer to her.

"Still. I can't help wondering what was in there," he mused, stretching his legs out in front of him. "Vanessa was so excited this morning. Compared to how annoyed she was when we left."

Arica nodded slightly. *Can I tell him about the trap?*

"No, it's safer not to," Bialsa reassured. "No need to let on we're trying to catch the culprit yet."

"I mean, it would make sense," said Arica. "Why would they have a secret vault behind a secret vault if not to hide something powerful?" She wasn't lying, so she wasn't so nervous about saying it.

"Yeah," he agreed quietly. He fiddled with his left hand, pressing his fingers into it like it hurt him slightly.

He would probably be an asset to their plan, even without knowing. The two of them in the tent alone, two of the four who'd even scouted Santsin Val, where someone could interrogate them with no one else even knowing. Hopefully, someone had seen him enter the tent and wasn't keeping it to themselves. Then again, this wasn't the most gossipy group.

"Do your hands hurt?" she asked, if only to break the silence.

"Just sore. It's usual," he dismissed, exposing both palms for a moment.

"How..." Arica caught her tongue, realizing she couldn't even see the gash she wanted to ask about anymore. "How do we know if Vanessa's lying?" she quickly saved.

Bialsa, did you see that? That gash on the heel of his hand is gone. Did he heal it?

"I guess we don't," Steen shrugged. "I guess we could always…"

"No," Bialsa answered evenly. "Not so thoroughly, so quickly."

Arica bit her lip as Steen frowned in thought.

"Maybe we should try to find out, though, just… out of curiosity. I don't like that she's hiding everything from us."

Her heartbeat picked up, but she bravely looked him in the face, betraying no suspicion.

"Me either, but I don't want to poke around. Not with this supposed traitor around. She might get suspicious of us… Like, can you believe how angry she was when we broke the forge?" She silently prided herself on the quick lie.

"She knows it's not you, not with your lack of training," Steen reasoned.

She frowned. *That wasn't what I wanted.*

Then he continued. "It's an old, old place. She had a reason to be upset. Who knows what we could've found."

It's him! Arica called in her own head.

"Jake's on his way!" Bialsa squealed in what felt like excitement. "Don't let him out of your sight for a moment!"

"Well, okay, you're right," Arica continued as if she wasn't aware that he was either not Steen or somehow different from the person she'd worked with the day before. "But it might be a little worse if I'm caught going through her things or something. And what about you? Aren't you worried?"

Steen gestured outwards with his hands. "Almost worth it, don't you think?"

She scowled at him a little. "Whatever."

He smirked a little, pulling his weight to a knee. "Well, I've got to go finish my chores."

"Wait!" Arica yelled suddenly, jumping to her feet enough to startle him. But she had nothing to continue her exclamation as he stared at her in question.

"Yeah…?" he prodded.

"Keep him here!" Bialsa fortified. "Jake's almost here."

"Um…" she reached a hand out towards him. "We're… alone," she enunciated, trying not to clench her jaw. Her pulse was so quick it was making her lightheaded.

Steen also looked conflicted about it but didn't leave yet. "I…"

"Just for a second," she whispered, beckoning with a hand.

"He's just outside the tent, two more seconds," Bialsa reported as Steen took a step back towards her.

"I don't think—"

Sword tip first, Jake swept the tent open and ducked in, cutting off Steen's words and Arica's hesitant smile. Both of them greeted him casually.

"Sorry. Am I interrupting anything?" he asked, his sword lax at his side.

"We were—"

Steen interrupted her with, "Yes, but it's fine."

Jake gestured at the last chest resting on the ground. "Just packing the last."

Arica's eyebrows lowered. Wasn't he going to do something about "Steen"?

The man next to her warily watched as Jake bent down to grab the chest, only at the last second looking up and regarding his friend.

"Hey, while I'm thinking about it," Jake casually addressed. "There's this sharp little chip in my blade. Could you fix it?" It took him barely a stride and a half to reach them. Then he outstretched the sword, holding it perpendicular to his arm.

Steen stared at it distastefully. "Not right now. I'm kind of in the middle of something."

"Use your touch," Jake prodded, the blade getting uncomfortably close to Steen's body. "It'll only take a second."

Arica backed up as he looked at her for help. She certainly felt guilty. Jake was going after him on her word alone, so what if she was wrong? It would probably ruin any tentative friendship they'd worked up.

"Not right now. I'll look at it later in a better light."

Then Jake's sword lithely turned in his practiced fingers, stopping against Steen's neck in only a quarter of a second.

Betrayal crossed his face, but Jake's was blank.

"As your superior officer, I demand that you use your touch this moment, or you will be apprehended," Jake warned coolly.

Arica ran to the other side of the tent just to be out of the crossfire, but Steen silently stared at Jake.

"Jake wants you to take the rope from his belt and tie him up," Bialsa reported.

Arica searched his waist with her sight alone but saw nothing.

"Take the metal off of my skin, I'll do it," Steen bargained. "This is ridiculous."

"Here," Jake directed at Arica. He dug into his front jeans pocket and pulled out a thin rope about a foot long.

She took it, holding it out. "Is this really going to keep him—"

She saw the purple haze around the guilty one, but only a second too late. Air exploded from his personal space, only big enough for Jake to recoil a step, but freed the weapon threatening Steen.

Before Jake could recover, Steen was sprinting for freedom. Arica could only think of failure as she flung her arms outwards, feeling warm and tingly. The tent's loose flaps stiffened as if at attention, sealing the room.

It was so effective that Steen bounced off, nearly throwing himself to the ground, but it was just enough for Jake to slide over. He didn't bother with the sword, instead kicked Steen's unstable feet out from under him before slamming his knees onto his back, pinning him to the ground.

"That was me!" Arica squealed in triumph. "Did you see that?"

She sprinted forward to help, realizing she still held the rope, but Jake snatched it out of her hand before she could do anything herself. It lengthened in his grasp, and he flipped it like a wadded-up sheet. Before long, it was thicker and at least ten feet, still elongating as Jake wrenched Steen's large hands behind his back so he could wind the rope around them.

He stood up, hauling the smaller man up without struggle, but still needed the rope.

"Here, Arica. Wrap it around his shoulders," he ordered, tossing her the end.

Jake grabbed the offender by the neck as Arica started walking around them in a circle, easily ducking under Jake's arm with each rotation.

Nobody tried to say anything, and it was wracking Arica's nerves. The rope slid under her fingers the way she expected it to, but watching the end, it didn't seem to move at all.

"That was good, Arica," Jake finally said. "I'm proud of you."

She didn't respond, but her grin was enough to show her appreciation.

She assumed Jake would stop her when they'd wrapped up their prisoner enough, but it kept going until the rope sheathed his entire torso.

"Here, it needs to be tied carefully," Jake guided, taking over.

Light once more fell into the room as Vanessa entered. She stepped to the side to reveal a copy of their tied-up traitor, only dirtier, with a different tunic and a rag wrapped around his left hand.

The shifter's jaw clenched.

"Well, gentleman," Vanessa sighed, sauntering in on light feet. "We have found our culprit."

"Get everyone out here, *now*," Vanessa demanded of Zak as she passed through the middle of the torn-down camp. Arica followed at her heels, with Jake and Steen hauling the prisoner behind her.

"And if ANYONE disobeys, arrest them."

Arica looked over her shoulder, but instantly regretted it. He was struggling, shifting into different people in a split second each time. Some of them she recognized, some she didn't. He was obviously trying to work his way free, but no matter how large of a person he chose, the ropes binding him would expand, then shrink again, keeping him tightly wrapped. Steen and Jake would just shift their grip in annoyance. For a moment, the shifter turned into the commander, huge and heavy, only for Jake to slam his forearm into his face and force him back to someone smaller.

Vanessa led the way from the tent to the pair of bulky horses they'd been using as pack mules, only pausing long enough to grab an old tree branch thicker than the width of both of her hands.

"Lay him down here," she ordered, pointing to the stone near the large animals.

Jake was less gentle dropping him than Steen, then hurried off as soon as he was free of the burden. Arica could hear him barking out orders.

People gathered as Vanessa vigilantly watched.

Jake returned, so Arica backed away from Vanessa and the discarded Dovevian who looked an awful lot like Kylen, the same mousy braid and dark blue eyes. But the anger on his features as he glared at the ground wasn't something she could've imagined on the young Zenian.

For the tone Vanessa had been using, it was taking too long for everyone to gather. Malon and Skah had shown up quickly, the vampire next.

A hand touched her shoulder, startling her.

"Is he..." Kylen mumbled, leaning over her to get a better look at the shifter who'd copied him. "Man, that's just... wrong."

"Least you didn't have to listen to your own voice," Steen argued from Jake's other side. "*That* was messed up."

Arica had to add her own opinion, shrugging Kylen's hand off of her shoulder. "It was really realistic."

Vanessa's arms crossed, her face blank as she watched her company gathering. "Now, we've only to wait for Ricken, Banen, and Elvy..." she announced to those gathered.

"Do you really think this man is one of them?" Zak asked, closer to her as doubt crossed his features.

Vanessa looked at him, her eyes glinting with mischief, but she didn't answer him directly.

"He fell for a quick setup between myself, Jrasko, and Miss Arica. I doubt he's been able to duplicate anyone for long, so I have every reason to believe that he has replaced and masqueraded as one of us for some time. Maybe for a long time. Your participation and appearance have thus dismissed my suspicions of each of you."

Arica watched Zak sigh in relief as Elvy worked her way through people towards him, combing her fingers through her wet hair.

"But don't expect more information until we've had the time and sources to dispel any other suspicion," Vanessa continued, scanning her underlings carefully. "Kind of you to join us, Ricken."

Arica searched for him, finally spying the dark-haired warrior behind his sister.

"Well, does anyone know where Banen has gotten to?"

Everyone else broke out in worried whispering and Jake shifted his weight, setting his hands on his hips, an inch from his sword.

Vanessa beckoned to Kylen, whispering something when he came toward her. He nodded once and jogged around the horses.

Every morning they had to line up the stuff they were carrying themselves, mostly their personal things, so nothing got left and nobody ended up with way more stuff. This was where Kylen went, carefully picking down the line until he found what he wanted.

Two bags fell at Vanessa's feet, a dark green bag and a smaller brown one.

Arica stared at the shifter, his eyes closed as he lay on the ground as if he knew he was defeated. Or maybe he was planning on how to recover from it.

Vanessa wasted no time going through Banen's bags, crouching down on the ground over them. She tossed out the larger, more useless effects as the entire group waited in bated silence.

Arica didn't know what Vanessa was looking for until a small wooden box made an appearance and was set on the ground. With barely a twitch of her finger, it cracked down the middle, a loud popping accompanying it like a can of soda exploding in the summer sun, but Arica was the only one to startle. The pieces fell to either side.

"She just released the magic in it," Jake explained after leaning over her.

Vanessa dug through the mess, pulling out an innocent enough paper, some little wood sticks; probably pencils, a handful of black-painted coins, and some tiny opaque bottles.

"Well, what was the enchantment?" Arica asked as Vanessa unstopped a bottle and took a whiff, only to cringe and quickly replace it.

Crouching down and setting his elbows on his knees, Jake was barely shorter than her, but at a much better level to talk to her. "Likely either something that keeps it anchored to a spot that another Dovevian has access to or one that lets it and another identical container occupy the same space inside. Or I suppose it could've been one to keep anyone but himself out, obviously not effective."

"Why hasn't anyone, like, named these enchantments to keep them straight?"

"They have," Jake sighed, rubbing his forehead. "But they're in Raellic."

After sweeping all the contents back into the bag, Vanessa stood up to address the group once more.

"We've caught our culprit. But don't think for a moment that my guard will be down, or that I'll be sharing sensitive information. As you've all heard, we found little in Santsin Val but struggle and death. We found the bodies of their commander and his second, with no knowledge of the fate of others."

Vanessa reverently paused as if sympathizing with everyone's silence. The air grew heavier, as impossible as it seemed.

"But press on, we will. As easy as it is to assume, I'll not keep our next destination a secret. We have no choice but to follow the Dovevians' path to Castle Kopion. Just know, not even I know what we'll find. Or if the situation there is the same as here. None of my attempts to reach out have been successful. Thank you for your cooperation. Ready to leave."

Movement exploded throughout the group as they worked to do as she ordered. It wouldn't be too long before they were moving, just waiting for scouts to start off.

Jake was one of the few who didn't move, so Arica stayed next to him until he went and helped Vanessa, who fetched a pair of harnessing ropes from a horse. They each tied one to a side of Vanessa's branch, then tied the other ends to either horse, and their prisoner lengthwise to the stick. They had cut the cart up smaller in order to handle the rougher terrain, so it seemed a plausible solution.

Arica knew it wouldn't be a comfortable ride for him. But it almost sounded better than walking more.

"We'll have to watch him closely," Vanessa advised as she stood back to admire their handiwork. "If he's who I think he is, you won't meet a slicker bastard."

Eyes still closed, but lips moving slightly, he looked like he was meditating. *If he's doing something he shouldn't be, they'll catch on, won't they? Can Dovevians telepathically communicate?*

Jake and Vanessa had all but said there was no way to do so without the andromaes, but were the king's dudes restricted in the same manner?

"Come," Jake barked, snapping her out of her thoughts, but she couldn't tear her gaze from the person. He'd killed someone and pretended to be them. Banen.

Then the color drained from her face.

"Wait, Jake," she gasped, tearing after him as he stalked away. "Wait. Jake, wait. Wait!" She grabbed his arm and used her weight to slow him.

He glared at her tiredly. "We need to—"

"I have something really important to tell you," she blurted. She released him as his eyebrows lowered and he turned closer to her. "When we were in that crypt thing, trying to find a match for the gold seal thing..." Her jaw shifted wordlessly as she tried to form the correct sentence. "I... I saw a body. I think it was Banen."

Arica squeaked in terror as his large hand snatched up her wrist. "You saw a *dead body*, and you didn't think to *mention* it?" he spat.

Her eyes were frozen wide open, but an anger boiled just underneath her fear. "I-I... It was a *crypt*," she yelled.

"That I mentioned had been closed. For a *long* time."

She jerked her hand from his uncomfortable grip and stepped out of reach. Jake's expression humbled to light annoyance.

"Exactly. Why would a fresh body be there? I'm sorry, I don't know how bodies decay in a sealed environment, or whatever, I just..."

"There's nothing we can do now," he dismissed, shrugging. "Thank you for letting me know. Come help. We need to get moving as soon as we can."

24

ANDROMAE OPINIONS

"**I** love the rain," Arica sighed, staring into dully-lit clouds. The old trees drooped their rain-heavy leaves and limbs over the thick, spongy undergrowth. "But this is ridiculous."

As miserable as it was being unable to get dry enough anywhere, she was glad to be out of Akvelia's caves. The ground alone was so soft that she'd gotten a better night's rest than she had since leaving home. So soft she almost worried that she'd walk into a sinkhole, and not notice until she was halfway in it.

The only one really enjoying the lack of sunlight was the vampire, Kasper. She'd spotted him running about effortlessly, bouncing off tree trunks like a brawling kitten. Only when she saw him catch a small rodent of some sort did she stop watching his animalistic behavior so intently.

Letting the tent flap fall to muffle the soft pitter-pattering, Arica retreated into the cold tent. She wasn't the only one wasting time out of the rain. Elvy was in the opposite corner, braiding her fluffy red locks into little rows with painstaking precision, and Ricken had come in to fetch something for his sister but stayed to dry off for a bit.

Malon, Steen, and Jerim were all camp lookouts while Rapier monitored their prisoner, with an occasional checkup from one of the others.

Arica did one of these checkups before going to gather her things more thoroughly but ended up regretting it. The shifter had chosen the commander's physically adept form, down to the same clothing.

The real thing stood not two feet from him, both hands around his sword with the tip buried in the dirt an inch. He barely moved or acknowledged her, but the fake icy blue eyes stared her down intently as if begging her for help through his gag.

She shook off a shiver and headed back to her designated tent.

The air inside felt sticky again, so Arica tried to pull some of the moisture from the air, as Jake had taught her the day before. But all she could do was *think* about gathering it up, unsure if it worked. Well, someone else would notice at some point, anyway.

Wondering why she'd grown bored when the alternative was rubbing deeper sores into her feet, Arica pulled out the little paper from her satchel. She wasn't completely sure, but paper seemed to be quite a rare thing when trekking through a rainforest, so she was saving the suspicious piece to doodle on. So far, she'd drawn quick sketches of flowers and leaves she'd seen on the walks and wavy, unrealistic landscapes which she'd used to practice her shading with the makeshift little pen.

As she unfolded it, she grew more interested and fearful of the little paper. Most of her doodles had been on the back, avoiding the foreign handwriting, but someone else's weren't. Long, detailed stems curled down the edge, growing up towards the letters before blooming out in beautiful long, sloping flowers that, even in black ink, looked vibrant. Almost real.

"Who did this?" she mouthed, staring at the drawing with a bitter expression. It had been in her pocket since the day it had appeared. Nobody else could've held it.

She snatched up the stick, and without any more hesitation or thought, scratched out a response.

Who are you?

It almost ruined the entire page, her ugly letters, but she wasn't playing games. For a long minute, she stared at the page, wondering if more ink would appear.

Ricken rose to his feet and made his way out of the tent.

The page stayed the same.

Arica let it fall to the side, her gaze shifting to the empty satchel. What had Jake told her? Something about an enchantment where two containers could occupy the same space? She snatched it back up, but before placing the page in it, used her limited origami skills from fourth grade to fold it into a rather crude flower. She made sure a petal plainly displayed her question.

"I must be crazy," she mumbled, carefully setting the flower on the bottom of the bag.

She only stared at it for a few seconds before closing it. *How long should I wait?* She was glad that the little white andromae had gone with her master because the last thing she needed was Vanessa finding out she was talking to strangers. Was she even going to get in trouble for it? There had been no outspoken rule against it.

She glanced at the redhead, wondering how long she was going to be working on her hair. It was strange; even without a cellphone and an endless supply of beauty products, Elvy's personality often reminded her of her friends back home. Much tougher, dirtier, but just as haughty sometimes, and almost as giggly when around those she liked. Even while faced with impending danger, as they consistently seemed to be.

Shaking her head to clear her thoughts, she checked the satchel, and her heart skipped.

The paper was gone.

She mentally checked through all of her things, wondering if she was missing anything that she'd placed in it originally, but couldn't think of anything, at least nothing important.

The next minute she spent checking the bag, and glancing at Elvy, hoping she didn't notice the suspicious behavior. But her back was to Arica, sorting and carefully organizing all of her things. She doubted she'd get caught peeking into an empty bag over and over.

Finally, it was back, re-folded into a smooth square with barely a hint of the origami shape she'd made in the soft material.

With shaking hands, she unfolded it, scared of what it was going to say. Maybe scared it wouldn't say anything. But there it was, the same elegant handwriting.

My name would have no meaning to you, should I dare to hope.

Her shaking didn't stop, but her face grew warm.

"If I was back home, and had gotten this in a text, I'd have blocked it by now," she whispered to herself.

Reason was staring her in the face, though. This wasn't her phone; it wasn't at home; it wasn't some stalker, a bored prankster, or a scammer. This was a magic person, talking to her through a magic bag in the middle of a magic war. Maybe someone who could help her out.

So, she wrote: *At least tell me whether you're a good guy or a bad guy.*

The process started again; the wait frustrating her more than it normally would. But there was an answer soon enough.

What is good and bad in a full bloody war? You ask the wrong questions, but the answer you need is this: I am interested in helping you.

She thought for a minute. Who could this be? The man from the lawn came into her mind, the one who'd thrown her the satchel. The handwriting was so delicate, even with the dark ink. She'd never met anyone with such pretty handwriting, let alone a man. It had to be him, though. Didn't it?

You say that like it's a good thing, she scribbled, hoping it was legible. *Whether you're with me or not, you've got ulterior motives for helping me. I doubt it's out of the kindness of your heart.*

Elvy passed over her as she once again placed the paper in the bag, leaving her alone in the cold tent. Only her need for clarity kept up the game.

The paper read: *Would you believe it's merely to satisfy my curiosity?*

What did she know about him, or these people at all? Nothing. The rules didn't apply. So would it be so ridiculous to believe him? She simply wrote: *No.*

So shall it be for your entertainment, my name? You don't know me.

You said that already.

But we've already met.

Arica pressed her lips together. He was just toying with her, wasn't he? *I already assumed you were the man from campus,* she replied.

I said I would entertain you, did I not? What fun would there be in candor?

She rubbed her face, trying to decide what to do. Her sarcastic side was itching to pounce on him, but they were getting nowhere, and the only reason she was doing it in the first place was to gather information. Still, she ended up with something less than helpful.

Maybe I will recognize your name, though. And I'll know you're supposed to be my enemy.

This time, the response broke their rhythm and took longer for her to receive. She'd almost wondered if he'd given up when it returned, mostly full but folded up with a crisp, clean page just like it.

If that's how you feel, I think I'll keep it to myself.

If it would be this difficult to get a name from him, then she wouldn't get anything out of him other than frustration.

Arica took the blank page to write her response on. *Why? I already know you aren't a Dovevian.*

What makes you so sure?

She thought for a bit before she answered. Was this sensitive information? She considered her phrasing, hoping she wasn't betraying anything this way. *You met me in my hometown. You obviously weren't from that century, or the planet. And I know the Dovevians don't know about Ellteria, or whatever you want to call it.*

She felt confident about her discretion until she saw his response.

What makes you think we don't know?

"Oh, no," Arica whispered to herself. Whether on purpose or not, he'd used "we" referring to the Dovevians. But what was worse, if they *were* aware, Vanessa had to be warned *immediately*, even if she didn't want to admit she was talking to potentially dangerous strangers and giving away information.

They can't know, she jotted almost frantically. *Garal has made no move to take over or take on any presence there.*

The wait for his response was the longest yet. She didn't realize just how worked up she was getting before she wiped sweat from her hairline.

Finally, it came, but instead of the papers they'd been using, there was just a small torn piece.

I no longer hold an interest in the king's endeavors. If he wants to know, he can find out for himself.

Then she found the full page again, with additional dialog. *I am not the king's lapdog.*

I didn't mean to insult you. I just don't know you. What do you want? She sat back after it was back in the satchel. Was this a good thing, or a bad thing? The king didn't know. That was a pro. But how long was it until this guy spilled it to him?

What would it take to prove my curiosity to you?

Your name, your touch, your private journal, maybe even your still warm heart. Without even thinking, she delivered it into the bag. He was starting to really irritate her, and she wanted him to be aware.

My, you've quite the price, darling, but I'll see what I can do. Though, I should warn you. Just touching my heart would corrode yours.

So you are a Dovevian, she confirmed, hoping he wouldn't start over again.

I never said I wasn't.

"What do you want from me?" she angrily enunciated as her fingers scratched out the words. She took a breath, knowing this wasn't a good way to feel, even towards an enemy.

Nothing, the message said, but it wasn't all she found in the bag this time.

A small device lay in the bottom, circular like a Frisbee, split down the middle with only a small ball hinge that let the sides grind against each other in opposite directions.

She went to scribble out her confusion again when she noticed he'd added more.

Do you trust me now?

Glancing at the disc, she didn't know the answer.

I don't know what this is.

Something that helped us, but will now help you. Well? Do you trust me?

Again, pushing her towards his unknown goal.

If I say yes, what terrible thing will you do to me? What crucial information will you extract from me and use to kill all of my friends?

I see you've been welcomed to DeRael properly.

She couldn't help smirking a bit. *Is your handwriting getting sarcastic, or is it just me?*

I digress. My answer is, once again, nothing. I have no need for power. My mortal needs are extravagantly met. My only intention is my own amusement.

So I'm just a toy to you?

If you'd like, darling, but I think of it as investing in a future partnership.

She smiled in modest triumph. *See, now your intentions are coming out. But I'm not taking over both groups with you to form Lise's Evil Mercenaries Incorporated.*

Why is it called such?

Because you're Lise?

I am not.

She lied back down on her bedding in defeat. *Worth a shot*, she tried, using her upright knees as a desk.

I am also not trying to take over anything. Except for your trust.

Why me? Why do you want to help me? Why do I need to trust you? We're strangers.

The paper was missing for a long while this time. It was a good thing they were taking the time to scout.

Shall I be honest? Since I'm demanding such trust from you?

Yes, probably.

She expected some sort of confession, but all he said was: *I have another gift for you.*

A quick search of the bag made it apparent that it was still empty, save the other paper.

What is it? she asked.

Something I made. Trust me.

You're just words on a paper that keep magically appearing.

Am I? I do have a name. I'll tell you, eventually. Here, as promised.

She looked again, but there was nothing, so she set the paper back.

If there was anything dangerous, she'd go straight to Vanessa or Jake. If she died, well, at least it was just her and not everyone there.

She waited a few long minutes before checking again, wondering what on earth she was trying to achieve this way. But when she did, there was a piece of jewelry with it. A simple, fragile silver cuff with little blue gems dotting the middle.

Use it. I'd hate to see someone so pretty face down in the mud, back full of arrows and bullets.

He didn't need to know she wouldn't wear the cuff, but part of her wondered if it mattered. She stared at it. *I'm in so much trouble.*

Vanessa stormed between the soggy tents, mud caked to her knees and splattered across the rest of her. Behind her, Jake followed with longer, slower strides, and even though he looked much calmer, *he* was the one with blood and dirt smeared across his face.

Arica felt like she'd gone unnoticed as their leader went through the camp with a bloodlust in her eyes and her jaw locked tight.

"What happened?" Arica asked as Jake approached, slowing. Rapier paced past him, looking almost as irritated as his superior.

"We were ambushed by a few of the Dovevians. Nothing gigantic, but they knew where we were headed. Vanessa had to pull back sooner than we wanted. We never even got a good look towards Kopion. They shouldn't've known we were there. Steen was the first. He barely made it, but he'll recover quickly under aid, I think."

He finished, and both of them looked in the direction Vanessa had stormed, then started a mutual dash after her.

"Does he still look like the commander?" Vanessa demanded as she passed Kylen, who barely managed a nod before she wrenched the thin blanket from the sitting prisoner.

Sure enough, it was still Rapier's doppelgänger, down to the outfit.

Vanessa stood over him as a crowd gathered, staring blankly. Then she looked up and spoke a foreign phrase.

As if he understood, Rapier balked, but Jake pounced like an awaiting tiger and tackled the commander to the ground.

"Vanessa... please," he begged as his hands were pinned. Jerim and Derrick came to Jake's aid at his request and helped drag him to his feet.

"He's trying to create a rift between us," the blond said breathlessly. "Ask me anything."

The crowd that had gathered around them was silent as Vanessa looked over her shoulder to him. Her arms folded, and she took a few steps. "Sabina," she called, her gaze trained on him. "Make yourself known, andolviam."

As requested, a slate blue hawk tore into the air, not from either Rapier's direction, but Zak's. She perched on a tent pole a few feet above all of them.

"Can you discern these two on your own?" Vanessa asked clearly.

The hawk's feathers ruffled, but Arica couldn't hear anything.

"You all insist on remaining mute?" After a long moment, she resituated herself in front of Rapier. "It's almost as if they feel unsafe to allow anyone else into their network. Almost as if someone could've seen things they normally wouldn't know."

Rapier's stance drew more confident as he gazed at her. "Then bring me back to your tent. Whatever I need to do, I'll do it, I can't stand this, you need people you can trust."

Sour guilt rose in Arica's chest as she watched him stand his ground under Vanessa's accusations. But a soft smirk slowly passed over Vanessa's face as she took a step backwards.

"What do you think, Jrasko?" she asked lower, then glanced back to the Rapier tied on the ground. "Would he be desperate enough to replicate our relationship?"

"I wouldn't put it past the little creep," Jake said, his grip on the commander unwavering.

Vanessa shook her head, then waved a hand at Derrick. "I'm done playing games. Bring them together."

They complied, dragging the standing man to the ground next to the gagged one.

"Why doesn't she have him prove he's got his touch?" Arica asked, and out of instinct expected Jake or Bialsa to be there to answer. Neither were, but Steen glanced up at her.

"I would guess—"

"I took it from him," Vanessa announced, staring Arica down with a proud tilt to her chin. "Well, Mr. Maloney did in my stead. With this man caught, I decided it was safer to keep him from influencing anyone with what little control he has over it." She glanced at both Rapiers, then back at Derrick.

"It will hurt him," the dark man cautioned.

"I know."

She stepped back, and like a wave, the crowd of Zenians fell back with her, giving Derrick more room around the pair of men. Even Jerim let go of their prisoner, trusting his tied hands to keep him on the ground.

Arica expected something dramatic. Some booming power, an explosion or a whoosh, but the magic he used crept on them, silent and slow. A soft mist gathered at its master's feet, not unlike the revenant's deadly fog. Tentacles of darkness grew from it, reaching out for the identical pair.

Derrick barely moved a muscle.

A silent tornado of smoke snaked around them, hiding them in darkness. A gasping breath, the breather shrouded. The smoke roiled as if alive. A flash of white, almost a pair of eyes in the darkness.

Arica took an involuntary step backwards into someone.

A twitch of Derrick's hand, or maybe not even that, and the thick darkness dissipated.

One of the Rapiers fell over, his body convulsing as if wanting to throw up, but unable to. The other, the one who until minutes before was free, was untouched.

She pointed, but people were already on their way to grab him. "Nobody takes an eye off of this one. He's the shifter."

Elvy and Skah on either side jumped for the struggling false commander, reinforcing the fact he'd lost and wasn't getting away.

Aaris tore the gag from Rapier's mouth and helped lift him from the dirt.

"Seize Malon," he groaned before Aaris was even untying him. Vanessa was at his side in the next moment, pushing him upright. His eyes were slit in pain as reddish blood dripped from his nose.

Chaos erupted as Parel and Damad, closest to the young woman, weren't about to disregard the commander's orders. Ricken jumped to her protection and Skah let go of the standing Rapier to reinforce.

"Stand down," Vanessa ordered, drawing her short sword as she jumped to her feet. She took two steps after the boys before they grudgingly let them restrain Malon, even without an explanation from the commander.

Then she turned back to their actual prisoner as Rapier's hands went free and they passed the ropes over.

Arica jumped as a hand touched her shoulder. Jake was still closer to the middle in front of her. She thought no one else was behind her.

"Take these," a voice whispered soft enough she couldn't discern the voice's owner. "You're the only one I trust with them right now."

She twisted her head over her shoulder as a hand slipped into her palm.

Zak's expression was serious, concerned almost. "Yeah?"

"Sure," she managed, expecting him to slip something small into her fingers. But his warm hand felt empty. He held it there for a moment, but she kept her own limp. It felt tingly, like holding a vibrating phone too long. She desperately wanted to ask what he was doing, and why it required skin contact, but his stealth kept her from drawing any extra attention.

As soon as he let go of her, he casually took a few long steps closer to his original position, leaving her wondering what he'd done. A quick scan of her hands proved they looked no different.

At Vanessa's orders, they instead used the enchanted rope on Malon, who had a resting glare as Jerim shoved her around. The shifter was just restrained with a pair of wide cuffs.

"Take them both to my tent," Vanessa ordered flatly.

Nobody wanted to argue, and she didn't give them a chance to, but even as Damad and Jerim hauled the prisoners up, Skah and Ricken were close behind, eager to keep track of Malon.

Jake bumped Arica's arm, nodding in the same direction they were going when she looked up.

"Let's go listen," he said.

"As long as we don't get in trouble..." she mumbled, following along behind him. She looked at her hands once more, but they were unchanged.

They crowded into the small tent. Jerim and Damad took their leave. Rapier entered last, and while dazed, he didn't look particularly hurt. Vanessa immediately looked to him for an explanation.

"It wasn't complicated," he said, dabbing at his bloody nose with a sleeve. "At first, Asriel tried to bribe and threaten me. It was too late that I realized he was only distracting me. It was then Malon knocked me out and helped trade our places." Then he looked over at Ricken, who scowled so hard he looked like he should've been the villain in a cheap movie. "I think she's been taken over by Anraquella."

Vanessa nodded in thoughtful agreement. "Anraquella would've had a chance to possess her in Neva, so perhaps she's been passing back and forth. So long as we keep her cuffed, they're one man down."

"So are we, though," Arica pitched in without thinking.

"I prefer our chances without Anraquella even without Malon," Vanessa said in finalization. Her hand waved, and the air around the pair clouded like a bubble, then darkened until they were barely visible. Then she held out a hand to Ricken and Skah on the other side of them. "Will you please go through your sister's things and bring me anything that seems even slightly suspicious or unfamiliar?"

"I will," Ricken mumbled obediently, his scowl barely lessening.

"They didn't expect so many of us this morning," Jake mused aloud, earning a brief nod from Vanessa.

"We were lucky they let little Ransom lead," she agreed. "It may have gone differently otherwise."

Jake lifted his chin with a haughty expression. "And for perhaps not the last time, my hesitation letting Rapier whisk you off has paid off."

Vanessa dismissed him with a wave, then set the hand against her lips, looking down at the Dovevian pair.

"What do we do about Anraquella?" Rapier then asked, as if he was the only one who wanted to get things done.

"As I said, as long as she's under a field or shackled, she can't pull herself back into her own body. So, we'll keep them together and as protected as we can. Hopefully, there are no more surprises meant for us."

Then she looked at Malon's bodyguards and bowed her head slightly. "Thank you for your concern. You may leave now. She's in fair hands."

Arica looked away, feeling bad for the pair, but they left without a fuss. It wasn't until the tent's flap was securely closed that Rapier turned to Vanessa with a proud look in his eye.

"I heard them talking when I was barely conscious. It was brief, but it's news all the same. The Dovevians are holding siege against Castle Kopion. They've been trying to break into the tunnels underneath, but they're too broken up and collapsed."

"I find it amusing they've the patience for that."

Rapier shrugged. "Unfortunately, they have all the time they want. They have the king's mortal army surrounding it, and their own barrier. It sounded like they haven't killed anyone, and aren't really sure who's in there. So they may be fighting for an empty castle."

"I doubt they would go to so much trouble unless they knew at least *someone* was there," Jake reasoned. Then his head and shoulders violently shuddered.

"You okay?" Arica asked.

"Headache suddenly. It's nothing," he dismissed as Rapier continued.

"Well, whoever is there, they're not coming out. And we won't be able to get in until we dispose of the Dovevians."

"If I knew for sure who this was..." Vanessa glanced over her shoulder and into the corner that withheld the pair.

"It must be Asriel. I can't imagine anyone else has gotten this same magic," Rapier said, but Jake shook his head, arms folded as he leaned against the sturdy tent wall.

"There was another a few years ago that had to have touched their target," Jake said quietly, closing his eyes. "And the one who didn't actually change, but projected the image into your mind."

"As hard as it is to believe, it is certainly becoming a more common variant of the metamorphen touch," Vanessa agreed lightly. She stared at the shifter, one hand rubbing something small in her palm, the other clenched into a solid ball.

Jake let himself drop into a crouch, squinting his eyes like they hurt.

Rapier looked at her, his expression cold. "Make him tell you."

There was a long pause, but in the end, she nodded towards the pile of deceitful Dovevian.

Rapier got a hold of the shifter as their cocoon dissipated once again, then hauled him to his feet. He'd kept the commander's base look but now had darker hair, smaller eyes, and a sneer that looked nothing like the usual professional look.

He threw him into the dirt, his hands unable to keep him from planting face first.

"Get up," Rapier growled, kicking the prisoner's legs.

Vanessa suddenly moved, grabbing him by the front of the shirt and throwing him upwards in an impressive display of strength. "Show me your face," she spat, with no room for reasoning.

"I'd rather provoke more anger and fear," he whispered evenly, his smile nothing but pleasant.

She pulled a short knife from her belt in a flash, then slashed it towards him. He covered himself with his arms, so the blade slit through the fleshier part of his forearm.

Arica gasped, her feet pulling her body back flush with the wall of the tent.

"Change!" Vanessa ordered.

"Knock it off," Jake mumbled, but he didn't direct it at Vanessa, more into his hands as if talking to himself. "*Knock it off.*"

Blood splashed onto the ground as Vanessa rounded again, her jaw offset. This strike she directed more towards his hand. The next was closer to his elbows, slicing both even as he stumbled backward.

Rapier stood, his hands clenched, eyes trained vacantly on the shifter without making the slightest move to help.

"Jake," Arica said, kneeling next to him.

His mouth was open slightly, locked as tightly as his eyes, until he forced a few words. "Try to touch her. It's... Bialsa."

"Bialsa... why?" She touched his knee softly enough that it wouldn't've bothered a dozing kitten, but it fell under her weight, steadying on the ground instead. He was shaking his hands like he was trying to concentrate, but he still had a pained expression.

Arica stood up as Vanessa grabbed the shifter by the shirt and pressed the knife against his throat, her thumb against the flat of the blade.

"I'll take all too much pleasure from killing you," she hissed viciously.

Arica's mind went a mile a moment. She certainly didn't want to get close to a woman wielding a weapon so carelessly, but couldn't come up with a better plan. She snuck up behind her.

"Arica," Rapier growled scarily enough that she stopped in her tracks, her eyes flicking upwards. His glare was harsh, and she kept the eye contact but ultimately decided she had to stop her leader regardless of consequences. She jumped forward, only after remembering the importance of skin contact. She decided to grab her by the skin just under her sleeve above her elbow.

There was no instant reaction. In fact, Vanessa didn't seem to notice that she was being touched.

"Perhaps we'll see you when you're drained of your blood."

Arica felt different. It wasn't entirely clear, but she could feel the intensity of the anger inside the woman like the sun blazing directly on her skin. She could feel the hurt and reason behind it, the desperation for the justice this death would bring, though it felt disjointed like it wasn't hers to feel.

Maybe not even Vanessa's.

Her breath slowed, trying to keep her heartbeat from going crazier than it already was. But this wasn't all she did. She reached away from the heat, pulling at the calm and wisdom, things huddled in the very corners of Vanessa's mind to make room for the rage. It dampened, suffocating under Arica's rearrangement.

Vanessa took in an impressive amount of air in one breath, one backwards step righting her footing. Arica tightened her grip, just in case.

The knife fell from Vanessa's hand, then she whirled to Jake bent on the ground.

Rapier shoved her out of the way, grabbing the shifter on his own.

"My hand," Vanessa demanded breathlessly, desperately taking Arica's fingers. "Don't let go."

She led her to the corner closest to the tent opening, where an old-looking chest awaited. She flung it open and dug around with one hand. Arica knelt just to keep her arm from being bent awkwardly as she held on.

Then Vanessa pulled out a small leather bag and tossed it on the ground. It was wide, but barely two inches long. Regardless, she reached in and stood up, pulling out a familiar golden greatsword as if from the ground itself.

Arica had no idea where this was going even as Vanessa dragged her back towards the middle of the tent, then slammed the point of the blade into the dirt.

"Let go and stand back," Vanessa requested. She seemed to be entirely in control again, and Arica didn't know what was going to happen, so she obliged, walking herself into the corner.

Vanessa placed both hands on Skotjretant's hilt, then stood with her feet apart. She uttered a quick sentence in another language.

A wave of energy visibly pulsed from the ground around the sword, but she couldn't feel it as it passed over her feet.

Vanessa let go of the greatsword and backed up a step or two as a white snake as thick as Arica's leg and twice as long as Jake was tall whipped under the edge of the tent. Porcupine-style bristles sprang up along her back as she twirled around the sword, coiling her body in a circle without actually touching it. Once the full length of her body piled halfway up the weapon, she lifted her head and bared long fangs, but not at her summoner, instead at the Dovevian with red, dripping wounds along his arms.

Rapier released him and stumbled back, grabbing the edge of the cot instead.

A tiny bat dropped from a pocket in his cloak and burst into a large gray-blue hawk mid-air before perching on the pommel of the sword.

A rusty bobcat shouldered into the tent, paws bigger than its face. It bounded up to the other two andromaes, then lazily sat against the snake.

"How *dare* you," Vanessa snapped. "You refuse to speak for three days, then pull a stunt like this?"

Bialsa's scaly head turned to her master, fangs still extended. They stared each other down for a moment before Vanessa shook her head. "Speak to all of us so we can hear your childishness."

Arica jumped when the ice-blue snake eyes turned to her.

"We want this cretin done with!" the girly voice projected to the room's occupants.

Her pointed head faced back to the shifter, on his rear in the dirt, blood smeared across his body.

Jake finally stood up, but he looked worn out and out of breath.

"There's no use keeping him, we've got him, why not rid us of him now?" demanded a voice that was only different from Bialsa's with a note indicating haughtiness.

Vanessa's arms crossed, her body language difficult to read. "And you, Rune? What say you?"

The bobcat looked over his shoulder at her. "I don't want to intrude." His voice was still barely different, high and feminine. "But... Would it be too much to disable his powers?"

Vanessa's chin rose slightly.

The tent's light level increased as Zak parted the entrance. "I don't mean to... Rune, you *are* here. He was panicking..."

"They all were," Rapier said with a slight, tired nod. Then he beckoned Zak in and the tent closed.

"I know how the three of you hate the Dovevians, especially this one." Vanessa nodded once, her voice sharp. "But you will *never* give me orders again. Bialsa, you know better, especially after last time. Sabina, I never thought you'd put Jadrion's feelings behind yours."

Bialsa's intimidating jaws snapped shut, and Sabina ruffled her feathers, shrinking her body in on herself.

Then Vanessa looked at the bobcat. "Rune. Your chaos did not help. In fact, Jrasko looks rather beaten. But at least you were trying to cool off the others. Thank you."

Last, strangely enough, she rounded on Arica. "And you." Her tone was calmer, her eyebrows rising. "You used an emotional power."

Her face flushed hot, unsure how to respond when Zak shuffled nervously and spoke up. "I... I gave them to her. They're Rapier's. I heard the andromaes grumbling, as you all did, and decided they might help in the hands of someone who was unaffected."

Vanessa gave him a curt nod.

"They weren't yours to give," Rapier argued quietly.

His superior whirled to face him. "And mine? Were they mine to give? After abusing them, I didn't want to give you much of a say."

Arica cast her eyes on the ground. Had he really done something so bad as to warrant his own touch being taken?

Vanessa's next words were calmer, but no less commanding. "You may return them to him, Zakary, whenever you're able."

As she finished her sentence, a dusty gray rabbit wriggled its way into the tent, then hopped toward the trio of andromaes on huge back feet, somehow ignoring that all three forms could easily snap it up for dinner.

"Oh, my," Vanessa said as it took an adorable leap onto the top layer of the white snake and faced Bialsa head-on.

It then turned, sniffing the blade with a quivering nose, and looked up at the high master.

Her lips parted, and Arica could only guess that it was talking to her.

Then she walked forward, hands held out to the strange animal.

"Garient, Colten's andromae," she murmured. "He must've been just close enough to feel the summon."

"But... why's he..." Zak mumbled in confusion, but he didn't finish the thought.

"The andromaes don't die with their owner because of loyalty or mental connection," Vanessa answered.

Garient sniffed at her outstretched hands, then hopped into them. Bialsa unraveled herself, shrinking in on herself until she was a much smaller snake lying at Rune's feet.

"Their lifespans are only about eighty years naturally. They connect with us and feed off on our immortality. When we die, it severs this connection, and they die with their source of life." She cradled the bunny to her chest, where it grew longer front paws, stretching out. The nose flattened, the ears receding into the skull until it more closely resembled a small pointy-eared dog.

"Garient was with Colten only a few years. His own lifespan isn't up yet."

"What happens to him now, then?" Arica asked, frowning at the still animal.

"He'll either link with another Zenian or run off into the woods and live a normal andromae life," Vanessa said.

"Good to see you again, Garient," said one of the andromaes. She could only guess that it was Sabina. "But what are we going to do about..." The hawk turned its head backwards to look at the Dovevians.

Vanessa took a few steps, the little dog jumping from her arms as she went.

She stood over the bleeding Dovevian, then set her boot on his shoulder. "Well, what will it be? Will you show us your true face? Or shall I sic my hungry andromaes?"

As the shifter looked at her with a face of disgust, it changed, not the expression but the entire shape of it. His hair grew out and darkened, his muscles shrinking somewhat. He ended up a thin man, about Vanessa's height, with shoulder-length hair the same color as hers, and a humbly handsome triangular face.

Unlike just about everyone she'd gotten a close look at, he didn't seem to have a single scar or mark, and even the open wounds on his arms healed over remarkably fast.

"As I thought." Vanessa grabbed him by the front of his new purple tunic and hauled him up.

Everyone was silent as she dragged him back out of the tent, then followed behind her out of a mix of obedience and curiosity.

Arica looked back at Malon for a moment. How fast someone could be taken down on a mere word. Something moved in the corner of her vision, drawing her attention to the middle of the tent.

A tiny navy blue bat clung to the canvas, shivering. She wouldn't've thought much of it if not for the coloring. It watched her.

Another andromae?

"Uh... hey, Jake," she called, staring at it for another long second before turning.

Zak stopped her at the entrance, holding out a hand. She knew exactly what he wanted and gave him skin contact.

"You used 'em good," he mumbled, staring at their hands as if this was going to help him see what he was doing. He let go almost as quickly.

"I didn't know what I was doing," she said breathlessly. A cold, empty feeling washed over her like she hadn't eaten or inhaled in a week.

Jake stepped closer, pulling his gaze from Commander Rapier. "Yes?"

She stared at him. "What?"

"You called my name."

Arica watched his eyebrows lower, then glanced at Zak, who nodded for a second.

Jake shifted, leaning an arm on his sword. "What did you need?"

"I... don't remember," she mumbled.

"It's okay," Zak said, setting a strong hand on her shoulder. "Sometimes losing magic, even if it isn't yours, can be... traumatic. We'll get you some food." He waved a beckoning hand and followed Vanessa.

She stood just past the cold fire pit, still clutching the prisoner in front of the gathered company, which looked like it specifically waited for an address. "I'd like to introduce you to our newest solved problem." She jerked his face up the chin so he could see the group better, and the majority could catch a look of his face of defeat.

"This is Asriel. Many of you have heard of him, but for obvious reasons, have yet to meet him as he was born. He is a master of physical form, my elder brother, and, most importantly, the right-hand man and spy of King Garal."

Arica grabbed her own arms, trying to shield them from the cold. The crowd looked neither impressed nor anxious.

"This is good news for us," she began softer, then looked behind her to Jadrion. He came forward, taking Asriel by the shoulders and giving her use of her hands again.

"They've always been tricky... but this is almost *desperate*. They're pulling out all the stops, which means we're on the right track. It means there's something worth fighting over in Kopion, and that's likely at least *some* of our brethren. But as fortunate as I feel for having found out about these two, I'm also disturbed by it." She looked over at Rapier, who sported a worried stare holding the Dovevian. "The little I've heard from Kopion almost concerns me; I'll not deny it. We have to be prepared for war."

With this, she turned on her heels and stalked to Jake. "Make sure we're all rounded up. We march immediately."

With a stiff nod, Jake left to do as told, but Arica felt Vanessa's gaze and stayed put.

"I... I can barely use a sword," Arica piped up without encouragement, her pulse quickening. "I have no actual power. I can't do any... 'war'."

Vanessa placed a few fingers on her lips, staring vacantly at the ground. "You'll have a bodyguard, and we'll spend the next few nights in full training. Dinner will be quick tonight, and we'll have a hard start in the morning." Then she looked up, her expression blank.

"Ready to leave. Gather your strength for a few minutes. Maybe I'll have some time to teach you as we go."

Arica nodded, realizing she'd given her an order not unlike those received by everyone who'd already left. She went without another word.

25

COMING CLEAN

A rica looked over the tops of hundreds of flourishing green trees from the plateau they'd stopped at for the night. It was so much flatter than she was used to, so different from the towering mountains back home. She'd never known that her line of sight could reach so far.

The evening before, they'd sent Jake and Aaris ahead to search for signs of struggle and Dovevians, and they'd found the distant castle. From their position on the top of the bluff, several of them said they could see the landscape of it, but to Arica, it all looked the same.

Still, she looked. She looked until each tiny green leaf faded into each other, and soon trees blended into one another before whole plains of land were tiny pinpoints. Even after Zak had pointed in the direction and tried to guide her eyes to the hypothetically distinct patch of land around the castle, her brain wasn't having any of it.

Her calves ached, and the blisters on her heels couldn't be soothed by Jake's oils anymore, but she felt better standing static for those few minutes. The littlest bit of bending and her knees would creak, she could already tell. Besides, the weak sunlight felt good on her dirty skin.

"I'd kill for a burger and a milkshake," she whispered into the wind, hoping some helpful genie was listening to her wishes.

Instead of focusing any longer on her growing craving for dairy and sugar, she considered the problem of her illicit pen-pal. That chilly morning she'd found herself with a few extra minutes as she cuddled in her cloak. It was a mistake to make contact. Even with her intention to draw more information out of him, she'd only given out more and frustrated herself.

She pulled the folded papers out of her pocket, then stepped a few yards to a tree with a trunk sturdy enough to rest on.

Are you awake? she'd asked after five minutes of reasoning. *Hello* was too cold. She wanted him to think she trusted him, but *hey, what's up?* was too pally and left room for misunderstanding, even if he'd spent more than a few minutes in the real world.

I'm not a vampire, he'd answered, to which she'd both thought and wrote; *I think you've just given more away.*

You've probably more clearly seen the only vampire in our following, anyway.

She'd thought about this but ended up choosing honesty. *Really, I didn't get a significant look at you. All I know is you're tall. And kind of ripped.*

Ripped? He'd only asked as if this had a speckle of importance.

Strong, muscular. For knowing of my world, you don't get a lot of the lingo.

I've not spent much time there, to be true. Was this all you wanted of me?

She'd paused, wondering the same. *You patronize me. Why not the other way around?*

I thought the Zenians were the 'good guys', or are you finally reconsidering?

I've always wondered, she'd told him realistically. *How do I know who is and isn't? Then again, you're the ones killing left and right 'cause it's fun.*

I kill no one for fun alone. Either way, you're welcome to join me anytime; I'll show you who's being unnecessarily aggressive to the other side.

This is where she'd stopped, sweaty and nervous. He wanted her to join their cause, after all. But even in her worries about whether the Zenians were 'good' enough, she knew as a fact that the Dovevians were not.

She continued to stare at the conversation. He'd had the effect on her he'd wanted, she was sure of it. She hadn't gotten the bravery to reply. Until reading through their conversation again in the sunlit trees.

I actually wanted to ask about the jewelry; she scratched out before quickly stowing it in her bag. She looked around again, checking for peepers. The camp still settled below her, but that also meant there was a better chance of someone seeing and questioning her behavior. It didn't stop her.

Yes? Was all it asked of her.

What is it?

Try it on, he replied simplistically.

Her fingers reached into the satchel for the smooth metal band. It was really pretty. But she wasn't brave enough.

She tried again. *But what does it do?*

Try it on and find out.

No.

You don't trust me.

You're a stranger that won't tell me the truth. So no.

I haven't lied once.

She looked up from the paper, her eyes squinting hard. Well... he may have been right because he'd told her practically nothing.

I know, she finally wrote.

But you have.

Sweat beaded on her forehead, her whole body flush. Had she? Even upon re-reading all of their previous conversation, she didn't feel as if she'd said that much. Had she gone overboard and accidentally given something away without even realizing? Those people were master manipulators. They could probably take away a million things from her simplest answers, the simplest questions. Eventually, she went to respond, but the paper wasn't there anymore.

It returned a few moments later with a new message. *Have I scared you? I meant no harm.*

No, but I'm still wary of you. You talk like a friend. But I know we're on different sides.

We are friends, regardless of sides. And regardless of sides, I intend to help you.

Why?

Darling, we've been through this.

Tell me your name.

And this, maybe you've a partiality for tedium?

She let out a long sigh as someone called her name. *Can I be honest?* Back in the bag, the paper went. She hoped it was quick, so nobody approached her while writing.

Please, read the paper.

Then she picked up her writing utensil and scratched out a final response.

You're confusing me completely. I honestly don't know what to do with myself. Part of me wants to believe you, trust you, and help the Zenians with your help. But everything I've learned about this place, especially today, is that the Dovevians, the guys out to get us, will do anything to harm and infiltrate us. I'm not the first person you've tricked. And even if I don't know your name, and I can't ask anyone about you, I do know one thing. You've got to be pretty desperate to come to ME to get what you want.

She slammed the paper back in the satchel. Tears streamed down her face.

Her eyes shut. They were getting to her, and she didn't even need to fight them off with a sword, though she may have preferred it.

Then she gathered all of it up into her arms, carefully tucking it so nothing could fall out, and raced further into camp.

Parel was making dinner with whatever their hunters had scavenged, as he usually did, but the only other one even close to the fire was Kylen.

She continued her search, sticking her head in both closed tents and peeking into Vanessa's open one where Vanessa and Derrick knelt over a rather gory gash in Elvy's thigh. She found several people doing various things dotted about, but not the one she wanted.

As she was about to yell his name and declare him missing in action, she heard a yell of triumph from behind a tent and went to investigate.

A patch of flat ground reached to the horizon for about twelve feet before what she could only assume dropped to a steep incline. Gravel made up the ground of a soft slope to the left, the wet forest reaching towards them to the right. Probably the reasoning behind the unsheathed weapons lying next to Jake and Zak. Their attention remained on a little wooden box between them, and the dozen colorful dice scattered inside of it.

"Hey, uh, Jake," Arica said as she approached.

He responded without looking up. "Yeah?" A few of the little dice moved on their own.

She twisted her ankles, anxiety and embarrassment reddening her face. "I… need to talk to you."

Zak grinned at his opponent as Jake leaned away from the game, rubbing his stubbly jaw.

"I'm in the middle of something," he mumbled, glaring at the unrelenting box.

"But... I really need to talk to you, please. Now, please. Right now."

The calm urgency in her voice was enough to get him to look at her, but she wasn't sure he was going to move.

So she jerked her head and started up the gentle slope, hopefully towards a little privacy. It took a moment of held breath, but soon she could hear him following.

There were plenty of trees to conceal them, but she didn't want to hide so far that if they were in trouble, nobody would find them. Jake didn't argue or question her as she pulled him behind an old, rough oak tree almost wide enough to hide both of them completely. Then she turned, and without saying a word or even stopping to wonder how he'd react, held out an armful of trinkets and pages.

"Uh... what is all of this?" he asked, fumbling to catch it all as she forced it into his hands.

"I've been secretly talking to someone I believe is a Dovevian," she blurted in monotone.

Against her assumptions, his expression stayed neutral, but he lifted the first page, his violet eyes following the messy lines of dialog.

"I... have a satchel. I... found it. Anything I put in it, he can take and vice versa," she admitted, her voice quiet. Her palms rubbed together in nervousness. She wasn't sure he'd completely heard her.

He scanned the first page quickly, then looked over the second like he wasn't reading them thoroughly.

"I didn't know what I was doing," she said much softer. "I wanted to get information or something... But then he was giving me things. And now... I don't know what to do... I don't think I'm helping anything." Her hands rubbed her own arms a little. "I was scared, so..."

"So, what did they give this first time?" he asked blandly.

Arica pointed to the thick stone disk.

"And this, second?" he asked, hooking the bracelet with a finger.

She nodded, the wait viciously eating at her nerves.

Last, Jake looked over a charcoal sketch she'd found the night before of an incredibly detailed towering stone castle labeled simply with *my view.*

"Well?" she finally whispered, egging him on to his verdict.

"If it's harm you're worried about, you haven't caused any." He looked up from the sketch. "Yet."

"So... you're not mad? I didn't do anything I shouldn't've?"

He let out a breath through puckered lips, then shook his head decisively. "Listen, anyone else in this camp would immediately tell you to march your brave ass down to Vanessa and come clean. I'm strongly suggesting that too. However, there are also two reasons I could warn against it."

As if to fortify his words, he crouched down, barely under her height, but could look her right in the eye. "One, I know her. I know that the second you do, she'll cut all ties and disregard your entire... investigation. And two, I also know that sometimes, doing something behind her back can be what we need. I can't tell you how many times I've salvaged a battle by disobeying. Don't tell her that, though."

Arica folded her hands together. "Really?"

He put a hand on her elbow, giving her a soft, encouraging smile she'd only seen a time or two before. "The best advice that anyone will ever give you is to follow your instincts. Experience is powerful, but you can never know what's going to happen next unless your *gut* tells you."

Jake set the papers on the ground and anchored them with a few fingers. "I don't know who this is exactly, but he knows enough to be a Dovevian for sure. Experience would keep me from humoring them because I know how their fetid schemes can turn out for us. I know every single one of them, and what they've done to resemble monsters. That's why I want you to go to Vanessa."

He lightly poked her arm. "But if you think this could help, then I won't tell you not to. You don't know enough about anything sensitive, so unless you were telling them exactly where we were at any given moment, I don't think you can do much harm."

She shook her head in clear reassurance. "I wouldn't. But what about... the real world, the portals?"

"Don't tell 'em," he suggested seriously, making her realize that he really *hadn't* thoroughly read their banter. But she kept it to herself. Was there anything any of them could really do, even knowing one of them knew? "I'd hazard a guess that this is one of the young ones, so you probably won't get much we don't already know. If he slips up and mentions any positions, please let us know. But..." he stopped, giving her a sly smile. "Do be careful. Even the baby Dovevians have a few years on you."

Her face warmed, and she cast her eyes to the ground. "As many as you, though?"

"Point taken," he grunted.

Then he grabbed the bracelet and stood up. "Well... it's made of silver, so it won't hinder your magic." His brutish fingers handled the delicate jewelry with care. "And it has an enchantment, but it's just a very basic protection spell. Nothing you don't already have."

He slipped it onto his tendinous wrist, and Arica couldn't help but smile. "The blue really goes with your eyes."

"I'm not dying, so it's probably all right," he shrugged, took off the jewelry, and tossed it back to her. "Maybe just a piece to earn trust before a planned deception."

"So, what about the sketch?" Arica asked, gathering the rest of her evidence.

He glanced at the contents distastefully. "I mean... It's not a poor plan. But it doesn't matter. I'm sure Vanessa is already working on a strategy, and I wouldn't doubt this to be a trap."

Arica frowned, wondering what he meant exactly. "Plan? I meant... Is it Kopion? What plan?"

She noticed him raise an eyebrow, then shift back for the picture of the castle. "These little arrows, the Xs and symbols? He has a plan laid out for you."

Her hands gripped the page, eyes digging into the little pen strokes he'd pointed out. She hadn't noticed them on her own.

"The weirdest part of it is, this isn't what Kopion looks like right now."

"What do you mean?"

"As I said. Anyway, Vanessa has her own plan. Please be careful. You won't lose anything if you cut all ties now."

This guy wants me to do his dirty work. Or he wants to help. But Jake was right about something. Vanessa would never condone such an act.

"Bottom line? I'm telling you to show Vanessa," Jake sighed, setting his hands on his hips. "Sounds like dinner's ready. Care to accompany me?"

Rain poured down so heavily that it drowned out even Arica's ragged breathing; a constant roaring like the static of an old radio turned all the way up. Even though she'd wrapped up in both her cloak and the thick fur blanket she carried around, her skin was cold to her own touch.

All of her senses were on edge, but she had to get back to sleep. Hopefully the storm wouldn't wake her again.

As she rolled onto her side to recover her night, however, a hand grabbed her shoulder. She let out a quick scream, but the hand's owner quickly shushed her in a familiar voice.

"Are we being attacked?" she gasped, not realizing her voice would be so groggy.

"No, no, we're fine," Jake said, barely audible even speaking normally. "This tent is flooding. Gather your things. Everyone else has already moved."

The bottom of her bag was wet, laying in a puddle of rain, and he was right. Elvy was dragging her things out ahead of them. He grabbed her by the forearm, not giving her a choice, and hauled her to her knees. Her pants resisted her movement, sticking to her skin. No wonder she was so cold.

"Well, where am I going?" she asked, frantically trying to get her hands to work correctly.

Jake grabbed her first pack, slinging it over her shoulder. "With us. Come on."

As soon as they had everything, including a bunch of wet stuff, and had gotten to the opening of the tent, Jake reached back and grabbed her spare hand. She braced herself for a sudden shower, but as they stepped out into frigid air, the rain split over them and fell to either side. It was barely any quieter, but the small blot of orange flame in front of them had a calming effect.

Mud sucked at her boots, but Jake's firm hand kept her from tipping over. She hadn't remembered the terrain being so rough the evening before. Luckily, they'd set the other tent on the top of the hill. The swooping boughs of a dozen oak trees had done a pretty thorough job of covering it there.

"Are you all right?" Jake called back, probably regarding her trembling hand.

"No," she responded, but doubted he'd heard.

Once closer to the larger tent, the noise quieted as the rain filtered through millions of large star-shaped leaves.

"Wait," Arica said, releasing Jake's hand as he ducked into the tent. "I'm going to take my boots off."

He let go of her so she had full use of her hands. It didn't take long to shed the boots and the additional five pounds of mud caked to them. She quickly followed into the shelter.

She'd worried about bothering other people, but it looked like most of them were awake or shifting about, anyway. Several tiny points of light were in use, casting abstract shadows into all corners of the room. It was warmer there, not by a lot, but with everyone crammed in closer, it helped.

Arica followed her large companion, who stooped almost in half. She was upright, with only an inch or two to spare. Her clothes dried as she walked, lightening her load and warming her.

She was careful between the two rows of people, avoiding feet and bags and the occasional weapon.

Jake led her all the way to the rear end of the tent, where his things already lay.

"The far end is mine so I'm not constantly tripping people when shifts trade," he explained quietly.

Jake shifted his bedding against the far wall, which swayed in and out almost peacefully despite the pelting rain. He carefully laid out her things, then gestured to it.

"This will have to work," he mumbled.

It took a few minutes to work her way into the newly dry bedding, get shifted around, and completely settled in, even though Jake was practically asleep by the time she was finally comfortable. Her fingers couldn't be touching any other skin, as cold as it was. Then she stopped moving and stared up at the ceiling.

Sleep, she thought wistfully, but her eyes stayed open. She could still hear the rain, and maybe some movement back towards the front. Someone snored, but they weren't close. She turned her head to the right, wondering who the lump was, but he was almost lifeless. They'd all hear her wrestling around, she was sure of it, so she stayed still until she started itching.

"Maybe they should put you on the next watch," Jake mumbled from underneath the arm crossed over his face.

Arica scrunched down but faced him so she didn't have to talk so loud across the extra space between them. "Sorry. I don't know why I feel so awake."

"Adrenaline."

She watched him for a second, just an arm and part of an ear exposed to the cold. Then she turned her face back to the ceiling.

It was so peaceful. She remembered many camping trips where they'd end up rained on. It didn't feel much different, staring up at the tent's top. Being small, listening to the rain and her father's deep snoring, hoping she could stay warm.

The memories made her feel more content. There was no reason to think about magic or big heavy swords or all the strangers she had to exist with. Just the tent protecting her from the cold, rhythmic raindrops and the black sky.

"There are some sleeping tablets in my bag if you want them," whispered Jake sluggishly.

"I'm okay, thanks," she said back.

He shifted, pulling his arm back under the blanket, and used the other to prop his head slightly upright. He blinked slowly but kept his eyes on her.

"Are you okay?"

She nodded, glancing over at him. "Are *you* okay?"

"This is something I've been doing for a long time," he whispered.

She smiled. "Running through a forest, without a place to live, chasing after people with demon powers?"

"Pretty much the theme of my entire life," he concluded.

They both quietly snickered.

"Well, at least you've got this weird little group. Family."

"Not always," he mumbled. "Sometimes you end up alone. Sometimes there is nobody else. And never can you fully trust family. Not until they earn it like everyone else."

Arica sighed and rubbed her dry eyes. "I mean, my dad was a marine but on the occasion he was home, he was extremely aggressive with my mom, always. I've hated him since I was a lot younger than I should've."

"Was, huh?"

"Yeah. He's gone now. While it was hard, I'm kinda glad." She let the heavy words settle against her, spreading silence like snowfall as if this would be enough to get them to sleep.

Then Jake waved a lazy hand in a circle making her chuckle.

"I didn't mean to be cryptic," she whispered dismissively. "He wasn't a great guy by American standards. Vocally abusive to us, physically abusive to my mom. Luckily, because of the marine thing, he wasn't around much, but it was plenty to break my mom. She's really unstable and I love her, but I'm the only kid who'll even talk to her anymore. My older brother, Travis, rescued me and my little brother from her when we were teenagers. People think my relationship with him is weird, but he's always been more of a parent to me than anyone else. I still can't imagine being betrayed in some of the ways you guys have. I don't understand how your family can be so cruel."

"You just have to learn," Jake whispered softly. "It can sting, but... you still learn to get over it."

"Like Vanessa?" she suggested, almost sadly. "I've never met someone so..." She wasn't even sure what word to use. *Ambitious? Cold?* "Adjusted to loss as she is."

"She's had enough gain as well," Jake muttered.

She turned, shifting onto her stomach. "Yeah. But, I mean... Husband. Father. Brother, uncle, cousin after cousin..." She leaned her chin into her hand. "But at least not her son."

Jake smirked, raising an eyebrow in her direction. "Proud of that, are you? I'll not deny it."

She couldn't help grinning in triumph. She'd still been slightly unsure of whether she was right. "I pieced it together the other night. Well, it wasn't hard."

He closed his eyes, brow still raised and smirk still on his lips.

"Like, I probably could've guessed way sooner, without being in so much mortal danger, what with the facts. Like, you do practically whatever you want, and Vanessa is totally okay with it. And how you're jealous of Rapier, but not because you want her for yourself. Just you want her *to* yourself. And the way everyone trusts you know exactly what she'd do. But mostly because Zak and Damad were talking about you the other night. And I guess Steen flat-out said it the other night, I just didn't take it literally at the time."

He made an *mmm* sound with his lips but said nothing intelligent.

Arica smiled, just looking at him for a minute. Then she crawled a few inches closer and placed her chin on his outstretched elbow.

"You're a *momma's boy*," she giggled in a whisper.

He let his heavy hand press on her face, unenthusiastic, but she laughed quietly and slithered back to her spot.

He shifted again, leaning more to his other side.

"Guess that means your dad is probably a Dovevian. Drake, I'd guess?" she asked, hoping it wasn't too touchy of a subject.

"Didn't end up mattering," Jake said. "Family found organically is better than family forcibly conforming to specific roles."

Arica let a warm smile spread across her face as she watched Jake's eyes fall closed. "Yeah... it is."

26

I'LL SHOW YOU MINE

A ten-foot sheer drop onto mossy boulders gaped in front of Arica and Jake. A stream rushed from under their feet into the wide mouth of a cave and further into the ground. Soft sunlight filtered through the oak leaves, a kaleidoscope of light brushed over everything.

"Wow," Arica breathed, picking her way across the soggy ground. "This is what you wanted to show me? I've never seen anything like this in real life."

Jake was barely ahead, looking over everything carefully. "I suppose I shouldn't be surprised it's intact. It's only been about ten years."

"I was ten that long ago," she mumbled, more for her own benefit than his. "How did you find this spot, anyway?"

She followed him to the edge, where he easily collapsed, throwing his long legs over the edge. Hers she crossed, settling onto the soft, cushioned ground.

"I didn't. It was a friend of mine. She was always exploring where she shouldn't've and dragging us into it."

Arica glanced at him, smirking. "Sounds like someone I know. Was she one of your previously mentioned wives?"

He gently shook his head. "No. They were a long time ago."

She was hoping he would continue about them, as she was curious, but didn't want to ask in case it bothered him.

The water splashing down from underneath them was crystal clear, the light spray cold but refreshing in already cool air. She could only imagine how pure it tasted. Inside the mouth of the cave, it got dark quickly so she couldn't see into it thoroughly, but it seemed like the water was gently going downwards. She wondered if the little stream had carved the entire thing out by itself.

"I..." she started softly, staring into the water. "This is so beautiful. It feels good. I don't really know why, but I like it."

"DeRael is like that," Jake agreed softly. "It's got a lot of magic running through everything. It shows." He turned, looking right at her for a moment.

"I feel like... this is a good representation of how I feel about all of this. It's beautiful, kind of scary, but I have this... temptation to jump in and just... go. Find out what's down there, what you're all about. Maybe die, but open my eyes to... everything. Life, magic, just understanding." She met his eyes. "I wish I could just throw away that..." She let out a quick laugh. "*Ridiculous* instinct and sense of fear keeping me alive and just see..."

Letting it trail off, she looked down the cave and took a deep breath, squelching the swelling fear in her chest. She started when Jake leaned closer.

"Then go," he challenged steadily in her ear.

She let out a nervous laugh. "I'm trying, I really am. I actually dried my shoes this morning. Without lighting them on fire."

He sat back up straight but nudged her with his elbow. "Not your representation. I mean this. Throw away your human instincts. Go."

Arica looked up at him in shock. "Go? Down there?"

"Why not?" he shrugged, giving her a mischievous smirk.

She looked at the little cave, mouth hanging ajar. "You want me to throw myself into a tiny rocky river, running down into a hole to fall into a cave system to be trapped forever alone?" she demanded, only looking at him near the end of her sentence.

"I didn't say I wouldn't follow you," he reasoned nonchalantly.

"What if there's lava? Or we just get trapped? Or fall a million feet to our deaths?"

"We're at too high an elevation for lava, and if we fall, we'll just climb back up."

Arica regarded his expression, searching for any sign of teasing, or the lurking presence of a *gotcha!*, but it wasn't there. "You're strangely serious about this," she mumbled.

"The best way to learn is to do. Maybe someday you'll be struggling through a cave by yourself, or stuck in a river. But this time there'll be someone to help you out." He pointed at himself, then gestured outwards. "Look, I'm not gonna try to convince you to. I was giving you the option to learn."

Her hands rested on her knees as she wondered what she'd ever done to deserve his torment.

Tilting her head to the side, she listened to the chipper singing of a hundred birds. The water gurgled, mixing with air as it fell. Leaves rustled around them.

She set her hands on the ground on either side of her and pushed off.

Her ankles took her weight, the shock of impact throwing her to her knees, but the thick moss underfoot felt like falling onto a thick memory foam mattress. It prickled under her palms, a rough, strange texture. She brushed off both her hands and knees and stood up.

The jagged path worn into the ground was wider than she'd thought from above. She took a few tentative steps following the flow, turning when she heard a thump behind her.

Just as he'd said, Jake was only steps behind her but had an expression that might've suggested that he was just taking a stroll in her direction. Arica smiled but kept up her determination to explore.

Along the stream, the edges of the stone were crumbly, held together with woven moss, but not sturdy enough to keep her weight once loose. She followed it step over step, carefully testing the ground with her foot each time. Once at the end of the opening, she reached out and used the cave wall to steady herself.

The shelf grew narrower, and she thought about turning back. But she crouched down and reached into the cold water. It was about a foot above the waterline, but the water itself was only a few inches deep.

She splashed into it, her boots watertight as they'd proven before. The rocks underfoot shifted more than she expected, so she kept one hand on the bank for stability.

Her eyes didn't strain to see as she got deeper into the dark. The ceiling lowered and within a few minutes, she could reach up and run her hand along it.

"It seems like it's flowing heavier. This whole thing could be flooded," she observed.

Realizing that the space would be much more cramped for her larger friend, she glanced back to make sure he hadn't left her alone. There he was a few feet back, following silently even in a noisy stream.

"You should be a ninja," she whispered in a spooky manner, then sloshed forward again.

"A what?" he asked with genuine confusion.

Her foot found another sturdy place to step. Until she picked up her back one, and the rocks crumbled out from under her, pitching her to the side.

She caught herself on the edge and grabbed a heavy root protruding from the wall. She struggled a little, trying to pull her leg out of the snug crevice. Freezing water soaked into her clothing, adhering it to her skin.

Carefully adjusting the rocks around her knee, she slogged her way up. She was almost all the way out before realizing how well she could see. A quick check told her it wasn't Jake's doing, but she wasn't sure where the faint light was coming from. Then she noticed an echoing splashing sound and looked down.

Arica scrambled away from the edge, forcing her leg free and out of the spacious hollowed cavern below them. She could see where the stream ended. The wall sharply dipped a few feet in front of them, letting the water pour over the edge into a large pool in the cavern below.

"Wow," she breathed, leaning closer but out of danger. There had to be outside light filtering in from somewhere, but she couldn't spot any for sure.

She could see pillars around the lake, some intact but some broken into pieces. The closest wall was smooth, with a texture, maybe some kind of carving in it.

"Is this a ru—"

She felt just the faintest vibration under her fingers. Then the rocks underneath her hands crumbled, and half of the wall followed suit. She didn't have the chance to pull herself up, and fell, unable to breathe or scream, just arms flailing for something to grab onto. The cold water continuously attempted to drown her as it fell with her.

Then gravity loosened its hold on her, her fall slowing considerably in the air. It was almost calming, even if confusing. Until she splashed into deep water, enveloped in a heartbeat.

Arms thrashing in slow motion, she tried to figure out which way was up. Her lungs were already out of air. Her muscles ached with the penetrating cold. Waves returned to her, buffeting her around.

Her knee brushed solidity, so she pushed off, regardless of direction. Her lungs screamed for air.

Finally, she broke the surface hand-first. She was so desperate for oxygen that she sucked up just as much water, only to cough it back up violently. She lost her strokes long enough to slip back under the water. Panic raced through her.

She'd seen the edge of the pool just barely after surfacing, and worked her way over, kicking and struggling to keep her head over the water. Her hand grabbed the cold stone edge, confirming her safety net. She took a few breaths between coughing up water and shakily pulled her body against the stone.

But she had a much worse problem, she realized, looking above to where the water poured from, a steady sparkling stream as if it had never been disturbed.

Then a head surfaced amidst the mess of white churned water and loose dirt.

"Whoo, that's brisk," Jake howled, shaking his sopping hair out.

Arica may have laughed at him, had she not been coughing up her lungs and fighting cold and terror.

With much less struggle, Jake pulled himself through the cold water to the edge she clung to, then silently helped her climb up onto it.

Her clothes made a sound like a wet fish flopping onto the stone. She stopped moving and lay on her stomach for a minute, her throat and lungs on fire.

"If I'd known that surviving that would hurt so much, I would've just drowned," she choked, her voice nasally.

"I would've dragged you out either way," Jake calmed, churning up white water as he dragged himself onto the edge.

"Just let me die..." she moaned, rubbing water out of her eyes.

"Maybe tomorrow." The big man stood up, his clothes clinging to his body and his cloak hanging limp and heavy. But Arica wasn't ready to move just yet.

"Don't think I'm unaware of what happened," she panted, looking up at him.

He raised an eyebrow, wringing water out of his sleeve.

Arica rolled her eyes. "I saw the glow in the rocks before they broke. I know you made us fall on purpose."

His smirk was not a nice one, but he didn't seem to want to deny it. "And the relevance of that...?"

"You could've killed us!" she shrieked, astounded at how that could've been irrelevant.

"Ah, but I didn't. I slowed you down too. You should be grateful."

"Yeah, well, how about now I'm suspicious that you brought me down here to kill me, or extract information, or just turn evil and take advantage of my inexperience." She rolled onto her back, her clothes squishing in her puddle.

"We'll see what happens," answered Jake.

Arica pushed herself to her knees, shivering. It was already cold in the spacious cave, the water just made it much, much worse.

The stone she rested on was suspiciously flat. In fact, looking around, she noticed that most of her surroundings looked purposefully formed. They were on a rectangular platform, two short pillars standing to either side, supporting a cracking roof. Three sides were open to the cave, overlooking the flooded pool, but the back wall was more or less intact, covered in worn carvings.

Some pictures were barely recognizable beyond random swirls and lines, but some still told stories of rich kings and warriors sporting bows and, sometimes, some kind of vine-like weapon.

"Are these from those elf guys, too?" Arica inquired, fingering a low carving of a crude humanoid figure surrounded by swirling runes she could only assume was magic. "What do they mean?"

"These ruins are all from the Sceztiak, yes. Though I don't know what any of this is saying. Their era was long before my time," he answered with a strange reverence.

"That's quite the feat," she teased without thinking.

He grunted in response and turned around to face the pool again.

It had once been a beautiful place to be. The platform was higher than any of the others, but through the clear water, she could see evidence of three other edges of the pool, all of them with rubble strewn out. It looked like the water flowing from above had worn through the roof, then had torn down the walls over time, spilling out into the rest of the cave, and maybe more ruins.

They wandered out of the pool area, and Jake allowed Arica to be in the lead.

Most of the ceiling dripped with water, though there was only one other waterfall similar to the one they'd fallen out of. She followed the cave a little further to a place where it narrowed, but she could tell it opened up to light further on.

She wouldn't have guessed it was nearly as huge and open of a cavern as it was, and she couldn't help feeling tiny upon making her way into it. They stood on a long, wide ledge that looked out over the lower recesses of the cavern. She would've expected her entire small town to fit into the bottom. The openings in the roof were frequent enough that most of the huge ravine was lit, the bigger holes draped with long green vines and moss.

"I really can't believe this," Arica whispered, keeping her feet spread for balance as her dizziness grew.

The walls weren't all natural, with ruined buildings big and small, tiny from the distance, maybe once the location of an entire city, washed away by rivers and time. The most noticeable depression snaked from one end of the cave to the other, eventually trailing down and disappearing. Even though it had once been a river, it was dry and empty, like much of the space.

Then a realization crushed her awe. "How are we supposed to get out of here?" She pressed a hand against her chest, wondering how such space could make her feel so claustrophobic. "We've been gone so long, they're probably wondering what happened. Maybe freaking out," mumbled Arica with a bit of desperation.

She hadn't noticed until that moment that Jake had wandered away from her along the edge, his cloak calmly swaying behind his shoulders as he took in the scene.

The ledge they'd come out on ran both ways, but not for long before stopping abruptly against a wall to one side, and turned into a steep, dangerously spiked slope on the other. The closest opening to the sky was much closer to the middle of the room, hundreds of feet past the edge of the ravine and way out of reach.

She looked back at Jake, who kicked loose rocks over the intimidating edge.

"I see you cooking something up over there," Arica accused, folding her arms.

He shrugged, glancing in her direction. "I'm trying to decide whether escaping is worth the backlash I'm going to get for this. Even though I *really* want to."

"If you can, do it, please. I'd rather not be eaten by whatever thing is crawling around down here. Five-foot rats, or a gang of Velociraptors. Vampire bats, and cave spiders bigger than my head." A shiver ran up her spine just thinking about all of it. She took a few long steps closer to the experienced warrior.

"Do you remember our conversation about touches?" he asked, still staring over the edge.

She nodded and took a few more steps.

"Well, I think it's time I show you mine."

The mischief in his eyes was clear, but she didn't know his intentions. Her lips parted to ask, but before she could, he pushed his cloak back and stepped off of the edge.

Her jaw dropped as she froze. "Did he just..."

He was gone.

She scrambled to the edge, knowing he was planning something dramatic when a wave of pure force threw her back. She grabbed her arms over her head as it stopped, but before she could try to recover, a second wave hit, skidding her entire body several feet and tearing exposed skin against the raw stone floor.

In frozen terror, she waited a few long moments. Finally, it felt okay to breathe again and she gasped, lowering her arms.

"What... on Earth..." she mumbled, shaking palms pushing her off of the ground. She'd scraped her right arm raw. Her hip felt tender as well, but she ignored both of them and moved to the edge of the ravine, crawling just in case there'd be another gust.

She wasn't sure what to expect, but as she looked down into the cave, she could see nothing different but a few displaced rocks. The problem was, it was still relatively dark below them, a straight drop into the old river path. So, if Jake was wandering around down there, or splattered across the rocks, she wasn't going to spot him.

With his brief blasts of pressure, though, she wasn't sure how he'd expected her to see exactly what his touch was.

Arica cupped her hands around her mouth and called his name as loud as she could. Her heart pounded hard, her voice echoing into the cave over and over. But there was no answer and no evidence of his existence as she searched over everything within sight.

Her eye caught movement, just enough that as she looked for it again, it could've been a trick of the light. But there it was again, in the dark corner below the slope that started to Arica's right-hand side, just the slightest shift of darkness. Then she caught sight of something that was definitely moving in better light, a pitch-black length of muscle, visibly sliding over the stone even from her height.

"I swear to God, if that boy just changed into a giant python, I'm going home immediately," she whispered with a shiver.

She climbed to her feet, brushing off her knees. She followed along the edge the opposite way Jake had, down towards the slope to see if she could get a better look at the mass of whatever it was moving down there.

It had to be Jake, didn't it? He'd changed. It explained how he'd acted.

She slid on loose rocks, coming to a stop right before it really began to decline, then leaned over the edge. She'd already fallen enough for one day, but she had a better view of a creature darker than the shadow itself, a dull obsidian black. But all she could see of it was a thick, meaty leg that quickly climbed out of the light.

Her jaw loosened as the overall shadow climbed into view, stalking closer to her. It was still very far away, so she couldn't judge size perfectly, but it seemed gigantic, a hulking, four-legged body with a sloped back and powerful chest. His neck was long, curved forward to a head that reminded her of a horse's. All the legs were as large as the one she'd seen, but the front ones looked awkward. It took a minute of watching it climb up the rocks, a wide, squarish stance, to realize that it was because they were bent forward, nothing like a horse's in shape, but with similar joints on tip-toes.

"Wow," Arica mumbled, the only other sound the shifting of rocks under the beast.

She waited several minutes, awed, watching the incredible animal climb. Eventually she made out a pair of fluffy, almost ragged wings cupped in the air for balance, wondering how she could have missed them even as camouflaged as it was. She made out the paws and the sharp, curved claws that allowed it to climb so well.

Arica thought it was trying to climb up to the ledge again, but eventually, she realized it was too big to even fit on it. So what was he doing?

It climbed nearer to the ceiling, a steeper way than if he'd climbed up to Arica. He'd found a bowed spot in the stone, just above him.

She wasn't sure what his plan was until the giant claw reached up and started raking into the stone. The sound alone was incredible, a low rumbling that made her wonder if the earth would start shaking as well. There were no sparks, as she might've expected, just scraping and crumbling as he tore through the stone as if it were soft clay or loose soil.

She was so intent on watching the beast tearing through the ceiling that when she caught movement to her right, she jumped hard enough to lose her footing and slipped onto her shoulder.

The slithery tail had made its way onto the ledge, flicking around not unlike a cat's would as it readied to pounce, just slower and on a much larger scale. She followed it off the edge, to where it draped above the enormous drop and eventually led to the animal itself. It was ridiculously disproportionate no matter how big the creature itself was.

Without thinking about how dangerous it could've been, Arica stood up and chased after it, slow, and crouched as it lethargically twitched about ten feet to either side.

She didn't know what she was doing, but couldn't help herself. She wanted to remind him she was there. And, admittedly, she wanted to see how soft he was.

She jumped forward on her knees, slamming her hands down on the tail, hoping he would feel it enough to know she was there and wouldn't drag her off the edge.

Her hands were barely big enough to wrap around and touch the ground on either side of the tail, certainly not big enough to go all the way around the diameter of it. It was also very soft, to her satisfaction, thick skin an almost impossible black, with short fur just as dark.

There wasn't any way she was strong enough to hold it in place, but it stayed under her hands, barely tugging against her grip.

The loud scraping stopped.

She looked back to the tail's owner, whose shoulders he'd worked into the large hole he'd dug in the ceiling.

Arica felt the tail curling around her before she noticed what it was doing. The end of it was a lot skinnier, about a foot of long, thick pieces of hair that looked similar to a porcupine's coat.

She stood up, letting it go in case he needed it back. But instead of retreating, it whipped up and wrapped around her.

"I don't like this," Arica shouted across the room, unsure how good his hearing was. It wrapped once around her waist, once around her chest, just under her arms, then wrapped around her shoulder and across her neck. It didn't choke her, but she wasn't able to turn her neck.

Then the animal finished wriggling through the hole above, and more light burst into the cavern below it.

Arica knew what was coming next, but didn't have time to object before it swept her off her feet and dragged her over the edge of the cliff. Her breath caught with the sensation, but she never made up for it as it quickly pulled her towards the hole. She wanted to duck, even though the hole was plenty big for the animal that had crawled from it first.

Sunlight hit her face, but all she could see was the gigantic animal in front of her, piercing red eyes bigger than her head, observing as he lifted her from the cavern below.

Yet as soon as she'd cleared the ground, the thick coils around her were loosening. Her knees hit the ground first but even braced for it, she rolled, prickly weeds tearing at her hair and clothes.

The animal took a gigantic step over her, not even coming close to crushing her, yet she felt the wind he caused. She rolled onto her hands, getting up once again so she could watch.

Even with the sun beating down, it wasn't a lot easier to see the thing. It was so dark and reflected little light. In fact, it seemed to pull some of it in around it, making the details and lines of muscle hard to depict, almost shadow-like.

The solzetair, for this is what she was sure it was, galloped away, light on clawed toes, tail spiraling around behind him. The ground shivered a little, but not enough to worry about keeping balance.

Then the pair of front paws spread as giant wings opened up, fanning the air a few times before jumping.

Arica expected him to show off, do some flips or a crazy dive, but he just climbed up a few hundred feet and hung in the air, twisting around for a few seconds.

Then he faced her and dove.

She wanted to run in some direction but didn't know what would be best. She doubted he would try to hurt her, but wasn't sure he was going to be so smart about it. As the gigantic animal sped towards her, she ended up throwing her arms over her head and crouching. He passed over by many feet, then slammed into the ground a hundred yards away.

Wind pulled her hair and clothes towards the spot hard enough that she leaned away from it to keep balance, the shadows shifting like a rolling cloud, but it was gone just as fast. She got back up and searched the area but couldn't see him. She was alone in a field surrounded by old, thick trees. But at least she was out of the cave.

"Jake!" she called as loudly as she could muster, but her lungs felt as if they were permanently out of breath.

There was no answer, but with the creature gone, he had to be somewhere. She could see kicked-up and disturbed dirt but wasn't positive that it wasn't from climbing out of the cave.

A cloud drifted over them, hiding the sun's intense glare.

Arica caught sight of something black lying in the dirt near her, and with excitement, she raced to grab it. It was a feather, about the length of her arm from shoulder to wrist. She pulled it through her fingers, feeling the fluff. The entire thing was just as dark and dull as the rest of the animal.

Finally, she spied a man-shaped figure a ways away, moving slowly but towards her. She settled onto the ground, playing with the feather, wondering if he'd let her keep it.

It was only a few minutes later when hiking Jake reached her with several similar feathers he'd gathered on the way over. He'd raised his hood to keep off the sun but didn't look winded or ruffled.

"Come on," he called as he approached. "We're a little further off from the rest than I thought. Even though I cut some distance coming out of there."

Grinning, Arica took his offered hand and stood up. "Really? You just pulled the biggest surprise ever, and now you're just back to business? Was that whole freaking dragon thing concussion hallucinations?"

He smirked, then held out the three feathers. "Solzetair. Here, you can keep them, or you could sell them. Make a quick fortune."

"Then do your thing again. I'll pull a couple more," she teased, fluffing one against her shoulder.

Jake patiently beckoned her with a hand, urging her into a walk. "I'll admit, I'm rusty. It's hard to do, and I haven't done it much in recent years."

"What, aren't you 'allowed' to?" she scoffed, trotting after him quicker than his own legs needed to move.

He faced more towards her but wasn't catching her gaze. "It's just dangerous. I could get in trouble if I'm seen."

"Oh," Arica sighed. "Well, that's the same thing that Drake is then, isn't it?"

"It's a hereditary touch, yeah," Jake agreed stoically. "Long line of Damages were the same. Drake does it a lot, part of the reason Vanessa hates when I do it. It's... difficult to tell us apart."

"I suppose I can understand that," Arica agreed. She ran her hand down the length of the feathers again.

Jake reached into his cloak, presumably his magical bag, and ended up pulling out a mess of leather straps, then worked them over his shoulders underneath his cloak as they walked.

"So, I understand what you were saying at the castle a while back, Jake. Assuming actual dragons are... Reptilian... I can see how it would be hard to mistake them and those, ah, solzetairs. I mean... where do they, like... live, anyway? It would be hard for something that big to hide. And eat."

With the leather holster fully strapped to his back, he pulled out the long sword strapped to his hip and carefully slid it into the leather one. "I'm not sure if any real ones are alive anymore. Technically, they're invasive to DeRael, they're a type of demon, but them and the dragons keep each other's species pretty scarce."

"How so?"

"They're the perfect enemies. Solzetairs are extremely sensitive to heat and flame, especially that of the dragons, but their claws and fangs are some of the few things that can pierce a dragon's hide, their venom all but lethal. Well, to anything really."

Arica stared into the sky for a bit, nodding thoughtfully. "I don't think I'd want to face either hostile."

Jake shook his head in agreement, then undid his belt.

She was slightly surprised until he pulled the thick metal sheath off of it and held it out to her. "Put them in here for now. I'll try to line your cloak with them tonight, keep you a little warmer and keep them somewhere safer."

She took it thankfully and carefully stuffed the feathers into, hollow first. It was almost the perfect size for them, only about two inches of the tips sticking out.

Jake looked down and caught her gaze. "Got a little jogging in you?"

She rolled her eyes but smiled. "Worried we won't make it before they start a search party?"

He stopped in his tracks and bent his knees, placing one hand on the ground. "Maybe I just want to see who's faster," he challenged *almost* seriously.

She fake smiled with her teeth showing. "I don't think it would be much of a race, dragon boy."

"You saying you're gonna win?" he demanded, as if truly insulted.

She couldn't help snickering a little, then shrugged. "Okay. Go!"

27

BATTLE CRYING

J ake didn't leave Arica in the dust like she expected, even when she slowed to a jog after about thirty yards. He stayed back, doing some awkward gait between walking and jogging.

Arica assumed he knew where he was going from seeing it as a solzetair, so she trusted his direction.

As they got into the trees, Jake worked his way ahead of her to lead. She tried copying his complicated gait, using trees and branches to propel himself or re-balance or change directions, perfectly jumping over roots and puddles and through narrower trees. But all she managed was to stumble through the underbrush, making him stop and wait every dozen yards. She was probably the worst scouting partner he'd ever had.

Luckily, it wasn't much longer before they found a trampled path and followed it about forty feet into a clearing, where they caught sight of a few companions.

"Zak," Jake called, jogging up to the man closest to them as he talked to Kylen.

"Oh, hey," Zak greeted, glancing behind Jake at Arica.

"You haven't stopped because of us, have you?" Jake asked breathlessly.

"No, we—"

"Jrasko!" Vanessa shoved her way between Kylen and Steen, then threw her drawn sword back into its case. "Seven, where is your head? Where have you been?"

Jake put up with her as she pushed both of his hands out, quickly scanning him. But when Jake's lips parted to answer, she interrupted angrily.

"Look, I get it," she snapped as she grabbed Arica's hand, looking over her skinned arms. "Sometimes, you need alone time, but you know better right now. We've an entire army of Dovevians that could be on us in moments..."

Arica's face scrunched in disgust. "W-wait, we weren't having sex, if that's what you mean."

She shot a glare at Jake as he snickered.

Vanessa held out a hand, cutting off any more objections. "I don't care, really don't, but we have to go now. We spotted Drake flying close."

"Well, no, that was me," Jake admitted through his teeth.

Arica shrank back as the rest of them froze.

Then both Vanessa and Jake moved simultaneously, her sword swiping out as his forearm rose to deflect the flat of her blade. She swung it back around, this time throwing a small knife out that would've pierced his neck had he not twisted backwards.

"You are going to kill me," she seethed. "Get up to the rest of the group. We've more ground to cover." Then she discarded the sword to the side and stormed back to the gist of the group.

"Should've stuck with the first suggestion," Zak shrugged apathetically.

Arica forced her hand to unclench.

"She still would've swiped at me," Jake mumbled. He stooped to scoop up the abandoned sword.

"I don't think it would've helped solve the solzetair problem, though," Arica reasoned.

Jake gave her a look of disbelief, then gestured outwards, giving her the impression he still thought that was better. Then he mounted the slope after Zak and the others.

"Just for the record," Arica added, giving him one last look of disdain. "It's your reputation getting us in trouble. Not mine."

She followed, using her hands to climb the incline until it flattened out.

Everyone spread out as the treeline receded. Near the head of the group, Arica could see Rapier gesturing, talking to several people.

Jake slowed to let her catch up. "At least she—"

A shadow swooped over the landscape, blotting out the sunlight as it passed over them.

"Seven's sake," Jake mumbled, watching it disappear behind the treetops. "That one isn't me."

"Jrasko!" Vanessa called, anger drained from her voice. But he was already mounting the nearest tree to climb through its branches.

Arica's heart jumped into her throat. Only a few yards ahead of them, she saw Vanessa raise a hand up into the air, her commander repeated the gesture. Then she raced closer, but Arica stood dumbfounded. What was going on? And what was she supposed to do?

Vanessa called her son once more, but he wasn't listening.

It was too late by the time she reached Arica. A huge black silhouette climbed out of the treetops in a pulsing flurry of leaves. It launched into the sky, bulky wings flapping desperately.

"Damnit," she swore, her breath heavy. She stepped back a few feet, getting a good look around. "He's going to kill himself."

"What? Why?"

Vanessa swallowed, glancing back at the rest of the company with a look so worried and unsure that Arica wanted to freak out on her own. "He's not anywhere near as strong or controlled as Drake. And he knows it."

Arica followed her to join the rest, still wanting answers. Others seemed to be awaiting the same. "But then, why would he just go?"

"Adrenaline, maybe. Distraction, probably," she said. "We've all started pulling out our secret weapons. Though I fear this one is more trouble than it's ultimately worth."

Arica took a deep breath as Vanessa threw out a few orders, the first going to Zak to watch Arica, which she resented, but didn't argue with. Everyone was already tense, armed, and split into several groups. Arica felt slightly dizzy suddenly and blocked out Rapier's report on the Dovevian's current position.

"Whoa there, filly," Zak called, dropping his sword to catch her. "Breathe, now, breathe. Don't panic."

She tried to obey as he lowered her to the ground, just focusing on basic human functions instead of once again being attacked by evil magicians. She gained enough control to keep herself sitting upright.

"It's okay, I know it's scary," Zak continued enthusiastically. His hand rubbed her back.

She closed her eyes briefly, her consciousness slowly returning to full function.

"I promise we'll hang back, okay? You don't need to do anything but follow up."

Nodding, she took a deep inhale, then opened her eyes and sat up a little straighter. "Thank you. And I'm sorry," she whispered.

"Happens to the best of us." He shrugged, his grin warm. "My second proper fight, an awry spear barely grazed me. *Grazed.*" His forehead wrinkled, smiling as he snapped his fingers. "Like that, I was gone. Finally woke back up on my face as they were cleaning up."

Arica smiled at the thought of it, then rubbed her eyes, looking around the abandoned clearing. Maybe she was faint for more than just a minute. "This place is..."

"Terrifying?" he tried, sighing. His hand still rubbed her back, a soothing gesture. "I know. Like I said the other night, it'll take some getting used to, but you can do it, even if you need help like the rest of us."

She took a painful swallow but nodded. "Who helped you?"

"Well, me 'n Rapier were the only Ellterians when I joined up, but I guess there was a fella before me at some point. Anyway, he was a bit of help."

Her mouth dropped open. "Rapier is from the real world, too?"

"New York, I think. But it was a long time ago."

"He's the last one I ever would've pegged for not being native," she admitted.

"And believe it or not, Derrick was some... help. If not hindrance, but..." Zak shrugged, then unhooked her canteen from her shoulder. She took a long musty drink from it, missing the ice-cold filtered stuff from home, but grateful for it anyway.

"I'm ready," she sighed, capping her drink, then stood up.

They followed the trail into the trees but found their own path through. She didn't know what they were doing, let alone what the Zenians were up to.

"Head on!" Vanessa called close by.

Arica looked up and found her standing on a tree branch, hanging over a wide valley in the ground that was too wet to have much growing in it. She could see how rain could easily gather there but it wasn't holding it.

Rapier repeated the command further away, but Zak kept his even pace through the trees.

"Explain what's happening, Zak," Arica panted, barely keeping from slipping on damp leaves on a steep spot.

"The Dovevians staked out on the other side of that ridge right there," he said, gesturing across the dip. "On neutral ground, our numbers actually do something. I don't know what form we're taking yet, though."

"Are they really wanting to fight us?" she asked, audibly nervous.

"Likely. Though it won't surprise me if they end up making us chase them. I don't like that they are aware we're headed this way. It's only a matter of time until we walk into a trap, regardless of how careful we're looking."

Arica spotted a few of their pals just below them, hiding along the trees skirting the clearing.

Ricken scowled like he was eager to bash heads in with the unusually bulky hilt on his short sword, but Elvy was stiff against one tree, her eyes closed. An arrow was knocked and half-drawn in her little wooden bow.

Parel and Skah looked out into the area around their hiding spots.

"Are we holding?" Zak asked, getting Ricken's attention.

"We are," Ricken grunted, nodding at the other three. "You're babysitting."

Arica let her sight fall on the ground, even as Elvy addressed her. "Are you all right now, hunny?"

She smiled a little, shrugging. "I'm fine."

"It's okay," Zak tried, crossing his sword over her body as if to keep her from continuing. "We'll just hang back until we're needed."

Frowning, Ricken went back to looking out.

"WALK ON, VANGUARD!" came a scream from across the field. It wasn't a voice she recognized.

Arica and Zak both jogged closer to the others, finding places to peek without immediately being seen. There was no movement more than could be natural, especially as a drizzle started up. It didn't seem like a good sign, in her mind at least.

"Sounds like Lise is calling out again," Zak said quietly.

Arica was close enough to Ricken to hear a low growl. "Corrin was calling a minute ago."

Her heartbeat raced in anticipation. Was she going to sit back and watch actual violence? Were they going to make her join? The last thing she wanted was to use the little sword that she'd successfully whapped Jake with *once*.

Vanessa called out an order from a distance, power in her voice.

Arica tensed, but nobody around her moved.

Parel swore in a foreign language, so Arica shifted her position to see the furthest part of the treeline. She wasn't sure what she was seeing, but there was movement through the trees. A lot of it.

On their side, a stocky grayed man slid down the steepest part of the ridge and landed perfectly, sword readied even though he looked as calm and emotionless as ever.

Behind Derrick, Jerim jumped down a little less gracefully, then came Kylen and Steen.

Arica couldn't help admiring how controlled and precise their movements were as they slowly advanced. Even Kylen, who looked nervous at the back of the pack.

Then she got a better look at what was emerging from the trees on the opposite side. Men dressed in matte black armor and silver masks that were smooth but for the necessary openings. She couldn't guess how many there were, but they marched forward in lines of about twenty.

"Are we in trouble?" Arica asked in a whisper.

Zak glanced over briefly. "No, they're just soldiers. Derrick could take them all out by himself."

"But it means at least some of Garal's army is at Kopion," Ricken argued.

"I thought we already knew that?" Arica wondered aloud.

In her peripheral vision, she saw the large body of Parel shift, enough that it made her antsy. Then she noticed all eyes were on her.

"Maybe *some* of us knew that," Parel mumbled.

Ricken whispered something under his breath, but Arica could only guess that it was hostile.

With her face warm, she elected to ignore them and went back to watching.

As soon as the four Zenians reached the middle of the field, a call went out first from Vanessa, then was repeated by Lise across the way. "HOLD ALL."

Lightning flashed across the sky, reminding her that her friend was up there somewhere. She had no idea what he could be doing, but she hoped he was okay.

"Why are they holding?" Arica asked quietly, sure Ricken and Zak could hear her.

Nobody answered.

The wave of black soldiers stopped, facing the mere four Zenians. Did this mean that the Dovevians were behind them? Did it mean all they had to do was get through some mortal soldiers to be on their way? But there were at least two Dovevians calling the shots; this had already been established, and it didn't include the one in the air.

Arica could feel her own heartbeat pulsing slowly, waiting for something to happen. Was this part of battle, waiting, staring, until all the soldiers were starving and exhausted?

Then, the four select sprinted forward with no audible order.

Derrick only took a few yards before he stopped, and with barely a wave of the hand, he sent a dozen soldiers reeling backwards into their companions.

The other three went for a more physical assault.

Zak grabbed Arica's arm as an attack called for the rest of the Zenians, but it wasn't Vanessa's voice, more likely Rapier's.

Their closest set of friends ran onto the field, but it was then a cry rang out and a few better-equipped soldiers bombarded the Zenians below.

Zak shook his head. "The Dovevians are hiding within the army. Looks like Derrick has a hand on them, though."

"What are we—"

Thunder boomed like the biggest firework show she'd ever heard, but it was nothing compared to the roaring scream that ripped through the sky as it lit up in terrifying flashes of grays and purples.

Arica's hands flew to her mouth, her ears ringing with the scream's echo. "Was that—"

"One of the solzetairs," Zak shouted grimly.

The ground vibrated, only a little at first, but it grew to a quake hard enough that both of them slid on wet ground. Arica's feet desperately tore through dirt, but she was determined to get back on them. Her hands and sleeves came up caked in mud.

"Can't be good," Zak mumbled, holding both of his hands out as if he was drunk.

She instinctively grabbed his forearm as she stumbled forward, balancing them both. "Are we going to the battle, or are we…?"

Zak used his sword to gesture in a half circle. "We'll just kind of circle around, keep an eye out and stay—"

Arica took a step forward to follow him, but instead of solid ground, her foot went through some thick underbrush and into thin air. She let out an ugly grunt as her stomach hit level ground, her feet landing in soft, churned-up dirt in a little hole about two feet below her. The weeds and leaves she'd broken free stuck to her, obscuring her vision.

"Did I just fall into a trap?" she panted, frozen in place.

"It's just a foxhole," Zak said, crouching to help pull bushes out of the way.

"You must have huge foxes here." She unhooked her cloak from around a sharp, sturdy root and set her elbows on the level ground.

"Maybe a large wolverine."

She had her arms tensed to lift her weight out when unusual colors edged into her vision.

"What?" Zak inquired after a few seconds. He knelt, holding his hands out for her.

Instead of taking his help, she crouched in the large burrow. The tunnel downwards immediately shrunk, probably big enough for a skunk or a red fox.

"So why is this…" She trailed off, mostly talking to herself.

Upon falling in, she'd disturbed a lot of dirt. But the top layer was densely packed, as was the entrance around the actual fox hole itself. She focused on most of the looser, damp soil on the opposite side, sure this was what her vision was pulling her towards.

Before she knew what she was doing, she tore a few handfuls of the soft dirt up and let it sprinkle to her feet. It was so silky, no little sharp rocks. Had she not been following her primal urges to dig, she might've marveled at it for a bit, let it run through her fingers.

"What are you doing?" Zak questioned with genuine surprise. He jumped back about a foot when the soil under his feet loosened.

"Sorry, little critter," she mumbled as she discarded whole armfuls of soil down the hole. At least it wouldn't come up and attack or spray her.

She pushed her arms into the soil once more, and this time her fingers reached all the way into cold air.

Looking up at Zak's confused expression, she smiled nervously. "I don't know why I started this, but there's something back there."

She pulled another armful forward, then shifted her feet to free them. There was still a mound of dirt in her way, but she could see some space behind it. A few scoops later, she decided her hole was big enough. Caked in dirt from head to toe, she wriggled into it on her stomach.

Sure enough, just beyond the loose dirt was a much bigger tunnel, smooth and straight. Her heart raced, terrified of what could lurk in it, but for some reason, she kept army-crawling forward.

"Am I supposed to follow you, or... guard?" Zak called, his voice muffled.

"You can watch my back," she answered, finally deep enough that she could get on her knees. "It looks like it'll go a little way."

She heard a muffled, airy *thump* when he landed on the loose dirt.

She wasn't going to wait around, so, figuring he could keep up on his own, she crawled forward into the dark. Zak was one of the thinner warriors, not much taller than her either, so it wasn't difficult for him to follow.

Roots occasionally reached down to tickle her face and bare arms as she went, once in a while too thick not to break before she could continue through them. She tried not to think about spiders, mice, or the moist air filling her lungs.

"Arica, wait!" Zak barked, so alarmed that she immediately turned to see him on his knees.

He lightly touched the side of the tunnel. "There's residue of magic everywhere," he murmured.

Arica reached out and ran her fingers over the packed dirt, seeing and feeling nothing she didn't expect to. Prickly brown dirt.

"What do you mean? I thought you had to be terrible to leave much of a residue at all," she reasoned.

"This wasn't done discreetly. It was done to last."

"That's it!" she announced. She crawled forward again. There had to be a reason why she felt so strongly about continuing.

"Arica, wait, it could be dangerous," Zak said, his tone serious.

She didn't stop. "I know what I'm doing," she lied. "Just come on, cowboy."

He did as told and followed her around a tight bend and into a wider passageway where they moved into a crouch.

A throaty yell vibrated the dirt above them, very close. Arica stopped, a hand bracing against the wall when Zak almost pushed her over.

"We're under the fight," Zak confirmed quietly.

She pressed her hand against the dirt above them. "I'm not sure this is secure. I don't want to be trapped."

His hand touched her knee, then her shoulder, then followed her arm to where her hand was.

"Getting a little too familiar?" she whispered, trying not to shiver under his cold touch.

"Sorry—"

"Can't you see?" she blurted.

There was a pause, and he pulled his hand away. "Can you?"

"Well yeah, there's..." she glanced from where they'd come. It turned into a black void just like further into the tunnel. She had no idea where the dull glow was coming from.

"Arica," Zak whispered gravely, and told her what she already knew. "It's pitch black in here."

"Let's just keep going," she insisted.

As they went, they could still hear the commotion above, the clanging of swords, the occasional boom of magic, and some muffled calls. It only got louder as they went. The simple fear of being trapped kept her trudging on.

"What's that?" Zak asked, drawing her attention to a crack in the ceiling. She hadn't noticed the light change, but it was a little more yellow.

She stopped to examine it as a passing pair of boots rained dirt on her. It wasn't very big. Her boot shuffled to give her a better view, but she kicked something loose. She found an old wood-handled shovel on the ground.

"What are you doing?" Zak asked as she looked over the handle.

There was a tiny carving of an arrow, pointed towards the head.

"It's... the right size," she mumbled to herself. *Am I going crazy?*

She pushed Zak back a few inches, then shoved the shovel into the crack. An indent waited in the packed dirt, the perfect fit for the handle. It looked like it stuck from the ground above, but she wasn't sure how thick the dirt was from their heads to the forest floor.

Glancing back to see Zak's look of bewilderment, she could only shrug. She didn't know what she was doing either. A heavy *clank* rattled them, vibrating the wedged shovel, chased by a heavy *thud* that shook the grass roots above their heads.

Moans of pain followed the feminine shriek. "DAMNIT, CALLOVOI!"

Arica glanced over her shoulder and gave her companion a meek smile before continuing the race down the tunnel.

"How did you know... that Sutlie would trip over that..." Zak panted as he followed.

Pushing her hands along the walls to force her legs faster, she called back, "I didn't!" *Probably wouldn't've done it if I had.*

She saw another disturbance in the tunnel ahead, and all she could think to herself was, *Act fast.*

A worn spear relaxed on a crude wooden contraption in the middle of the passage. She immediately slammed the spear's shaft into place against the wood brackets, then twisted the lever, setting a simple gear-and-chain pulley into place.

With a grunt, she slammed her boot down on the lever, loosing the spear out of the tunnel. The old contraption creaked quietly.

Arica wasted no more time crawling over it further into the tunnel. It wasn't long before the space widened out and she could finally stand up.

Zak bumped into her but sensed that it was safe to stand up. "How big is this spot?"

She looked carefully, trying to make out the defining lines around her, but wasn't completely sure. The edge to her left curved out, and she could see the other side of the cavern but couldn't tell how far it was. The middle of the ceiling rounded up like the inside of a bubble, but she had the feeling that they needed to stick to the flatter edge.

Someone let out an aggressive war cry above.

"Run," Arica urged, grabbing Zak's cold, muddy hand so she could lead him through the dark.

Her hand ran along the edge to make sure she was staying against it, as her vision slowly revealed how large the space was. Several dozen feet to the other side, nearly the same to their destination. Arica wasn't completely sure she knew where they were going.

They slammed to a stop when the ground shook, a low, forceful boom that rattled the packed dirt all around them, showering them in it.

"What was that?" Arica gasped, looking at the roof. Did it look looser now?

"Sounded just like something Der—"

She grabbed him by the shoulder and jerked him into a sprint, cutting off any more words. She could see the second tunnel, but were they going to make it?

The sound was clear, a grinding, crackly noise that only pushed Arica faster. Tendrils of light flooded over them. Zak could finally see where they were going and barely overcame her before he started dragging *her*.

They dove for the entrance as the dirt crumbled. Air whooshed around them as they crashed into an unrelenting wall.

She never imagined that the sound of a thousand pounds of dirt collapsing would be so *soft*.

Until the screaming started.

Arica choked on the dusty air as she picked her sore limbs out of Zak's.

"Anyone alive down there?" a voice called, the air too thick to recognize it.

Gasping for breath, Arica scrambled for the opening. Heavy rain quickly weighed the floating debris down and helped Arica see the mire of bodies and dirt. It looked like a giant bowl of human brownie batter.

Horror quickly replaced amusement. The deadly tons of dirt could've swallowed up any of her companions.

It was bouncy, so uneven that she struggled to walk across it. The closest person was mostly a boot and an upper shoulder, possibly a woman's, but she wasn't completely sure.

She noticed a shadow and looked up.

Along the torn edge of the collapse, Derrick and Jerim stood, only one of them with a look of awe at the mess. Dark liquid dripped off the edge of Derrick's lax sword.

"I... think that was you, mate," Jerim teased, hitting his companion in the arm, but he got no reaction. He pushed his hair out of his face, a deep amber color in the rain.

"What are you doing down there?" Derrick asked before glancing over at Zak with no more than the twitch of an eyebrow.

"Um... I don't know," Arica admitted sheepishly.

The surrounding dirt shifted as the woman near her worked herself out of the dirt, gasping as soon as her face could find genuine air.

Even speckled in dirt, the blonde-and-black streaked hair was familiar, Sutlie probably.

Arica quickly stepped over and started pulling dirt off of her.

"Leave her, Arica," Zak insisted, jerking her away from the struggling Dovevian.

"But—"

"Stay down," Derrick barked. He stomped his foot down against the edge of the hole, causing a good amount of dirt to follow the rest, showering Sutlie with enough to weigh her down again.

Arica shook a bunch out of her hair.

"Come on, let's get out," Zak urged. "Look, that spot looks sloped enough to climb out."

She saw the spot he was talking about, to the side where it had piled up close to the edge, but it was still about four feet of sheer climb.

Everything was heavy with rain as she pulled herself out of the pit. Zak was on level ground first, unsheathing two short swords.

As soon as she was on her feet again, he tossed one at her. She fumbled to catch it, but it ended up in the dirt.

"Can't leave you unarmed," he said with a snicker.

"I have a sword," she admitted. "I just don't know how to keep from harming myself with it."

Zak started after the gist of the group, where weapons still raged. "At least this way, you won't look like such an easy target!"

Arica looked behind her as he left, watching for Jerim and Derrick, but they'd already moved on. She was too turned around to know which group had come from which side, but she could see that a good third of the low field had collapsed.

The rain made it harder for her to see very far. Her face felt frozen, though most of the dirt had washed off.

Instead of charging into battle as her guardian had done, she skirted the edge and hung in the weeds. Maybe anyone who would kill her wouldn't notice her.

She could feel the pressure of occasional magic, but mostly she noticed the swords banging around. It was chaotic, nothing like she'd ever seen in movies.

For a moment, she tried to watch Derrick exchanging quick blows with a sprightly fellow, a long sepia ponytail flying in circles with him, but it wasn't easy. They wavered in and out of shadows as if a spotlight couldn't decide which to light up.

Rapier slammed blow after blow onto the sword of a large Dovevian she thought Bialsa had called Siddek, sparks shooting in all directions every time their swords connected.

Kylen and Elvy both fought a thin, duel-wielding Dovevian that looked too young to be any kind of warrior, but he wasn't letting that stop him. All four swords spun like crazy, but none of them came close to hitting their dodging targets.

There were only a few of the identical soldiers left, mostly distracting while the Dovevians tried to get in critical blows, but the Zenians were on top of it.

Steen blocked a damaging hit from a shorter Dovevian with blond hair, then threw a soldier off balance just by slamming him with his shoulder.

Aaris and Damad were back to back, pushing back enemies on all sides, mostly with powerful blasts of air directed at their feet.

"I have to help," Arica mumbled to herself, bouncing the sword in her hand. Then she glanced at the blade shiny with rain. No, the only thing she'd do was force someone to rescue her and hinder them more.

So, she crouched down a little further and stayed out of anyone's sight. At least, so she'd thought, until looking above the ridge not far from her hiding spot.

A tall man stood above the fight in a sleeveless coat, his head hooded. A blackened sword hung relaxed at his side. It wasn't until she saw his eyes she knew—even across the distance—he was looking right at her.

How had she not noticed how out of place he'd been on her campus? Like most of the Dovevians, he was a grayed pale like he never got out of their evil lair, and around his thick, defined arm was the pair of wavy black bands she'd seen before on others. His eyes looked like they had dark war paint around them, obvious even under the shadow of his hood.

Little evidence suggested he was going to kill her, but she couldn't erase the feeling of looming danger. She didn't know for sure it was him scribbling with her. She didn't know if he actually wanted to help her and meant to betray his own people.

He carefully inclined his head as if to acknowledge her, then took a few long strides along the ridge away from her.

"DRAW BACK," he bellowed across the field, drawing out the words to be as clear as possible. "OUR BUSINESS IS WITH THE CASTLE."

The cries and screams of battle didn't change. But as Arica watched, eventually, the Dovevians slogged their ways backward as the Zenians chased them down and swung with renewed vigor.

Soon they'd be crawling back up the mountain, and Arica was right in their path.

Aaris and Parel chased the giant Reganold her way, even though they had no chance of keeping up with his ridiculous strides.

Crouching and using her hands to keep her steadier, Arica worked her way through the tall underbrush along the edge. She focused on reaching the other side, even as she heard footsteps much too close to her.

"Arica!"

She looked up as Zak grabbed her arm and dragged her to her feet, far enough away from the Dovevians that there was no use for cover anymore.

They were nearly back to the collapsed pit, the fighting all but over. Arica wanted to make sure there wasn't anyone still struggling to get out of it, but as soon as she peeked over the lip, she regretted it.

The Zenians were dragging the bodies of the fallen soldiers to the edge and piling them in. She was only grateful that most of them still had so much armor on that they weren't any worse than bloody piles of clothing.

Still, she stumbled back and away from the edge, shoving Zak back.

"That's horrible," Arica mumbled through her hand.

She followed Zak's tugging until she spied the old, worn spear sticking out of the ground a few yards away. A piece of black fabric hung from the shaft, but there were no bodies or parts under it.

Oh, good. Maybe I didn't do any real damage.

Zak grabbed it like he was just going to pull it out, but it stuck.

Arica tore off the fabric to find the spear's head, but it was wedged into a freshly cracked boulder bigger than her head.

"That's a surprise..." he muttered, then yanked with both hands.

The boulder cracked just enough to release the spear, but a chunk fell at Arica's feet, the surface cut almost perfectly smooth.

She bent, grabbed a handful of mud, and spread it across a row of small hollows stretched across it like an ant-eaten log.

You've only seen an example of what I can do.

But as worrying as this was, the last word embedded in the rock was the most worrying.

Arica.

Her heart raced dangerously, pulling oxygen from her brain.

"I don't have the brainpower for this..." she whispered breathlessly, then stood upright.

Zak stared after their companions, leaning heavily on the spear as he worked forward. "Come on."

Before sprinting after him, she looked over her shoulder for one last look at the Dovevian causing her so much trouble.

There he stood in the same place, but this time the white-blond Dovevian that barely looked old enough to be fighting waited at his side, his hands and sword shaking in anticipation.

Then Arica's secret companion caught her eye for another moment, nothing but a curious gaze as he set a hand on the other's shoulder.

So what does he want?

28

VOICE OF REASON

"As much as I'd like to, Enileny, we can't keep marching," Rapier reasoned to Jerim as they approached the camp. Arica trailed along behind them as she'd lost her guide in the chaos of cleaning up. "I don't even know where Vanessa or Jrasko are yet."

Then, before the redhead could answer, Rapier cupped his hands around his mouth and yelled out orders. "Pitch one tent! Vanessa's will be for the wounded."

The atmosphere of the camp's residents was dark, a tangible mix of defeat and exhaustion. Most of the depression Arica felt, however, was her own. Her brain was still slowly digesting so much. Dozens of dead laid out in dirt. A confusing message placed just so. The sudden and possibly permanent disappearance of her closest friend. Or maybe her biggest worry, the confirmation that her secret confidant was in fact a Dovevian.

The pulse in her temples threatened a headache.

"Teres, are the fields up yet?"

Arica looked to the left where Derrick and Aaris stood a dozen yards away, both on a rise overlooking their clearing.

Derrick said nothing but raised a fist that Rapier seemed satisfied by.

Zak was on the ground in front of them, helping Parel patch up an ugly, bloody gash on the big guy's shoulder. Arica, unsure what else to do, followed Rapier through the middle of the camp to where a few people circled around an already giant fire.

She looked back when she heard a loud yell.

Dragged towards the smaller tent by both Damad and Skah, Ricken struggled to keep his limp, crooked leg under him. Blood splattered on the ground from his already-soaked side as he fought back like he was still on the battlefield.

"Careful, you've got—" Damad tried, but stopped to concentrate.

Elvy approached the three of them cautiously but stayed far enough back when Skah let go entirely. She then used a bit of momentum and slammed into Ricken from behind, throwing the injured man into the dirt.

"Derrick," Elvy called desperately, taking a few long strides back towards the edge of camp. "I'll need you with this one!"

Arica saw Derrick's descent as he started towards the smaller tent. The sound of steel hitting steel distracted her, making her turn back towards the fire.

"Young ones, thinking they're impervious even on the brink of death," Rapier grunted to nobody in particular as he discarded his sword into a growing pile of weapons. Many grotesque and disgusting substances caked the blades.

Arica stayed by Kylen as Rapier barked a few more orders.

She let her weight fall on the ground next to the other young Zenian, glancing across the weapon pile at where Steen rested with a stone in one hand and a sword in the other. Both of his hands were sheathed in thick leather gloves.

"Here," Kylen urged, pulling a wet rag out of a pot sitting against the fire. Then, like a game of block stacking, he jerked a dirty sword out of the pile and handed both items to Arica.

"Isn't it usually the job of individuals to keep their weapons clean and sharp?" Arica asked, scrubbing dirt off the short, plain blade.

"Not when you've got someone around who can do it in a fraction of the time," Kylen explained, nodding at Steen.

Steen acted like he hadn't heard the compliment as he finished one and set it to the side. A few weapons were already laid out, shining like new. Then he held his hand out to Kylen, who handed over a freshly cleaned one.

Arica stopped scrubbing to watch Steen's process. He held the hilt of the long, skinny sword in his left hand, parallel to his body. Then, fingers barely moving off of his knee, the edges of it slowly shone. It was only about thirty seconds of this before the metal glowed around the edge, a precise half inch of it all around.

This was the point when Steen picked up the rock again, a dark, wet stone. The sword sizzled and steamed as he roughly stroked the stone along it with long, precise movements.

"I thought you couldn't use magic on common metals," Arica said as she handed over a less-than-perfectly clean sword.

"*You* can't," asserted Steen. "My touch is a little different. Still can't make or destroy it, and I can't do it when I've skin contact with any."

"He does some useful and cool stuff with it, though," Kylen interjected cheerfully.

"And since we can't all go around just using swords of gold and silver..." Arica added, trying to prove she understood.

Kylen pulled out a skinny blade, then found a couple of long arrows.

"Are we really fixing Elvy's arrows?" he asked, looking up at their blacksmith.

"She said they were her last ones, so I don't see why not. Just don't cut yourself on them. They're probably still acidic."

Arica looked up as she heard a cry for help.

Vanessa stumbled forwards through the mud, all but supporting a much bigger person with her shoulders. His upper torso and right arm were completely wrapped in her cloak, only leaving his left for her to drag.

"Jake," Arica gasped, abandoning her chores to help.

Mud caked both of them from head to toe, and even though Jake was trying, he was obviously struggling to stay completely conscious and only kept Vanessa off balance.

Arica sprinted towards them, hoping to help somehow, but Rapier got there ahead of her. He slipped between the pair, hauling Jake up by the unwrapped arm, and gave him an extra few inches to lean on.

They made a little more progress. Arica followed, unable to help, when Jake's knees buckled out from under him completely.

Rapier barely caught him, battling Jake's generous relationship with gravity, and Vanessa tried, but mostly had her hands on his chest, avoiding his entire right side.

"Seven, lift him up," Rapier panted.

The two of them lifted the limp body and propped him mostly in Rapier's arms.

They half dragged, half carried Jake into the same tent they'd dragged an unwilling Ricken into, staggering most of the way. Arica followed behind at an okay distance, curious but unable to butt in until she saw Vanessa wave a hand at her, urging her in.

There was a row of cots where Vanessa's usually was, taking up the width of the space. Ricken was in the far one, a scratchy blanket covering all but his dirty, sleeping face. Elvy was bent over Damad, pouring a blue liquid over a few animalistic scratches across his neck.

"I'm glad you've survived," Vanessa mumbled, wrapping an arm around Arica's shoulders and pulling her out of the way.

Rapier finished pulling himself out from under dead weight, leaving Jake half hanging off of a cot.

"I apologize for stranding you, but I had more pressing things to take care of."

Arica glanced at Jake again, then shook her head. "It's okay," she whispered with stress. "What happened?"

"Where's Lord Teres?" Vanessa asked, looking up at the commander. "Go fetch him."

"He'll be right back, so he promised," Elvy whispered, even though she stared with worry at Jake.

Vanessa glanced back at Arica. "I tried to chase them in case I could distract or help. I was at the site as soon as they crashed into the trees. Jake was struck when the lightning lashed out. I was sure both of them had fallen, but when I arrived I didn't see Drake, solzetair or human."

They watched as Elvy finally jumped over to Jake. Arica briefly wondered why they weren't doing anything themselves. Surely a thousand-year-old dignitary would know at least as much as a medical student, probably *her* medical student.

"Rapier, report," Vanessa requested as she wiped her face clean with a rag.

"No Dovevians were severely hurt, but most of the soldiers they sent were killed. You and Jrasko were the only two unaccounted. No casualties, though I've been told Ricken is still in awful shape." He nodded at the sleeping warrior on the other side of the room. "The minor injuries of others have been treated, more or less."

"We'll have to see where Lord Kisok stands tomorrow," Elvy added, digging through her bag so slowly that it was almost torturous for Arica. "He might improve through the night with Teres's coaxing."

Vanessa nodded stiffly, then took a deep breath and crossed her arms. "We did well. Their plan was to thin us out before we march on Kopion. I sent Bialsa to try again to alert Commander Herak. Hopefully, they were able to make a little progress from their end while the Dovevians were distracted away from the castle. She'll also be giving me a better picture of what we're up against."

This all sounded reasonable to Arica, so she didn't ask questions.

Elvy peeled the dirty cloak back from Jake's torso, so Vanessa approached to help her. It stuck to his skin.

Arica had to cover her mouth and look away as they revealed the skin underneath. The entire surface of his arm was charred black, covered in dark, sticky blood, and dirt. Other than being dirty, his clothes were still completely intact, so Elvy dug out a knife and started cutting away the shoulder of his shirt.

"Where's Lord Teres?" Vanessa mumbled anxiously, her expression only one of worry. She helped work his clothes back, revealing that a lot of his side and shoulder were also charred, but not as bad as the arm.

It looked papery, fragile, so much so that Arica convinced herself that he'd been wrapped in paper bandages that burned away. The smell itself wasn't as bad as she might've expected, almost familiar, but was also strong considering most of it was the same old swamp smell she'd carried in her nose for days.

"Kind of... porky..." she mumbled to herself.

Then Elvy pulled the arm outwards, laying it a little further from his body.

"That's awful," Arica gasped, both of her hands against her chest.

With nothing else to do, Vanessa stepped back, folding her arms. "He looked worse as an animal. Drake tore out most of the feathers in this wing. Several of the bones shattered. I wouldn't assume anything, but the injuries looked like they transferred well when he changed back, so I don't think anything is more than fractured."

Arica shook her head, feeling slightly disoriented. "It doesn't... make any sense. I mean, transforming itself, but having wounds transform with you...? It... hurts my brain to even think about."

Vanessa waved to Elvy, pointed at a gash in the meaty part of Jake's calf, then looked back over her shoulder at Arica. "Just because you don't understand doesn't mean the science is absent."

Derrick entered just as Arica's face turned red, excusing her from any garbled responses.

"Give me room," the sullen man ordered, and all three ladies backed up as far as the small space would allow.

"Jadrion, go supervise cleanup and setup," Vanessa directed.

As the commander ducked out of the tent, unnatural blue light grew to life along the canvas above them, giving Derrick more than enough light to see by.

Curious as ever, Arica watched closely to figure out what Derrick was doing as he bent over the mess of skin and clothes. One of his hands braced against the cot, then the other went to touch some of the burnt skin but didn't actually make contact. Instead, he let his hand hover about a quarter inch away, fingers flat.

The room grew still and silent, all eyes on the healer and his patient.

Arica noticed the air between Jake and Derrick's hand distorted, only confirming her confidence that he was using magic.

She wondered if his special powers had anything to do with the bands on his arm. It was the one he was using. *All the Dovevians have them, right?* The ones she could remember. She had never been remotely close to the dark tattoos, so she hadn't noticed before how they were made up of tiny symbols, none of which looked familiar, though they had a slight hieroglyphic look to them. The band above his elbow had bigger symbols, each separated, but the one below had smaller ones, with each of them linked to the next by at least one black stroke.

Derrick waved a hand at Elvy, who handed over a small pair of pliers.

"It doesn't look any different," Arica said aloud, upon noticing the patch that Derrick had been focusing on.

He didn't look up as he monotonously said, "You can't heal something dead."

She shut her mouth and just watched as he slowly, carefully, used the tweezers to peel up a bit of the char until he could discard a few small pieces.

Arica repressed her gag reflex and focused once again on the Dovevian's tattoos.

Setting down the tool, Derrick looked up at Vanessa before blankly stating, "There's venom in his blood."

Vanessa's shoulders fell as she let out a frustrated sigh.

Pulling away the torn-up shirt, Derrick didn't have to search long before finding a mark over Jake's hip. It was a large red bite mark in an elongated shape, leveling from about the lowest ribs to just past his jeans, but it wasn't anywhere near big enough to be from a solzetair.

"He's immune to the venom," Vanessa dismissed stubbornly.

"As the demon," Derrick said.

Vanessa stared at the bite with distaste, her arms tight across her chest.

"He's not dead, so a resistance, but it's evidently working on him."

Vanessa set the heel of her hand on her forehead, and Arica suspected the men were waiting for her to tell them what to do.

Then she let her hand down, pacing back away from the cot. "Just do it," she huffed.

Elvy pulled a few things out of her bag, then handed a knife to Derrick.

Arica didn't know what they were going to slice, but never would've guessed he'd set the knife in his own palm and give it a quick, precise cut. It wasn't particularly deep, but small beads of dark liquid immediately gathered.

The redhead carefully mixed a white powder into a tiny jar of colored oils with a little tool, nodding as soon as it was fully mixed.

Derrick tipped his lax fist over Jake's open mouth, allowing a few strings of the viscous blood to drizzle out of his palm.

Like a flash, Elvy was there, pouring water from a silver canteen after it.

Vanessa froze, watching their progress as Derrick set his clean hand flat over Jake's heart. There was silence for a few long heartbeats, until Jake breathed in heavily, muscles tensing. Derrick didn't move, but Elvy set her hands on either side of Jake's head.

"Stay still," Derrick suggested placidly as his patient squirmed ever so slightly.

Vanessa sighed, mumbling into her hand, "Bad timing, boy."

Then the Dovevian looked up and nodded at Elvy, who promptly emptied the white paste into Jake's mouth.

"Come on," she mumbled encouragingly, even as Jake continued fighting out of unconsciousness.

Derrick waited another minute before removing his hand, and Vanessa took it as an okay to check the same spot they'd looked before.

"Much better," she sighed with relief.

"Still at risk of infection," Derrick mused as he did the same thing from before, passing his hand over the charred layers of flesh. "We'll need to wash the dirt away, carefully. Find something to numb the pain."

This statement brought Arica's attention to Jake's face. He wasn't moving, but his jaw was locked, his eyes squeezed closed. She didn't want to be in everyone's way, but there was such little space in the tent that she decided it didn't matter where she was.

She squeezed past Elvy, who dug around in her bag for more things, then situated herself near Jake's head, against the tent wall and mostly out of the way.

"Master Damage, do you still have any of that dried root?" Elvy asked.

Vanessa made a humming sound as she picked up a bag and dug through the pockets around the outside. Eventually, she came up with a tiny leather pouch and handed it over.

Elvy made the little elixir within a minute of rushed stirring and checking. She poured a small amount on a clean rag and held it out to Arica.

"Cover his nose and mouth, he'll breathe in plenty of it," she urged softly.

She did as told, using both of her hands to gently secure the rag over Jake's face. She focused on Derrick's hands as he reached across the larger man to the bite marks, doing the same slow waving movement. The little gauged, wet marks slowly healed over under the Dovevian's presence, weaving new tissue into the wounds. It only took him a few minutes to cover the bite, front and back, before he returned to the burned patches.

"Do we have enough clean cloth to wrap him in?" Derrick asked evenly.

Vanessa set a hand on her chin for a moment, then grabbed her blood and dirt-soaked cloak. "I'll make something work."

Elvy scooted to the corner of the tent, grabbed a pail, and set it near Jake's feet. Arica couldn't help watching it fill with water on its own, then begin to steam.

Derrick moved so suddenly as he reached across for more rags that Arica jumped. He dipped one of them into the hot water, then held it out to her. Nervously, she took it, not knowing exactly what he expected her to do. It was hot enough that it stung her hand, but she kept her mouth shut.

"This is done," Derrick directed, pointing to the lower section of his side. "But don't touch his arm."

Biting her tongue, Arica walked around the cot to the place indicated and started to scrub away dirt, dry blood, and dead skin. Charred pieces easily flaked off under the pressure, leaving red, cratered flesh exposed.

Derrick wrapped the arm in bits of shirt and laid it across his chest, giving her access to much more of his ruined skin than she ever wanted to see.

He's right-handed, heavily, as he admitted, she thought, glancing up at Derrick as he worked. *I hope he'll be able to figure it out.*

"So... the blood thing. Is it a regular thing you do? Feeding people your blood?" she asked. Apparently she was the only one who ever needed small talk.

"When it's needed," he answered, indifferent to her teasing tone.

"How did it fix the venom?" she asked, this time seriously.

"My blood is poisonous, so strong it can neutralize almost any other toxin," he recited monotonously.

"So, it kills the venom, then you cure the poison with something else and it's all good. How do you even find something like that out, though? Did someone try to lick your wounds one day or something?"

Derrick didn't change his hand's pace at all, just as blank as he'd been at the start of the conversation. "It was an accidental finding, a common occurrence with my superlative abilities as they develop. All being advantageous in their own manner."

Arica's eyebrows stitched together before she looked up at the strange man. "I don't suppose the word 'humble' is in that big head of yours?"

"Yes. Having modest behavior, a lack of arrogance, in some cases, that which is poor and of inferior quality." Then he looked up, serious as ever. "I have a lexicon in my belongings. I'll lend it to you if you'd like."

"Excuse me?" she blurted without thinking. She was struggling to understand how he'd meant it.

Then he looked up and gave her a forced, stiff smile that only affected his mouth. "Of course."

There was no point in trying to continue talking with the man, so Arica focused on her task.

Vanessa returned shortly, carrying an armful of bleached cloth. Arica couldn't watch, but they carefully wrapped Jake's arm before Derrick started his tricks on it.

"Arica," Vanessa addressed, her voice betraying her exhaustion. "Go eat. We've done enough for tonight."

Arica shifted her bag higher on her shoulder as she stepped carefully between crowded bedrolls in the low tent. Without Jake, she wasn't sure exactly where she was allowed to be. Maybe there were some unspoken rules to sleeping arrangements.

Eventually she settled on a vacant space between two other claimed spots and unfurled her own bed. A few people came and went from the shelter, most still eating or arranging weapons.

So, when she pulled out her little magic satchel, she wasn't worried anyone would spy on her. A crisp, new message lay on the bottom.

I saw you, it accused. *You look stronger than last. Dirtier, as well, but tougher, more threatening.*

Arica leaned back on her full bag, frowning. "Of course I look different," she sighed, tiredly. "New place, new people. New... life." All of that seemed fake now. Had school ever existed? Was her family just her imagination? Why did that seem so far, so false, when she was in a land of magic and danger? She shook her head and those thoughts away so she could answer the inked compliments.

I look threatening?

Instead of overthinking things while waiting for the response, she closed her eyes and focused on her breathing to relax. She was so tired, yet the day's events kept her alert.

Eventually, her nervous checking turned out to have a reason.

I said more, the Dovevian boasted. *I could still kill you with nigh a glance.*

Arica bit her lip, trying to read into the words. *Why didn't you?*

His answer was roundabout, as so many of them had been. *Do you still hesitate to trust me?*

I was surprised you didn't come after me; she said truthfully, remembering the towering person a spear's throw away.

This relationship is a painful one, is it not?

She wasn't sure if she had time to write circles with him, so she got straight to the point. *Just get it over with. Why do you want to help me?*

You're a sharp young lady, yet nobody's given you the credit. I want to be the first.

Why?

Will you do something for me?

She put the papers down. "This is it," she whispered aloud. *The moment he tricks me into helping him and the Dovevians and makes me seem like a traitor.* Even so, there lingered a desire to get an upper hand over him. To help the Zenians finally get what they needed.

She smiled a little. Because a twenty-year-old girl could tip the scale on a thousand-long war between occultists.

"Right," she giggled, picking up the pen to scribble a quick, *What?*

His answer was anticlimactic. *Give me two stones.*

That's an odd request, she replied sincerely.

Do it and go where you cannot be heard. Within screaming distance, for your safety, but outside of your working fields.

Arica's brain started working hard. This didn't sound horribly deadly, but she still hesitated. The Dovevians were cunning and nasty. Would it be dangerous to give a Dovevian a rock, though? Were fingerprints special in DeRael? Would it give him the coordinates of their camp? And why did she need to leave the force fields?

She hit her head back on the hard casing that should've held a weapon but instead held a bunch of oversized feathers. If Jake had been available to come, she'd give him the decision. But she'd have to be brave.

Brave enough to give a rock to a bad guy.

She slipped out of the tent, thinking no harder.

The sky was dark, the stars like silver glitter on a black sheet, but the moon had disappeared an hour before. It kept the Zenians' large fire an obvious point of reference. Not that she planned on going very far.

Arica walked past the long, quivering shadows of her teammates, as casually as possible, while clutching the satchel to her chest.

"This is not suspicious," she slowly mouthed for the tenth time since leaving her bed.

She reminded herself to stay casual, but couldn't help looking back over her shoulder at the campfire. Everyone all but ignored her, a helpful enough occurrence.

Her heart skipped in shock when her gaze caught a pair of black eyes strongly trained on her.

Her arms tightened around the satchel as the Dovevian's knowing stare penetrated her. Was she inadvertently doing something so suspicious that Derrick couldn't help but recognize she was up to no good?

Just before she gave up the mission for good, Derrick completely loosened, leaning over and responding to something Jerim had said to him a moment before. Arica waited with hesitant breath, but he didn't look at her again.

A shiver ran down her spine as she hurried to move on.

Just taking care of business, she recited, in case anyone asked what she was doing. But as she reached what she could only assume was the edge of the protective barriers, neither Damad nor Aaris graced her with anything other than a quick nod of acknowledgment.

She let out a bit of breath she hadn't noticed she'd been holding. She was officially exposed.

Fingers shaking from either cold or anticipation, Arica began using the toes of her boots to scrounge around for a pair of stones, as per the request.

"Do they need to be big?" she muttered to herself. "Smooth? Does it matter?"

The ground was spongy under her feet, covered in short, soft grass. There didn't seem to be an abundance of rocks, but there had to be some somewhere. It was the outdoors, after all.

She climbed a little hill, happy with the resulting vantage of the campfire below, with an easily accessible escape route downwards and enough loose gravel for her to pick through.

After discarding several oddly shaped ones, and many that she'd deemed too small, she found a pair that looked and felt about the same, and set them into her bag. A boulder gave her a comfortable enough place to rest, even if it was a little cold. Like everything else in the entire area.

Hugging herself, she remembered the solzetair feathers in her things down below. Jake had told her they'd made a good lining for her cloak, but just thinking about them made her wonder if there was anything they could do for him now. Maybe some magical property, maybe just more warmth for his injuries. Then again, if solzetairs were so flammable, maybe he didn't need a bunch of feathers creating an even bigger chance of being lit on fire again.

She checked the inside of the satchel after several minutes. To her surprise, one of the pair still rested on the bottom, but it was different now. It glowed softly. A note lay underneath it, so she slid it out and squinted.

"Hold it in your hand, and speak," she recited slowly. But she didn't touch it. Instead, she wrote, *I'm too nervous that it's going to do something painful to me. I don't trust you.*

She was impatient to get the ordeal over with, so checked the bag every two seconds or so until the response came.

I promise it's nothing dangerous. Pick it up.

Arica closed her eyes. "I'm... an idiot," she griped, reaching for the glowing stone. It was pleasantly warm and fit perfectly in her hand.

The glowing dimmed a considerable amount.

"What the heck am I thinking?" she whispered, setting the heel of her hand against her forehead.

"Maybe that you should've placed your trust sooner."

Arica jumped, looking for the owner of the deep, fruity voice in the dark trees. "Where are you?" she squeaked, trying to control the shivering taking over her body.

"At my comfortably furnished post. You don't think I'd be over there, knee-deep in muck and drenched to the bone, do you? Here I have hot, clean water in a bath, clean linens, quality food—"

"I get it, you're being treated like a prince, and I'm here looking like a swamp witch." She kept glancing around the hill, making sure she wasn't being tricked, but eventually rested her eyes on the rock in her hand. "You sound like you're sitting next to me."

If anything surprised her again, she was sure her heart would throw in the towel.

"Magic, dear. It's a usual luxury in the Dovevian rankings," he boasted proudly. "Though I know that using them for mere satisfaction in The Zenian Court is to transgress the more basic of laws."

Arica fell quiet, cupping the stone between both of her hands. The previous bravery she'd felt had dissipated the moment she'd heard the elegant tones. Would it be so hard to drop the stone at her feet and walk straight back to her bed?

"I hope after all we've been through, you aren't still afraid of me?" he asked, sounding almost sincerely concerned.

"Maybe," she finally spoke, her voice weak. "But I'm still not convinced that you're not trying to get to the Zenians through me."

"A fair enough assumption, given my standing."

She could practically hear a smirk, maybe one similar to Jake's frequent amusement at her naivety.

"What do you want?" she demanded, stronger after clearing her throat. "I feel like I'm cheating on my friends."

"I mostly wanted to see if you trusted me," the voice admitted playfully.

"Look," she moaned, both hands roughly rubbing her tired face. "I'm not even supposed to be here. I just wanted to make sure I wouldn't hurt anyone else with this stupid... And..."

"You belong here," he whispered, almost evilly.

"What makes you so sure?"

"Because you *are* here. And because of you, the tides of this war have a chance to shift. Because of you, and *me*."

She sighed, wearily staring up at the sparkly sky. "Why are you still playing at this? I have a better description of you now, there's twenty people that I could go ask right now. Find out who you actually are."

"So why don't you?" he inquired curiously.

She felt a pressure on her chest. "Honestly... I'm terrified of putting a name to your face. Because I'll also know your crimes."

"Everyone makes mistakes," the Dovevian tried to reason, but even he didn't sound completely convinced.

"Like, what do you think we do all day? The stories I've heard? Most of you guys have killed your families, or tried to. Murdered, raped, purposely crippled. You make animals suffer and hunt people for entertainment. Betrayal, martyr, deceit, they're all things you guys are guilty of let alone your basic lack of humanity. And it's all of you. Lise, Asriel, Siddek, Ransom, Drake, Sutlie, Reganold, Anraquella, Nian, Navin; you're all garbage. Then you get King Garal, who's behind this entire bloody WAR!" She swallowed tightly, forcing her shoulders to loosen, then took a calming breath. She was going to draw attention. "But please, continue to tell me how wonderful you all are."

"It's mostly true," he answered simply, his voice even. "Considering our customs are grossly exaggerated in the eyes of our enemies. But perhaps I underestimated your knowledge on the subject."

"Well? Are you going to tell me which one is yours?"

She heard a low chuckle before he answered. "How do you know you've even *heard* my name?"

Arica paused, wondering if she was missing something. "Are you... trying to tell me you're like... some secret weapon? That the Zenians don't know about?"

"I've never lied to you, and I won't start now," he said in a way that made her wonder if he was trying to be sweet, and coming up just short. "No, one of the names you mentioned is, in fact, mine. As are a *portion* of the crimes."

Waiting for him to continue, Arica fingered the stone, but he said nothing more. "So, you won't tell me?"

"As I mentioned before, I'm mostly here for my own entertainment. But if you guessed, I'd be disinclined to lie."

"Well, you seemed in charge somewhat..." she mused. Then she sharply inhaled.

"What?" the Dovevian asked with mischief in his voice.

He didn't fight; he called the shots; and he wasn't as aggressive or dim as the other Dovevians she'd caught whiffs of. And he knew about the portals, about Earth.

He's the king.

Arica dropped the rock into her bag as if it had stung her, silencing the Dovevian. She snapped her bag up and started climbing back down the hill as quickly as she could without hurting herself.

"I need to ask about the king."

29

SAVING DeRael

Aloud metal banging violently jerked Arica from the bloody scenes ac-companying her fitful sleep. The clanging continued even as a woman started shouting out instructions.

"Andolviam! Up and out, ladies and gentlemen, we've only a few minutes to eat!" Vanessa called like a stern mother after her children.

But unlike children, the Zenians around Arica immediately hustled to life in the barely existent light of dawn.

Finally, Vanessa's banging stopped, and movement increased.

Arica wasn't sure if she was irritated or grateful. Grogginess clung to her, her overactive mind freely acting out the battle from the day before, and the realization that night. She'd never gotten the chance to ask about King Garal before everyone was down for the night, but she hadn't tried very hard. The more she thought about it, the more she was convinced she was wrong.

She packed up her bags faster than usual, everything exactly where it needed to be. But she was still one of the last people out of the tent.

Morning chill hung heavily in the air. The fire they'd made was so small that all it could do was warm the underside of the large pot Parel dished food from.

Her dishes were ready to go, so within moments, she sat next to Kylen with a bowl of liquefied oats. She blew the steam from it then took a bite without concern for the temperature.

As a kid, she hated it when her mother cooked oatmeal. It was slimy and gross, so why would she want it when she could have a bowl of crisp, sugary cereal? But there in the middle of the forest, the sweet, sticky, minty dish was absolutely delicious. It was her only outside source of warmth, and she knew it would keep her from feeling hungry again for quite a while.

Even as focused on her breakfast as she was, it was hard not to notice Jake as he stalked over to the fire, eyes narrow and body stiff as he accepted his meal.

"Jake!" Arica said with a mouthful. He looked over as she jumped from her seat, but his expression didn't change. She watched as he carefully lowered himself to the ground close to her, his injured arm hidden in his cloak.

"How are you feeling?" she asked quieter. Though it was becoming more apparent.

He set his bowl on his lap and clumsily chased a spoonful. "Enough," he grunted.

She frowned, then sat back down, observing him. His hair clung to his face and neck, but his injured side faced away from her. His sleeve hung empty, his arm bandaged securely to his chest.

He shot her a glare for staring. "I'm fine, I promise. Been through much worse."

Arica averted her eyes quickly, but couldn't stifle her concern. "Your eyes are really red," she mumbled passively.

"It's the hullek; for pain," he answered in a low tone, then took another bite.

Finished, she set her dishes to the side to wash later. She leaned her elbows on her knees and pulled her cloak tighter around her, staring into the fire.

"What happened?"

Jake took a few more slow bites without answering her question, but she didn't press. Then he climbed to his feet. She assumed he had things to do, and didn't want to talk to her, but as he took a step away, he beckoned her. "Come on."

Arica let out an inaudible sigh. What trouble was he going to drag her into this time?

Against his reputation, he brought her barely far enough away to even be worth moving, but possibly out of earshot. He sat down on a low branch so thick it could've been some confused fork of the trunk. Arica had to jump to pull herself next to him.

"Glad to see you're actually surviving DeRael," he started almost sourly.

"Yeah, well, apparently I'm some crazy war machine," she said with a wave of her hand. She caught another whiff of a rich scent that, while she couldn't place, smelled very familiar.

He let out a grunt that was pretty far from a laugh, but that's how she took it.

"But I mean, aside from almost being buried alive, all I really did was hide," she reasoned. Even though it was only partly true, she didn't want to brag about what she'd done without knowing exactly what it was.

"What about you?" Hopefully urging him into a story, she settled in, trying to get more comfortable despite the rough surface. She would wish she was back there after a few more hours of walking.

"He didn't even see me coming," Jake started with a long exhale. "But that advantage was pretty short-lived. I barreled into him, nearly snapping his neck with one bite, but—"

"Well, that's great!" Arica cheered prematurely. "Means he's poisoned too!"

Jake shook his head. "Dovevians are immune to most poisons. This one included. I had a good start, but haven't as much experience fighting solzetairs. We clawed, and bit, and tore, keeping air under our wings throughout. At one point, he'd caught me up in his tail, trapped my wings, but he wasn't strong enough to keep us both up. I could feel the energy in the air as lightning struck around us. Drake let me go, and a moment later, it hit me. All I can remember is blurriness, orange light and... falling. I think he attacked, but I couldn't move to stop him. Vanessa must've scared him off around then, otherwise, there would've been a lot more damage."

He squirmed a little, visibly uncomfortable.

"Lived to die another day," Arica sighed, rubbing the palm of her own hand. She looked over his skin a little, able to better see the red, blistered area just over the collar of his shirt. His neck, ear, and cheek, while not charred black and dead, had turned a bright red color, like he'd been out to the beach for three days straight without sunblock.

She watched him reach to his jaw to cure an itch, but he flinched when his nails scraped the sensitive skin.

Arica kicked around a few leaves bigger than her head. They looked like they'd fallen from their tree. "Is it weird? To think that you could just about live indefinitely?"

Breaking out of his own trance, Jake glanced down at her with a tired expression. "Nature will always catch up, eventually... Part of me wonders if this injury is its way of telling me to slow down."

"Sure," Arica whispered, her cheeks warming. "Since I just decided I don't hate you, suddenly you discover you're ready to die."

He smirked tightly, then shook his head. "I've been feeling it for a few years now." They turned quiet, then suddenly he let out a long, heavy sigh. "Nah, I probably still have a few hundred years of babysitting and torture left..."

"Good." She smiled but didn't look up at him. Maybe he understood her humor a little better than she thought. She leaned away as their shoulders almost touched. She didn't want to hurt him, and he was shifting again.

Without thinking, she reached out, letting her fingertips touch his pink cheek. It was burning hot, but instead of recoiling like she expected, he pressed against her cool touch, closing his eyes.

She let her entire hand spread across his cheek, then softly she asked, "Are you okay?"

"Probably." He shrugged, casually pulling away. "Think I'll look any less intimidating missing a limb?"

"Probably more," she giggled lightly. "You really think you'll lose it?"

He titled his head slightly, then gestured at it. "I can't even feel any pain in it. But even if Elvy and Teres say it'll be fine, I'm still preparing to lose it."

"Hope you can fight left-handed."

"Not as well." He met her gaze. "But I'll learn."

Without thinking, Arica carefully climbed to her knees and leaned close to him. She ran her knuckles down his neck, feeling the damaged skin. She didn't really know what to expect, so as she touched the edge just under his collar, it felt so unrealistic, like the smooth, crunchy bubbles of burnt cheese on a casserole.

She carefully tugged the collar down, but most of that had bandages. *Alcohol,* she thought to herself, the scent stronger now. It was something she easily recognized this close. *He smells like whiskey.*

Jake turned his head, the resulting crackling sound reminding her of stepping on dry leaves. He shut his eyes, grimacing slightly.

Arica leaned over, steadying herself by setting a hand on his opposite shoulder, then carefully kissed his jaw, the heat feeling much more intense on her lips than her fingers.

"I hope you don't get a fever," she mumbled, her brow furrowing.

Jake frowned, tilting his head at her as she backed up. "I'm fine," he repeated flatly.

Her hands went up. "Forgive my concern, oh noble warrior."

As he smirked, she let her fingers rest close to his burn. "You know... there was one day my best friend was trying to get me to pick a date. I had to admit that I liked odd guys and traits, that the handsome ones are too plain for me..." She swallowed, not sure why she was telling him this, but forged on. They paused for a moment, staring each other down. Then Arica shrugged. "Well, if I'd known from the beginning that you were a thousand-year-old warrior in converse, with the hots for danger and pain, I wouldn't've dismissed you so casually."

She caught his gaze again, his a curious, almost accusative look.

"Guess I shouldn't judge a book by its cover," she added nervously, putting her arms around her waist. The pressure in her chest rose a little as she looked back at him and his false half-smile until she was uncomfortable.

He shifted, but it contorted his features into pain in a flash.

A pang of false guilt ate at her stomach as she let her eyes settle on the ground. "I'm sorry this happened to you."

Jake continued rubbing the sore spot without answering, but she didn't know how that could be helping. Maybe it was just distracting him.

Arica's fists clenched. "Why would your own dad do this to you?" she demanded angrily.

Looking up at her, Jake didn't look too serious anymore. "It's not personal, Arica. I've gotten a fair share of chunks out of him."

She rolled her eyes, turning her body away from him. "This whole Zenian family thing is messed up."

"The perks of being nearly immortal," Jake said, then clicked his tongue.

Arica glanced at his feet, spaced evenly apart with even weight distribution. Why was he always so level? She frowned, noticing Vanessa stalking around the newly abandoned campfire a few yards before them.

Jake glanced over at her. "She wants to talk to you."

"How can you tell?" Arica asked meekly as the intimidating woman approached.

Nobody said anything even as they separately made eye contact with their superior.

"Good morning," Arica tried politely.

"We've yet to see," Vanessa replied. She approached closer than Arica expected, then like the sting of a scorpion, she reached for the sheath at Arica's hip and drew out the sword.

Arica didn't have the response time to do much more than stare in shock, even as she offered it back to her.

"Show us what you've learned."

She resisted the urge to look at Jake for permission and took her weapon from her superior.

Arica shifted her feet on the level ground until they were spaced apart. The short, shiny sword was heavy in her hand. She expected an immediate barrage of attacks to batter her down. Instead, she had to struggle to turn around, following the circling steps of her opponent.

"When I was a young girl," Vanessa began, her voice strong. "The Zenian Court was a different group. We were advisors, scholars. Granted..." She let out a warm chuckle that made Arica smile a little. "I was trained to be a warrior, but only because I wanted to be one."

Arica grew dizzy following the woman as she circled her, but wanted to stay on her toes, if only to impress her.

Out of nowhere, Vanessa struck forward. Her feet graced the ground like lightning bolts, but her sword whipped out much slower. Even then, Arica barely lifted her weapon up in time to deflect the bigger one.

"But it's not... part of who we are."

She feigned to the right, but Arica fell for it and almost lost her balance.

"You don't have to fight," Vanessa said. "At least not more than enough to survive."

Arica heard Jake grunt behind her, but she kept her eyes on Vanessa. "I-I'm klutzy and so bad at it."

"We will work on it," she said with a quick nod. "You may find a technique you do enjoy or do well, or perhaps you'll struggle your way to a basic level of skill."

Arica took a deep breath. If all she ever did was train her reflexes to defend herself, she'd be fine.

Then Vanessa broke the offensive stance and rose to her feet completely straight. "Contrary to your apparent instincts, hunching over like a gorilla won't help. It'll only leave your own movement restricted and your body exposed."

"Oh," was all Arica could manage. She rose from her stooping position and straightened her spine—the way Vanessa's was—but it felt awkward.

Vanessa raised the sword in her hands up to her stomach, the point crossing over her shoulder. "The easiest form for you to learn may require the most grace, my dear. But it also may be the safest. The idea is to tire out your heavy-handed opponent as quickly as possible. You will try to achieve quick strikes, in and out. It does not matter where, we're not going for vitals or one-shots. Almost anyone will still deflect strikes that could draw blood. Low, high, strike often and quickly, twisting out of the way after each. Don't block any hits he may pull, just back away."

Arica was listening closely, trying to form in her mind just how this would go.

Then Vanessa lifted her chin. "Try it."

She let out a deep breath, staring at the elegant woman. She didn't want to, not because she worried she'd hurt her, but because she knew that given the chance, she herself was going to be hit.

Arica struck, but in the time it took her to retract her sword, Vanessa deflected it with hers, then slapped her across the thigh.

"Ow," she mumbled, rubbing the stinging spot, but Vanessa had no sympathy in her cold eyes.

"Faster. On your toes. You'll learn to balance, but you have to be lithe or you'll be cut in half."

Arica nodded, readjusting her grip. She couldn't even wear high-heeled shoes; how was she supposed to jump around in clunky boots?

She tried, though, this time going for a low strike. Blocked, as expected, but she knew where the offending sword would come from as it made its own pass towards her. She skittered out of the way, barely catching her balance, but Vanessa missed her.

"Better," she commended in a light voice.

Arica smiled but got rid of it as she turned back, readying to go again.

"Arica," Vanessa then said, as if they were just having a pleasant walk through a park. "This is a conversation I have with all of my tyros, especially upon witnessing a first battle. You've seen the Dovevians now."

"I'm not exactly sure what I saw," she admitted as she blocked another strike.

"Still. They're dangerous and cunning. I want to make sure you know how seriously I take my position. And how serious I consider activity involving them is. Even an Ellterian may find themselves consorting with them."

Arica blushed, but hopefully it went unnoticed. She backed up a step, hoping to get a moment or two of peace before being attacked again.

Vanessa's sword lowered though, her gaze concentrated on her. "Do you understand?"

She forced a nod.

Vanessa's sword swung in a showy circle. "They'll lie, and use trickery. You may see or hear things you don't understand, or that scare you. Maybe things you desire or like. Don't let them convince you they're right, or good. They aren't. Don't even speak to them."

With this foreboding message, the sword in her hands felt heavier. She still dodged to the side, but her feet felt sluggish, and she wasn't sure she could move. Maybe it was just guilt. She glanced past Vanessa to Jake, almost to ask him if he knew where this was coming from. He just shrugged with a hand.

"And if I find out you are..." Vanessa lifted her chin slightly, bearing down on her even as her sword went lax at her side. "Well, I'll die before I allow the Dovevians or their sympathizers inside my court. Remember that."

"You have a lot of hatred for them," Arica said, but she wasn't sure what effect it was supposed to have.

"So would you. Which brings me to another point, especially after seeing the two of you."

They both glanced at Jake, but he gave them a quick glare. Blocking a sudden strike, Arica tried to focus both on thinking before she spoke, and not getting whopped again.

"Look, I-it... Barring the fact I am an adult and it's none of your business, there wasn't, nor will there be, any sex going on."

Vanessa attacked again, quickly enough to surprise her, but she weakly batted away the tip of Vanessa's sword.

"I didn't intend to pry. That isn't the path of conversation I was taking."

Arica countered but missed so badly that Vanessa didn't even bother parrying. Instead, she struck out, the edge of her sword barely missing Arica's neck but she didn't retract.

She froze, suddenly feeling less safe as the woman stared her down. The weapon tapped her shoulder.

"If you haven't yet felt the pains of love loss, this isn't the place to start. Not if you intend to go home, nor indeed if you decide to stay," Vanessa said with dead sincerity.

"I wasn't..." Arica mumbled, readjusting her sword as Vanessa freed her. "Saying I loved anyone."

Vanessa raised her head, haughtily replying. "Don't gain closeness if you can't handle the consequences. Our job is a deadly one. Make friends, connections, relationships, and you will be hurt. A fact of our lifestyle."

She blocked Arica's higher attack but backed up a step instead of returning the favor. She gave the tyro an impressed nod, then swung back, her muscles actually tensing this time.

"Seems a little pessimistic," Arica grunted, ducking to avoid a hit to the side of her head.

"Heartbreak, death, corruption. Lovers torn asunder, infants torn from mothers, parents torn from children, siblings from siblings. It doesn't end. We are a species created for one purpose."

She paused, and Arica felt pride in Vanessa's increased breath.

"Protection, guardianship, over our people. Nothing more. Especially not something as trivial and mortal as love."

Arica raised her sword over her head, stretching her muscles. "Even if you lose people more suddenly, that isn't a good reason to cut yourself off completely, is it?"

Vanessa was ready when she flew at her, trying something new. But her "blunt force" theory derailed as Vanessa's powerful counter threw her to the ground.

"That is something you can decide for yourself," Vanessa said with a finalization that was hard to argue with as the young girl stared at her from the ground. Then she held out a hand. "Well, I'm not impressed, but I've an idea where to start."

Arica let her pull her up, still somehow surprised by the high master's strength.

"When we march, you'll be with me. We won't be able to spar, but I'd like to test your magic as well."

She wanted to respond, but almost as quickly as she'd arrived, Vanessa was walking away with long, determined strides.

Turning around, Arica returned to Jake, feeling the weight of failure. If she didn't like her progress with sword handling, she was going to be furious about how little control of magic she'd gained.

"Well then," Arica said before loudly clearing her throat.

"She's quite the ray of sunshine, aye?" Without waiting for an answer, he nodded and continued. "That's just like her. She's right, but don't take everything she says so seriously."

Arica kept her eyes down and kicked a rock away. Vanessa was the one who always seemed a little eccentric, but Jake had always been her voice of reason. If he agreed with her, Arica didn't know what she was going to do.

"Look, I don't know what you want to hear, or what you expect, but you don't have to listen to her. Love if you want to. You just have to know that if you do, you have to be prepared for the end. And know that it will, probably tragically."

"Are you speaking from experience?" she asked softly.

"Yes, a lot of it. I've fallen in love many times despite her. I won't again. Like her, I'm tired of it. At a certain point, one accepts the fact that loss is almost more common than gain, but we still have to keep fighting for everyone around us. The Dovevians are a different matter."

She tried to mask her disappointment and kept her voice steady. "So, you're agreeing with her."

"No. They are dangerous, but I also believe one needs to know one's enemy. I still think the young should be able to experience the things we have given up. I wouldn't take back any of my mistakes, I learned from them, have protected people because of them, despite the harm they caused. And I wouldn't take back any of my romances, even though they all ended... poorly."

"You mean they were killed," Arica said bitterly.

"Yes, mine, but it's not always the case." Then he raised his head to the sky. "You get people like Vanessa who are bad at choosing, or maybe just unlucky. But maybe that's why she's more bitter than I. At least I've had the chance to make peace. And in some cases, revenge."

"Which is where the Dovevians come in."

He nodded once. "They aren't helpful; I'll give them that."

"How much is a lot of experience?" she asked. "I'm just curious. Just how many people would one have to lose before having such a resentful outlook?"

"I don't know what a lot in your eyes really is, but a few."

"And still no kids?" Smooth, she scolded.

"I never said I didn't have any. Just none older than you."

She turned an inquiring gaze to him, prodding more information without prying.

He smiled slightly, shaking his head. "I've a boy. Lives in Togheraith, this side of Ballewine's mountains. He'd be... around ten now, I suppose. Maybe younger."

Arica leaned her hands and body on the tree behind her, smiling. "Does he look like you?"

"I wouldn't know." He shrugged awkwardly.

Her lips parted in surprise. "You've never even met him?"

"His mother wanted him to be safe," Jake reasoned softly.

"And that's what you wanted?"

"I've no say in the matter. But is this really a good place to raise a child?"

Arica turned her gaze to the sky. "Yeah, but... It's still your kid, you deserve a say."

"It's not as if it has robbed me of the... experience. Vanessa and I have taken up many orphaned children, some of which you have met recently. Some you will when we get to Kopion. This is what Vanessa was talking about, but don't let fear run your life, or you'll never live. In some ways, she's good about it. In others, skelt's more suspicious than her. Dovevians or not, bad things happen to all of us. It's just a price of immortality."

She continued to stare anywhere but at him. He wasn't making her feel any better about any of it, just making her more homesick, where at least she knew the rules and social expectations. Here, she felt she was just going in horrible, infinite spirals.

"I guess it doesn't matter," she finally murmured. "Because after this... I'm headed home."

"Are you okay?"

Arica forced her gaze from the trampled ground as they walked in procession. Zak walked just ahead of her, one hand in his pocket. They'd already had some casual conversation over the course of their morning march, but none of it serious. She didn't know how to start.

"Arica, you look..."

What do I say?

His eyebrows went up as she reached him. She still hadn't answered. He didn't object when she slipped her hand into his elbow and matched his walk.

"I... I'm okay," she whispered, trying to smile. "I just want all of this to be over."

"It will be."

Elvy waited behind them until Zak finally acknowledged her and beckoned her to him.

Someone stalked up from behind her, one of the few since she tended to linger at the back of the pack.

"Hey, you got a problem there?" Jake asked out of the blue.

"What?" Arica asked. She let go of Zak and searched the surface of her body for problems.

In the blink of an eye, Jake sheathed the little weapon he'd been playing with, then reached into the deep outside pocket of her cloak without asking permission.

Her heart skipped a beat as his gloved hand pulled out a small rock, faintly glowing with light. Her face warmed, realizing she'd gotten caught and would have to explain herself.

"Where'd you get this?" he asked, one eyebrow twitching up. "And who has the other?"

Arica stared forward, grabbing her own arm, then slowed her marching pace considerably. Jake caught on and did the same, but Arica waited until they were at least twenty feet behind the rest of the group before walking closer to him.

"The Dovevian talked me into leaving the safe field. He gave me this stone, and we talked for a bit, but I was careful."

Jake gave her a grimace. "You, ma'am, are brave. And that may not be a good thing."

"Why not?" she asked, clasping her hands behind her back as she skipped over a large rock in her path.

Jake grabbed her by the arm, jolting her to a stop. She realized he was serious and looked up at him with obedience.

"Bravery can get you two things around here. Fame, or death."

She raised her chin, looking him dead in the eye. "Like everything else?"

"You just have to have sense as well," he whispered, gaze softening. Then he looked up and whistled through his teeth.

Parel and Steen both looked back, the cook with a slightly dazed, breathless look, the blacksmith with a stern, mildly annoyed one.

"Breather," Jake barked across the space between them.

Neither of the other men responded, but Steen gave a nod before they went to make up the few steps they'd lost.

Then Jake turned his head back to Arica and held out the rock. "Though I suppose I more than encouraged it. So, are you gonna talk to him? The glowing means he's already holding the other one."

She blushed again, but gingerly took it from him. It didn't look like she had a choice.

"Uh... hello?" she called quietly.

"I was wondering if you'd died in your sleep. I suppose you're on the move now, however," the strong, familiar voice resonated, still throwing her off with its clarity. She didn't let on the trace of relief she felt upon hearing it, nor did she know why she'd felt it.

"Already trying to get information out of me," Arica teased despite Jake's eyes on her.

"On the contrary. Would you like to know what I'm up to?" he warmly offered.

"Plotting the destruction of my friends and family?" She avoided Jake's gaze as he snorted. *I need to just get to the point.*

"I'll admit," the Dovevian sighed, completely oblivious to the ancient Zenian on standby. "This joke is becoming tiresome..."

"What joke? We're enemies, aren't we?" she whispered, feeling a little cocky now.

"Unless I was to become an asset to your cause."

Finally, she looked at Jake, but her expression was a mix of confusion and surprise.

"What, like our... inside guy? A spy?"

This got Jake's attention, but his soldier-like discipline kept him standing still and patient.

"Would you be opposed to that?"

Arica tried to think clearly, but her mind raced with possibilities too complex to delve into yet. "Can you do it without getting caught?"

The Dovevian let out an abrupt, deep-chested chuckle. It was closer to an evil laugh than she'd ever heard for real, but much warmer and real. "Now you're insulting me," he said in a slightly higher voice.

"Let me," Jake snapped out of the blue, his hand outstretched.

She stared at it for a moment, involuntarily pulling the rock closer to her chest as if it was her most prized possession. *What if he ruins this? I could make this guy help me. Jake's prejudice could end it.* But she looked up into warm violet eyes, her fingers loosening on the stone.

She averted her eyes. "I need you to listen."

"All right," the person on the other end responded obediently.

"Do you trust me?" she demanded strongly, looking at Jake before giving him a reassuring smile.

Jake nodded once, a serious expression as the Dovevian answered, "More than you me."

"Well... I told someone that I was talking to you. Not Vanessa, she and Rapier still don't know, which is against both of our better judgment, but we both also believe that we need all the help we can get with this war. And I know he is going to help us do that. Will you talk to him?"

There was silence for a long minute, plenty of time for her to fidget and convince herself he was angry with her and had given up on helping. But, eventually, he was once again responsive.

"Who is it?"

"Ja—uh, Jrasko... Damage." Jake seemed well known among the Zenians, but she didn't know if the knowledge also carried to the Dovevian part of the world.

"No," the voice snapped, more hostile than she'd ever heard him. "Frankly, I'm upset you think I'd trust anyone else for a moment."

Her heart dropped as she looked up at her companion. "He says he doesn't want to talk to you," she whispered, even though the rock would still take her voice to the opposite one.

Using his teeth, Jake jerked the glove off of his fingers, then took the rock from her anyway.

"Look," he started, glaring into the trees. "I should go to Mistress Damage about this this moment, but I haven't. Just tell me how you plan on helping us. I'm open to outside help, but I'm not risking any tyros for it."

She averted her eyes, repressing a smile. *He's protecting me from the big-bad bad guy.*

"So, let's talk," Jake finished with expectation.

He stood, the rocked hand awkwardly outstretched for some painfully long seconds, in which Arica imagined what kind of evil plans the Dovevian was laying out for him. She could only guess.

Eventually, Jake shook his head, then dropped the rock back into Arica's hand. "He won't speak."

She cupped it tenderly, realizing how tired she was getting of doing this back and forth with all of them. "Hey, um..." *Still don't know your name, pal.* "Dude," she tried. She glanced up at Jake, wondering if she should ask. Describe him to him. But what if that knowledge kept Jake from turning a blind eye to her shenanigans? It felt more and more important by the word.

"It's me again. You can talk to me, right?"

"I don't agree with letting others meddle," he answered, his voice much more stern now. "But I'll let it go. For now."

She squelched the guilt in her gut saying she'd done wrong. "What do you want me to do?"

"Check the satchel."

Instantly, she dropped her heavy bag off of her shoulder and pulled the drawstrings apart. As she'd set it, the satchel was on the very bottom of the bag, folded as if it was empty.

"I don't know Vanessa's plan," the Dovevian continued as she worked to free the bag. "But I'll guarantee it's not the right one. If you try to destroy us, you'll die before you do. Just a fact. I've a plan but you're to swear you won't tell your leaders. The Damage boy, fine, as long as he slips it to no one else. Does he agree?"

Satchel in hand, Arica carefully set the rock on the ground. Hopefully, he would notice his own rock cease to glow. She reached into her magic bag but felt nothing new. Just their pages, the writing utensil she used, and his little pot of ink. Then she pulled out the sketch of the castle. It was warmer than the other papers like it had been drying in the sun.

Sure enough, she opened the diagram of the castle's grounds and the surrounding forest to find new markings and ink, along with small but clear words dotted about the surface.

"He says he's got a plan, but we can't tell anyone else. He wants you to promise, too."

"I don't like this," Jake growled low. Like an animal cornered by an invisible presence.

Her breath heavy, Arica faced him again, a lavender outline of the man's instructions lingering in her vision. "I know... but we need to trust him," she begged solemnly. "I just... I just know."

He frowned, running his hand through dirty hair. "Okay... fine. I won't tell. But I won't promise that I won't try to save lives if I see the chance."

Arica beamed, then picked up the rock again. "He'll do it," she announced with confidence.

"All right. I assume you know of the fields?"

She nodded, but he never saw it.

"It's how Herak and Miss Marc are keeping their base under control, only instead of just repelling magic, it repels everything. So, to keep us out, they've sacrificed—"

"Being able to leave," Arica concluded.

"Yes. Now, what do you know of magic itself, little one? The way it has to have a continuous source—"

"Or a weakness," she finished, scolding herself afterwards for being such a teacher's pet.

"Right," the Dovevian continued in the same helpful, instructive tone. "It's been two weeks. They're either dropping like flies in there, or there's a weakness."

"This doesn't sound right," Arica admitted, her voice shaking a little more than before. "You want me to help you find the weak place so you can get in?"

"No. I think I know where the breach is. Ransom and I nearly found it, but I drew his attention elsewhere. I've marked it on your map because I'm not the one who needs to infiltrate it. You are."

"Why would we need to infiltrate our own base?" she asked with extreme doubt.

She glanced up long enough to see Jake's scowl. He picked up the things she'd left on the ground, urging her to follow the beaten path.

"Because regardless of how many Zenians you have on us, you'll have to retreat, eventually. And when you do, we have an enormous trap set. You'll be lucky if a handful of you survive."

She squeezed her eyes shut. Jake was being patient, but she had to resist the want to tell him. Taking a deep breath, she gathered her strength. "So, how do we stop it?"

"The trap is complicated. I won't go into specifics, but it's set up in a perimeter far around the base. You may have already passed this way through it."

"But, a lot of these guys can sense, and have been looking for, things like that, sense magic," she told him with skepticism.

"Quiet. It's reserved, not active yet. We've spent a lot of time enchanting the area, but we've always retracted it back, just leaving the imprint. Nothing that Miss Vanessa would suspect, maybe a tiny trace here and there. Either way, it'll be able to trap you when you try to head back out, like inwards angled spikes in a box. The problem for us is, to keep it undetectable, we have to wait until you're in here to activate it. To do that, it would take... three to four of us. So unless Vanessa is planning on killing every last one of us—"

"She wouldn't be opposed," Arica mused.

"—before letting a single person retreat, you need a way to escape unscathed."

"And you know how to make it look like we did it without you being a traitor?"

"It's gloriously simple. You won't be able to kill all of us. You know this, regardless that your numbers will nearly double. They're malnourished, wounded, and weak. You can't lose any more than you already have, even though I suspect that our little surprise attack didn't achieve our desired effect."

Arica couldn't help rolling her eyes. "Tell that to Jake and Ricken."

"And I apologize," he impatiently excused. "But let me continue. You can't kill us off, so there's only one way to escape. Don't shatter Kopion's field."

Arica stuck her hand in her pocket, letting go of the rock but kept her fingers close to it.

"What good could we get from keeping their field up?" she said quietly.

Jake looked at her tiredly, then shrugged a little.

"Why?" she asked, after touching a couple of fingers to the warm object.

"Tell us, would it be easier to patch up a cage or build an entirely new one from scratch?"

"You want us to trap the Dovevians," she concluded gravely.

"Indeed. You infiltrate the base, make it a little obvious when you open the field. You'll only have a few minutes to get Herak and order everyone out. Meanwhile, I'll be directing my comrades to the break. We'll want control of any augments, artifacts, and hostages, to force you to retreat into our trap. I'll leave one man to guard the break of the barrier, but it should be easy for your friends to take care of him, kill him if you need to. Then you leave. Once on the other side, patch up the break."

"Trapping you guys in the base?" she suggested carefully.

"It won't hold very long. The patch will be the weakest point. We'll all know this. I'll have to do whatever I can to break it in order to keep suspicion off. Have Výan Deli'ampy—one of the Kopion Zenians—do it if he's still alive. Then escape the area. Your friend, Jrasko, may be of some use, as he can direct his mother back as soon as we're inside the base. Tell her and her commander your plan if you need. Have any of you take credit for this; do not tell her it was me. If everything goes well, I'll contact you afterwards."

Arica looked up at Jake again, her pulse racing in anticipation. But her Dovevian wasn't quite done.

"Then we can start on a plan to take over Endré and the king."

30

THE LIAR, THE THIEF, AND THE BAD GUY

From behind a couple of trees, Arica watched a pair of hauling horses shoot into a gallop, carrying Zak and Damad off at a pace that shouldn't've been possible after their journey, but looked effortless for the athletic steeds. Vanessa directed her commander while pulling her hair up out of the way. Pieces of oddly shiny-looking leather armor waited at her feet, ready to be donned.

Arica pushed herself between the close tents, trying to keep the noise down. She wanted to watch the preparation unfold, but she had her own mission.

They'd certainly made it out of the swamp. The trees huddled together, their trunks much thicker, most of them towering around them hundreds of feet, forcing their camp to be more spread out than usual. This was all good for her, as she slipped to the entrance of Vanessa's little tent with barely anyone in sight.

Her heart wracked against her chest, her hands shaking as warm air enveloped her. She thought her heartbeat was bad until a pair of scarlet eyes pierced through her from the corner. She jumped back.

The vampire said nothing as she regained her breath, but neither did he look away or blink. He crouched, unmoving, next to the bound Dovevian lying on his side, facing away from her.

This hadn't been part of the plan, but regardless, she ignored the painful gaze and walked into the room as if it belonged to her. As described, there was little in the tent for furniture but her target; a large trunk sitting next to a set-up cot.

She tried to keep from acting nervous as she pulled Jake's key from her pocket. Hesitating was going to be more suspicious than just getting the item.

Please, please work, she begged as she inserted the key into an obvious yet plain keyhole in the middle of the trunk's face. She had to pull it away from the tent a bit to keep the lid off of it, but as soon as she had, she again doubted herself.

The trunk displayed a surreal, precisely packed array of objects that belonged in a wizard's basement or a pharaoh's tomb. The only one she recognized was the red leather book tucked in the upper corner, still the size of a pocketbook. *I can't do this. I shouldn't be stealing.*

A guilt ate at her stomach. Surely the vampire would sense her fear soon. What if her touch accidentally activated something? Or what if Vanessa would sense that her fingerprints were on these objects?

Yet, she felt a pull to the contents. Maybe it was the look of many items made of rare metals and gems, like the compass with a faceted face, delicate strings of silver wrapping around it and over the top to create a protective cage; or the pair of ostentatious gold daggers that were grotesquely melded together at the tips; or the lantern made of hammered steel for all but a bottom made of a swirly pink opal-like stone.

Then again, maybe it was just her mission urging her on.

The need to leave Kasper's sight got her going. She carefully pushed apart a green gem set in old, broken wood and a silver box about the size of a cigarette carton. Just as Jake had said, a cylindrical container sat underneath. She pulled it out. It was a perfect size to sit comfortably in her hand, small enough to hide in her fingers if she needed to conceal it.

The flap of the tent parted, but before she startled, she recognized the bandage-wrapped shoulder working through it.

"Have you gotten the item Vanessa needed?" Jake asked as he glared at the vampire.

"Uh, yeah," Arica called back, then closed the chest, making sure it was securely locked before standing up.

Jake wearily watched Kasper, jerking his head towards freedom instead of verbally directing her out.

She scampered out as fast as she could.

"Come on," Jake ordered under his breath, using his body to herd her around the tent, presumably back to safety.

"You don't think Kasper would let Asriel go, do you?" Arica blurted.

"I don't know if he *would*. It doesn't matter. He couldn't undo Asriel's bonds; he barely has the magic to warm a cup of tea anymore."

Arica shrugged the thoughts away, then held the cylinder out to her partner.

"Perfect," he whispered without making a move to take it. Then he scanned the area, triple checking that they weren't being watched, but it fed the anxiety in Arica's stomach.

"All you'll have to do is place it on the ground and push the ends together. It'll keep the barrier from breaking more as long as it's there."

She nodded, carefully placing it in her pocket. "I don't enjoy stealing from Vanessa, though. This seems really wrong," she murmured. "Why didn't you do it? She probably wouldn't care if you were messing with her stuff, especially since you have a key."

Jake met her eyes. "You're the one calling the shots now. Technically, I'm still in charge of your safety, so I'm just here to make sure you don't die."

Faking a smile, she nodded weakly. "I just need to focus."

"Do you have everything?" Jake asked.

Arica pulled the wrinkled, rolled-up map from the folds of her cloak, with it the talisman that the Dovevian gave her, and the bracelet as well.

She looked up at Jake, holding out the bracelet. "I'm going to wear this."

He gave her a nod of consent, so she slid the cuff onto her wrist and held her breath. Nothing happened, just as when he'd tried it on.

"Okay," Jake urged gently. "Remember the plan?"

"Yes, but let's go over it one more time. Just in case," she said as she unrolled the map.

"We still have to see where we end up on the battlefield, but assuming that she marks me injured, I won't be in the vanguard. I doubt you'll be marching. But, whatever happens, we'll then sneak out to the forest bordering the castle. There's a pathway here.'" He pointed at the map. "Up the mountain, a rough trail, but enough to follow. About a quarter way up and we'll work our way south to the weak spot that your Dovevian found. Are you sure you haven't seen him, or know anything about him? I really want to know who we were dealing with."

"No," Arica lied through her teeth.

"Well, anyway," Jake continued. "You use the talisman to break the barrier and Vanessa's artifact to keep it contained so we can repair it. Then we split up. I stay out of the way until the Dovevians go to charge into the castle and start pushing everyone back. Then you..."

She waited a minute for him to continue before catching on. "Oh! I'll go southeast along the wall and slip into the meat cellar using the window. Then I'll go upstairs and find the commanders."

"Your Dovevian will lead them the opposite way along the perimeter towards the staircase to the rooftop balcony. Sneak to the inner chambers. Based on regulation, their wounded should be in the grand hall. Then you only have about ten minutes. He'll give you the signal when they pass the barrier. You have to be ready to seal it five minutes after that. Take out the Dovevian standing guard, then seal it up. I'll have to get everyone going within minutes."

Arica nodded obediently. "Okay, what if I run into problems?"

"If someone comes and tries to stop us on the way up, I'll distract them and you go on alone. If Vanessa doesn't listen to us, then we'll be in hell either way."

"What if the Kopion guys don't listen to me? They don't know me," Arica blurted, her heart dropping a little.

"Randa will recognize your name, don't worry," Jake reassured.

She took a deep breath, then stuffed everything back into her pockets. "This is insane..."

"Welcome to DeRael," he breathed, awkwardly shrugging. "Time to go join the pack. Once Vanessa calls the attack, that'll be the signal for all three of us. Tuck the rock into your sleeve. If you need to talk and fight, it'll still work."

She nodded affirmatively. Then they heard a call from the loud commander, a signal for their last instructions.

"For those of you still here," Vanessa yelled from her position on top of the little wagon, looking down on them as Jake and Arica joined. "You're my core. We've already stationed the barrier around their front. Your primary aim is to get through the Dovevians and pull them away from Kopion enough that Commander Herak can break the inner field and to help him pull out his forces. We're going through the middle, down the courtyard where the soldiers split. I don't want to call a retreat until we've broken through to our second half, so don't hold back on them. The barrier will keep them from converging behind us, but once we're whole, they won't have a chance against us."

Arica dropped her hand into her pocket, touching the warm rock. "They're focusing on breaking the field from the courtyard," she whispered. "Wanting to get to it before there's enough of your force to stop us."

"We'll keep them from it long enough for you to break your own spot and gather up the Zenians," the deep voice soothed.

She released the object before leaning over to Jake. "Will the outer field be a problem?"

"No," he dismissed. "As soon as we flee, it'll be down in a moment."

"What about Vanessa? She seriously seems like she just wants to be rid of the Dovevians once and for all. I don't think she's going to be okay with just fleeing and leaving them kind of trapped."

She looked up, to see him chewing on his lip again, something he must've done to concentrate. Eventually, he looked down at her. "You're wrong. You don't know her like I do. Let me handle her."

She pushed for answers, but he ignored her quiet begging as Vanessa started splitting the rest of the Zenians into groups.

Finally, Jake stood taller, cleared his throat, called Vanessa's name, and spoke a string of foreign words.

Arica glared up at Jake as Vanessa met his gaze, her eyebrows rising slightly.

She responded similarly. Her words sounded like an inquiry, but his only response was a mischievous smirk.

"What did you ask her?" Arica bugged, bumping his hip.

"Shush," he scolded lightly.

Vanessa jumped from her perch, waving an arm through the air as she landed on light feet. "To position! Arica, you're with me."

Arica felt her stomach twist. It wasn't part of the plan.

Jake pulled her into a crushing hug, surprising her. He never seemed the huggy type, but he proved to just be relaying a few last instructions in her ear.

"Play fight, keep safe, switch who you fight next to and run as soon as you have a window. Meet at the trailhead."

He let her go, her cheeks warming a little as the scent of cedar and whiskey lingered. She turned to follow Vanessa.

"Come," the high master beckoned with an arm out until Arica passed her at a jog, intending to catch up with the rest of the group. Vanessa stayed annoyingly close as they found a quick pace, but maybe it was a good thing. The Dovevians wouldn't make such quick work of her.

She didn't have any idea how long they would have to walk, but soon enough, they crested a hill to see the mess before them.

The hill gently swooped down into a wide open valley, where hundreds of black-clothed soldiers formed neat lines. *But where is the castle they're supposed to be protecting?*

The Dovevian's sketch wasn't accurate at all. An overgrown courtyard of tall birches sat where it should've, yes, but beyond that, there was nothing but a flat expanse of stone, running a long way to a perfectly smooth mountain face. The grass and trees slowly curled around the air, acting as if something had simply cut the entire building out of the mountainside and deleted it.

"It's... invisible?"

"Not the most practical camouflage," Vanessa mused in response.

They approached more on the right side than the middle, which meant they were already close to the trailhead, but looking out across the rim of their little valley, and how spread out and few their force was, she couldn't help feeling a little desperate.

We don't have a chance. She quickly pushed such thoughts out. They had an easy fight against humans, and they outnumbered the Dovevians. Plus, they had twice the people on the other side of that invisible barrier. *And it's my job to get them out before anyone gets really hurt.* Hopefully, her secret friend could help.

Vanessa unsheathed the massive greatsword from the holster on her back, her dominant arm strapped into a bulky, complicated-looking piece of steel armor that didn't match the rest of her light coverings.

Arica couldn't help but eye it. "Nice armor."

"I've worked on it for a long time," she murmured. "Intending to gain an edge with this blasted sword."

With a slow flourish, she lifted Skotjretant straight out and gave it a twirl. The blade seamlessly slit through the air with a low *whoosh*, then in mid-air froze, pointed towards the army below.

Then Vanessa let out an inhuman scream worthy of a dozen banshees. Everyone around them exploded in obnoxious cries and whooping. The army responded similarly, and Arica made out a few distinct positions probably filled with Dovevians. Vanessa threw the point of her sword out towards their enemy, a small red spark traveling up from hilt to tip. The signal flashed across the valley.

Her surrounding companions nearly trampled Arica as they charged forward into battle, but she stayed as still as their leader, watching.

Elvy's feet slowed sooner than anyone else's, her bow steady as she loosed a few arrows into the crowd. One person from each of the three positions did the same, but she couldn't imagine how effective it really was.

Arica turned, eyeing the trees up to the edge of the invisible fortress. It was likely her imagination, but she thought she could see the makings of a little path that would lead in the right direction. Her feet ached to sprint for it, but Vanessa tapped her shoulder, urging her in the wrong direction.

They were much slower descending into the valley, but it didn't look like the rest of the Zenians were all that pressed for help. They cut through the soldiers with ease. Arica didn't feel any less anxious. Not just the clatter and bang of steel and leather and bone, but the yells and *screaming* of the participants. It was unnerving, but she was thankful that she could keep her eyes down to the gore she wanted only to imagine.

Arica jumped back as Vanessa swung her sword in a wide circle, obviously gunning for a pair of disjointed soldiers trying to catch Zak off guard.

Arica looked away before she saw the result. *This seems way too easy*, she told herself, eyes drawn back to her goal.

"Where are the Dovevians?" she asked shyly.

"Waiting," Vanessa sneered, her practiced gaze sweeping across the mass of soldiers still lying between them and the castle. "Their army is a distraction. They're watching, so we'll have to find them and target them."

She then pointed across the field opposite them. "Derrick's drawn out Lise already. Which isn't—"

Arica looked to find what had stopped her words.

Atop a knoll further away from the courtyard, their secret inside man stood watching, a stained black sword lax at his side.

"And so the drawing begins," Vanessa announced in a low, fierce tone.

Arica followed the thin woman's quick footsteps towards him, sure she was going to be in trouble for ruining the plan.

Sure enough, as they approached, his dark, paint-smeared eyes didn't train on the actual threat to his safety, but the defenseless girl behind her. Arica threw an arm out, pointing at Vanessa in an effort to explain herself. His lips pressed together, focusing back on their problem.

Obviously at a disadvantage, given how her opponent was on higher ground, Vanessa slowed, staying just out of reach.

He was so much more intimidating up close, a tower of tarnished muscle and magic. Maybe it was the tattoos around his arm, the black makeup, or maybe it was the vicious expression in his dark eyes that made her worry, wondering if this was really the man who'd spent so much time teasing her just to get her to listen.

The ground around Vanessa's feet erupted with hot steam, propelling outwards and tearing up the dirt towards the Dovevian before stopping a few inches from his feet. He gave her a funny look of disbelief, then returned the favor as a powerful wave of air, only for Vanessa to bat it away before it could throw her off-balance.

"FENGRA," she roared. She stalked a few yards up the hill, though it made her more vulnerable. "I hope you're ready to die for this land, Drake."

"Damnit," Arica cursed under her breath. She'd suspected, after everything she'd heard about and from him, but she didn't want to truly put a name to him.

Vanessa's sword bounced off Drake's but struck hard enough that it nearly threw him off balance entirely. Her new piece of armor was definitely helping.

"Finally handling that accursed sword, my love," Drake growled, his last word breathy as he shoved the greatsword back with his own.

Vanessa twisted left, swiping underhanded in a strike that would've split open his side, unlike when she would whap Arica with the flat. And unlike with Arica, the strike elegantly deflected off of Drake's sword and was returned nearly as fast.

Arica looked back towards the treeline. They were still too close between her and her goal, but maybe if she just began a sprint, she could get away and only later explain to Vanessa what she was doing. Luckily, it didn't seem like too long of a run for her already exhausted feet. Her eyes followed the edge of the treeline from the invisible fort, all the way to the tiniest indent in the trees. Hopefully, where she'd meet Jake.

She hadn't realized how close the fighting couple had gotten. She had to duck out of the way so Vanessa didn't have to save her. What she didn't expect, though, was for her to still be within danger's reach. A long arm scooped her up like a toddler.

"Stop," Drake demanded in a powerful tone, twirling in a half circle so he could point his sword in Vanessa's direction.

Arica struggled against the meaty forearm pinning her, her feet shoving against his knee, but he barely moved. His intentions might've been completely innocent, but her heartbeat raced, and she gasped as if her final moments drew close.

Vanessa's expression was one of absolute venom, but her giant sword froze in place.

"Be quick," Drake growled through his teeth, his breathing and tone reminding her of a bear that was much too close. "This has to end *now*."

"Let her go," Vanessa demanded calmly, more a threat than a plea. She took a few determined steps closer, poising her weapon.

Arica screamed as Drake stepped forward, swinging to deflect another strike.

He suddenly freed her; her fall so quick her knees buckled on impact, throwing her into prickly grass. She crawled a few feet, her head spinning too fast to see which way it was.

Trees. Go towards the trees.

She dragged herself up, using her hands to help pull her forward a few steps before she'd balanced enough to run.

Her vision cleared, and even though the sounds of metal on metal still slammed against her eardrums, she felt as if she was home free.

Her arm ran warm with tingling that at first she thought to be adrenaline or from being squished in Drake's arm, but when she glanced down, she noticed that the little bracelet was the source. It buzzed lightly, glowing just the faintest amount.

"Jake said some of them are activated by touch," she said to herself.

She kept running.

There it was, the trailhead. It had to be. There weren't any other paths that wound towards the back of the hypothetical castle. Where was Jake, though?

She crashed through some underbrush, probably startling all the animals in a thirty-foot radius. Overgrown weeds shrouded the path, hardy, prickly plants forcing from the old cobble and clay path.

She slowed up a steep incline. Her blood raced with anticipation, but she knew if she tried to sprint the first part of the hike, she'd be miserable for the rest.

Finally, the path evened out for a bit; the greenery receding from this evidently airless soil trampled from many years of use.

Arica could see along the path a little further, where it rose back up again. She could also make out the smooth cliff face through the trees. She wasn't sure how far they needed to go.

And where's Jake?

Without a sound, a gigantic beast dropped onto the packed dirt in front of her, coat white as snow with paws at least the size of her head. She screamed, tripping when she tried to retreat, then fell flat on her butt.

Teeth bared, the animal had an offending stance, massive paws spread out. The shape of the head and snout was a little longer than a cat's would be, but her fur was short, her body meaty.

"What are you doing?" the animal screamed, even though her mouth didn't move. Her voice remained tiny, like a fairy's in the throat of a dragon. "Master Damage *insists* you return to her."

This was relieving; she wasn't about to be eaten, but she still had a major obstacle.

"Let me pass you, Bialsa, I've gotta get to the castle!" she yelled back and struggled to her feet.

"You have your orders and I have mine, back to the meadow immediately!" she argued in a girly voice. She took a few long strides forward, hundreds of pounds of muscle rippling with every movement.

What do I do, what do I do? Arica backed up a step as the huge snowy beast stalked towards her, mouth closed but head lowered, silver eyes boring into her.

"I won't hurt you, but I have to bring you back," Bialsa said.

Arica ran at her.

There was no plan. She was just going to run and see what happened.

Bialsa wasn't expecting to be rushed. The animal leapt back, a few paws pulling away from the ground like a much smaller cat's might've.

Arica had every intention of charging past her, hoping she wouldn't be able to chase her through the thicket ahead, but Bialsa wouldn't let her get that far. One leg swept towards her.

Panic. She was going to be pulled off her feet and forced to fail. The displaced air of the approaching paw tickled her skin. She threw her arms forward.

It didn't touch her, but started from her arms; a wave of power that threw the quarter-ton creature backwards. The heavy body crashed into a few trees. They snapped as they slowed her.

"Oh my god, I didn't mean—" Arica screamed, her hands flying to her mouth.

Bialsa stopped on her side, still, as a few leaves settled onto her white fur.

"She's fine, just go!"

Arica looked back even as she started forward again, meeting Jake's gaze. He mounted the last few steep steps up the hill. A rust-colored wolf bounded up ahead of him, scampering to the bigger andromae.

"Stay with her, make sure the Dovevians don't find her," Jake ordered to the smaller of the two. His pace quickened to catch up to Arica.

Her worry was not only for the poor animal but also the owner, who was likely to be furious. Unfortunately, she didn't have the time to waste lamenting.

"Wasn't that Rune?" Arica asked, slipping into a thick spot of branches along the path.

"He still listens to me sometimes. Later."

She nodded.

With Jake in the lead, they went faster than she had on her own, what with all of her slowing to make sure there was indeed evidence of a path. It was more than another minute or two before they'd strayed from the path just a little and sidled up against the edge of the cliff.

This close to the barrier, it wasn't possible to see through to the other side. In fact, it was so cloudy that she might not have been able to see the castle through it, whether it was invisible or not. But she couldn't stop staring at the shiny surface and the tiny hints of the colors surrounding them, almost opalescent.

"Well, he was right," Jake said grimly as he stopped. "It's definitely weaker here." As if he radiated five hundred degrees, the bushes shrank back, giving them a little breathing room.

Arica let her lungs deflate as she reached into her pocket for the disc-shaped item.

"You don't think… this is what they used to break ours back in Neva… do you?" she asked quietly, fingering the colorful stone.

"I think it would be naïve to believe otherwise," he mumbled, craning his neck as he inspected the curvature of their bubble.

"Seems kind of… messed up to do the same to these guys."

"At least we have it now," he reasoned a little louder, then held out his hand.

She was about to hand over the disc before she realized he probably wanted Vanessa's cylinder and pulled that out of her pocket instead.

"How can you tell it's the weak spot, anyway?" she asked, concentrating her vision on the shiny wall in front of them.

Jake held a hand up but wasn't close enough to touch it. "Just feel the energy it's emitting. It's not nearly as strong."

She couldn't feel anything of the sort, so she focused on her plan.

"Twist the circles together and set it flat against the field. It should work immediately," he said, his breathing heavy.

The stone sides were barely even offset, but out of fear of breaking it, she was careful. Just pushing them didn't merit any movement, but when she stretched her fingers over it and twisted, they ground together and clicked into place. Her fingers tingled with a buzz, but it wasn't quite enough vibration to see.

"Hurry," Jake whispered, looking over her head anxiously.

Arica held the device between her palms, took a few steps closer to the field, and reached out.

It drew towards the solid energy, but not until it touched was there a reaction. Ripples distorted the smooth surface, originating perfectly around her hands. Then she pulled the device back as hard as she could.

It was silent, the breaking. She could see the distortion as she pulled it away, then the tearing. A hole appeared in front of them and the edges webbed out across the rest of the field.

Worn stone bricks peeked out a foot or so past the barrier. Within seconds, the space was plenty big enough to pass through.

Jake twisted the two ends of Vanessa's artifact, then knelt down in front of the quickly growing crack and set his own enchantment.

The edges of the tear blurred, stretching out towards the artifact like a vacuum. The cracks webbing out on all sides slowed but were already much too big.

"Well." Jake sighed and pushed himself to his feet. "No turning back from here. This'll be hard to ignore."

Arica nodded, staring at the break. Her feet were frozen.

He looked at her, still breathing heavier than she thought he should've been. "Do you have this?"

"Um... yeah," she whispered lightheartedly.

"Okay. You've only a few minutes. I'll stay here and replace this after they come through. It's breaking too fast. Get going."

They kept eyes on each other for another long moment. She turned to leave.

"Arica."

She watched him pull out a golden trinket almost the size of his hand. He tested the weight of it before holding it out.

"The hero crest?" she asked reverently, then took it.

"Just in case you run into trouble."

She nodded, tucking the item into a pouch. Then Arica bolted into the passage.

The surface of the barrier was slightly warm, but much firmer than she thought it would be. She ran her hand along it as she turned right, jogging between. There was more light than she might've expected, but it was still dull, the barrier acting like thick clouds filtering the sunlight. Her shoulders occasionally bumped either side, once in a while so narrow that she had to sidle awkwardly. The worry that she might hit a place where she'd get stuck stayed with her, but she pressed on anyway.

She headed in the opposite direction from the bare cliff face, or where it had been without the castle. She thought she'd have an excellent view of the battle below, but there were too many trees and the castle wall in the way. It felt odd that she couldn't hear it either. In fact, the only thing she *could* hear was her own feet crunching through untamed grass, and an unnerving clunking as her sword whopped against her thigh as she jogged.

Eventually she came to a little window, only half of it poking up over the ground. It was the first change in the wall lower than her head. She almost started moving again, as it seemed way too small to accommodate her, but she wasn't sure if she'd ever find anything else.

She tucked her hand into her pocket and touched the warm rock.

Drake had told her he'd keep his in his sleeve, so he could listen. She instantly heard labored breath, but surprisingly enough, nothing else.

"I'm in. I just gotta get to the Zenians," she told him as she dropped to the ground by the window.

"I'll call to retreat up the—" he yelled.

She didn't know how the enchantment worked, but it seemed that she couldn't hear anything outside of vocal.

Then Drake's voice quieted to a weird, raspy whisper. "Don't leave until we're in. You won't have much time."

"I know," she agreed with worry, then took her hand off of the item.

Arica's legs fit into the window just fine, but the room was so dark she didn't know how far she'd be falling. She twisted around before slithering the rest of her body through the little window. She was barely small enough.

Her plan had been to keep her shoulders above the edge of the window until she knew how far it was to the ground. But as soon as her waist freed from the tight space, she lost her balance and crashed to the ground, landing on her shoulder and side.

"Ouch." She sat up and touched the tender spots scraped raw on the rough stone. She got to her feet, a little shaky but determined. At least she wasn't being gutted on the battlefield.

The room wasn't huge, though it reached high above her. Empty racks lined three of the walls. The doorway in the middle of the fourth had a wooden door cracked with age. The smell was unpleasant, an old, moldy stink, but wasn't particularly strong.

She slipped into a wide room that appeared to be an abandoned kitchen, with several fireplaces, counters, and cupboards. There was no fire or windows casting light, but there was enough from *somewhere* to see basic shapes.

It was eerie, so quiet and cold. Her steps echoed so loud she figured that if anyone lived, they'd find her in a minute or two.

There were too many places a monster or a hundred could hide. She jogged through a spacious dining hall absent of chairs, or any cloth or adornments along the giant, solid table.

By all evidence, nobody had been there in weeks.

For the first time since the plan came together, a terrifying thought crossed her mind that almost stopped her dead in her tracks.

What if nobody was left? Was she just walking into a base full of corpses, like Santsin Val, but messier? Or, maybe, Drake had planned the entire thing to capture her. The only thing keeping that thought from becoming more stable was the *why?* Maybe if he was tricking *all* of them to join the others, then they'd be able to kill all the Zenians at once. But... he wasn't.

Whatever the intentions of the Dovevians, or the condition of Kopion's occupants, she pressed on.

There was still no resident evidence as she found her way into a large hall. At least it smelled fresher.

Which way?

She was losing track. While she could see enough, the dark rooms of the vast building all looked similar: abandoned and cold. Even if a group of Zenians hid in a room somewhere, it could take her hours to find it.

Arica looked around again. Maybe her best choice was to wander around yelling. Or maybe it was time to backtrack. She looked over her shoulder to gather her bearings, but instead found a pair of figures only a few feet back. She jumped back and clasped her hands over her mouth, unsuccessfully squelching a scream.

The two men stepped closer, swords extended towards her in the dark. The shorter of them flipped up a long torch as it flared to life. He watched her carefully, irises so dark they barely reflected the light. Long black hair contrasted a sharp, ghostly pale face.

"Who are you?" the other asked quietly, his slender brown eyes narrowing. He looked really young, her age at most, but in a sleeveless coat, she could tell his leanness was balanced with the standard strength of a Zenian. There was also the matter of a few old scars, though the most noticeable one interrupted the short brown hair just above his ear.

He gestured at her with his sword.

Her lips parted, but nothing came out. She did her best to shake off the stunned look, then cleared her throat, her heart still racing. "S-sorry, you just... terrified me. Uh... I'm Arica." She held her hands out in a show of surrender. "I need to talk to your boss. I'm here to help."

The boys traded looks of doubt, perhaps communicating. She noticed the pale one had pointed ears hiding within his straight, shiny locks.

The young one looked down his nose at her with suspicion. "Are you with Vanessa?"

She started to nod, then paused, then nodded some more, trying to keep her voice level as she said, "Yeah, yeah. She sent me to get everybody out. So you *are* Zenians?"

He gave another worried glance, this one shorter before sweeping his dark eyes over her. His sword lowered, but he still used it to gesture. "I'm Lyrenel. This is Výan."

Výan. This is the guy. She tried not to be suspicious, but took an extra long look over him, studying his lean face. She needed to remember him. "Can I talk to your commanders? We're in trouble."

"This way," Lyrenel said calmly as he turned and gestured at his companion.

31

THE COMMANDER

"Do we take her to the sanctum?" Výan asked, his voice scratchy and deep.

Arica walked between her two new companions, matching their rushed pace through the abandoned halls, led only by Výan's soft torchlight.

"We're still expected to return with Caldaryze, so yes," Lyrenel directed, leading into a long hall.

Columns lined the far side, the shadows between them dark enough to hide just about anything. Even as embedded into the rock as the fortress had seemed, it was dark, and Arica had sensitive eyes.

"Caldaryze. Isn't he a Dovevian?" she asked, silently questioning her fact retention.

"Yes. We picked him up as we retreated from the caverns."

She took an extra glance around at the cold, quiet innards of the castle. It didn't feel like a home. Maybe that was just because it had turned into a prison. "Why is this guy separated? Shouldn't he be guarded?"

"Just keeping him out of the way," Lyrenel reasoned, barely turning his head to her. "The Dovevians prefer to keep their tyros intact. We may need him if they break in."

She heard his boot hit a lower step before she'd even seen the stairs in front of them. Her heart raced. She'd been inches from an unexpected, jolting step downwards. She turned to make sure Výan was still following. His footsteps were eerily quiet.

"You guys were scouting for them," Arica said with the realization. "Trying to find where they'd attack."

"Us and half a dozen more," Výan murmured almost aggressively.

She hesitated as she followed the young Zenian down the steps, the disjointed details of her plan fading into further chaos. *And I can't just wing it. I need those commanders.*

Slipping her free hand into her pocket, she found her little communication device but heard nothing from it. "We had to take a detour," she breathed. "But I'll be back on plan in a few minutes."

Lyrenel glanced back as they reached the bottom of the steps, but seemed to understand what she held, and didn't respond.

"Where are you?" Drake asked in a whisper. She repeated the question aloud.

Lyrenel glanced at her as Výan overtook her and turned right into a low, inconsistently shaped room made of stone. "Back end of the lowest level. The cellars," he finally answered.

This, she also repeated, but the Dovevian didn't respond.

Arica took another few steps until she was only one step above the stranger.

His soft brown, almond-shaped eyes studied her.

"This isn't going to be one of those moments where I'm led to an empty cell, but don't realize what's going on until I turn around and the door is closed... right?" She grabbed her forearm, fidgeting in place but kept his gaze.

He held himself proudly, shoulders squared and spine erect. His thin lips held a sternness, but there was something there in face just under the surface. Curiosity?

Lyrenel's gaze finally broke, his shoulders loosening. "There aren't any cells down here." His arms folded across his chest. "I'm just trying to get a read on you."

She let out a nervous laugh. "I guess I was doing the same."

Then Lyrenel nodded, indicating for her to into the low room.

A pair of men sat around a small table. One had a much older look than most of the Zenians she'd met, with a salt-and-pepper beard, matching shaggy hair, and leathery, light brown skin. He slouched in a wood chair, fiddling with a small wooden box and some small, colorful game pieces. An empty plate and a half-filled jug of water sat on his other side. The other man, however, was propped up on his chair, limp, like a macabre doll.

The conscious one watched them approach. "Co—"

"We're to hurry, Fallian," Lyrenel interrupted as Výan unshackled the prisoner's wrists from the legs of his chair and straightened him onto the floor. He had relatively handsome, young features, a firm jaw, and dull red hair that had barely grown in from being shaved off. A good portion of his skin was black and purple with bruises, but what wasn't had the telltale gray tinge of a Dovevian, even in the flickering candlelight.

Fallian's bushy eyebrows lowered. "We—I thought we were going to keep Caldaryze out of—"

The sound of heavy steps on the stairs cut him off. One of them extinguished the small candle, and all three unsheathed weapons.

Blue light trickled down the stairs, but it was impossible to see the footsteps' owner until he'd turned the corner. Her Dovevian companion.

Arica reached out like lightning, grabbing the hands of the two closest Zenians, Fallian, and Lyrenel. What she didn't expect was a violent retraction from both of them. They shot in opposite directions, weapons blazing at her as she gasped.

"N-no, I was trying to help—" She looked back at Drake. "I don't know what to do," she whispered breathlessly.

Nobody attacked, but Drake held a finger to his lips as his light reached them. But for good reasons, none of them relaxed as they watched the dangerous enemy like a group of curious cats.

Drake tilted his head to the side, violet eyes sweeping over his unconscious companion. "It appears clear," he called, his deep voice booming in the enclosed room.

Hands still raised, Arica stepped further into the corner, away from Caldaryze as Drake slowly advanced.

The Dovevian held up four fingers, then pointed up the stairs.

A distant voice responded with boredom. "Then come back."

"Orders?" Výan breathed, posed to strike at any moment.

"Stay *put*," Arica enunciated quietly, hoping her confidence alone would make him listen.

Výan cast a furious gaze over her. "*Why?*"

"Just listen," she whispered, glancing at the other two.

Fallian was obviously unhappy, but he also waited for somebody to say something, and Lyrenel looked more curious than worried. This was good only because if they indeed wanted to attack, there would've been nothing she could do to stop them.

"Nobody mentioned they were in the castle," Fallian stated quietly.

Drake strolled within reach of the trio of iron points, then lazily batted the closest one with a black leather bracer. "There's *five* of my companions within vocal distance, so *shut the fuck up*," he hissed, his head twisting to meet gazes with all four of them in turn.

Drake reached for their prisoner, then glanced up at Lyrenel as the thin man's sword reached for his neck. He froze, but his expression didn't change.

"Do you mind?" he whispered in a mocking tone.

"I can't let you have him," Lyrenel murmured with a finality that would've been hard to argue with.

"Wait a moment," Drake called, once again for the benefit of the other Dovevians. "I found Caldaryze. Wounded. They *left* him here." An eyebrow tweaked, his gaze still bearing down on Lyrenel.

Arica imagined his voice, but he only needed his cocky, questioning smirk. *Your turn.*

A soft growl of annoyance rose in Lyrenel's throat as he withdrew his sword, standing down.

Drake smirked, bending down, and easily picked up his friend's slight frame. He gave Arica one last look, then walked away with his arms full.

Then the sword switched targets fast enough that Arica jumped, nearly impaling herself on it as Lyrenel glowered. She kept the gaze despite a quiver in her muscles that she couldn't pinpoint the source of, and for a long time, they waited in silence.

"There's nothing else. We might as well move on from this area," she heard her Dovevian command through her stone, though she could still hear him at the top of the stairs.

"They're moving on. We should go," Arica suggested softly. Lyrenel's glare didn't waver for a moment. She jerked her head to the side, then went to leave, but after five steps, she was blocked by Výan's glistening sword tip. A gasp jerked through her as she threw her hands up.

"You were right," he growled low, baring even closer to her, but she didn't dare back into either of the others. "She's a Dovevian spy."

"I-I can explain!" Arica begged quietly.

"It wasn't hard," Lyrenel murmured as she turned back to him, her heart racing. "Vanessa would never send in a *tyro*."

"No, you're right," she panted, outstretched hands trembling. "That was probably a terrible choice of lie. But I swear, I'm here to help. Jake's outside if you don't believe me. I-I can prove I'm a Zenian, I... I'm Amer—Ellterian." She let her hands twist palmsup. "I have some of Jake's solzetair feathers... Although you probably can't tell them from Drake's."

None of them moved, almost as if they expected an order from someone else entirely.

"Look," she spluttered, trying to form actual words. "I'm conspiring with Drake Damage to get you guys out of here safely. If you know Vanessa at all, and I barely do, you know she wouldn't've accepted his help. Hell, I only got Jake because I didn't tell him who was helping me." She shrugged so hard her shoulders threatened to pop from their sockets. "I get you guys are hesitant, but, like, I don't really see another choice right now."

"Our other choice would be securing another Dovevian tyro," Výan threatened, taking a practiced step closer and closing her into the triangle of potential pain.

"J-just trust me," she begged, her knees shaking with stress. "Look, you don't even need your swords. I barely have any weapons. You could probably take me out with a toothpick."

"We can't take any chances," Lyrenel murmured, then nodded at Výan.

"Oh, I know!" Arica gasped, then went to stick her hands in her pockets.

"No," Lyrenel snapped, crossing the few feet between them. Výan froze in place.

Arica's hands instantly went back in the air as she stared into his stern eyes. "Sorry. Bag tied to fourth and fifth belt loops."

His eye contact didn't waver as he pawed at the satchel, then pulled the single heavy item from the bag. A big golden seal.

"If that doesn't tell you something, and you really don't think the commanders will care, then... I guess you'll just have to stab me," she said blankly.

His expression softened slightly, a flash of curiosity on his lips as he looked over the item. "Where'd you get this?"

"Jake gave it to me a few minutes ago, in case I ran into trouble. I found out it's Khantarian, probably a Zenian's from way back in the day. Well, and before that, I actually found it hidden in Jake's storage chest. But between those things, I used it to dispel a revenant."

Lyrenel gave her a questioning glance, but she didn't blame him. She'd lived through the whole thing and didn't believe half of it. Then he gave a single, stern nod.

"Mistress Damage must be thrilled with you," Výan mumbled, begrudgingly putting his sword away.

Hands still up, she shrugged. "So? We gonna do this, or can you take me to Commander Herak now?"

Lyrenel's jaw stiffened behind lean cheeks, but his sword lowered.

"Are you sure we can trust her, sir?" Fallian asked hesitantly.

Sir?

Lyrenel gestured at the other two, then smiled stiffly as he offered Arica the crest back. "Master Commander Lyrenel Herak, at your service, ma'am."

Arica finally caught sight of some actual light, though dull and flickering. She walked in the middle of her three companions as they passed under a towering archway into a foyer. Two gigantic doors led into the main hall, propped all the way open. Braziers on the sides of these doors were the source of the light, though they burned low. A bunch of bedrolls and belongings sat in a haphazard pile across from where they'd entered, near the enormous doors.

She'd given them what information she could, but the commander hadn't hinted at what he planned on doing with it.

Lyrenel approached a droopy-faced guy and the stocky gorilla-armed dude he was bandaging. "Russel, is Lady Marc back yet?"

He shook his head, his long blond hair tucked securely behind his ears. He pressed the last of the tape onto the man's bicep. "I haven't seen her. Mettis is back. Aven..." He made a noise as if pained, then looked back at his work.

"Should we round again?" Fallian asked almost tiredly.

Lyrenel's lips pressed together for a long pause. Then he met Arica's gaze. "No. I want to see this break our savior is on about. Gather the—"

"Lyrenel!"

They looked across the open doors to the corridor opposite where they'd entered.

A woman pranced towards them in shin-high boots, wearing various pieces of armor, including a shiny baby blue mask over half of her face, even covering one eye. Her white blonde hair was kept back from her face with a loose ribbon.

She slowed from her jog, a long, silky cloak fluttering down around her. "The barrier is broken. We have to be ready to fight," she said in an airy, andromae-like voice.

"No!" Arica blurted, throwing her hands out in front of her a bit more dramatically than she'd intended. Then she felt exhausted eyes on her.

"Who's this?" The blonde asked softly, her uncovered eye wearily taking in Arica's little, less than threatening physique.

That's got to be Randa, she decided. The stories she'd heard fit the odd woman perfectly.

"Okay, look, my name is Arica Tanson, and we have a plan! But we only have a few minutes. We broke the weakness in the barrier, so we need to get everyone out. Then we can seal it up behind us and give ourselves a few minutes to escape the Dovevians."

Nobody moved but her, as she wondered if this was even going to work.

Lyrenel glanced at Randa, meeting her gaze. "There are Dovevians already searching the corridors. They've retrieved Caldaryze. We have to leave one way or another, join the fight. We'll regroup."

"We just need to get out," Arica reiterated softly, feeling the weight of their decisions. "As fast as possible."

"We could retreat up the mountain," Lyrenel agreed, glancing between the two women.

Randa let out a soft, tired sigh before answering. "There stands thirty hundred between us and the Nevarians. If the Dovevians are in the castle, we're surrounded and on our own."

Lyrenel threw her a dramatic shrug. "So we leave them here. Rejoin the high master and rain Iylcaobonaste upon them until she calls for release."

With an incline of the head, Randa silently agreed.

Lyrenel cleared his throat loudly, palming the pommel of his sword. "Send Nahlie to draw back the scouts. We'll round on the southern tower. Warn them to keep close watch and not to engage." He turned to the guys sitting in wait. "Lord Tramnovich, help Juyterm get Aven out of harm's way before joining Master Damage."

"Sir, yare wanting him out fast and injured, or reallae fast and injured?" the stocky man asked in a heavily accented growl.

"Just don't die, Duekov," Lyrenel suggested tiredly. Then his gaze landed on Arica.

Her hands spread out. "I'm not much of a fighter," she said nervously.

"No, but you've been on the battlefield; you've seen the weakness of our barrier. I may yet need your help."

He returned one last look, as if making sure everyone understood, then ushered Arica into a jog.

Arica's head crested the tower's floor onto a platform with a waist-high rail around it. A sheet of rainbow surrounded them. Lyrenel reached the edge and leaned forward, his shoulder blades protruding awkwardly from thin shoulders.

She joined his side, looking out over the front of the castle. Thousands of small black ants spanned the courtyard below them, broken up only by a dozen tiny circles that puffed and exploded with magic and practiced swordsmanship, no matter how many swarmed in on any of them.

Still, a thick layer of soldiers stood between the troupe of Zenians and the gates of Castle Kopion.

"Once through, Mistress Damage will open the shield from the courtyard. If the Dovevians don't break it from the inside first," Lyrenel narrated.

"It's easier to break from inside?" Arica asked. This wasn't information anyone had thought to give her.

"No. But it is easier to break with magic on both sides."

Black-robed warriors converged on a Zenian but immediately blasted back in an almost perfect circle around them. The swarm thinned out the closer to the courtyard she looked, before everything disappeared behind the roof in front of them.

A soft, faded boom echoed off the castle walls like rolling thunder, a black and purple bruise blossoming along the shield in front of them. The roof vibrated, large pieces breaking away and cascading to the ground. Lyrenel stared, concentrated and stiff.

"Are—are you doing that?" she asked softly.

He blinked. "Hopefully it'll distract the Dovevians long enough for everyone to slip away."

"I can't believe you've kept this place under control this long," Arica murmured.

Lyrenel turned back, his lips pressed straight. "That's what we do, Miss Tanson. We survive." He beckoned with a single hand.

They returned to the innards of the old castle, and while Arica was still turned around, she could tell they weren't headed for her makeshift entrance.

"Quietly," Lyrenel murmured, slowing to a sneaky jog along the wall.

She mimicked his pace and walk, and even kept one hand on the wall as she went. The natural light dimmed, but Lyrenel did nothing about it. She could see okay as it was.

They passed across a huge cased archway leading into a dining hall and continued towards the rear of the castle.

Arica smacked into Lyrenel's toned arm as he flattened himself against the wall and unearthed an iron longsword. A pair of figures walked on the other side of the corridor, both heavily cloaked from head to toe. They walked slowly, close to the wall, but unalerted. And unrecognizable.

Arica saw Lyrenel's chest expand with a deep breath, but she snagged his off arm and dragged him back. "No," she whispered, continuing to tug as she snuck into the closest doorway. Luckily, he didn't resist, letting her lead him into a small alcove full of dusty junk.

She waited, sticking her hand against her communication device. "Is there anywhere safe anymore? Are we trapped?"

Lyrenel didn't notice her movement, so answered in a soft whisper. "They'll move on."

Hurried footsteps echoed off the stone corridor, much louder than even their labored breathing. She wasn't positive, but in the shadows, Lyrenel's eyes looked like they were barely focusing. She could still see light from *somewhere*.

"So," she whispered, leaning her head on the wall. "Do you come here often?"

Lyrenel's weight pressed lightly against her as he peeked out to check their surroundings. "Mmm-hmm," he murmured, straight-faced. "It's a great spot for sex."

Her eyebrows went up, suddenly less keen on being nearly chest to chest with him. "Ooookay."

A shout rang across the hall, familiar, but it wasn't enough to swear it was Drake's. "Hey! Where's Netosi?"

"Ransom was trying to corner the Kyrganite girl, so he ran to help," called a tempered male voice in a softer accent.

Lyrenel grew restless, handling his weapon, then peeked around the doorway.

"Did you see what they did to the barrier, Damage?"

"Of course. We'll have them surrounded by the time they get through it. I told you this was the better idea. Anyway, Anraquella nearly had a pair of them driven in Ransom's direction, so un—"

"Hey you! Stop right there!"

Arica gasped as Lyrenel slammed himself against the doorway as fast footsteps echoed, but instead of coming after them, a bald man in a billowy cloak tore past them.

"Nriallea just turned the corner," Lyrenel whispered, but his muscles readied, his grip shifting.

"Commander, don't," Arica whispered, trying to grab him, but he slipped out of her grip and bolted.

"Behind you!"

Arica threw herself around the doorway to catch a peek.

Lyrenel threw a blazing attack at the stocky, bearded Dovevian, but he countered as quickly. Drake took long, deliberate steps towards them in the long hall, but as his gaze flicked upwards and met Arica's, he spread his hands out to his sides in question.

She just shrugged as best she could. She was winging it and there was nothing she could do about it. Instead of helping, the towering Dovevian switched direction.

Arica bolted from the closet. Maybe it wasn't the safest, but she went to Lyrenel's side. He countered a swipe from his opponent, throwing the bigger man's arm to the side, then grabbed the hilt still in his hand and slammed it through the Dovevian's other forearm into the wooden pillar behind him. He let out a wail, but it stuck.

A piece of brick flipped up in front of Arica's foot, tripping her. Her kneecap smacked the ground hard enough that her teeth clattered. A boot haphazardly flipped her onto her back. Her breath caved as a shiny, paper-thin blade tip brushed the front of her shirt.

Drake's face was blank as he tipped his head to the side, his blade effortlessly static. "You're not very good at this," he murmured.

"That's what I keep trying to tell everyone," Arica whined breathlessly.

She jumped harder than the Dovevian when a long piece of jagged wire flipped around his off arm, skin-tight before he could even move it.

"Funny thing about arteries," Lyrenel said loudly as he dragged Drake's arm a little closer, holding steady to the handles of the little wire saw. "They're very easy to reach. I'll have yours gushing before you can lean into the sword. And even if you do, any wound you'd have time to inflict upon her could be coaxed to heal within the next fifteen minutes."

Arica's gaze switched from him to the sword tip against her sternum and back, doubting his statement with her whole being, but couldn't form words to express so.

"Or you could let her go."

Drake's jaw tightened as he glared at Lyrenel. A few superficial veins popped in the trapped bicep, but Lyrenel's stoic expression remained with his challenge.

"As you wish, Commander," Drake finally announced, flourishing his weapon up and away from Arica's personal space.

Lyrenel released the saw, grabbed Arica's arm, and wrenched her up with surprising strength. He dragged her out of the hall and into a room stacked with old, broken racks and chests.

But she chanced a glance over her shoulder in time to see Drake wrench his companion's sword from his own arm and hand it back to him. As he turned, he caught her gaze and gave her a mischievous smile she couldn't read.

"After the rebels."

Arica turned and sprinted after the commander, but he was halfway in a small room, waiting, ready to slam the door as soon as she stumbled in.

A layer of rainbow magic formed over the old wooden door, but almost immediately, soft, muffled bangs pounded against it.

Lyrenel paced away from it, wiping a blackish smear from the tip of his sword.

"They want hostages," Arica whispered.

"If we're lucky."

She looked around the room as a light blared near Lyrenel's shoulder. No windows, no other doors, a small room of shelves holding dusty bottles and kitchen tools corroded with rust. Like it hadn't seen light or life in a hundred years.

"Could we... carve through the walls to escape?" she asked softly. After a moment, she looked back.

He was quiet but for his evening breaths as he sheathed the weapon. A patch of red spread on the brown fabric of his tunic, low on his stomach.

"Oh, my—I didn't realize they got you," Arica whispered, stepping to help, but as usual, she wasn't any.

He unbuttoned his coat, but instead of a newly torn wound or a knife erupting from it, there was a pile of blood-soaked gauze strapped tight around his waist.

"It's fine, I just tore it again," he murmured, throwing down a visually empty bag. He knelt to rifle through it and pulled out some tape and more fabric.

"We can rest for a minute, anyway." Arica sat down, happy for the excuse.

Blood leaked from a large, open gash in the center of an abdomen muscle, simultaneously rubbed raw and scabbing, so she slid to help. She held the bandages to catch the seeping liquid as he ran a few pieces of thick tape to close it back up.

"What happened?" she asked, cringing as a deep breath soaked the fresh bandage.

He exhaled through his teeth, but his hands were steady. "Kisok got me when they pushed through the caverns beneath the castle three d-d-day—"

Arica's muscles tensed to jump up, her first instinct he was having a stroke or something, but he shook his head like he was getting water out of an ear.

He continued as if nothing had happened. "Three days ago."

"And it's not better?" she said softly.

"We haven't a master of healing like you Nevarians. We make do."

He'd taped enough she felt brave enough to press the gauze against it, but his stifled groan startled her enough that he had to take over.

"I still can't believe you lied to me," she scoffed, wiping blood on her jeans.

Lyrenel cleared his throat, drawing her attention to a sharp, soldier-like stare. "I didn't lie," he said with barely a shake of the head. "You expected me to trust you, and you didn't even know your commander's name."

He stood, belting his coat closed before shouldering his bag and sword.

"Yeah, b-but you scared me, it threw me off. And I'm like brand new here. I can barely remember anyone's name, let alone the first name of a dude I hadn't actually seen before. And it's not my fault you look like a twenty-six-year-old teenager."

"How new *are* you?" Lyrenel asked over his shoulder.

"Uh, two weeks ago I had running water and a cell phone, so…" She was sure someone had mentioned this guy was one of those who knew about her world.

"You are Ellterian," he stated as if remembering. He looked closely around the room for something invisible. "Well, I'm sure you've some stories I'd like to hear sometime."

"I haven't done anything cool or exciting," she admitted nervously. "Or anything at all, really."

"Then maybe you shouldn't be trying to save us all by yourself," he murmured.

She nodded softly, glancing around again. A door stuck out at her, though she was sure the first time she'd looked, there wasn't one. Except, it wasn't a door. There was no handle, no hinges, not even a change of material. Just the slightest shift of color, an almost… purple.

Arica lurched forward and placed her hands on the freezing stonework. Not even a seam stuck out. She didn't want to be known as the girl who saw random, colorful boxes.

"I think there's something here," she called softly.

"I don't remember what's on the other side of that. I think it comes out into the crypts. We'd have to round back to the greathall, and I—"

"No, it… It's something else." She wanted to explain better, but she knew nothing more. The weirdest thing was that he listened. He joined her side, gently touching the stones.

"There's nothing here."

"Okay, but if hypothetically there was… How would one… break it, or open it or whatever?"

Lyrenel filled his lungs with air and held it for a long moment, then shook his head. "A hidden keyhole? A spoken word, perhaps? It could be any number of things, and there's nothing to say it would lead anywhere helpful, anyway."

She looked over it again. If there was a keyhole or a lever, she'd notice. *Right?* She touched her forehead, the muffled noises of threatening power dulling behind her. "An important phrase. Okay, um..." Lyrenel dodged a step back as her arms flapped with an annoying realization. "Freaking duh. I know what it is."

She glanced into curious coffee eyes as if waiting for permission, but didn't wait long.

"Ersiasevaer," she enunciated.

It didn't have the effect she'd been hoping for. Nothing opened, nothing groaned, and no monsters awoke from their dusty slumber. However, Lyrenel's expression had changed from casual curiosity to concern.

"I know it's Raellic, but I was taught the phrase," she explained quickly, but this didn't cure his confusion.

"By whom?"

She paused, trying to blot out the noise. Maybe they weren't getting out of there. "Uh, it uh— It's a long story, but Jake told me what it meant."

His eyebrows stayed low as he glanced at the wall, his lips pulled into a tight frown. "Teurm ekh adaot."

Light grew at the bottom of the section, a perfect match to her vision. The wall softened under her touch, allowing her to sink into a silky, warming clay. She almost resisted, but within moments, she could feel cold air on the other side. Sinking was unneeded, though, because after another few, the stones faded from existence altogether, leaving an open spot into a dark, narrow hall.

"Does that mean anything to you?" Arica asked as Lyrenel shouldered past her.

He said nothing, his body blocking one side of the passage, his light shining across the other. He turned and with barely a wave of the hand, the buzzing stopped and the wall returned to stand as it always had.

"Come."

32

MAGIC OF THE REALM

Arica rounded the corner behind Commander Herak, her breath short. She may have been running for her life, but that wouldn't suddenly give her a swimmer's lungs.

They reached an oddly shaped room. The walls rounded in the middle and fanned out at an angle. Tall wooden pillars stabilized the stone ceiling, but there was only one piece of furniture in the room, a high table with detailed carvings filled with gold.

Her hands struck out, anchoring her against both sides of the narrow passage. "We still haven't made it to the back of the castle, or the break in the field. I'm kinda scared for the rest of your buddies."

"Well, this'll help," Lyrenel said, jogging to the fancy table. "It'll give us time, at least."

With his touch, a low tone went off, a pleasant buzz she could feel in her hands and feet. In fact, a lot in her hands. She found a groove under the left one along the wall, the perfect width to slide a finger in and feel the smooth gold embedded within it.

She followed it a few feet, but she saw no indication of it stopping as it led back down the small hall.

"What is this?" she asked as she returned.

"An augment table," the commander murmured. "Designed to soak up and store huge amounts of magic in case of emergencies. We didn't think Kopion had one."

She couldn't focus on any one thing carved into the table, but it looked mostly decorative and abstract rather than painting a picture. Except, a rather deliberate circle pressed in the direct center of it about the size of her hand.

She reached into her pocket and once again handled the heavy crest, eyeing the slot in the middle. "So basically... an augment table and a hero seal are the same kind of—"

"They gather the raw magic of this realm. Dovevian magic comes tainted with that of Naornagosau, Solyve's plain," he explained in a hurry, his eyes focused on his task. "If we dispel it, forcing ours upon them, it will weaken them. Allow us a chance to escape."

"How do we get outta this room though?"

He held up a single finger and finished his pass around the table. "That should about—"

A *crack* tore at Arica's eardrums as the table split into pieces, only the gold embellishments holding splintered wood together. The buzz grew intense.

Then Lyrenel jogged to the pair of window shutters. "How about we break some bones?" he suggested lightly.

Arica hesitated, fingering the seal as she stared at the table's center. Maybe it was the gold or just the sentiment of the thing that urged her to keep it. Still, it obviously belonged there.

She leaned forward, barely touching the precarious table, and gently placed the seal against the lip of the indentation. She kept only the very tips of her fingers hugging the piece as it slipped into place perfectly.

The tone changed, barely noticeable.

Light flooded the dingy room as Lyrenel yanked open the windows. She didn't know what the next step would be, but didn't expect him to tug at the stone frame. Like sand or loose cobble, it crumbled away under his hands, only a handful or two before he dragged whole armfuls of dusty material away from the wall. Before long, he'd created a hole big enough for both of them a few feet from the shiny barrier.

He barely gave a look back before leaping over the low, jagged wall.

Arica gasped and sprinted to the edge. "Are you insane? I didn't know you *actually* wanted to break some bones."

The fall wasn't as bad as she expected, but it was still over fifteen feet, about four from the pulsing field of energy.

"I'll catch you," Lyrenel offered from below her, on his feet and unscathed.

She suddenly felt dizzy and grabbed the wall for support. "I'll break you," she managed, her head light.

"I'm a lot stronger than I look."

A shiver ran up her spine, the unnerving height having no argument about being the most intimidating thing she'd approached that night. *After all I just did, jumping to my death will not stop me.*

"Just for the record," she called down, setting her hands on the edge of solid stone as he had. "I'm NOT falling for you!"

She launched over the edge, trying to mimic Lyrenel's jump. Her shoulder slammed into an unforgiving barrier, knocking the air out of her before she dropped the last few feet into a stranger's arms.

"We'll see about that," Lyrenel grunted.

As soon as he set her back on her feet, she started forward, hopefully leaving her anxiety sickness behind. He was right behind her.

"We just met. Are you always this flirty?" she asked quickly.

"Uh, is it *that* strange when confrontation is my only way to see the sun again?"

"No. That seems reasonable."

Lyrenel grabbed her arm, slowing them both to a stop as his finger touched his lips.

He slipped his sword out of a thin leather sheath, holding it parallel with his forearm.

Arica could see the edge of the break. It was much taller than before, but there wasn't any sign of the Dovevian that might've been on patrol.

Nevertheless, Lyrenel led her slowly, the noise of each step as controlled as possible.

A shoulder came into view from the other side of the field, just inside the tear.

Arica didn't know how he could tell it wasn't one of his guys, but he went after him, sidling up against the field, then jogged forward as lightly as possible.

His swipe should've been deadly, but the target whipped around with an inhuman agility and deflected the blade with a plated arm guard.

The pale, humanoid creature didn't have any weapons, but still, Lyrenel avoided the swipes of long hands with sharpened nails, swinging his sword back about fruitlessly.

The vampire, Patryk, she remembered. Maybe Drake left him here because, as Vanessa had also said, a vampire should be an easy opponent for a healthy Zenian.

Lyrenel certainly wasn't in over his head, but in the small space, the vampire had an obvious advantage. So Arica sprinted forward to help push the fighting further away from it.

Her sword came from its sheath much more clumsily than she intended, but she kept it in her hands. Luckily, Lyrenel had edged to the other side, so she didn't worry about hurting him. But this wasn't any disadvantage for Patryk.

The vamp pulled a short knife from his belt as a defense to Arica's unplanned strike. His little knife batted away her sword with such force she stumbled into the unrelenting field.

He spun at Lyrenel, narrowly missing a long slash to the chest from the commander's sword.

Plan it this time. Go for the head. She took the hilt in both of her hands, prepared to throw all of her strength into smacking him with the flat of her blade.

It went fine—her swipe controlled and strong—until the vampire turned in a circle and flung out his covered arm, slamming the blade hard enough to fling it from her grasp.

Then Patryk rounded again.

She threw an arm forward; the only thing that could defend her with her sword on the other side of the vampire. There was no way her sleeve was going to stop the knife. She knew this but didn't have a choice.

A sudden burst of blue energy pulsed out of Arica's bracelet and created a barrier that bounced them in opposite directions against Patryk's strength. Luckily, Lyrenel was there in a moment, slamming his sword vertically into the vampire's chest. He quieted under the blade.

"Whoa," Arica gasped from the ground, staring at the unmoving undead.

"New bracelet?" Lyrenel guessed with a lazy gesture.

"Yeah." She glanced at the cuff cupping her wrist innocently enough.

Lyrenel held out a hand. "Come on. This won't hold him long. I don't suppose your sword tip is silver?"

She shook her head, taking the offered help.

Then Lyrenel slashed horizontally across the vampire's neck. Blood squirted from the severed veins like a water pipe finally bursting under pressure.

Arica jumped back, squealing, then covered her nose and mouth.

"Must've been feeding on the injured," Lyrenel said passively as he gestured towards the front of the castle. "That'll take a bit more time to recover from."

He held his hand out to her as the stolen liquid's arch lowered to a trickle. He was nice enough to help her step over the growing puddle and the undead body, then retrieve her sword.

The galactic barrier looked a lot more fragile than when she'd left it, cracks webbing out as far as she could see. The hole still widened, slowly, but visibly.

"They broke the artifact you were using to hold it," Lyrenel observed, kicking over a charred, cracked version of Vanessa's little cylinder. "Must have been strong enough to leave a lasting effect. It should have shattered. Not bad."

Arica looked at the ground, her chest settling since they'd finally stopped running and fighting. With it, a fear blossomed, tightening her lungs and throat. "Yeah. I had a lot of help." She looked again at the deteriorating barrier. "So, can Výan fix this?"

"Maybe. If anyone can. But it won't hold long."

Arica looked around, nervous. Lyrenel's long weapon bounced anxiously in his hand. She had to resist reaching for the rock. Maybe she was mad at his actions, but if Lyrenel was correct, the Dovevian already knew what they'd done, and he was probably furious.

She caught Lyrenel's gaze and glanced at his blood-soaked coat. "I didn't even think—Are you okay?"

"No," he sighed, then shrugged a shoulder. "Has your Dovevian said anything since we foiled their plan?"

She shook her head, trying to shrink in on herself as a sick feeling crept over her insides. At least he still trusted her.

"Fucking *Drake*."

Lyrenel leaned to look past Arica as she jumped in a half circle.

Jake leaned one hand on a tree trunk, his features stern but pale. She guessed by his stance he'd only just arrived.

"Your Dovevian?" he scoffed, then shook out his short hair. "The most grossly devious one over there. This was the stupidest thing I've *ever* been a part of."

Arica glanced at Lyrenel, unsure what to say. The *hatred* in Jake's eyes was so strong she worried that some of it was towards her. But when Lyrenel's expression was soft with sympathy, she looked back.

"We can't really go back now... We have to follow through with it," she mumbled meekly.

His body stayed rigid, his bloodshot gaze boring into her. "Should have made you tell me who he was." His voice was low, way too familiar, even though the same tone was someone else's.

Arica swallowed hard, unable to look him in the eye anymore.

"Don't listen to him," the commander soothed. "He's in a lot of pain."

She barely looked long enough to see Jake shifting uncomfortably like he was going to object just with body language when something else distracted her vision.

Two women and a man crested the hill on the overgrown path, two she recognized as new friends, Fallian and Randa, but the third was a younger appearing girl with soft cheeks, a cool, light skin tone, a boyish haircut, and a double-ended ax strapped to her back.

"You finally made it," Randa chirped, leading the pack.

"And no one else, Commander Marc?" Lyrenel asked, folding his arms.

"Cahlkal is running for Vanessa."

Neither said anything else, but they both turned to the break and approached the wall of the castle as a pair of Zenians rounded—Výan and a man with low eyebrows, in leather armor and holding a longbow.

"They're bringing Aven through the workrooms," Výan reported, turning his head to the stretch of wall facing them.

"We're nearly there then," Lyrenel murmured, hand outstretched but several inches from touching the stone slabs.

Arica expected some kind of explosion, even just a minor one, but there was a soft pulse, forcing Lyrenel to take a step back to regain balance. Then the wall crumbled into dust about three feet wide with enough height to squeeze an average person through.

Randa barrelled into the dust first, but Lyrenel was right behind her. Both came back dragging a body wrapped in a blanket, a tanned, average-built fellow whose features barely existed behind skinny strips of bloody gauze wrapped around his head.

"Out," Lyrenel ordered, quiet but firm as he adjusted his half of the burden into Jake's awaiting arm. "Regroup with Mistress Damage. She'll lead you from there. Výan, once everyone is out, fix this mess of magic."

Fallian supported another Zenian by the hand, a pretty woman with long black hair and thick makeup. She held a rag to a gash in her forearm, her voice low and raspy as she said, "Yare lucky yare so resourceful, Commander, or I'd be missing my arm about here."

"Just looking out for you, Lady Naemaoskr," Lyrenel said with a curt nod.

A few more Zenians finally trailed through, totaling out to be about fifteen Kopion Zenians altogether.

"Herak!"

Arica turned with the commander to see who was yelling so angrily but saw Jerim walking up the slope between Zenians, his face contorted in frustration.

"Where's my child?"

Lyrenel's expression was apathetic. "We had to leave him behind."

"How dare you!" the soldier roared, stomping up towards the commander, but Randa threw her arm out over him, stopping him in his tracks.

"He's a Dovevian, Jerim, not a priority. You know the Dovevians won't hurt him," he reasoned coolly.

"He was *hurt*," Jerim began, pain breaking on his features, "If he dies—"

"Then I'll be responsible for the end of another enemy, and you can all thank me," Commander Herak growled with clear authority. "You should be with Mistress Damage's company, retreating, Enileny."

"Come," Randa urged gently, pulling him backward. He glowered at the commander another moment, then turned and followed Randa's beckoning.

Stalking to the hole again, Lyrenel took one last look, then stepped back. "That should be everyone. Otherwise, they're dead meat with those Dovevians. Have at it, Výan."

Arica looked over her shoulder for Jake. He stood a little ways away, waiting. Výan pushed purple streaks of magic, a more visual display than she'd ever seen, into the barrier. It gathered across the torn edges of the field like faint lavender salt crystals.

"Go with them, Arica," the commander then ordered out of the blue.

She jumped slightly, hearing her name, but the order also surprised her. She hesitantly turned to follow it before glancing back at the field.

"Wait..." Nobody stopped her as she sprinted back up to the surface of the field, next to the elven guy. Then she reached out and pointed above her.

"Concentrate it here."

She half expected some snotty remark or for him to just disregard her, but the magic grew where she indicated, slowly curing to match the rest of the barrier.

"Well, that made quite the—" Výan muttered before she interrupted.

"There!" She wasn't sure exactly how she could tell where it was weakest, but she felt like a cat after a laser pointer, seeing the dot only with a sixth sense. Something she couldn't understand, but her finger knew where to point.

"Hurry," Jake barked behind them.

They both continued their task.

"Lord Damage," Lyrenel called as if he wanted to start up a pleasant chat. "What happened, anyway?"

"Long story," Jake grunted almost resentfully.

Lyrenel let out a quick snicker. "Solzetair bite, an imprint of lightning, burns, a few broken bones... Tried fighting Drake in the air, didn't you?"

Arica looked over her shoulder to see Jake pull his cloak closed tighter, then support his weight against the tree again.

"Maybe not that long. And you, boy?"

Lyrenel smirked softly, glancing over his bloody coat, but he did nothing to cure the source. "I went too lax against Lise and earned the badge for it. Luckily, his aim is terrible."

There was silence for the last few long moments as Výan listened to Arica's insightful encouragement. Only once they had about a foot diameter circle left did Jake stalk forward. He said nothing, just reached forward between them and stuck his arm in the last bit of space opened.

Loose metal pieces clinked together before landing on the other side of the field.

A hand roughly grabbed Arica's shoulder and started dragging her back. "Wait, what was—"

"Seal it up," Jake ordered without room for any argument. "NOW. Then *run*."

Arica wanted answers instead of blind orders, but Jake's grip on her arm wasn't resistible as he dragged her a little faster than she could comfortably keep up with.

She could hear someone crashing through weeds behind her, but couldn't look back.

Jake swore and let go of her arm. She almost tripped, but clumsily stayed up, keeping most of her momentum. She didn't know where her partner had gone, though Lyrenel had to keep from slamming into her.

Then she felt a gust of wind so strong it cut an attempted gasp short. Trees cried out in agony, the ground shaking as a colossal monster clumsily stumbled through forest greens.

Arica barely got a glance at black fur and a stringy, torn-up limb dragging along the ground before something solid hit her back so hard the wind again escaped her lungs. She slid across the ground for too many yards to count.

Her lungs and chest constricted as she stopped on her stomach, too stunned and bruised to even breathe. The ground shook again in a slow beat. She finally sucked in a deep breath, resolving to lecture Jake for being so dramatic.

Just before the mountain erupted into orange chaos.

A surge of hot wind threw her an extra few feet, scouring her skin and barrelling through her clothes and hair. She wasn't sure if she'd heard the whoosh of fire, or if her ears had made it up as she was being thrown. Everything was too bright. Even with her eyes closed colors danced everywhere. Her ears rang and her skin tingled even against the cold dirt. Her cheek and arm stung, scraped up from rocks and broken branches.

A scream pierced through the ringing a thousand times more agonizing. It wasn't human; so loud she could feel it vibrating her bones. The ground trembled under the writhing animal.

Arica forced her eyes open, but all she could see was a blur of orange and yellow light.

Cold hands touched her shoulder and arm.

She had nothing left, so she fell asleep.

33

THIS WAS ALMOST AN EPILOGUE

Arica allowed the weathered door to fall in place as she faced the yard outside her own small quarters.

The estate they'd made their temporary home was heavily influenced by Revenal's temperate climate. Many small buildings substituted a single large one, only attached to each other with decorative arbors and vine-laden trellises spanning from a circular frame around most of the structures. Flowers in beds of soft soil lined carefully tended stone pathways in giant squares.

It was peaceful and amazing, and Arica would've appreciated it more than anyone… except for being constantly plagued by the fear of the openness of the estate. There were so many places dangers could hide. It would be simple to pick them off or swarm into the grounds, or send dragons in from above.

Too many nights she'd spent distracting herself from all the things that could go wrong.

The warm spring air was comfortable as Arica weaved in and out of streaks of moonlight across the flat path. She kept a small green book clasped to her chest. She'd forgotten the little defaced botany book until four days before. Her things had remained untouched for two months. For two months, she'd only needed her sword, her mentors, and the supplies the Revenan lord had provided.

She'd finally dumped the bag onto her bed and amidst an impressive layer of dirt, the book had fallen open. If she hadn't known any better, it was random. If she hadn't known any better, someone else would've left the message.

She opened the book to the memorized page number, walking on auto as she glanced over the writing in red ink lining the spine of a page listing the properties of a Revenan flower. She twisted the book in her hands to make sure she'd read it correctly.

Eight words. *Four days at midnight. The infirmary. He's back.*

The book snapped closed, and Arica focused back on her steady walk. Nobody passed her; the estate fast asleep and silent.

Shaking off any more distractions, Arica let the stone under her feet lead her in a half circle to the other side of the estate. Her destination was a larger square building made of thick, lacquered wood planks stained a dark color like most of the others. This one was different just because of the delicately painted orange symbol to the right of the door signaling medical essentials; half a realistic heart shape, the other half segments of citrus.

The door swung open smoothly under Arica's encouragement.

Vanessa looked up from the large leather book resting in the crook of her arm, her eyebrows arching.

Arica didn't answer the questioning glance as she slipped in and shut the door, then followed Vanessa's gaze to a high couch.

Jake slouched, legs askew, his eyelids heavy even as he watched Commander Herak poking at his intact arm. Tight cloth held the other against his torso.

"You're back," Arica chuckled lightly.

Both men looked up as if they'd been too busy to notice she'd come, but Lyrenel was quickly back to leaning over his work.

Jake tilted his head, forcing a smile. "More or less."

"It could be less," Vanessa said as she placed a firm hand on Arica's shoulder.

Then he let out a ragged cough that sounded like he was trying to get rid of his lungs entirely. Arica couldn't help cringing in sympathy.

Lyrenel froze until he'd regained control over his lungs, then reached for a short table on his other side already set up with items and tools. He pressed a short piece of sticky tape to Jake's arm.

"You know I don't like those," Jake grunted. A reddish-brown crystal about the size of a fingertip was embedded in the middle of the tape, pressed into his skin.

"Funny that you think that'll change anything," Lyrenel scoffed.

Jake shifted his legs, leaning back as he glanced at Arica. "Not allowed to *breathe* on my own anymore."

"No, that's something I insist you do, otherwise we'll have to send you back to Kallé Corve with Teres."

He earned a quick sneer. Then Jake turned his attention to Arica.

"Are you okay?" she asked tentatively.

"Enough."

Vanessa lightly squeezed her shoulder. "I do need to speak with you for a moment. I did what I could with the little spot of magic we found by the river, but it wasn't strong enough to tear into your world."

Arica nodded softly, her gaze frozen on the hardwood floor. "Oh."

"I'm sorry, but give it a little time. We will find something."

A calm settled on her shoulders. *I'm not... disappointed.*

"What did you need here?" Vanessa asked lighter. "Are you hurt?"

"Oh, I..." Her fingers teased along the uneven pages of her book to the corner. She flipped it open, only a few pages from the right one, but stopped one page before, and read a note in the same style of red ink near the spine.

Page 127.

She'd been through the book over and over, but every time she saw new things, no matter how hard she tried to flip the pages sequentially. Even with Vanessa practically breathing down her neck, she had to find out exactly what this was about.

So, she turned to page one hundred twenty-seven. Immediately, she wondered how she hadn't noticed this page before. It was originally blank, possibly a passage for sketches, but had been filled with a small print. Unfortunately, it was in a unique script, maybe a different language. Probably the one she'd already run into so often before.

The only exception was a sentence at the very top of the page. *For High Master von et Vanessa Malkalli Leadd-Damage.*

Arica looked up and held the book out.

"What is this?" the woman asked in her usual doubtful tone, but she took it anyway.

"I don't know, but it's for you."

A mix of accomplishment and nervousness grew in Arica's chest as Vanessa shifted into a slow pace, her eyes moving along the straight lines of symbols.

What could that message be? And who wrote it?

"What is it?" Jake asked as Lyrenel pushed his head to the side and went at it with a long, skinny tool.

Vanessa's expression hardened, but she didn't respond as her eyes trained on the pages of the old book.

Then, with only the sound of her silk dress fluttering around her, she left the room.

Arica stared at the guys, a sudden tension settling on her.

Lyrenel glanced at the empty doorway as he pulled off bloody rubber gloves. "What did you do?"

"She doesn't really have to do much to get anyone riled up or confused," Jake dismissed.

"Hey, I..." She gave up and just frowned.

Lyrenel condensed his stuff to the table, arranging bloody tools and vials and swabs.

Jake remained still, lacing his fingers together as he stared tiredly at Arica. "Tell me a story."

A smile erupted across her face. "I guess you probably don't remember a lot after you passed out." She meandered over and sat on the arm of the couch, her knees practically in his lap.

"Impressive, isn't it?" He laid his head back, eyes slowly drooping.

"I'm sure you're tired from your trip, but don't fall asleep just yet," Lyrenel warned softly.

He rolled his eyes, then turned his body towards Arica and waved an impatient hand.

"Well..." she said, trying to decide where to start. "Just before Výan sealed the break, this *really* stupid guy—wait, it was you—threw in a couple of fire volts from lord knows where, and we all turned and ran."

"Yeah, that sounds like me," he murmured.

"Then—maybe you were counting seconds—you turn full beast mode and start throwing trees around with these thrashing movements. Your tail swoops into Lyrenel, Výan, and me. The mountain explodes, throwing all of us for, like… a hundred feet. You kept most of the impact off of us, though it still broke Lyrenel's knee."

She followed his gaze to where Lyrenel stirred clear fluid in a glass with a twisty metal spoon.

"I'm fine," he quickly reassured. "What you didn't know was that we'd just activated an augment table. You probably didn't think it would be that bad."

Jake's eyes narrowed. "I thought Kopion didn't have an augment table."

"We didn't think so. *She* found one."

They both gave Arica soft, quiet looks. She shrugged softly. "But you're on the ground drenched in flames. It took like five of them to put you out. Luckily you made it pretty far from the mess, but before Vanessa can get to you, you completely pass out full solzetair. We couldn't do anything. It was only like twenty minutes before everyone was gathered up and retreating. We didn't see any of the Dovevians for a long time, but eventually someone spotted another solzetair headed northeast. No idea who made it out of there."

"Master Damage has been gathering information to find out who of the Dovevians still stand," said Lyrenel. "So far, it looks like most of them survived intact."

"That is disappointing," Jake murmured.

"We probably would've left you there if you hadn't popped back into this body." Arica gently pinched the thin fabric shirt at the shoulder. "Which I still don't understand."

"Basic principles of magic," he grunted. "It takes energy to keep up even a touch. I was out of it. Would've died within minutes without help."

Arica had to avert her eyes for at least a moment. "Yeah, well… I don't know whose idea it was to take you to Kallé Corve, but…"

"Teres's," Lyrenel said, looking up from his work. Then he held out the clear glass filled with a pinkish-colored liquid. "Well, it was Teres's suggestion to hole you up to heal. Master Damage, of course, decided where. Luckily, Kallé Corve wasn't far."

"And I guess you know the rest," Arica said with a cheerful shrug. "Derrick and J… Joy—"

"Russel Juyterm," Lyrenel said with a nod.

"—the awesome medic dude from Kopion dragged you back the way we came and set you up to heal for a bit, then you came to meet us."

Jake handed back the empty glass, his face scrunching up.

Lyrenel took it and said, "I'll be right back. Stay with him." He gathered a few things, but Arica watched him leave with a sinking feeling. Then she forced her head to Jake.

His lips stretched tight, but she was pretty sure it was more a grimace of pain than anything. Then he asked the very thing she was hoping to avoid. "Have you spoken with *him* since?"

She sighed, hands poking her own knees with boredom or awkwardness. "Haven't had the nerve. Do you think I should?"

He gave a short but finalizing shake of the head. She wasn't exactly sure how to feel about it.

She hadn't touched the rock since leaving Kopion, but it weighed heavily in her front pocket. It still lit up occasionally. More recently, it had started its call nightly. But she couldn't bring herself to take it, no matter what. She didn't want to talk to him, or anyone who could've found the other after Kopion's explosion.

She let her shoulders slump, watching as Jake's eyes slid closed.

"Hey, Lyrenel told you not to sleep yet." She moved closer to the back of the couch, then reached out towards his face. His neck and cheek had healed over, but the skin was a little rougher than it should've been. A much bigger hand rose and grabbed her wrist.

"Why are you touching me?" he mumbled, eyes slitting open just enough to see her. "Stop it. I know; it's bad."

"I'm sorry." She tugged it, but his grip kept her there.

His gaze tiredly passed over her to the wall.

"I heard your back is the worst," she slipped, not even stopping to wonder if he needed to hear something like that.

"I can feel it," he said with a quick nod. "But everything just aches."

Arica pressed her lips together, her throat sticking with guilt. "You... you're a hero."

His jaw locked for a minute, then he shook his head. "No, you don't know what it's like being a part of this group. This is just the type of conviction the Zenians demand."

She couldn't help smiling in disbelief. "You almost died, Jake."

"And it wasn't the first time. It wasn't even in the top ten." He finally released her hand.

Arica let her gaze fall, forcing a hard swallow as her chest tightened. "Yeah, well... then maybe I don't belong here, after all."

His knuckles gently touched her arm, slowly sliding down the length of it. "Maybe you don't—"

Arica would never find out if there was more to that. Vanessa slipped into the room almost silently, but heavy footsteps followed as Aaris and Lyrenel entered as well.

"And, as far as I can see," Lyrenel said clearly. "He looks much better, inside and out. Some ways to go, but good progress. How do you feel?"

Jake shrugged, but his injured side remained considerably lower. "I've been through worse. Might as well hand me a sword."

"I'll hand you this instead," Vanessa said as she shoved the little botany book in Jake's face. He fumbled to grab it.

"What... Isn't this your book from Maramore?" he mumbled, a brief glance in Arica's direction.

"Yeah." She pushed a lock of hair behind her ear. She didn't *want* all her stuff out in the open. "After we left Kopion, I had to tell Vanessa everything."

"Good," he said with a forced smile of sympathy.

"Drake, his presents, the books, the messages I found, the whole plan around Kopion... Showing you everything."

Vanessa shifted her hands to her waist, her posture proud. "Yes, I would like to know your reasoning behind allowing a tyro to walk around with a Dovevian in her ear without alerting me."

"I knew. That was enough."

"I don't believe you," she murmured, her stare so sharp that Arica had to avert her eyes.

"She said something that..." He let his hand fall on his thigh in a movement of surrender. "Well, I don't know how but it reminded me of McCarter."

"I keep hearing that name," Arica mumbled under her breath.

"For purposes that are slowly taking shape," Vanessa said, then gestured at the book.

"What's it about, then?" Arica asked, looking between her and Aaris, who remained silent.

"You and Lord Maloney reported that during the battle near Akvelia, you were using the setup of an underground tunnel," Vanessa said in her professional tone.

"Uh... yeah, more or less."

"How did you find it?" The question wasn't quite an accusation.

"It was just chance. I fell into an animal burrow close to it. I don't even know," Arica admitted quieter.

Then their leader turned to Aaris, arms loosely folded across her chest. "Would you care to explain further upon the things you mentioned a few moments ago?"

The quiet Zenian hesitantly nodded, his expression concerned, but he spoke clearly. "It was many, many years ago, but we did hollow out a stretch of swamp, McCarter and I. He never exactly mentioned why, but I wasn't one to question."

"Was it the same place Arica and Zak were playing through?"

Aaris's shoulders rose. "I wouldn't know. I can't even remember exactly where we did it."

"So, we used an old dugout. Why's that such a big deal?" Arica asked honestly.

She glanced back when Jake let his hand fall to a cushion with the book tight in his grip. He stared at the ceiling. Did he look grim?

"Because it wasn't something previously used. Hypothetically... he dug it *for* you."

Arica's eyebrows lowered a little, but Vanessa started a slow, thoughtful pace around the room.

"My only..." she whispered softly. "I knew he was powerful, but simply the idea that he could have implemented something like this, so specifically..."

"Just..." Arica huffed with frustration. "Just start from the beginning, slowly."

"Maybe we'll catch something we haven't, anyway," Lyrenel agreed solemnly.

Vanessa set her hands on either hip, raising her chin. "Fine. McCarter Bonds's Touch was—to put in a grossly simple term—sight towards the future. Every moment of every day, he saw and anticipated everything. The only drawback was that the further he looked, the more unstable his sight was. Days were a stretch, weeks were difficult, months or years excruciating. Therein lies my doubt that this could be possible; the biggest flaw to the theory that any of this could be his hand."

She pointed at the book, still pinched between Jake's fingers.

"The theory being that he set up a path for you, Arica. That book was on a shelf in Maramore, yes?"

She couldn't get her throat to do much but wobble, so a simple nod would have to do.

"He knew you would pick this book exactly. You followed the path he knew you would."

"How?" Arica demanded, almost interrupting her. "I could've picked up any of those books."

"But he knew which one you would choose."

She rolled her eyes with as much exaggeration as possible. "Okay, but the book literally just fell on the bed four days ago. It *happened* to open to the page saying Jake would be back in four days. Are we just supposed to assume every little thing we do is set in stone?"

"Not in the least," Vanessa admitted in a soothing tone. "I suppose I misspoke. You followed nothing; the path he made followed you instead. There were many things you could've done differently, but had you, McCarter's design also would have been different. He paved it after he'd seen what you would do. He wrote his notes on the pages you would see, dug the tunnel where you would walk, placed things where you would look. The only problem I see... is how he did it."

She stepped a few feet back towards the door again, holding her own arms. Her features grew tired, a strange look for her.

"It's been so many years since I sent him away. He had to have seen so far... Hundreds of years. It doesn't seem possible. But I suppose it doesn't really matter, does it?"

Arica didn't want to disturb the quiet, but nobody else seemed that eager to understand why. "Okay, I just don't understand why he would do any of this."

Vanessa let out a deep sigh, blinking hard to revert to her normal stony self. "Foremost, so you would trust him. Somehow, he knew he wouldn't be here to do anything personally."

Aaris raised a hand subserviently, only speaking when both of the women had their eyes on him, and Vanessa had given him a nod.

"If he knew that, you don't think he knew he'd lose all sanity, and that you would be the one to disable him?"

"I don't know, but he never tried to stop me if he had. You know what really throws me..." She took a step backwards, then tiredly lowered herself to the couch at Jake's side, eyes staring at nothing. Then her gaze flicked up to him. "He wrote these notes in Endreyan. I banished him around... 2650, yes? Endreyan wasn't introduced until around 2730. It didn't *exist*. If this is all true, then he saw these things clearly enough to write in a language that nobody, not even he, knew."

Nobody interrupted her as the room filled with a tension of reverence.

"Normally I'd suspect Dovevian tricks," Vanessa then added, her voice disturbing their silence. "But only he could've known to write what he did."

"Which..." Arica looked over in time to see Jake's eyelashes flutter as he rolled his eyes.

"You don't want to hear it. Long and subjective, most of it. He was a romantic. 'Daren't the life of my love spared by the wrath of our God find herself so woeful—'"

Vanessa snatched the book from his grasp before his grin could spread any more. "It doesn't sound like that," she growled.

Arica struggled to keep her jaw from clenching any more than it already had. Her teeth were growing sore. "That still doesn't answer my question. Why *me*?"

"It was just the first step," Vanessa admitted thoughtfully. Then she glanced at the book, her features darkening slightly. "He knew you would be the only one willing to give my husband another chance when we needed it."

Arica turned her body enough to look at the book. "That's what it says?"

"After proving it is indeed himself, McCarter tells me, in essence, that Drake's show of merit helping us in Kopion, assuming reports are correct, should give me enough reason to hear him out, even though he knows it isn't nearly enough for me. Then he asks that I try to set aside my rancor and trust in his intuition, though he's aware I would never do such a thing. Finally, he demands that I do nothing to sway you, Arica, from your path. To allow you to take advantage of Lord Damage of the Dovevians all the way to the gates of obsidian." She lifted her chin with pride. "Where we would once and for all take back the castle, the throne, and the lives of DeRael."

Arica waited for her to continue, but her lips pressed closed, a hardened expression coming over her.

She looked at Jake instead, then Aaris, then Lyrenel as well, but none gave her any more information. "So... what do we do?"

Vanessa let out a deep sigh, closing her eyes briefly as if she had to pull herself together. "I never, ever thought I would agree to such impetuous means of ousting the king, but... the lengths this has gone to, maybe it's the only chance, so... Get out your stone, Miss Tanson. We have to speak to the Dovevian."

She did as she was told; stood up and pulled a small bag from her pocket, and with it, the heaviness of not only solid stone, but the unknown. She could see the creases of worry and perhaps even fear in the face of their leader but didn't know what this was going to do to her.

The glowing stone fell into her palm easily. She held out her hand, and Vanessa held it, cupping the item between them.

"I shouldn't've doubted the word of a prophecy, even one from the enemy's side," came the resounding voice of evil with no encouragement. Vanessa's eyes slid closed.

Crap.

Then a deep chuckle fell upon their ears. "So sayeth the madman."

THE END

PRONUNCIATION GUIDE

Akvelia (awk-VAIL-ee-uh)

Andolviam (an-DOHL-veeyam)

Andromae (AN-droh-may)

Anraquella (on-ruh-KWell-uh)

Areun (ar-YUHN)

Atork (ey-tork)

Atvotshio fengra (at-VAHT-shey-oh fenk-ruh)

Aunseyant (on-SEY-awnt)

Ballewine (bal-eh-wahyn)

Banen Sraota (BEY-nen srey-OH-tuh)

Bialsa (bee-ALL-suh)

Caldaryze Enileny (cawl-duh-REEZ EN-i-LEN-ee)

DeRael (deh-rayl)

Dovevian (doh-VEV-ee-an)

Duekov Tramnovich (dwey-kov tram-noh-vich)

Ellteria (el-TER-ee-uh)

Elvy Ann Ent (el-vee an ent)

Endré (EN-drey)

Ersiasevaer (er-see-UH-suh-VEYR)

Garal Leadd (GAIR-all LEE-ed)

Ilcoaboanaste (eel-cow-bohn-ast-uh)

Inalbaent (in-ALL-beynt)

Jadrion Rapier (JEY-dree-an reyp-ee-er)

Jerim Enileny (JER-im EN-i-LEN-ee)

Jrasko (DRAY-soh)

Kallé Corve (kal-EY cohrv)

Khantaria (kan-tahr-ee-uh)

Kopion (kohp-ee-on)

Kujra (koo-druh)

Kylen Kisok (kahy-len KAHY-zik OR KEE-sok)

Kyrgan (keer-gan)

Lise Kisok (lahyz KAHY-zik OR KEE-sok)

Lyrenel Herak (LEER-en-el HAIR-ak)

Madellian (muh-del-ee-on)

Malon Kisok (mey-lon KAHY-zik OR KEE-sok)

Malsydon (mal-si-don)

Maramore (mar-uh-mohr)

Nahlie (NAW-lee)

Naornagosau (nawr-NAG-oh-saw)

Neva (nev-uh)

Nevaria (nev-ar-ee-uh)

Nian Netosi (NEE-an net-oh-see)

Nriallea Naemaoskr (nree-A-lee-uh ney-MOUS-ker)

Parel (PAR-el)

Pelekan (pel-EY-kan)

Raellic (rayl-ek)

Randa Marc (RAN-duh marc)

Revenal (REV-en-awl)

Ricken Kisok (rik-en KAHY-zik OR KEE-sok)

Russel Juyterm (RUS-el joy-term)

Sabina (suh-BEE-nuh)

Santsin Val (sant-sin vawl)

Sceztiak (skez-tyak)

Siddek Helim (sid-ek HEL-im)

Skotjretant (skot-dri-tant)

Soas Entdi (soh-as ent-dee)

Solyve (sol-iv)

Solzetair (SOL-zeh-tehr)

Steen Callovoi (steen CAL-oh-voi)

Tauria (tahr-ee-uh)

Teres (TAIR-ez)

Teurm ekh adoat (tyurm ek ad-owt)

Togheraith (toh-ger-aith)

Tolstolryn Dohvevna (tohs-tol-rin doh-VEV-nuh)

Turrales (tur-AL-ez)

Valkosce (val-kose)

Veyber (vey-BAIR)

Výan Deli'ampy (vahy-an del-ee-awmp)

Vyte (vahyt)

Zenian (zen-ee-an)

The adventure Continues...

The air even in the wind was acrid and smelly. The dirt underfoot, soft, but so uneven that every step was a chance. As they approached the billowing warmth of the town, the thick smoke and ash parted as if controlled by giant magnets, revealing only the charred musculature of an entire town.

In some places stone walls stood precariously, but most of the remaining pieces and parts were thick frames, some sharp and directed towards the sky potentially making the entire area a giant spike pit for a solzetair.

The warmth should've been inviting, but it was invasive instead, chilling and unwelcome.

The smoke and ashes settled in behind them, bringing darkness and blocking them from an unburnt world. Gray was all that existed anymore.

They followed the uncharacteristically quiet Dovevian all the way to a large pad of stone set a foot or so above the even dirt. There were noticeable divots for support beams, but nothing else was left of the large building.

Drake stopped in the middle and turned to the Zenians, hands casually in his pockets.

"What is it you're revealing, Damage?" Vanessa demanded as she approached him, arms crossed and demeanor still despite the threat facing her.

Drake just turned his bright eyes to her, a smirk slowly forming.

Arica stopped and stood still as a soft, warm breeze blew across her face. It grew into a small, controlled whirlwind of coal dust gathered up from the very edges of the framework. The dark specs hung like a silent snowfall until there was a considerable amount weaving together, forming solid lines.

It was a minute before Arica realized it wasn't random. They were forming a picture, a shadow of what the room once was.

Her attention was drawn to the middle of the room, where lines of coal had grown thicker. They formed a wheel bigger than Arica's body that slowly turned with the push and pull of a large arm.

Drake gently nodded at his artwork. "If you've never seen—"

"I've seen engines," Vanessa spat with annoyance. "What was wrong with this one?"

"They've applied this steam power to improve their iron mines and general farming, but this last month they've been working on designs to mobilize it of its own power."

The powder loosened, but instead of falling, it hung in the smoky air before drifting in slow motion.

"The Dovevians wrecked an entire city because some guys want to build a car?" Arica asked.

Drake shrugged, displaying a palm. "This is better than another apocalypse, isn't it?"

"Do you really think my father is capable of creating another apocalypse?" Vanessa asked, her eyes narrow with deep exhaustion.

"I'm not saying he is, and I've no proof he's trying, but there is something afoot, and he's already done it once."

Arica watched Vanessa for a long moment, but her still frame and blank expression told her nothing.

"History is looping," Drake said in a stronger, definitive tone. "Wylture Delmn fell to Dohvevna once. DeRael fell to Garal's apocalypse. Each loop is shorter, and I've a suspicion we're looking at another pass. I don't want to do it anymore. I'm tired."

Vanessa took a deep breath through her nose and she moved a small step in the scorched ground. "As am I."

"Why is technology, or... or self-sufficiency a bad thing for Garal?" Arica asked. "Why wouldn't he want to rule a society that achieves more than building castles and making food?"

"Humans are a threat to magic. They're a threat to aunseyants," Drake said nonchalantly. "As it's always been. The more they can do without it, the more obsolete we become. Science, in theory, could advance to a new magic that is unrestrained, harnessable by anyone willing to learn. A power strong enough to become godlike. It is the work of the Severed to control mankind. Why would they need protectors, servants, guardians like us if they weren't capable of being overthrown?"

"Gods? I thought we were guardians of humankind," Arica whispered.

"That may be where Zenians and Dovevians differ the most."

"You still sound committed to your cause despite all claims," Vanessa mused, looking over her shoulder at him.

"I am. I serve Solyve and his lesser siblings. But I do believe Garal has become the very thing he has feared. I know he's power-drunk. High King is too trivial a title for him." His shoulder tensed into a shrug as he met Vanessa's gaze with an uncharacteristic sobriety. "There's talk that if the Dovevians continue his work... he may become a god. We have to stop him."

NEED MORE RIGHT NOW?
FIND MAPS, LORE,
UPDATES ON UPCOMING
PROJECTS, AND MORE AT

WWW.KJERI-REES.COM